CONVICTION

AN ASH PARK NOVEL

MEGHAN O'FLYNN

Copyright 2016

First printing, September 2016

This is a work of fiction. Names, characters, businesses, places, events and incidents are either the products of the author's imagination or used fictitiously. Any resemblance to actual persons, living or dead, or actual events is purely coincidental. Opinions expressed are those of the characters and do not necessarily reflect those of the author (though any opinions regarding political figures or card games are probably accurate).

No part of this book may be reproduced, stored in a retrieval system, scanned, or transmitted or distributed in any form or by any means electronic, mechanical, photocopied, recorded or otherwise without written consent of the author. Pirating is for jerks.

All rights reserved, including the right to be a bastard pirate. Unless you're Orlando Bloom. (Swoon.)

Distributed by Pygmalion Publishing, LLC

*For my mother
who didn't raise no fool and who also managed to
teach me the appropriate use of double negatives.
I am what I am today because of your love and support.
But that won't stop me from kicking your ass in bridge.
You've been warned.
I love you, Mom.*

WANT MORE FROM MEGHAN?
There are many more books to choose from!

Learn more about Meghan's novels on
https://meghanoflynn.com

PROLOGUE

ASHLEY JOHNSON FELT the hatred the moment she stepped inside the courtroom from the door behind the judge's bench. It thickened the air, choked the breath from her lungs, and severed the hope that she'd managed to scrape together while waiting in her cell. There was no hope in this room. Just anger. The cuffs on her wrists jangled obscenely in the condemning hush of the courtroom.

They might as well kill her now. It would be preferable to the slow agony she would suffer imagining every major event in her daughter's life—her birthdays, her college acceptance letters, her wedding—from inside stone walls.

The jury's eyes burned into Ashley from their box on the right side of the room, and her legs tried to buckle. Maybe she deserved some of their judgment. It was true that she'd made some bad choices.

The choice to be with Derek was the worst one of all.

She tried not to look at the front of the courtroom as she passed, tried not to see the stand where Derek's dead body had been turned into a poster, his sightless eyes watching and accusing her even through the film of death. The wall behind him was splattered with the bloody remains of his skull. Every time, she tried not to look, but every time, she failed.

Frank Griffen sat, shoulders square, mouth set, his black-rimmed glasses frozen halfway down his nose. But his pinky fingers twitched like he could feel the energy too. Not that he ever sat perfectly still—his mouth or fingers or eyes, something was always moving. He wouldn't have been her first pick for a defense attorney, but she was broke. And he was good enough. If he got her out of there.

Eyes forward, don't look at the jury. Don't look at the poster. Don't look.

Behind Griffen, Detective Eddie Petrosky frowned, squinting—agitated. Griffen said the detective'd had that look since some serial killer had gotten away on his watch last year, but to Ashley, those lines of irritation on Eddie's forehead showed that he gave a shit. Down the row, Dr. McCallum, the shrink who'd interviewed her before the trial, sat watching, his enormous belly squished against the back of the pew in front of him. He had deemed her depressed, testified that she'd likely been suicidal the night Derek died. He hadn't been wrong. She had often prayed for death though she'd never come close to acting. It was a fantasy, slipping away when things got too hard—but not a fantasy she wanted to embrace.

Her feet seemed stuck to the floor as she scanned the rest of the crowd. Her caseworker, Diamond's caseworker, sat in the back. Some lady in a short skirt sat across the way, maybe a hooker waiting on her own court appearance. The one person who might've offered her hope, or at least a reassuring smile, was nowhere to be found. He'd visit on his own time, he'd said, and if she tried to stir things up without his consent, he'd leave her to die in prison. She couldn't even think his name, for fear it would tumble out of her mouth. The guard behind her coughed, probably annoyed that she'd stopped in the middle of the courtroom, or maybe he was trying to remind her to move.

Then she saw her. Diamond entered the courtroom, her baby girl, already grown bigger in the months since Ashley'd been locked up. And with her, Ashley's dead boyfriend's mother: Lucinda Lewis, Diamond's grandmother, if you believed the birth certificate. Lucinda glared at Ashley.

Ashley resisted the urge to run to her baby, to kiss her and hug her and tell her everything was going to be okay, that her mommy was coming home soon, and they'd be a family again. She wanted just one moment with Diamond. To smell her. To hold her. Instead, she watched her baby pass her by and disappear behind Lucinda as the woman turned to the seats. Ashley's chest constricted.

Derek's idiot brother, Trey, had shown up today too, his red bandana tucked haphazardly into his jeans pocket. Derek's aunts held hands as they followed down the aisle after Lucinda and slid into one of the long benches that held families like church pews—the law's last shot at redemption in a city where there was more blood than holy water.

The guard prodded Ashley forward so hard she stumbled into the table where Griffen sat. He jumped up and helped her to her seat, and she sank into the chair next to his, noting that Griffen's bony nose was leaking again.

He swiped at his forehead and then his nose with an orange handkerchief, then shoved it into his pocket more violently than seemed necessary. He didn't look at her, but she could see the tightness of his mouth. Not a good sign.

Tears burned behind her eyes though she wouldn't give anyone the satisfaction of watching her cry. Not the jury and definitely not the prosecution. She didn't want everyone to head home tonight feeling superior because of her pain. It was bad enough they were all free while she was locked in a cage, especially when she didn't deserve to be there.

She'd made bad choices, that was true. But she wasn't a killer.

Her throat threatened to close on her, and she swallowed over the tightness, trying to remember what Eddie had told her. *We'll figure it out, Ashley. I'll find a way.*

But he hadn't. Neither had the one she'd expected to get her out of this mess; the one who was supposed to care. But maybe he'd been a mistake too.

Where is he?

Like a shotgun blast, the bang of a gavel reverberated through Ashley's shoulder muscles and shivered down her back. Church was in session. She relaxed her fists in her lap and raised her eyes to that fat bastard judge, Clarence Delacour.

"We have already heard from the prosecution. Are you ready for closing arguments, Mr. Griffen?"

Griffen stood and walked around the table, buttoning the front of his suit jacket with twitchy little movements. He was barely taller than Ashley herself, but the set of his shoulders was rigid and determined, and this made him seem much larger. He walked to the jury box and put his hands on the rail, his grip soft like he was polishing the wood with his index finger instead of making a point.

Ashley tuned out after his "Ladies and gentlemen of the jury." She knew there was reasonable doubt, or at least Griffen had told her there was. But she also knew what the prosecution thought: that she'd come home, found her daughter injured, and bludgeoned Derek in the head with a blunt object, probably the hammer she'd used to hang a picture earlier that morning. A hammer that was now missing, which Griffen had assured her, was a good thing. Defendants had been released for less.

Ashley's neck was damp with perspiration by the time Griffen cleared his throat and strutted to the podium for his final statements.

"Ashley Johnson was ambushed," he said. "When she came home, the living room was dark, and she was unable to see what remained of her boyfriend. She walked through the room without turning on a light and into Diamond's bedroom to check on her little girl. And when her back was turned, someone stuck a syringe in Ashley's neck and carried her to the bathtub. She almost died at the hands of the same person who killed Derek Lewis. Our lack of another identifiable suspect does not equate to Ashley Johnson being guilty."

Griffen turned and caught the eye of someone behind

her, and Ashley sat straighter. *Is he here? Did he come?* Out of the corner of her eye, she watched Petrosky nod to Griffen, the detective's face softening a fraction before reverting to its usual stoniness.

Griffen turned back to the jury box. "This girl did not kill Derek Lewis. And if you make the mistake of convicting her, you will be allowing a killer to go free."

The silence in the room felt heavy, like it was closing in on Ashley from all sides, until the judge spoke again.

"Is the prosecution ready for rebuttal?" Delacour's eyes were on the clock on the side wall—not on Ashley, not on Griffen—as her lawyer walked back to his seat. Obviously, the judge thought she was expendable. Like trash. Maybe she was. Maybe she had always been.

Shannon Taylor, the prosecuting attorney, rose to her feet, thin and blond and a fucking bitch. "Ready, Your Honor."

Ashley looked down at her hands, and the cuffs glinted like crude bracelets that weighed down her soul instead of her wrists.

Taylor cleared her throat. "At just after five o'clock on the evening of February fifteenth, a noise complaint came into the station, stating that someone was arguing at the apartment Derek Lewis and Ashley Johnson shared."

Ashley's hands trembled. She pressed her palms together and squeezed them between her knees.

"When police arrived at six-thirty, Derek Lewis was alone at the house, alive and in good health, and informed the responding officers that Johnson had gone to the drugstore and then to drop off their daughter at a neighbor's. Both of these statements were later verified. What Derek didn't know is that he had only four hours to live."

In her peripheral vision, Ashley tried to see what the jury was doing, but her vision was blurry. Her face burned.

When Taylor spoke again, her voice was softer, but her words somehow rang throughout the courtroom. Aggressive. Dangerous. "At seven-thirty, Ashley Johnson arrived for a job interview at an all-night garage where she was described as 'distracted' by the owner. After the interview, Johnson disappeared." Taylor cut her eyes at Ashley, and Ashley's stomach twisted.

"No one seems to know what the defendant was doing during this time, but she was gone for long enough that she neglected to pick up her daughter from her babysitter's home. When the sitter had to leave, she dropped young Diamond home with her father, Derek. And at eleven o'clock, when Ashley Johnson finally returned to the apartment, she found her daughter with a fresh bruise on her lower back and another on her leg, marks the sitter testified were not present earlier that day. Indeed, the one on Diamond's hip was a clear imprint of Derek Lewis's belt buckle."

Ashley's breath came hot and fast as she saw Diamond in her mind's eye, saw the bruises on her sweet baby's legs. *She's trying to get to you, trying to make you react.* Her leg muscles shook with anger. She swallowed hard.

"Ashley Johnson may have put up with Derek hitting her. She might have been neglectful herself, not bothering to pick her daughter up on time. But the defendant wasn't about to let her boyfriend get away with hitting her little girl." Taylor paced in front of the jury box. "Johnson found Derek sleeping on the couch. She grabbed a hammer, walked behind the couch, and hit her boyfriend in the head, again and again and again." Taylor mimed each strike, and the jury winced as they visualized Derek's head being smashed to bits.

Ashley could see it too, the blood, the fragments of skull and brain, gooey clumps landing on the wall. She tried to focus on the prosecutor instead. Better to look angry at the false accusation than pissed at her dead boyfriend whose corpse was even now staring back at her from the easel, his face bloody and eerily blank. *Well, ex-boyfriend.*

"Ashley Johnson panicked, got rid of the murder weapon, and wiped down as many surfaces as she could, but she only managed to smear the blood. She did leave one intact handprint on the wall in the hallway, though. Her fingers. Her palm. In Derek Lewis's blood."

Ashley focused on the blond knot at the nape of the prosecutor's neck, trying to ignore the jury. Every frown, every sympathetic look, was horribly wrong. If they were going to let her go, they'd look more hopeful, wouldn't they? Their faces said they'd already decided she'd had a good reason to kill him—and that she had, in fact, done it. She inhaled through her nose to push back the nausea.

"Panic, ladies and gentlemen. Panic, in a severely depressed woman already stressed to her breaking point. And the defendant realized there was nowhere to go. The mess was too big. She had no money. No one to turn to. No options, no way out." The pause was deafening, a ringing silence that hurt Ashley's ears.

"So she prepared a syringe from Derek Lewis's stash with a deadly overdose of heroin, left the front door ajar to ensure that someone would find her daughter, then climbed into a full bathtub and injected the drugs into her own neck."

The jurors' eyes swung to Ashley's table, and she saw pity and an agitation she almost couldn't bear to acknowledge. The air thickened further until the heaviness of it clogged her throat entirely, blocking her breath. *Jesus, help me, please...*

Taylor stilled, placing her hands on the polished wood of the jury box. "Just after midnight, a neighbor happened upon Johnson's open front door and found Derek dead on the couch, Diamond in her crib, wailing, and Ashley Johnson unconscious in the bathtub, the water pink with Derek Lewis's blood."

Ashley prayed silently. Please, God, help me. I'll go to church every Sunday. I'll do anything.

"The defense wants you to believe that she was framed. But Ashley Johnson had both motive and opportunity to commit this crime."

Yes, she'd had both of those things. She'd had the opportunity. And some nights, even now, she lies awake in her cell praying God would send Derek back just so she could kill him again for hurting Diamond. No, she hadn't done it, she knew she hadn't. But the way the police had interrogated her, repeated their questions over and over, every word from their mouths wrapping around her throat like a noose that would eventually strangle her…sometimes she doubted her own innocence. Was it possible she'd lost it on Derek and blocked the whole thing from her mind? Had the memory of the sharp needle sting in her neck as she bent over Diamond's crib been a hallucination, the start of some kind of psychotic break? Why would anyone want to kill her? She was a nobody. Maybe she really *had* killed Derek. But Eddie Petrosky didn't believe that, and if he could trust her, then she could trust herself, too. She clenched her fists, and her face flushed with fresh determination.

Taylor's shoes echoed against the wooden walls as she strode back to the podium and gestured to the photo of Derek's corpse. "We can all sympathize with a mother protecting her child. But this is not the way. If we accept vigilante justice, if we set a precedent suggesting that we can harm those who get in our way, that we can take the law into our own hands, then we fail. Society fails. Derek Lewis wasn't perfect. He should have been punished for his crimes but *in accordance with the law*. This isn't about whether you like the victim or empathize with the aggressor. Even if you think Derek Lewis deserved to be punished for what he allegedly did, Ashley Johnson did not have the legal right to inflict that punishment."

The world was fading around the edges, every sound like the shush of Diamond's breathing when Ashley used to rock her to sleep—hazy and hot and peaceful. Those hours had been a reprieve from planning how they were going to escape from Derek.

Derek did deserve to die. *But I didn't do it.*

Taylor stared pointedly behind Ashley, probably at Diamond.

Don't look, Ashley. Don't.

"Ashley Johnson needs to suffer the consequences of the crime she has committed. She and others like her need to know that one cannot simply take the law into their own hands and kill someone who does them wrong. You must return a verdict of guilty of murder in the second degree."

The quiet seemed alive, squirming around Ashley, and the judge's scrutiny wiggled up her sleeves and down her back. Shannon Taylor walked back to her chair and sat, and Ashley listened to the rustling of shoes on the floor, the sound of jurors preparing for dismissal, the audience collecting their things.

Beside Ashley, Griffen blew his nose, a low, hollow honk. Behind her, Diamond cried out. Ashley watched Shannon Taylor and clenched her fists, her eyes burning with unshed tears.

1

Shannon Taylor left the courtroom with a pit in her stomach. She should have been happy. It had taken less than two hours for the jurors to return a verdict of guilty. Ashley Johnson had buried her face in her hands and sobbed until they took her away while Frank Griffen looked on after her, his face drawn and pale.

I'm right. I have to be. All the evidence had pointed that way, but damn. If only she'd been prosecuting Derek Lewis for abuse, then the tension in her shoulders would have abated with the verdict, not intensified. Being right didn't always feel good. It should, but…

Her stomach growled when she passed someone on a wooden bench in the hallway eating a sub sandwich. Maybe she'd get some sushi. No, Mexican. She glanced at her watch. Maybe fast food, though she'd probably regret it later tonight when she was sweating her way through grease-induced cramps at the gym.

Shannon kept her eyes on the marble floor, where cracks in the once-opulent stone threatened to snag the heels of her shoes. It was freaking depressing, watching Ash Park crumble. You could almost feel it in your bones, pulling at you, like the earth itself might slit you open and shove the bad inside so you could never escape.

She pushed through the front door and hurried down the steps, eyes forward, ignoring a beggar's call for change in favor of keeping her footing as she made her way toward her car.

"Taylor!"

Shit. Shannon turned to see Detective Petrosky approaching, his blue eyes bright with what looked like hatred, but Shannon knew it was just his resting bitch face. Or maybe it *was* hatred. He was good at his job, but damn if he wasn't a dick, especially when it came to his "girls." Sex crime detectives probably all ended up like that eventually—they either cared too much, sensitive to every nuanced attack, or they stopped caring at all.

"You shouldn't be here, Petrosky. You know there's nothing else to say."

"There's plenty more to say, Taylor. Someone else was in the house earlier that day, fighting with Lewis. Someone who got loud enough for the cops to show up. It wasn't her."

"Just because you know her doesn't mean she isn't a killer."

Petrosky ground his teeth. "I don't know her."

"You know her well enough. You set up that job interview for her, and—"

"She needed a leg up."

"And she got one, didn't she, when you threatened the garage manager with a parole violation if he didn't give her the job."

Petrosky stared at her, all ice and daggers. She gave it right back.

"She didn't kill him, Taylor. She was set up. Someone drugged her and tried to kill her too, and just because your ex-husband decided to prosecute—"

"Roger has nothing to do with this, Petrosky."

"He's the head prosecutor, he sure as shit does."

She shook her head. "I went for murder two because she was guilty. We've been over this. She was depressed, Petrosky. Her friends admitted it. Ashley Johnson herself admitted it. Dr. McCallum, your favorite department shrink, testified that even without the depression, years of domestic abuse can cause a person to snap. Add to it that Johnson *saw* her daughter hurt. It doesn't make any sense that a killer would murder Lewis, then sneak up behind Johnson and give her drugs. They'd have smashed her skull in too."

"Not if they wanted to frame her."

For god's sake. Shannon crossed her arms.

"They never found the murder weapon, Taylor. If she was going to kill herself anyway, why would she get rid of evidence?" Petrosky advanced on Shannon close enough that she could smell the sharp tang of booze under his mouthwash.

Who the hell does he think he's fooling? She should turn his alcoholic ass in. "People do strange things when they're in panic mode, Petrosky. Johnson didn't start the day wanting to die. A subsequent suicide once she realized what she'd done makes more sense with her history, and no one else had a motive." Derek Lewis was a small-time drug dealer, and no one had mentioned any bad blood between him and others in the neighborhood. He didn't even owe anyone money. And someone after the drugs themselves sure as hell wouldn't waste them by pumping them into Ashley Johnson's veins. Johnson had killed him. Panicked. And once Johnson knew she was fucked, she'd tried to take her own life. Case closed.

Petrosky's nostrils flared. "Someone else fought with Lewis that evening, Taylor. Ashley might have been scared, angry, but she didn't kill him."

Shannon sighed and edged toward her car. "I know, I know, it was the mystery person at the house."

Petrosky matched her step for step. "What about the later phone call, after Lewis was dead? The call about the supposed gunshot? There was no bullet damage, no powder residue, no other witnesses who heard a shot go off, nothing. We never even found a gun." Petrosky ran one thick paw down his face, sighing like an exasperated bulldog. "And if

Lewis did have a gun, if Ashley had access to it, why didn't she use that to kill him? And how'd the caller even hear it? The call originated miles from the apartment."

"Doesn't matter." Shannon reached her car, clicked the unlock button, and slid inside. "Someone else found her before the call even came in."

"But the caller didn't know that. They called to make sure we got her while she was still clinging to life, maybe even wanted to make sure the baby was okay."

"Right, because all cold-blooded killers who meticulously frame someone else end up feeling so guilty that they risk detection to protect the kids in the house."

"Your snot-nosed buddy Griffen agrees with me."

Snot-nosed. Perpetual allergies to dust he'd told her once in college, during their days of pizza and study sessions and sneaking into the courthouse through an unalarmed back window to smoke pot. Back when they used to wear jeans and T-shirts instead of suits, and the plastic bands on their wrists were pink for breast cancer—before they realized that awareness wasn't doing shit for research and tossed them out.

"Of course, Griffen agrees. If you're right, his client really is innocent, unlike the throng of people he usually defends who just pretend to be." Shannon grabbed the door handle, and Petrosky backed up.

"I'm going to figure out who did this, Taylor. Someone has to do their job correctly."

"Fuck you, Petrosky." She slammed the car door and left Petrosky standing by himself in the parking lot with his hands jammed in his pockets.

SHANNON WHITE-KNUCKLED her car from the parking lot onto the freeway, her neck muscles as taut as violin strings. A Styrofoam coffee cup rolling across the pavement tumbled under her tire as she flew by, the crunch not nearly as satisfying as it would have been if it were Petrosky's head. But it helped. To the east, stray orange construction cones, dented and abused, littered the shoulder amidst signs warning of steep fines and imprisonment should you kill a worker. As if there was ever anyone out working on this road. She hit a jagged pothole hard enough to lock her seat belt.

Shannon rotated her neck, Petrosky's voice echoing in her head as she pictured Ashley Johnson's glassy eyes. Then she remembered Lucinda Lewis, her arms around her granddaughter, her eyes swollen with the knowledge that her son was never coming home because of what Johnson had done. She loosened her grip on the wheel and punched the stereo button. Def Leppard.

Shannon cranked the volume and watched apartment buildings grind by along the side of the freeway, their windows ugly and vacant. Metallica came on next, pounding through her speakers as apartments gave way to office buildings, then finally to townhouses and the occasional movie theater or shopping center or grocery store. When at last she pulled off onto the ramp toward the hospital, The Offspring was screaming at her about getting away. *If only I could.*

The hospital was an eighties relic, an appropriately sick-looking building of brown brick with bay windows protruding from the side like giant, water-filled blisters. And the inside was no better. The interior of the hospital always made her nose itch with the smell of antiseptic, made her eyes hurt with its too-bright fluorescents.

The women manning the reception desk did not acknowledge her as she passed, not that she really expected them to—if she worked here, she would have tried to distance herself too. Even as a visitor, she focused on the sights and smells and sounds of this place, forgetting for three glorious minutes of transit why she was there.

Shannon pushed the elevator button, and a curly-haired woman with a nurse's badge—*Sadie*—scurried up beside her, wearing rubbing alcohol like perfume. Sadie pulled her mouth into a grin, but any joy was surely painted on her mouth like the lipstick on the women at the reception desk. Always there—expected, but it couldn't possibly be real.

On the third floor, Shannon gave Sadie the obligatory have-a-nice-day nod, and Sadie returned it, though it was only a polite formality—more a wish that wouldn't likely be granted to those getting off on the oncology floor.

To her left, a long nurse's station beckoned with smiling, sympathetic people in scrubs. Shannon's muscles twitched, one step from dragging her back to the elevators, not because of the smell or her sore eyes or the god-awful way everyone in this place pretended that the grief wasn't about to leap up and bite their faces off—but because *he* was here. Seeing him like this was almost as bad as she imagined his death would be, though she'd not have to wonder about that for much longer.

She walked down the hall and into his room without knocking, sure that this time someone else's brother would be there looking too small under the blue hospital blanket, tubes coming from his arms and nose, gaunt cheeks turning him into a caricature of himself. "We made an error," the ladies at the desk would say. "Your brother was ill from the radiation and the chemo we mistakenly gave him. He's on his way home now."

But of course, he was there, like always, shuffling a deck of cards on his meal tray with bony, yellowed fingers. His gray eyes flashed when he saw her, crinkling at the corners, and he was all teeth, face filled with joy—real joy. For a minute, Shannon forgot to be sad, and she was just Shanny, Derry's sister, twelve years old again and huddled with him on her bed while he taught her how to deal blackjack.

Derry slapped the cards on the plastic tray table, making it jiggle. His real name was Jerry, but she'd always called him Derry, short for Derrière, her childhood nickname for him.

"Shanny! My god, I thought you'd never show up. How'd everything go today?"

Shannon smiled at him and pulled a chair from the side of the room to the bedside. "Got a conviction."

He squinted at her. "You look less happy than you should for someone who just did her job like a boss."

"I had a little run-in with one of the detectives afterward. Someone who thinks the defendant didn't do it."

Derry raised an eyebrow. "He right?"

"No," she said, sharper than she meant to.

He picked up the cards. "Five-card draw, winner gets to tell Mom she's a bitch."

"Mom's dead."

"Oops, looks like I'll be the first one to tell her anyway." Derry stuck his tongue out, and Shannon's stomach heaved like someone had punched her in the gut. "Come on, Shanny, that was funny."

"You wouldn't know funny if it bit you in the ass."

"Let's have Dr. Coleman look at your funny bone for you." Derry winked at the doorway behind her, and Shannon turned to see Dr. Alex Coleman, almost impossibly handsome at six feet tall—dark hair, blue eyes, and straight teeth. He'd been beautiful even when they were children.

"He telling death jokes again?"

Shannon nodded. "You need to get him to knock it off."

The cards shuddered in Derry's hands as he shuffled and flipped them out onto the table. "What's he going to do, Shanny? Kill me?"

Alex sighed and walked around to Derry's bedside, giving Shannon's arm a brief, familiar squeeze, just like he'd done when they were little kid BFFs. Very first best friend, turned first love, turned first rejection, though, at the time, she hadn't understood why he'd refused her advances. At least he'd kept it in the family.

Alex put a hand on Derry's shoulder. "How are you feeling?"

"About as well as you'd expect for someone who's had poison pumped through their veins for hours on end."

"The infection in your leg any better?"

"You know it is. Don't pretend you didn't check the chart. I'm pretty sure poking through my records was the reason you scored me this fancy room at your hospital instead of letting the oncologist send me home."

"It is lovely and convenient for me to be able to see my fiancé on breaks between ER shifts." Alex's gold band glinted in the light from the overheads. They'd started wearing them the day after Derry's diagnosis. Now or never.

Shannon swallowed hard.

"Shut up and come play," Derry said. His ring finger had grown too thin to wear his band. "I'm *dying* for a chance to beat you."

"Asshole." Shannon scooped her cards from the table.

Alex rolled his eyes, sat on the end of the bed, and grabbed his own cards as Derry turned to Shannon. "Whatcha need, Shanny?"

Shannon tried to ignore the dark bags under his eyes and glanced at her hand: two fours, an eight, a queen, and a ten. She tossed an eight and a ten onto the tray.

Derry dealt her two back. "Alex?"

"None."

"None?" Derry shook his head. "You confident bastard. You better not be letting me win again."

"I never let you win," Alex said.

"In that case, I open with two weeks' worth of doing the dishes."

Shannon flipped a five and…a third four. *Three of a kind, suckers.* "I see your dishes and raise you making dinner for a week," she said.

Alex knocked on the tray to call her bet.

Derry snorted, pursing his lips with what looked like disgust. "Oh, Alex is taking the sissy's way out."

"Misogynist," Shannon said.

"Feminist," Derry shot back.

Shannon slapped her cards onto the tray. "That's not an insult."

"Obviously, you're not a Republican." Derry considered his cards for a moment, then slid them onto the tray. He met Shannon's eyes. "I'll see you and raise you my life's savings."

"Your life—"

"Take it or leave it, Shanny."

"I'll take it."

"Will you be getting your inheritance a few weeks early, or did you just make Alex that much richer?"

"Goddammit, Derry," Shannon said.

"Fold," Alex said.

"Sucker." Derry flipped his cards. Pair of jacks.

Shannon shrugged and swept her cards into the pile. "I assumed you didn't have anything."

Alex watched her, his eyes narrowed, but she ignored him.

"Huzzah!" Derry slapped the table knocking his cards to the bed. "If I keep betting like this, I'm going to be living in the lap of luxury right up to the moment I bite the big one." He winked at Alex. "Literally."

Shannon shook her head, but a smile was tugging at the corner of her mouth.

Alex stood. "I better get back down to the ER. Be back later." He kissed Derry on the cheek, squeezed Shannon's shoulder, and left the room.

Derry's eyes darkened as he watched Alex disappear through the door. "He doesn't deserve this."

"He loves you."

"Loves me enough to marry me for my money."

"You're the one who said no to the wedding." Derry had told her that he wasn't hitting the aisle in a wheelchair because it wasn't the memory he wanted Alex to have for his first wedding. Maybe for his second, but definitely not his first. "Love's all that matters, Derry. He wants you to be happy, and so does Abby." Her eyes wandered to the bedside table, where a skinny little girl rocking an AC/DC T-shirt and a blond bob stared into the room from a photograph. "So do I."

"You don't deserve this either."

"None of us deserves this." Tears smarted behind her lids. "How is Abby?"

"She's fine. Hanging in there, I guess. Do me a favor and do something fun when you pick her up tonight. She won't be ready until eight because she's going to Chuck E. Cheese with a friend, but…she needs to get her mind off everything. Pretty sure her little girlfriends don't have a parent dying of metastatic liver cancer. Did I tell you it's in my brain now?"

"I rented *Terminator*," Shannon blurted out.

Derry raised an eyebrow. "Nothing lifts one's spirits like blowing shit up. If only you could avoid blowing this game. I kick your ass every time." The brightness in his eyes was back—there'd be no more heart-to-heart talks, not today. "It really is too bad you guys are stuck with a clearly superior poker player, albeit not for long." He wagged his eyebrows.

"Jesus Christ, Derry."

"I'm going to tell on you when I meet him, all this taking-his-name-in-vain shit."

"Watch it, or you're going to meet him sooner than you think."

Derry put his hands up in mock surprise. "Shanny! Did you just threaten my life? I've got half a mind to toss you out of here."

"Lucky for me, you literally only have half a brain now. You'll probably forget this whole conversation by sundown."

"No doubt." Derry reached over the table and grabbed her hand. "I love you, Shanny."

"Love you too, Derry. But you're still an ass."

"Takes one to know one." Derry released her hand and sat back against his pillows. "Now deal. And this time, don't let me win."

Shannon avoided his eyes and shuffled the cards with shaking hands.

2

WHEN SHANNON LEFT THE HOSPITAL, the sun was sinking low in the western sky, turning the clouds into billowing plumes of fluorescent smoke against the newly budding trees. Her breath fogged in front of her—not quite spring, but it was trying. Though with Derry on his way out, everything would probably look darker soon: more drab, more boring. More dead. The thought of losing him tore holes in her heart until her chest felt like bloody cheesecloth.

She headed south, back into the city. Twilight was in full effect by the time she pulled the car into a strip mall that housed a pizza place and two vacant stores with For Rent signs in the front windows. Behind the strip mall was a nondescript warehouse with a sandwich board sign out front: "CrossFit Ash Park." She locked the car and headed for the entrance, an enormous garage door yawning open like the maw of some carnivorous beast.

The whoosh of air that greeted her inside was as cold as that of the hospital, exposed as the place was to the elements through the open warehouse door. But the air here was alive, not sterile and antiseptic. Warm rubber, salt, and ammonia, a mix of sweat and cleaning products, invaded her nostrils. It was like coming home—if home meant screaming hard work.

Backed by mirrors, the warehouse was filled with every piece of weight-lifting equipment she could imagine, plus kettlebells, acrobatic rings, and pull-up bars: the ultimate in police training. Park Kimball, the right-hand man for the chief of police, had opened the warehouse for tactical training last year. How he'd managed to afford the up-front costs on his salary, Shannon had no idea, but since then, he'd been offering classes three nights a week, weekend personal sessions for those entering the police academy, and free gym access for his friends on the force who needed a place to work out after a day of public servitude.

In the back of the room was an intricate setup of bars that looked more like a kid's jungle gym than weight-training equipment. Kimball stood on a dense gray mat beneath the setup, heaving a bar full of weights onto his shoulders and flipping them back down to his waist. Then up again. Then down. They called Kimball "Jackie Chan," a fitting nickname, especially when the tendons in his neck tightened with exertion. He dropped the bar with a thud and winked at Shannon.

She nodded back, though his gaze made her shoulders tighten. She hated that Kimball was closer friends with her ex-husband than he was with her—Kimball and his wife Amanda had invited Roger to Thanksgiving this past year, before the divorce was even official, while her invite seemed to have been misplaced. Shannon used to think of Kimball as family. But since her divorce, Kimball more closely resembled the misogynistic, xenophobic uncle she avoided at holiday parties.

"Ohh, look out! It's about to get stone cold in here, gentlemen!" Off to Kimball's left, Officer Isaac Valentine smiled at Shannon and hefted a barbell over his shoulders, perspiration shimmering on his forehead like diamonds. She grinned at him. Valentine was on the Ash Park force, a good guy and enthusiastic about his work, maybe overly so. And while Kimball was with Roger's bitch ass, Valentine and his wife Lillian had invited Shannon and her best friend to join them at Thanksgiving, conveniently forgetting to invite Roger. A department divided by divorce, like children in the midst of a custody battle. But here at the gym, any personal or professional strife disappeared in a haze of sweat. Plus, it was the one place Roger never showed up.

Next to Valentine, Detective Curtis Morrison's broad shoulders gleamed as he completed kettlebell thrusters, squatting with the ball, then pressing it overhead and back to a squat. Morrison caught her eye in the mirror and smiled. She tried to smile back, but the sudden image of Morrison's asshole partner—Petrosky, with his fleshy face, his five o'clock shadow—made the anger bubble up in her stomach again. Morrison's face fell. He always knew. She probably looked as irritated as she had last week when someone had cut her off in traffic on their way to lunch. She had called the other driver a goat fucker. Morrison had ordered lamb at the restaurant and asked her over and over whether she thought anyone might like to have their way with his meal.

She ignored the twittering in her chest and turned back to Valentine. "Five minutes before I kick your ass in kettlebell swings."

"Bring it, Taylor." Valentine dropped his barbell. "Nice work on Johnson today, by the way, especially considering you got screwed on jury selection."

So much for leaving her cases outside the gym. "Yeah, seems like Griffen always gets what he wants. Didn't help him this time, though."

"Hey, any of you catch the game last night?" Morrison asked. In the mirror, his face did not change, but she'd spent enough evenings with him to know he didn't watch any sports at all. That didn't stop Valentine from forgetting about the Johnson trial and going on about some pre-season nonsense. A bead of sweat dripped between Morrison's shoulder blades and down his back.

Shannon resisted the urge to mouth *thank you* at Morrison and walked through a doorway into the single bathroom, shivering at the chill in the air. She set her bag on the toilet. Hopefully, one day Kimball'd put in locker rooms.

In shorts, a tank top, and a pair of leather half-gloves to avoid tearing her hands on the metal bars, she yanked her perfectly blow-dried hair into a ragged ponytail and headed back to the main room.

"Let's make this happen!" Kimball called to her from the back of the warehouse, where he was swinging a kettlebell between his legs and up above his head.

Shannon shrugged. "If you really want it, Kimball. I've got all night to make you look like a punk."

Valentine hooted from the floor, where he was doing sit-ups with a kettlebell. "Shannon's going to mess you up, Kimball!"

Kimball paused with the kettlebell over his head and narrowed his eyes at Valentine. "What's with the gut? You look like a black Chris Farley."

Valentine's abdominals flexed in a perfect washboard with each sit-up. Shannon shook her head. *Men.* Very few women showed up there, limiting her options for female-to-female interaction, but one didn't need a vagina to be a good friend. She'd learned from her mother that women can be far more dangerous, far more hurtful than any man. She stood on her tiptoes and stretched her arms to the ceiling.

"I told you," said Valentine, "my wife is pregnant, and I gained a few pounds to make her feel better. That all right with you, you Jackie Chan-looking motherfucker?"

"Fine with me. I'm not the one who has to look at that fat gut every night."

Shannon looked at Kimball as she leaned over an extended leg, stretching her hamstring. He was huge—easily twice as big as he'd been just six months ago, protein shakes and weight training definitely piling on the bulk. The pressures of gym ownership. Even so, he still didn't have anything on Morrison. Shannon stretched her other leg and watched Morrison's blond hair catch the overhead lights like a halo as he hauled himself up on the rings, paused, and let himself drop in a perfectly controlled movement. His abdominal muscles flexed, and his arms bulged with effort, but his full lips were relaxed, calm, serene. Always so damn chill. She probably looked like a grimacing walrus halfway through her set of bench presses, though he was too good a friend to ever tell her that.

Valentine dropped the ball, sat up, and ran a hand over his stomach. "My wife can't get enough of this."

"Fuck you, Valentine." Kimball dropped the kettlebell and moved to the weight rack. "What're you doing later, California?"

"Don't call him that," Valentine retorted. "It's almost like Petrosky's here when you pull that shit."

Petrosky. Shannon's heart accelerated, and it wasn't from the impending workout. The way he treated his partner was bad enough, always acting like Morrison didn't know what he was doing. But to harass her after she'd done her job? Based on nothing but some crazy hunch?

Such an asshole.

Valentine grabbed a pair of hand weights and hefted them onto his shoulders. "I'm just gonna call Morrison 'Silent but Deadly' until he comes up with something better."

"Sounds like a fart," Kimball said behind her.

Shannon stalked to the bench and began adjusting the weights on the barbell positioned above it.

Morrison dropped from the rings and approached. "Need a spot?"

She nodded and leaned back on the bench, eyes on the bar above her chin. Morrison took his position at the head of the bench, his thick legs above her head but far enough away that his balls weren't in her face, which she very much appreciated.

He put his hands on the middle of the bar. "One, two—"

Gripping the bar in both hands, she inhaled, pushed the bar to remove it from the holder, and lowered it slowly, carefully. The muscles in her arms whined as she pushed it back up. On the way back down, she took a deep breath, her first full one all day. Morrison smelled earthy with just a touch of the lavender soap he used still lingering under the musk.

"Hey, Shannon," Valentine began, "you want to come to the art exhibit with Lillian and me tonight? Starts at six. Morrison might come, too, if I can convince him to blow off the rest of his workout."

Morrison winked at her. She couldn't smile back because the weights were taking all her concentration, but the silent encouragement in his eyes made her push harder.

Kimball snorted. "You're a bunch of fags, going to an art show."

The hair on the back of Shannon's neck stood up. She opened her mouth, ready to replace the bar and launch into a tirade about Kimball's choice of words, but Morrison beat her to it.

"We're cultured." He spoke quietly, but there was no mistaking the challenge in his voice.

"What are you doing tonight anyway?" Valentine chortled. "Playing chauffeur to dance class?"

Shannon suppressed a smile.

"Dana loves dance, asshole," Kimball said. "And I'm not about to deny my baby girl. Besides, Amanda has to work late again."

"Maybe your social-working wife got tired of looking at your flabby ass and found a real man," Valentine said.

Shannon's arms were on fire. She stared at Morrison's face, gritted her teeth, and lowered the bar again.

"So how about it, Shannon? You coming? We'll hit O'Doole's to celebrate your conviction afterward."

"Maybe," she wheezed as Morrison grabbed the bar. He helped her put it back into the holder, then walked around the bench and offered her a hand. Her grip was slick with sweat, but he managed to pull her to seated.

"I can't stay long, though," she said. "I have to get Abby at eight."

Kimball muttered something Shannon couldn't hear, then

said, "I'm done for today. Morrison, you'll lock it up for me? Got a long day tomorrow."

Valentine laughed. "Yeah, a long day wiping the chief's ass."

"Fuck off," Kimball spat.

Valentine ignored him. "I gotta head off too, get changed. Morrison, half an hour in front of the art gallery?"

"Not tonight. I need to drop off a file at Petrosky's after I finish up here. But I'm up for O'Doole's." He nodded at Kimball. "I'll clean the bars too. I want to squeeze in one more set of toe touches."

"Petrosky's got you by the nuts." Valentine shook his head, sighing with resignation. "Fine. I'll call you when we're heading to O'Doole's. Hopefully, I can get in and out of that exhibit fast, and we'll be over there in an hour."

"Later," Shannon said. She hated the way her voice was still strained from the presses.

Morrison watched them leave, then turned back to her. "Sorry about Petrosky earlier."

"He told you about that, huh?" She stood, wiping her hands on her shorts.

Morrison nodded. "He gets carried away."

"Your partner is an asshole."

"Maybe."

"That's it? 'Maybe'?" She met his eyes.

"He might be." Morrison's gaze was unwavering. "But that doesn't necessarily make him wrong."

Her chest heated. Morrison couldn't possibly believe that Johnson was innocent. Could he? "A jury found her guilty beyond a reasonable doubt."

Morrison's face remained unlined and still. His chest was just as unmoving—he may not even have been breathing. "I think there's always another side."

She frowned. "You say that about everything, but not all things are relative. Some things just are." She stretched her arms over her head, then locked them behind her.

"Some things. Maybe even this thing." Morrison smiled,

but it seemed forced. "Sorry, dude. How about you just enjoy your victory? You can tell me about whatever crappy movie you picked for Abby tonight. And if you have to sit through some princess nonsense, I'll play you in Scrabble again. Just don't let her see you doing it. Last time she whipped my butt, and my ego can't take another hit like that." He lowered his voice. "But seriously, think about Johnson. It might not be so cut-and-dried."

She shook her head. "You're lucky I like you, Morrison." He was probably the only reason she stayed in Ash Park at all after her messy divorce from the head prosecutor. It was hard to leave your best friend. Especially when they were one of your only friends. She didn't attach easily.

"Yeah, I know I'm lucky." He grinned. "So you going with us to O'Doole's? We can grab coffee first."

She dropped her arms. "I don't drink coffee at night. You know that."

"A glass of wine?"

"We're going to a *bar*."

"True enough. Silly me." He stood. Silent. Calm. Waiting.

She couldn't remember when he'd started this nonsense. Maybe he'd been serious the first time. Probably not, though. "Are you going to ask me if I want food so I can tell you I'm not hungry?"

Morrison shook his head. "Not tonight. Gotta keep you on your toes." He smiled and headed for the bars. She watched his back until he leaped to grab the first bar, pulled himself up, and turned his face to the ceiling.

3

O'Doole's crackled with the click of heeled pumps and the energy of forty professionals putting off bedtime for another hour. Valentine waved at Morrison and Shannon from the bar area and gestured to a booth in the corner. On Valentine's arm, his wife Lillian turned and smiled, petite until she turned sideways, then—*bam!*—her belly stuck out like a basketball.

Shannon rested her hand on her own stomach. *Abby.* She'd never regretted the surrogacy, not even when she'd found herself in Dr. McCallum's office feeling like an empty shell while the psychiatrist handed her tissues and a prescription for postpartum antidepressants.

Six years since she'd had Abby. Two since Derry's doctor had said "cancer." How things had changed.

Morrison touched her arm. "I'll grab us drinks. Red wine?" He met her eyes and smiled, and she nodded. At least some things stuck.

They sat in a corner booth far enough from the hubbub of the bar that they could hear one another. Morrison returned with the drinks, plunked the glasses in front of them, and took his seat across from her.

"To the best damn prosecutor I've ever met," Valentine said, raising his glass to Shannon.

Shannon clinked his cup with her own. Valentine had been first on the scene, finding Johnson in the tub and calling for an ambulance. He'd managed to preserve the crime scene too, not an easy task with EMS personnel. All she'd done was finish the job of putting Johnson away.

Valentine leaned across the table and lowered his voice. "Between you and me, though, I wasn't the least bit upset that Johnson took care of Derek. That asshole, beating on his kid, he didn't deserve to—"

"Isaac, enough," Lillian said, touching his elbow. "You're going to get yourself all worked up again."

Valentine shrugged. "You know what I'm saying."

Shannon did. Derek Lewis had hurt Diamond, and society wasn't any worse off after Ashley Johnson killed him. And Johnson *had* killed him, even if Petrosky—and maybe Morrison—didn't agree. She'd have to pick Morrison's brain later. Maybe. For now, she avoided his eyes and sipped her wine as Valentine sat back in his chair.

"Speaking of..." Morrison said, and Shannon swiveled in her seat to see what he was looking at. *Griffen.* Same suit he'd worn in the courtroom, one she'd seen a hundred times before. *Frugal bastard.* At least he'd loosened his tie.

Griffen slid into one of the stools at the bar, his posture erect but not quite as confident as it'd been this morning. He tossed something into his mouth and swallowed it dry. A pill? The strawberry-ash blonde on the stool next to him—familiar, though Shannon couldn't place her—laid a hand on Griffen's arm, her mouth at his ear. Looked like things hadn't worked out with Griffen's last stick-in-her-ass girlfriend, the one who'd said: "It's your friendship with Shannon or your relationship with me." Served him right. Shannon had always been there for Griffen, but there'd never been a romance between them—and no reason for her to be cut off like a gangrenous limb. Though if Griffen hadn't severed their friendship, she'd never have gotten so close to Morrison. And Morrison didn't date much, nor did it seem like he'd respond well to someone telling him to drop his best friend.

Then again...she'd never expected Griffen to drop her either. She finished her wine.

The strawberry-haired woman was looking Shannon's way now—prettier than his last girlfriend, thin, with wide eyes, full lips, and a fuller chest. Griffen was following her gaze, though he avoided eye contact with anyone at Shannon's table.

Morrison was already standing. "I'm going to say hi." His eyes were serene but still sharp somehow. "He's a nice guy. Can't blame him for doing his job."

Valentine sighed. "I'll grab another chair."

Griffen said something to the bartender, probably ordering his favorite martini—dry with two olives—and part of Shannon ached with nostalgia because she knew that. She waved Morrison down. "No, I'll go." He glanced at the couple at the bar and back at her and nodded.

Griffen looked up when she approached, but his smile was tight, and he refused to meet her eyes, opting to look over her shoulder at the table, or maybe at the wall. "How are you, Shannon? It's been a while."

"It has. Too long." She raised her glass. "To the trial being over?"

Griffen touched her glass with his own, his eyes on his half-empty drink. His face was still drawn and disappointed. No one likes to lose. Shannon turned to Griffen's date to introduce herself, but the woman beat her to it.

"Shannon Taylor, esquire," the redhead said knowingly. "I watched the trial."

Now Shannon remembered where she'd see her. "You were there this morning." *Behind Petrosky's stupid ass.*

"Had a case right before yours with Delacour." The woman extended her hand. "Where are my manners? I'm Karen. I work over at the rehab center, so I'm at the courthouse to testify occasionally if one of our guys gets into trouble. Though now I have another reason." She gestured to Griffen. "You'll have to excuse him. He's had a headache all day. I'm sure you understand."

Shannon nodded. He'd gotten stress headaches in college too, just like she had.

Griffen had downed his martini and was ordering another, his lips still moving, pursing and relaxing like he was already drinking it. He hadn't even looked at her. *What a dick.* Unless he felt guilty about how they'd parted ways. As he should, but...

Screw it. She reached over to the bar and squeezed his hand. "Nice job today. Really. I've been hoping you were doing well."

Griffen looked at his arm, at her hand, and then at Karen, who seemed stiff beside her though Shannon didn't really care why. He finally smiled at her—friendly, the way he'd been in college. "Thanks, Shannon. I've hoped all was going well with you too. So things are good?"

Some things. She pushed the flash of Derry's thin fingers from her mind and nodded. The silence stretched. "Anyway, I just wanted to come say, hey." She took her hand back and gestured to the table where Morrison and Valentine were peering over their drinks, Morrison impassive, Valentine almost...pouting. "Want to join us?"

Griffen looked over at the table but shook his head. Karen examined the group, maybe Valentine or maybe Morrison, as if still trying to decide whether they should join the party.

"I really appreciate the offer," Griffen said, "but we just stopped in on the way to my place. I need another ibuprofen and a little rest. Maybe a rain check?"

Karen frowned at the table and drew her eyes back to Shannon.

"Absolutely," Shannon said, trying not to feel too guilty about the way her chest relaxed. "You just let me know when." Shannon headed back to the table. She plopped into her seat and winced, her muscles already starting to ache from her workout.

Valentine sneered. "So how was our good friend, The Defense?"

Shannon rolled her eyes at him. "He's fine."

"Doesn't look fine. He looks pissed."

Shannon glanced over her shoulder in time to see Griffen and Karen heading out the door. Karen threw her a cool backward glance before she disappeared onto the street. *Griffen sure knows how to pick them.* "That's how I look when I lose, too."

"True enough." Valentine threw back the last of his beer.

Morrison was still staring after Griffen. "I swear I know that woman from somewhere."

"She works over at Breckenridge Rehab. You've probably seen her in court."

Morrison frowned, but his face softened when Lillian jumped.

"Sorry. Nothing like a baby kick in the ribs to wake you up."

"Did you decide what you're going to name that baby yet?" Morrison asked.

Valentine set his glass down. "All out of crazy hippie suggestions, are you?"

"For now."

"Thank goodness." Lillian yawned. "We like Mason. It was my grandfather's name."

"I love that." Shannon had considered naming her own theoretical children after her late grandparents: Evelyn and Terrence. They were probably the only reason she was halfway normal.

Valentine put an affectionate hand on Lillian's belly. "You making Mommy tired already, kid?"

Morrison pushed his drink aside. "Probably need to head out too. Long day tomorrow."

Lillian's belly rolled like a puppy under a blanket. Shannon watched it writhe until Morrison tapped her on the hand to leave.

4

When Shannon awoke the next morning, a hazy darkness enveloped her room. Thunderheads had already crept their way across the dawn and blotted out the morning sun. Storms today. She sighed and shoved her feet into her shoes.

Abby was still asleep, her short, straight hair plastered to the side of her head, her kitten Lucky curled against her neck in a way that made it look like he might suffocate her.

Shannon's heart skipped a beat. "Abs?" She touched Abby's shoulder just as Abby squinted through the dusky gray dawn, her slightly upturned nose wrinkling. Even half-asleep, she was adorable.

"Morning, Aunt Shanny." Lucky yawned and stretched his front paws.

Shannon sneezed. "Morning, Ab. Ready to get up and go to school?"

Abby put an arm around Lucky, and the kitten started up like a motor. "Nope."

"Understood. Let's do it anyway."

Abby pushed herself to seated, Lucky scampering onto her lap. "Will you make me pancakes?"

"Of course." Shannon smiled and left the room, easing the door shut behind her. Abby seemed so...happy. Normal. But what was about to happen to her wasn't normal at all. No kid should have to lose a parent. Well, no kid should lose a good parent, anyway.

The griddle was sizzling with blueberry dough when Abby finally entered the kitchen in a knee-length tie-dye shirt and aqua leggings.

Shannon flipped a pancake. "Nice shirt," she said.

"The kids at school think it's ugly."

"They don't know anything about fashion."

"That's what I said." Abby sat at the table, and Lucky leapt onto her lap.

"Oh. Good." What an amazing kid. Shannon slid the pancakes onto plates and topped them with fresh berries, then carried the plates to the table and sat beside Abby.

Lucky pawed Abby's hand as she picked up her fork. She giggled and shoveled a big bite into her mouth, watching as Shannon did the same. "These are good, Aunt Shanny." Three bites. Four. Five. "Daddy always says you're a good cook." Her face fell.

Don't do it, Ab. Don't bring it up. Shannon didn't want to think about her brother dying right now. Didn't want to talk about it now. But if Abby needed to...

Abby put her fork down on her nearly empty plate. "I wish I could make Daddy better. I was looking online, and there was an article about bone marrow transplants and—"

Shannon shook her head. "Abby." The cancer was everywhere: his bones, his liver, his brain. "We can't fix it." No matter how much they wanted to. They were helpless. Hopeless.

"When do you think he'll get to come home?"

"Hopefully, in the next week." Shannon pushed her half-eaten pancake aside and took Abby's hand. "They just wanted to keep an eye on that big infection he's got on his leg."

"That was my fault," Abby whispered. Lucky leapt from her lap and ran between Shannon's feet. "He was trying to fix my bike, and the wrench slipped and—"

"It wasn't your fault, Ab."

Abby's lip quivered, and Lucky clambered back on top of

her knees. She released Shannon's hand and stroked his head.

"The chemo for the cancer makes his immune system weak, Abby. It wasn't your fault. He loves you so much that he'd do anything in the world to make you happy, and if you told him he wasn't allowed to touch your bike, he'd probably throw a fit."

Tears pooled in Abby's hazel eyes. "I know."

"Your daddy is a stubborn guy. He'll have a little longer. And then we'll have to be strong, but we'll be together, okay?"

Abby bit her lip, "Will you get cancer?"

"No, I don't think so."

"What about Dad?"

Daddy, Derry. Dad, Alex. Pretty soon, she'd have only one of them. Shannon set her fork down so Abby wouldn't see it shaking. "We'll be fine. Your daddy just had wicked bad luck. We'll do the best we can to enjoy the time we have left." But there'd never be enough time. *Fuck cancer.* Shannon stood. "Did you get enough to eat?"

Abby nodded, her eyes on Lucky's striped fur. The kitten purred like an engine, and Shannon liked the little sneeze machine even more because of Abby's calmness as she stroked his back.

"Get your bag, okay, sweetie? We don't want to be late." Shannon picked up the plates and took them to the sink, her vision blurred by the tears in her eyes.

THE CLOUDS WERE heavy with rain or maybe one last snow, judging by the layer of frost on her windshield. *So much for spring.* Shannon parked in front of the Ash Park precinct and headed for the adjacent brown building where the prosecutor's office waited for her like an old, sullen dog someone had left out in the cold. The side entrance was unlocked, the lobby silent. She trotted up the back stairs. They'd never had the budget for security, and they didn't need it; if they had a crisis, they'd have a barrage of cops here in ten seconds.

In the bland, beige hallway, three framed paintings of watercolor butterflies hung at eye level, probably meant to convey a deeper significance than bugs or flight, but Shannon had never had time to ponder it. In all probability, neither had the three other attorneys who worked there with her, two men and one other woman. Their offices were at the far end of the hall; past hers and far enough away that she never had to see them unless they were brushing elbows at the office mailboxes. They didn't like her. Or maybe they'd just stayed away from her because of whom she'd married. She could hardly blame them.

Brown carpet muted the clacking of her heels as she turned the corner toward her office. Her heart dropped.

"Morning, Shannon." Roger McFadden stood just outside her door, six feet five inches of impeccable Brooks Brothers suit and flawless blond hair, smiling at her with his million teeth. The same smile he gave to every jury that was swinging in his favor. The same shit-eating grin he'd worn on their wedding day.

Bastard. Her chest heated with old hurt and new irritation. "Roger." She squeezed past him more aggressively than probably necessary.

His eyes bored a hole in her back. "Shannon. Nice work yesterday on Johnson."

"Thanks, *boss*." She shoved the key into the lock, and her keychain banged against the door, echoing down the hall. She needed to chill out, or he'd know his mere presence still got to her.

"You of all people don't have to call me that. Though head prosecutors do get some perks, I suppose." More teeth. He followed her into her office and sat across from her desk in one of the black leather chairs she had taken in their divorce settlement.

She sat reluctantly. *I should get a new job.* "What do you need, Roger?"

His eyes were tight, but it felt fake. "How's Jerry?" he said.

Shannon yanked a file from the top drawer of her desk. "Fine."

"Is he really? I thought he was—"

She slammed the folder on the desk. "He's as fine as he can be, Roger, you know what I meant."

His eyes blazed: angry, not hurt. "Just because we're not together anymore doesn't mean I don't care about your family. About Abby. About you. It's hard to work together when you hate me."

"You should have considered that before."

"I made one stupid mistake."

"Four. That I know of. They were just all the same type of mistake." *Why the hell are we still having his conversation?*

"You were just as guilty of finding comfort outside our marriage. The only reason you aren't attached now is that your rebound likes men."

She squared her shoulders. "Morrison isn't a rebound. He's just a friend, same as he was before we got married." Like she had the time or the desire to date anyway after dealing with Roger's bullshit. She wouldn't be ready for a relationship for a good long time—if ever. "And just because he also happens to be friends with my brother doesn't mean he's gay. Sexuality isn't contagious." *Dumbass.* She bit her lip to keep from saying it.

She should have let Roger think they'd gotten it on just to wipe that smug look off his face. Shannon glanced at the desk. Maybe he'd be humbler if she threw her stapler at him. "I'm not the one who came here to meet with you today, Roger. What do you want?"

Roger shook his head. "I just wanted to help. You're always so suspicious of my intentions. It's hurtful."

I'm not falling for your mind games today, Roger. She jerked the desk drawer open again and retrieved a pen. "If you're done badgering me, I need to get some work done."

"Actually, there is one more thing."

She raised an eyebrow.

"You've got a case there on your desk, a Reverend Jack Wilson, arrested after his six-year-old daughter died of a traumatic brain injury."

Shannon shuffled through the files on her desk, pulled Wilson's free, and flipped it open. "Jesus."

"Cops found the kid on the floor, Wilson holding a towel to her head. Said he dropped her. The cops didn't buy it because of the medical examiner's report that there were fractures in more than one cranial bone, but Wilson claimed she hit a toy on her way down, which could be consistent with the ME's report." Roger ran a hand over a face that was free of wrinkles, hair, and any telltale signs of a conscience. "However, there are...extenuating circumstances. The kid wasn't with his wife, and he'd only just found out about her the month prior."

A month ago. So he'd found out he had an illegitimate kid, realized it might hurt his pious career, and tried to get rid of her. "We've got another first degree? Second degree?" His rap sheet was clean, save for a few parking tickets. She flipped back to the photos.

"This is a tricky one. We're keeping it quiet to protect his mistress. If the press calls, no interviews."

"I don't understand." But she did. *Protecting other cheaters, eh, Roger?* Yet bringing that up would turn the conversation back to their relationship, probably what he wanted, and she wasn't biting. Shannon flipped to the photos of a little girl, snow-white skin, black hair, vibrant red stain from temple to ear. "Looks like Reverend Wilson needs to practice what he preaches."

"Probably so." Roger consulted his watch. "Protecting the privacy of the mother matters. It's the right thing to do, keeping it quiet."

Roger had never given a damn about the right thing. Shannon pursed her lips as she scanned the file. "I'm sure Wilson is glad for that. *Grieving* as he is."

"Grieving...yeah." Roger shrugged. "Anyway, the police reports are sketchy, and we've got a few days before the arraignment, so I'm thinking we'll drop the charges down, see what we can get easy."

Reduce the charges. Again. "It's not always about easy, Roger. What about justice for this child?" Shannon traced the little girl's cheek in the photo. "Poor kid."

"Shame. I'll let you get to it." His voice was dull, flippant even, and the hairs on her neck rose. "Have a good day, Shannon."

Asshole. Shannon glared at his back until the door clicked shut. She sucked a breath of paper and leather and stale air conditioning and opened the next new file.

Ishantey Webster, nineteen. Rape victim refusing to file charges. She could encourage Webster to testify, but if Shannon tried to force the woman to trial, she ran the risk of re-traumatizing the poor girl and would be accused of trying losing cases based on gut feelings that would never fly in court. Not that it would have been the first time. That was why Roger had the position he did and she was still stuck in the office taking orders from a man she never wanted to be beholden to again.

Somewhere outside, thunder boomed. She tossed the Webster file aside and pulled out Wilson. The reverend who had probably murdered his love child had apparently managed to buy himself a jet by telling parishioners Jesus wanted him to have it, or some such nonsense. Shit, he was worth a ton of money. She ran her finger down the list of witnesses. The girl's mother, the reverend himself, a neighbor who showed up when she heard screaming. The first responders. She rubbed her temples and winced. There had to be someone else—someone he'd confided in about it. Suddenly finding out you had an illegitimate kid wouldn't go down easy.

Shannon pulled her laptop from her briefcase to search for articles on Wilson. Lots on the jet, less on any open transgressions. But one article buried in the search results caught her eye: a blogger named Jason Delaney had written a piece claiming Wilson had been spotted at a local pub on several occasions—a big no-no for a holy man. Delaney's blog had since been shut down, but a larger website on crooked ministers had picked it up and reblogged it. The bar angle could be nothing, but it'd be easier to get a conviction if she had a witness saying he was freaked out about the kid. And nothing loosened the tongue like liquor. *Plead it down, my ass.* Maybe she'd give the detectives a call back, ask them about it. She tried not to look toward Roger's stupid office.

The sky was still threatening to open and drown the world when a loud rap at the door made her squiggle a ragged line across the page she was jotting notes on. *What now?*

"Who is it?"

"Morrison."

The hammering in her head lessened. "Come in."

Morrison let himself into the room and set a cup of coffee on her desk. "Didn't have time to make coffee this morning, so I got you a caramel…something. Oh, and"— he set a paper sack on the table next to the coffee— "kale Caesar salad. I know it's not your favorite, but it was that or Greek."

"I hate Greek. Feta ruins everything."

"I know."

She picked up the coffee and narrowed her eyes at him. "You buttering me up for something?"

He grinned. "Got one for Valentine, too, and Petrosky. I don't see any of us walking over to the deli today in the storm that's coming. Except maybe Petrosky—he doesn't give a crap about the rain or his hair."

"So, just making the coffee rounds then?"

"And I like to see you smile."

"You like to see everyone smile."

"True."

She cocked her head. "Am I smiling?"

"Nope." He grinned, and she stared into his Pacific-blue eyes until the crinkle ironed itself from the corners, and he looked down at his shoes. "Okay, so maybe I found some new information on Johnson."

Oh, for god's sake. "I'm not working on Johnson anymore." She sighed. "Did you find this supposed clue, or did Petrosky?"

"I found it."

"Did Petrosky tell you to tell me?"

"He mentioned you might want to know, yes."

Fucking Petrosky. "Hey, you guys are cool," she said in her best gravelly Petrosky voice. "Why don't you go talk to her, Surfer Boy?" But Morrison wasn't a fool, and he knew better than to come at her with bullshit. It must be good.

She crossed her arms over her chest and leaned back in her chair. "So, what is it?"

"A video."

"Of?"

"The pay phone where the anonymous call about the gunshot came from. Looks like a guy covering his face."

On the day of the murder, hours before Lewis was killed, a neighbor had filed a noise complaint about yelling coming from the Lewis place. It was an easily verifiable phone call from the same building, one that fit with the rest of the day's events: argument between Johnson and Lewis, Johnson takes off, lets the anger fester, then she comes home to find Diamond, and there goes his freaking skull. But at midnight, after Derek Lewis's murder, an anonymous tip had come in from a pay phone, blocks from the scene, claiming that gunshots were heard inside Lewis's apartment. Yet, like she'd discussed with Petrosky ad nauseam, they hadn't found gun residue on Johnson or Lewis or anywhere in the apartment.

"Whoever called did it from this pay phone so they wouldn't be seen," Morrison said.

"They hit that phone because there wasn't another pay phone nearby. There's what? Twelve working pay phones in all of Metro Detroit?"

"I don't think that's it. If it was an emergency, if someone had really heard gunshots, there were tons of open gas stations and liquor stores near the scene. And this lot's been closed for the last two months, which is why we couldn't get hold of the owners before now—whoever called probably thought the place was deserted already." His brows knitted together. "Someone else knew that something bad had happened at Lewis's apartment."

Shannon shook her head. "Like I've told Petrosky three thousand damn times, there's no way to prove that. Hell, maybe Ashley Johnson caught a ride down there and called after she killed Lewis to make sure someone found Diamond. She knows how long the cops take to respond from her arguments with Lewis; she could have made the call and still have had at least forty-five minutes to get back and kill herself. She already has enough of her day unaccounted for."

"Unaccounted for?" Morrison squinted at her, confused, and a wave of recognition hit her.

She set down her coffee. *She wasn't depressed that day*, Petrosky had said.

"Was *Petrosky* with her?" Her fists clenched under the table. "Was that where she spent her missing hours after her fight with Lewis and before she cracked his skull?"

Morrison cocked his head. "Petrosky didn't tell you? Maybe it's something he's—"

"Morrison, what the hell is going on?"

"She met with Petrosky to pick up some clothes. For her interview."

"What time?"

"He picked her up about an hour before the first noise complaint came in. That's how we know she wasn't the one arguing with Lewis."

Are you kidding? "You're telling me that Ashley Johnson's missing hours were spent with *Petrosky*?" she growled. "Why didn't he bring that up before trial?" But Petrosky wasn't responsible for the ache in her gut. She lowered her voice. "Why didn't *you* tell me?"

"He said he told you."

"And you believed that lying asshole?"

Morrison shrugged, but his face didn't change. Sometimes she wanted to slap him just to see if he'd flinch.

She leaned back in her chair, breathing around the block of concrete that had settled in her chest. *Why would Petrosky keep this back?* "Was Johnson fucking him?" Not that it mattered; it was too late for Johnson now anyway. And it was definitely too late for Lewis. Either way, screw Morrison's partner.

"Nope, he was just helping her out. She didn't want Lewis to know about it." He frowned. "I don't know, Shannon. Maybe Petrosky figured he'd wait until he had more proof to tie it all up for you. All I know is he took her to the Goodwill on Main and then to dinner at Holly's. There'd be people who saw them, cameras at the Goodwill. The server at the restaurant. His credit card receipt." He shrugged. "Like I said, I thought you knew."

"You really thought he'd told me?" Shannon's heart throbbed in her ears. She glanced at the wall between her office and Roger's and tried to lower her voice again, but it wasn't going to work for long.

"We've been friends a long time, Shannon. I've never lied to you about anything."

The hard edges in her chest softened. "You lied about liking Valentine's pumpkin pie last Thanksgiving."

"I didn't lie to you about it. Just to Lillian."

She sighed. Who had Lewis argued with? Who had called after he died? It really didn't matter, not now, but it would have been nice to know this information weeks ago. *Petrosky. What a dick.*

"Maybe we can talk about this more over dinner?" Morrison said.

"I'm swamped." She put her hands on the desk, shuffled her case files around.

Morrison watched her flip the Webster case to the top of the stack. "Coffee?"

"Never in the afternoon."

"Wine?"

"I don't drink."

He smiled. "Liar." He turned toward the door and paused with his hand on the knob, waiting. "See you at the gym."

She stared at his back but didn't respond.

He sighed, glanced over his shoulder, and nodded almost imperceptibly, mouth tight. Sad.

Good. He knew he'd screwed up. When she said nothing more, he turned back to the exit. "Until we meet under the barbell, Shanny." He eased the door closed behind him.

When she heard the clack of the latch, she grabbed the bag and speared a bite of salad as thunder rolled and rain and sleet attacked the roof like thousands of angry marbles. The kale was bitter but good, and probably healthier than the roast beef sandwich she'd planned on ordering from the deli down the street—not to mention drier.

She stared at the icy rain sheeting down her window and obscuring the world like she was trapped in a filmy bubble. No wonder Petrosky was so adamant about this Johnson case. And to hide all this for months was just...God, he was an asshole. Maybe even an asshole who obstructed justice. Unless he was just lying to get Shannon to look at the case. Or...did something happen during his time with Johnson that implicated her further? Was there something Johnson said or did that made her look guilty? Something he hadn't wanted to testify about?

That was probably it. Petrosky treated half these women like they were his own daughters. Probably because he'd lost his own so horribly. She poked at a cucumber with her fork. How would "Daddy" react if he found out some asshole was beating on his girl and her child? Shannon blew her hair out of her face, giving her frustration a voice. *Shit, could it have been...*

No way. Petrosky was a dick, but not a murderer.

She speared a final forkful of salad but tossed it, along with the carton, into the trash. Her throat had become too tight with dread to swallow another bite.

5
———

THE SLEET WARMED to a chaotic rain that had eased to a trickle by the time Shannon got into her car that evening. Wet earth and last season's leaves, their scents awakened by the melting ice, crept in through the closed car windows as she drove down Main Street toward the gym to sweat out the remnants of her agitation. On her right, the original Ash Park loomed from behind a wrought iron gate, its hinges long since rusted beyond use. Shame. In the back, knotty ash trees coiled in on themselves behind what was left of a park bench—all hiding in the shadow of the old elementary school, its windows boarded and forgotten. The year before, a serial killer had used the school to gut a prostitute and her son; left their bodies for the rats. Petrosky had taken it hard. Maybe he'd been close to that girl too, though he'd never said. Sometimes as Shannon drove by, she imagined she could still hear them screaming.

The CrossFit warehouse vibrated with the anticipatory energy of six regulars plus a curly-haired blond woman Shannon didn't recognize, all stretching their legs and doing warm-up exercises at the frantic pace of people trying to catch up after not doing shit all week. Morrison was already there, stretching his hamstrings, watching her wearily. He cocked an eyebrow like he was asking if she was still pissed. The hardness in her chest softened. It wasn't his fault Petrosky was a jerk. And Morrison clearly couldn't be expected to verify what his partner did or didn't tell her. Shannon nodded to him, smiled, and watched him grin back before heading to the bathroom to change.

But something was still gnawing at her insides, irritating the lining of her belly. In the bathroom mirror, her eyes looked sharp and blue, mouth too tight, forehead still crinkled with annoyance. Petrosky. He was a dick, but she *had* been wrong about Johnson arguing with Derek Lewis. Had she been wrong about Johnson killing him too? She shook her head. No. *Hell no.* She had done her due diligence on that case. Johnson had killed Lewis. The end.

Fuck you, Petrosky. She pulled her workout gear from the bag with enough force to tear the zipper.

When she emerged from the bathroom, Kimball was stepping to the front of the class and clapping his hands in a short staccato burst that meant *it's go time.* "Today we're starting with twenty laps around the warehouse," he said, practically yelling, though there was no other sound in the room save for the gentle patter of the waning raindrops on the roof. "Then suck it up for fifty double unders, hip-shoulder mobility stretches, thirty squats, twenty pass-throughs with a PVC pipe, and thirty overhead squats." Staccato hand clap. "And go!"

Shannon fell into step with Morrison as they took off around the interior perimeter of the warehouse. She took the first corner faster than he did, but he recovered and caught her before the next turn. Around and around and around. Third lap. Fourth. Shannon tuned in to the dull thunk of their shoes, the scrape of rubber against concrete, her own aggravated breath that had nothing to do with the run. *Fuck Petrosky. Fuck him in his stupid eye.*

"You okay?" Morrison asked.

He always knew, goddamn him. Ahead of them, the

woman with blond corkscrew curls bobbled, righted herself, and swiped an arm across her forehead. She was obviously new—she'd pass out halfway through Kimball's workout if she tried to maintain this pace.

Shannon caught Morrison's eye before refocusing on the path ahead. "I'm fine."

"Want to talk about it?"

"No."

"No?"

"Well...maybe," she panted.

They circled around to the front of the warehouse for the...fifteenth time? Eighteenth time? She had no idea, but Kimball was gesturing for them to come back to the main workout area. As the blond woman in front of her passed him, he ran his fingers over her arm, lightly, suggestively, and Shannon caught the woman giving him a wink. *Huh.*

Kimball didn't smile at Shannon when she passed. Or touch her arm or any other part of her. She would have kicked him in the balls. "Grab your ropes!" he barked, turning on the music: hip-hop.

Shannon headed to the middle of the room, where the jump ropes lay across wooden utility crates, one for each of them. She grabbed hers and got into position.

"Double unders, let me see 'em!"

"Is it about Johnson?" Morrison said beside her, his jump rope whipping through the air. How was he talking? She could barely catch her breath.

"Keep it going, people. Forty more," Kimball called.

Shannon counted, pushing every thought she had into her laboring muscles, the bounce in the balls of her feet, the rope whistling twice under for each jump.

"Ten more, people."

"Shannon? Is it about Johnson?"

"Lay 'em down, people, we're gonna stretch it out," Kimball yelled, and his voice had an agitated edge. Angry, even. Must have had a bad day, though she'd have thought the pretty blonde he was flirting with earlier might have taken the edge off.

"Yeah. Obviously, it's about Johnson," she said to Morrison. It came out breathy and strained. She sank into a deep lunge, one leg in front of the other, knee almost touching the floor.

Morrison lunged beside her.

"Switch legs." Kimball leveled a hard stare at her, then at Morrison, who was paying him no attention.

Shannon pulled one leg back and lunged with her other. "I—" The room was suddenly too quiet, maybe between songs. At the front of the room, Kimball lunged too, eyeing them with a furrowed brow and tight lips. When he caught her looking, he turned his attention to Bouncy Curls on Shannon's left, and his face softened. "Switch legs. Last set."

Shannon's heart was throbbing in her ears as loudly as the bass line by the time she completed her squats and pass-throughs. Every muscle in her upper body sang. Her arms ached, but she held the pipe and panted through the overhead squats. Shannon thought she felt Morrison's eyes on her as she completed the last ten reps, but when she looked, he was focused straight ahead, breathing hard, sweat glistening at the crook of his elbow and wetting the ocean wave on his T-shirt. *So he's human after all.*

"That's it," Kimball called. "Nice work."

Shannon strode past Morrison to the bathroom, where she wiped herself off and threw her suit back on so she wouldn't freeze in the chilly night air with her soaked gym clothes. When she emerged, wrinkled and exhausted, Morrison had already changed his shirt and was toweling his hair. He shoved the towel into his gym bag.

Valentine walked over to her from the entrance. *When did he get here?* She wracked her brain, trying to remember if he'd been there the whole class...no, she was sure he hadn't. And he didn't have a drop of sweat on him. Maybe he was just coming to do some after-class reps before heading home.

"Missed you in class tonight," she said.

"No worries, I'll see you tomorrow in court. I've got the spot after you with Judge Oliver."

She glanced around the room for the curly-haired lady who was probably halfway to screwing Kimball—there were cheaters everywhere, she would know—but the woman was gone. Must have run out as soon as class was over. Maybe out puking in the parking lot—that happened sometimes with the first-timers. "What are you in court on?" she asked Valentine.

"People contesting parking tickets. The usual shit for a flatfoot." He winked, but his face fell when Kimball cleared his throat from behind him. Kimball gestured to the warehouse door.

"Anyway, see you guys," Valentine said and headed for the bathroom.

Shannon nodded to Valentine and followed Morrison to the exit. As they passed Kimball, he waved goodbye with one terse jerk of the wrist.

"Did he just dismiss us?" Shannon said.

Morrison nodded. "He must have somewhere to go. Like always."

"Not in a hurry to toss Valentine out, though, is he?" And Morrison had a key, why would Kimball give a shit if they stayed?

A crisp breeze sharp enough to cut skin blew through the garage doors, mingling the reek of body odor with asphalt and soggy dirt. Morrison ran a hand through his damp hair.

"Want to get coffee?"

"No caffeine for me, I—" She stopped short at the garage door and stared across the lot. Her car. Something was wrong with her car. The back window had been smashed, bits of glass glistening on the ground. The papers fluttering across the lot looked like the yellow legal pad she used to keep notes. In fact—

Shannon dropped her bag and ran to her car. Her briefcase lay over the broken window, half in and half out of the vehicle, her files tossed on the pavement. She peered at the dash, expecting the stereo to be tampered with—or gone—but it looked intact. She clicked unlock to disable the apparently useless alarm, opened her car door, and reached across to the console where she had tossed her jewelry before going into the warehouse. Her earrings glinted in the overhead lights. What the hell? Not that she wanted to be stolen from, but if they hadn't broken in for valuables…

Morrison bent toward the broken window and peered inside. "You set the alarm?"

The pit in Shannon's stomach twisted. She sat back in the driver's seat. "Yeah, I did, but it only sounds if someone opens the doors."

Morrison's brows furrowed. "What did you have in the briefcase?"

"Just files from work." She closed the glove box. "Nothing identifying, just my notes. All my official files are at the office." She chewed her lip, thinking. She'd had information on a couple of assaults that looked like they'd get off. A child manslaughter case that would be settled with a plea. No paperwork worth taking. Shannon stared through the windshield across the lot. Kimball was approaching from the warehouse, phone in hand. Where was Valentine? This was his kind of thing.

Morrison knelt behind the car, trying to grab the remaining sheets skittering around the lot. "They all in here? Or most of them?" He passed her the papers he'd collected.

Shannon sifted through the paperwork. I…I'm missing a few pages on a sexual assault I got yesterday, though the main fact sheet is still here. And…Johnson's." She flipped. "All of Johnson's notes."

"Johnson? But—"

"I had some stuff left over from the trial, mostly from my final summation." She peeled back page after page. Someone took her notes? *Now?* No, that made no sense; the case was over. The sheets were probably wafting around in the woods that backed the lot or shimmying across the street, ready to disintegrate with the next rainstorm. Had to be. But...what if they weren't?

Goddammit all to hell. She needed a drink. "Let's go get some food."

"I just asked you for coffee. Don't you think you're jumping the gun a little?" His face remained flat, but she could feel the lilt in his voice.

"Oh, fuck off, Morrison. This is not the time."

He put his hands up in acquiescence. "All right, you've convinced me—dinner it is. We can take my car. I'll get a tow and file a report on this later tonight."

Shannon nodded mutely, her heart palpitating, and exited the car while Morrison peered into the night behind her.

RED VELVET CURTAINS STRADDLED every window, but abstract art hanging from wires on the ceiling kept the place from feeling pretentious—local stuff, maybe from the high school, all swirls in obnoxious colors. The waitress directed an irritating thousand-watt smile at Morrison.

Shannon glared at her until she walked away. "How'd you find this place?"

"A phone app. Got tons of great places around here, most of them out of the way."

She stabbed a piece of salmon, trying to ignore the errant creases in her blouse and how completely disgusting she felt. She should have gone home to shower. "Fuck today. I mean, seriously." She stuck the salmon in her mouth and forced herself to swallow, but her stomach flipped. She set her fork down.

"I understand. Sometimes life's tricky."

"Tricky? Jesus, Morrison, you've got all the passion of a paper clip."

Morrison smiled and sipped his water. "I'll let Petrosky know what happened. I'm sure he'll want —"

"Screw Petrosky. What's he going to do, look into it and withhold information again like a royal dick?" She took a gulp of wine and relished the gentle acidic burn as it slid down her throat and calmed her heart. Or maybe she just hoped it would calm her; her glass rattled against the table as she set it down. "You couldn't pay me enough to deal with him on a regular basis."

"He's a good guy. A little rough, but a good guy."

"Why are you so forgiving of him?"

Morrison shrugged. "He kind of reminds me of my dad, that closed-off demeanor. Not easy for everyone to love"—he gestured to her— "case in point." He waited while she grabbed her wine glass again. "Plus, he doesn't have any other family, not since Julie died."

Her heart seized. She hated that she still had a soft spot for Petrosky, but no one deserved to lose a child. "Is that why he helps all the working girls? Because of what happened with his daughter?"

"Petrosky's teenage daughter was not a prostitute."

"No, but she was kidnapped, right? Raped and murdered?"

Morrison nodded, eyes on the wall behind her.

"So is that why he does it? He thinks he's helping the girls?"

"I don't know. He just helps. Gives them food. Money."

"Clothes on the down-low."

Morrison pushed a tomato around on his plate. "A place to stay."

He lets hookers stay at his house? Her jaw dropped. "Why would he let those women stay with him? It's... Isn't he worried they'll steal his stuff? Maybe get in trouble if people think he's soliciting?"

"I think things get a little lonely for him." He took a bite of salad and washed it down with mineral water.

"Nothing like a hooker to make you feel less lonely."

Morrison laughed. "Indeed." He put down his fork, his eyes on her full plate.

"God, I hate this." She didn't have to say "the car"; she could tell he already knew by the way he nodded, knew that even the wine couldn't turn her brain off. She sighed. The break-in wasn't necessarily related to Johnson, but the timing was too perfect—just after Johnson's conviction, and whoever it was hadn't taken any other files. But why now? Why not before, earlier in the trial? It would have made more sense to take her notes then, whether someone was trying to help Johnson or incriminate the woman further. Shannon tucked a stray hair behind her ear.

Morrison watched her closely, his blue eyes locked on her, supportive, questioning. "You know it isn't a coincidence."

Not a coincidence...because he thought she'd prosecuted the wrong person. Was Johnson innocent? No. *But what if she is?* No, she had to stop thinking that way. "Whatever. I know you guys are going to have to investigate, but I don't need Petrosky all over me about it, which is the only reason I haven't confronted him about that information he withheld on Johnson. And I need evidence more conclusive than Derek arguing with a mystery person before you guys come at me on this again. I'm not about to go telling Roger that I convicted the wrong girl based on some random phone call and a smashed window."

"You're not worried about Roger."

She clenched her fist, released it. "Fine. If Johnson really is guilty and I go shedding doubt on her conviction, Griffen could appeal and get it tossed. Doubtful, but possible. I don't want to be responsible for a guilty person going free any more than for an innocent person being locked up." She drummed her fingers on the table. "You can tell Petrosky so long as he keeps it close to the vest. Which apparently he's good at doing if he's letting prostitutes live with him." She forked an asparagus spear but just stared at it. Her car. *Someone trashed my car.* She set the asparagus back on her plate and wiped her fingers on a napkin. Her hand shook.

Morrison leaned forward, appraising her and what was left of her fish. "You need dessert."

Her chest was tight enough that she feared she'd never be able to swallow. "I can't really eat right now."

"Trust me." Morrison summoned the waitress. "The usual, Kim." The girl grinned at him, shot daggers at Shannon, and left.

She raised an eyebrow at the waitress's back. "You come here often?"

"Are you trying to pick me up?"

Shannon stifled a smile. "I mean, come on, 'the usual'? And you're on a first-name basis with the waitress?"

"I've been here a handful of times."

"With who?" Was he seeing someone and hadn't told her? Her stomach tightened. Nah, he'd have mentioned it. They were buddies. Best buddies. Had been for years, since before she'd married Roger, and they'd had enough conversations about his stupid ass.

"I come alone," he said. "Usually at lunch. Been trying to get Petrosky to come too, but the one time he did, he ordered meatballs and bread to make it into a sandwich." Morrison shook his head and smiled affectionately. "I'd have brought you sooner, but you say you're busy half the time. Always eating at your desk."

"I also say I don't drink." Shannon nodded at her glass of wine.

"That's because you're a liar. But I still like you." He winked.

Kim returned with crème brûlée and two spoons, which she deposited in front of Morrison, without so much as a glance in Shannon's direction. *Looks like someone doesn't want a tip.* When the waitress was gone, Shannon reached over and grabbed a utensil, but Morrison stopped her short of actually spooning anything into her mouth.

"Let's play a game."

She furrowed her brows. "You're going to try that Zen bullshit again, aren't you?"

He chuckled. "Zip it and close your eyes. Have I ever steered you wrong before?"

Shannon leaned on her elbows, with her fingers laced together and perched her chin on her knuckles.

"Your eyes aren't closed."

She blew a stray hair out of her face and closed her eyes.

"Now inhale, and describe what you smell."

After a moment, the light scent of sweet cream invaded her sinuses. "Sugar."

"Try again."

"Vanilla?"

"More."

She sniffed again, the heat from his hand on the spoon tingling along her cheekbone as the scent of the food wafted into her nostrils. "Maybe...alcohol?"

"Grand Marnier. Okay, open your mouth."

She opened her mouth, and he laid a teaspoon of the dessert on the tip of her tongue.

"Let it rest there, but don't swallow."

She closed her lips and swirled the custard around the roof of her mouth.

"What do you taste?"

"Besides what I just smelled?"

"Yes."

"Fruity. Orange?"

"Orange peel. Did you notice that before?"

"Nope." She swallowed, easily, and opened her eyes. With her throat finally relaxed, she picked up her fork and finished her salmon. "That's a good trick, dammit. Plus, I bet it makes you eat less. I could probably stand to eat less brownies."

"Eh, you can eat as many brownies as you want, Stone Cold."

She shivered. "Ick. Don't call me that. It's creepy."

"Better than mine, though." He took a bite of the custard and held it in his mouth before swallowing, just as he'd had her do.

"I'll just call you Buddha."

"I can't live up to that." He leaned back in his chair. Shannon met his eyes, and for a moment, she was in the ocean, could almost feel the waves washing over her, her limbs floating in liquid salt. She picked up her wine again as Morrison's phone buzzed.

Morrison looked at his cell. "Looks like Petrosky's headed to the hospital on something," he said. "You want to swing by and see Derry? I told him I'd come say hi this week anyway."

Shannon's face was hot. Why was her face hot? She frowned at the wine glass and nodded.

6

By the time they arrived at the hospital, the crisp evening breeze had cooled Shannon's face. But Petrosky looked as irritated as ever, scowling at the ER doors, his cheeks pink with cold—or rage—a cigarette between his teeth. When Shannon and Morrison stepped onto the curb, Petrosky tossed his cigarette to the ground and headed inside through the automatic doors. "Domestic Violence case turned homicide," Petrosky muttered at the fluorescent hallway in front of them.

"Why'd they call us?" Morrison asked Petrosky's back.

"Abuse history. She called the cops yesterday and had him picked up. Tonight he shot her for her trouble. It'll be routine and over today, if I can grab the evidence." Petrosky pried an antacid from a roll, shoved it into his mouth, and stuck the roll back into his pocket. "I'm trying to get them to pull the bullet for me tonight, but they're giving me shit about it. I hate when they give me shit." He stopped in front of a door and leaned against the wall opposite. "That's why I'll wait here until I have what I need. That, and I want to snag this twat before he heads to Canada."

"Harassing the doctors might not be the best way to get what you want," Shannon said.

Petrosky kept his eyes on the door. "Always worked in the past."

Shannon balked as a thin woman with gray-streaked hair and flowered scrubs exited the room. The nurse smiled at each of them solemnly, though with tired eyes and lips that didn't quite curl up all the way. "They'll do what they can, dear," she said to Petrosky. "But we're backed up tonight, and they need to focus on the living before they get to your...er, request. Even the morgue is behind."

Petrosky nodded and took her hands in his. "Thank you, Frannie, I do appreciate you."

Shannon did a double take. Since when was Petrosky that...considerate?

The nurse nodded like Petrosky's behavior was perfectly normal. Shannon supposed it was, but certainly not for him.

"You go on and do what you have to do," the nurse said. "Find who did this to that poor girl."

"Oh, we will." Petrosky released her hands, and the nurse retreated down the hall.

Shannon watched her go, trying to remain calm by channeling her inner crème-brûlée-eating monk but ended up glaring at Petrosky instead. *Manipulative bastard. Just like Roger.* He didn't deserve a free pass on the material he'd kept from her on Johnson. "So I hear you withheld information on Johnson's whereabouts the day Lewis died."

"It didn't matter—you were still going to convict her." Petrosky twisted his head, and his neck popped, but his eyes stayed with her, defiant. "Easy win for the prosecution."

Shannon's heart rate tripled, and her shoulders went rigid. "I didn't take it because it was easy, you asshole. What could have been that important to Johnson that she would withhold something like that? That *you* would withhold it?"

"Maybe she didn't feel obliged to tell the person who was going after her."

"Okay, but—"

"I was only with her for a couple hours, well before

Lewis's murder. After dinner, she said she wanted to take a walk before her interview. I didn't argue with her."

"So really, she could have been doing anything. Maybe she was high as hell on smack before she even got to the apartment, killed Derek for no reason at all."

"And you wonder why she didn't tell you? Besides, heroin doesn't make people go ape shit and murder folks."

Shannon crossed her arms, the crème brûlée burbling in her stomach. "You're lucky I don't call you out for obstruction."

Petrosky shrugged.

"Shannon?"

She felt a hand on her shoulder and whipped around. *If just one more person messes with me right now, I swear to god—*

But it was Alex, his face drawn and pale, and her agitation melted into concern and settled heavy at the bottom of her stomach. "I didn't know you were coming up today," he said. His voice was strained.

"I...didn't know I was coming either." The words hung in the air between them, thick with unspoken explanations. *What happened?* Had Derry taken a turn for the worse? The doctors said he could deteriorate fast, but surely not within a day or two. She examined Alex's tense jaw, fighting the urge to run upstairs.

Morrison nodded to Alex, unsmiling, so he must have noticed that something was deeply wrong too. "Good to see you, Alex." Morrison glanced at his partner.

Shannon had almost forgotten Petrosky was there. "Oh, uh, Dr. Coleman, this is Detective Petrosky." Shannon gestured between the two. "Petrosky, Dr. Coleman."

Petrosky shoved his hands in his pockets, jaw tight, eyes narrow and suspicious. *What is that about?*

Alex ignored the slight and turned to Morrison to take his offered hand. "Good to see you again, Curt. Jerry said you were coming by. I just didn't know it would be tonight."

"Spur of the moment," Morrison admitted, peering into Alex's face. The worry lines around his mouth deepened.

Alex stepped back and addressed Shannon, lowering his voice. "Hey, if you have an extra minute, come on up to Jerry's room. I think it would be good for Abby to see you. She had a rough day."

Rough day. *Shit, not Derry. Please, not Derry.* "What happened?" The words trembled on her tongue but sounded okay in the air.

"Lucky...died." His words were *not* steady in the air—they vibrated from his lips, ragged and hoarse.

Lucky? "He was fine this morning!" If it'd been something at her house that made him sick, she'd never forgive herself.

"It wasn't...natural causes. Someone got to him this afternoon." Alex wiped at his eyes as if trying to unsee it, trying to make it not true. "They ripped him apart."

"Jesus." Shannon covered her mouth with her hands. How was that even possible? Alex and Derry lived in a beautiful lakefront home in a safe, upscale neighborhood. Not that money made people stop being crazy, but... "Did Abby—"

"No, no, I got there first, found him when I stopped there to meet Abby's bus."

"An animal, maybe?" It was a crapshoot, too hopeful. She knew the answer before he said it from the way he refused to meet her eyes.

"Whoever did it left a pile of limbs on the porch, neat, in a row. Couldn't even find his head, probably some dog grabbed it and carted it away. Or they kept it, sick bastards. I'll file a police report as soon as I get a chance." He still wouldn't look at her. "God, there was blood everywhere on the porch, you wouldn't think there'd be so much, he was so...small..."

Shannon's stomach heaved, and she sucked breath through her nose, the rubbing alcohol stench nowhere near enough to cover the tang of bile in her throat. "I'll come up in a little."

"Okay." Alex turned to Morrison. "Good luck with your case, gentlemen," he said and started down the hall toward the elevators. Toward Derry's room. To help her grieving niece to deal with a dead cat and a soon to be dead—

"Who's Lucky?" Petrosky asked.

"A kitten. My niece's kitten."

Petrosky's eyes stayed on Alex's back, his mouth twitching. "Your brother live near a bunch of psychopaths?"

"Nope. They live right off Square Lake Road." She watched Petrosky's jowls clench and unclench. What was she missing? "Do you and Alex know each other?"

Alex rounded the corner, and Petrosky's glower faded. Without another word, he turned and started off down the hall in the other direction, toward the front doors.

Shannon watched Petrosky's receding back and turned to Morrison. "What was that about?"

"Not sure. My guess is that Petrosky was here being, as he would say, a twat in the emergency room, and Alex called him out on it. Wouldn't be the first time Petrosky pushed a little too hard." He averted his eyes and looked in the direction Petrosky had gone. "I was going to stop up to see Derry with you, but this…you go ahead. I'll wait in the car for you."

He knew. He always knew. He'd known the night she found out Derry was sick when she'd curled up in the back of his car, and he'd stood watch outside instead of trying to placate her with stupid platitudes and bullshit ideologies about things being God's plan or whatever else people said. But it wasn't fair to make him sit around and wait tonight. "I can call a cab home."

"Nope. I'll be in the car. Got some paperwork I need to finish on the laptop anyway." His eyes were kind, stoic, but determined.

She pecked him on the cheek. "Thanks."

"Anytime, Shanny."

When she turned the corner toward the elevators, he was still standing there, staring after her.

. . .

THE ATMOSPHERE in Derry's room was dank, cold, morose. You could almost smell the despair that some said closed in at the very end of life, though it was probably only the fluids leaking from a body preparing to die. But this room was not only clogged with sorrow from the imminent loss of a loved one. Here there existed a more immediate tragedy—a child, bitterly grieving her murdered pet.

Abby slumped on the bed, her arms around Derry, her face pressed into his scrawny chest. Shannon resisted the urge to cover them both with a blanket. She couldn't stand looking at Derry's emaciated arms sticking from the hospital gown, the bones in his hands like hash marks counting down the days until he lost the fight.

Derry looked up as she walked in, his eyes glassy, his face wet.

"I'm so sorry, honey." Shannon crossed to the bed, sat on the edge, and put her hand on Abby's back.

Abby's muffled sobs wracked her lithe body. Shannon stroked her arm, against the grain, like she used to do when Abby was a baby—hurting for her, with her, but helpless to fix it. Derry kissed Abby's head.

Shannon raised her eyes to her brother's damp face. "Lucky was a good kitten. I think we'll all miss him."

Abby whimpered again, and Derry brushed her hair with his fingertips until her sobs subsided. "He'll be making you sneeze from the afterlife until you wash your sheets," he said.

Abby turned her face to Shannon, keeping her cheek on Derry's shoulder. "Lucky always thought that was funny. You sneezing." Abby sniffed, and Shannon handed her a tissue from the bedside table. "Remember when you sneezed so hard it made him jump half a mile in the air?"

Shannon smiled, but her lip quivered. "I remember." Her throat burned with unshed tears as she met Derry's red-rimmed eyes. She could feel it, the question, the worry, the fear. This was smaller, this loss. Soon his little girl would suffer one far greater—a devastating, heart-wrenching loss, and he would not be there to offer comfort. A tear dripped down Derry's cheek and onto his shirt. He stared at it, brows furrowed.

Shannon stood, straightening her blouse. "I think you guys need some time together. But I'll see you soon, okay, Abby?"

Abby nodded.

Shannon squeezed Derry's hand, so much thinner even than last week, more papery, more cold. She left the room before she could consider what that meant.

7

LUCKY'S FUR still lingered on the comforter in the spare bedroom when Shannon awoke the following morning, tiny white and orange hairs clinging to the yellow fabric. She stood in the doorway, staring at the sheets as if she had expected all evidence of the kitten to disappear the moment he stopped breathing. All night, visions had assailed her: his tiny broken body, limbs torn asunder, intestines spilling onto the porch, no longer whole, just a pile of pieces. When she'd finally drifted off, the dreams had been worse—knives and gore to the soundtrack of Abby sobbing, the coppery tang of blood in her nose.

Everything felt jagged and sharp. In the shower, the water seemed to slice at her skin, and when she stepped out, the chill of the bathroom tile froze her feet. Her silk blouse felt prickly against her flesh as she threaded her arms through the sleeves of her suit jacket.

She'd refused Morrison's offer of a ride to work this morning and called a cab to take her to the rental car place. She'd always had a tendency to isolate when things got hard, though, during her bout with postpartum depression, she'd learned to rethink that strategy. Loss and isolation don't go well together, Dr. McCallum had said. He'd also said she was so afraid things would go wrong that she'd rather destroy something perfectly good on her terms than leave it to chance and risk being hurt. He'd been right. It was probably leftover bullshit from years of convincing herself she didn't need anyone and was surely one of the reasons Roger had cut her so deeply. So...she'd connect with the guys. But later.

The cab reeked of stale cologne and garlic, or maybe that was just the driver. Shannon felt every bump on the freeway. The sun trying to peek through the fog was far too bright, the *shh* of the pavement grated like sandpaper against her eardrums, and though she knew she might only be trying to distract herself from images of torn-apart kittens, anger pulsed every time she considered the Johnson case.

Did it really matter that Petrosky had been with Johnson that day? Probably not. He obviously wasn't with her later that night, at the time of the murder. And just because someone else had fought with Lewis, so what? Johnson going missing hours after she left Petrosky didn't matter to the case unless it was something that implicated her or absolved her —and if it absolved her, she'd have told someone. At the end of the day, all this bullshit was just Petrosky trying to save one of "his girls." He couldn't stand the thought that this girl he'd tried to help had bludgeoned someone to death.

The rental car company was manned by a dour-faced soul with acne-like chicken pox who gave her the keys with barely a glance once her credit card cleared. Shannon thanked him silently; she had no desire to speak to anyone.

As she headed through the lot to her rental, Shannon pictured her car: windows smashed, briefcase torn open. It wasn't right, the missing papers, but she couldn't think of a reason anyone would care about Johnson after the fact. Even if someone else had been there the night Lewis died, they'd have been thrilled that Johnson took the fall. Unless...they thought the cops were looking for an accomplice and wanted to know what they had so far. That would make sense if Petrosky was poking around. Maybe. But an accomplice wouldn't risk alerting anyone to his presence just because he was curious about what they knew.

So, who else might have needed something from her? Shannon didn't have any other cases that were particularly evidence heavy, no other defendants that she could see being desperate to figure out what she had on them...except maybe the reverend. She'd focus harder on him. She'd look around on Johnson too. Worst case, she'd sent the wrong person to prison. Shannon sighed and rubbed her temples like she could squeeze the agitation out of her brain. Best case scenario, she'd affirm that Johnson was guilty and sleep a little better at night.

By the time she pulled up in front of her office building, Shannon had to actively resist the urge to drive home and go back to bed. She'd rather have walked across hot coals than go speak to Roger.

Her shoes clacked through the lot and up the stairs and thudded down the carpeted hallway to the door bearing the placard "Roger McFadden, Esquire." She opened it before he answered the knock.

Roger's eyes widened, but he recovered quickly, smiling into the cell in his hand. "Sounds good, honey," he said into the phone. Syrupy sweet. Must be a new lover—he'd lose that tone soon enough. Roger met Shannon's eyes. "And wear that lace thing I like." He smirked.

Shannon's fist clenched around the handle of her briefcase. *Don't respond, Shannon.*

Roger pocketed the phone and stood behind his desk, which was already piled with files and legal pads. Smug. Waiting for her to say something.

"I want to look at the Johnson case again."

The leery smile on his face fell. He came around the side of his desk and perched his ass on the edge of it. "You just got Johnson convicted beyond a reasonable doubt."

Shannon looked at the door, her hand still on the knob. She dropped her fist. "Some new information has come up, and I'm not sure if Johnson did it alone. I just want to be thorough."

"Then haul this 'someone else' in and charge them with

your new evidence, get everyone put away." He stood and strode back around to his chair. "My god, Shannon, I almost thought you were suggesting she was innocent." He grinned at her, all teeth. Predatory.

She stared at him until his smile disappeared. "I don't know exactly what to think. Someone broke into my car last night."

"So?"

"The only files completely missing were Johnson's."

"Coincidence. Or some whacko wanted to collect original docs on the trial he'd been following for the last month."

True. She hadn't even considered the people who turned murder trials into spectator sports.

Roger sat and slapped open a folder on the desktop. "How's the Lambert case?"

"The—fine. Finished with the preliminary stuff, got an arraignment coming up."

"Good." He made a note on his legal pad. "Simpson?"

"Dropped. She won't testify."

"Good."

She stood, silent, watching him.

Roger scrawled something on a page. "Let your boy toy worry about your car." His eyes remained on his files. "We're not reopening Johnson."

Shannon succeeded in not stomping out of the room, but she closed the door hard enough to rattle the office window. "Fuck you, Roger," she whispered to the empty hallway.

Inside her own office, her files were where she'd left them. She plopped into her chair and glared at them for a minute before diving in and busying herself with motions and appeals and all the paper-pushing bullshit that lawyers do, but no one ever sees. Nothing more glamorous than hours of legal research. She was grateful to drop the pen from her aching hand when her cell phone buzzed on her desk, rattling with a noise like snapping twigs. Alex. *Oh shit.*

Her stomach churned. "Alex...what's... Is Derry—"

"Oh, no, Derry's fine." His voice sounded as tired as she

felt. "I mean, he's...same as yesterday. I just wanted to thank you."

She squinted at the wall like it was hiding a secret from her. "Thank me for what?"

"The cop outside the house last night. Abby was really scared after what happened to Lucky, and with everything going on at the hospital, I didn't have time to file a report. Really helped Abby sleep better. And me too, honestly."

"Wait...outside the house?" *What the hell?* Why would anyone stalk her brother's house? Unless...did someone believe Alex and Abby were in danger? But it hadn't been Morrison; Alex would have called him by name.

The silence stretched on the other end of the line. "Didn't you tell him to?" A hint of worry had edged its way into Alex's voice.

Shannon pressed the phone to her ear to stop her hands from shaking. "Yeah, I mean...yeah. Of course. I just... Who ended up staying with you guys?"

"Detective Petrosky. I really thought he hated me from the way he acted yesterday, but now I think he's just a little... intense. Kind of a jerk, but looks out for people he cares about. Now I feel bad about reporting him yesterday afternoon."

"You called on him?" Of course, he had called on him. *Disagreement, my ass.* Now Petrosky's irritability at the hospital made sense.

"He was in the emergency room trying to bully my docs into—wait, did you not know that?"

Shannon was barely listening. Petrosky had stayed with Abby. But there was no way it was just because Abby was scared. He knew something Shannon didn't.

He knew there was reason to be afraid.

8

Petrosky's days of having inside information are over.

Shannon crossed the street to the Ash Park Detention Center, where Ashley Johnson was being held. From the corner of her eye, the back side of the courthouse loomed, gray and ugly, but achingly sentimental like a childhood friend. Even the frayed alarm wire in one of the center windows hadn't changed. Had it really been ten years since she and Griffen climbed through and wandered the halls, smoking weed and dreaming of prosecuting, of being big shots, of saving lives? Romantic, this notion, but they'd been just college kids, full of shit and brimming with naïve idealism. Of course, for the guilty, the courthouse was the place where it all ended. It was unfortunate that once you walked through the front door in a suit, the glamour disappeared.

Inside the detention center, Shannon put her briefcase on the belt for inspection and walked through the metal detector toward an officer whose uniform was stretched tight over her ample bosom. "Ms. Taylor." The guard's matronly smile somehow managed not to feel out of place as she took Shannon's briefcase and peeked into it.

"How are you, Beatrice?"

"Good, good. Grandkids are keeping me busy, I'll tell you what." She handed the bag back. "How's your daughter?"

"Niece."

"Right. Sorry."

"No worries." Shannon shifted the case to her other hand, trying to ignore the ache in her chest. "She's getting big."

"Oh lord, they do that too, don't they? Never stop growing!"

Shannon nodded her goodbyes and walked into the reception area, a glorified DMV with extra bars and more bulletproof glass. Behind a Plexiglas window along the far wall, Officer Anton Cook's face lit up as she approached. "Taylor! Who you here for?" He pushed a yellow request form through the metal tray under the glass.

"Johnson. Ashley."

Cook raised a bushy eyebrow that looked like a caterpillar that had crawled onto his face to take a pit stop before making a cocoon.

"Just some follow-up." She pulled the page toward her and grabbed a pen.

"Right on. You're the second one in two days."

Her pen stopped mid-scribble. "Who else was here?"

"Frieda Burke."

Frieda Burke. *Huh.* Johnson's CPS worker and Griffen's ex-girlfriend. The one who had made him choose between Shannon, his completely platonic college friend, and her, his lover. A tinge of disquiet settled between Shannon's shoulder blades like the tingle of someone watching her. Shit happened, and sometimes it sucked, but that wasn't what was bothering her now.

What reason would Burke have to visit Johnson after the trial? Johnson's daughter, Diamond, was no longer in Johnson's care, and social workers were always swamped.

"Hey, you seen Morrison?" Cook's eyes danced. He seemed oblivious to her unease. Hopefully, Johnson wouldn't notice either, though Shannon could play it off as irritability. Not like she was currently a paragon of relaxation. "I haven't seen him since last night at the"—*hospital*—"gym."

"Oh yeah, you guys and your exercise. He put a hand on

his gut. "I thought about joining, but Kimball is a little… intense for me lately." He held up a stainless steel coffee cup. "Tell Morrison I got his mug. He'll want it back eventually."

She nodded, still trying to settle her roiling belly. "I will."

Cook retreated through the steel door at the back of his little office box. Shannon leaned against the counter and glanced back at the empty chairs in the waiting area; the vacuum track marks not yet disturbed by visitors. Through the front door, outside, she caught a glimpse of a familiar figure: Petrosky, with his back to her, smoke from a cigarette wafting above his head like his face was on fire. *Stalker bastard.* No wonder she felt unsteady.

"Taylor?" Cook stood at the steel door to the waiting room, holding it open for her.

Shannon followed him through, and the door latched behind them, confining her in a claustrophobic tomb. She wiped her palms on her suit pants as Cook pressed a button, and a clear door of bulletproof glass slid open in front of them. *One more.* She took a deep breath, walked through the door, and waited with Cook in the next little clear box. The door behind them shut, and the entrance to the holding area opened.

"I put her on the end, last in the row." Cook gestured to the rows of halls. Shannon had always thought the place resembled a library, though instead of bookshelves, chest-high cinderblock walls were topped with black metal mesh that reached to the ceiling. "Thanks."

"No worries. I'll wait here."

Ashley Johnson was waiting for her on the other side of the mesh, mouth tight. "They said it was you, but I didn't believe them." Johnson's voice was soft and even, not a hint of anxiety or agitation. *Strange.* The first time Shannon had come, Johnson had cried through the entire interview. Maybe she'd been faking. Or maybe she was so hopeless now that she was numb. Despondent. During the trial, McCallum had said she was depressed. If she wasn't guilty and was locked up anyway, without her child…

Without her child. Shannon pushed thoughts of her own dark postpartum days from her mind and refocused on Johnson's now-trembling lip. There was the sadness. But sad or no, Shannon didn't have time to waste. "I know where you were the night Derek died."

Johnson turned her face away from the mesh, but not before Shannon saw her eyes widen with alarm.

"Why didn't you tell me, Ms. Johnson?"

Johnson shrugged and spoke to the side wall. "I didn't want anyone to get into trouble."

She couldn't really think Petrosky would have gotten into trouble for buying her second-hand clothes, could she? She must have met with someone else. Someone she'd be more nervous about getting caught with. So who would Johnson have to hide? "Why would they get into trouble?"

"I don't know."

The edge on the last word caught Shannon's ear. *Liar.* "Should I go ask them why they'd get into trouble?"

Johnson cleared her throat and stared at Shannon, chewing her lip like the wheels were turning in her brain. "You mean…Detective Petrosky?" she asked tentatively.

Shannon nodded and watched Johnson's eyes go from twitchy to steady and confident. Petrosky was not the big secret Johnson was keeping. So who was?

"Tell me about Detective Petrosky," Shannon said.

"Eddie was the only one who was ever really nice to me, never asked for anything in return. Gave me food, clothes, shoes for my interviews. Even let me sleep at his place a few times. Said if I had to, I could stay there with Diamond while I got myself together…I mean, if I had to because of Derek or whatever. I thanked God for Eddie so many times."

Eddie? Johnson was being pretty forthcoming for someone trying to protect a friend. "Where did you go that day after dinner?"

The alarm flashed in Johnson's eyes again, brief, but clear. She looked down at her wrists. "I just walked around.

Stopped at a gas station to change and went to my interview."

"And after the interview?"

Johnson's mouth dropped, but she recovered quickly. The hairs on Shannon's neck stood up. "I wasn't ready to go back," Johnson said. "I just walked."

Bullshit. It had been February, much too cold for an evening stroll. "Who were you with, Ms. Johnson?"

Johnson stared at the wall and said nothing. Perhaps she'd been with someone else, someone who'd brought her home. Someone who'd maybe still been there when she killed Lewis. Someone she was protecting. But Petrosky was wrong. Johnson was a liar and a killer. Whatever she had been doing, it wasn't anything that would absolve her or she'd spill it.

Johnson leaned toward the screen, eyes finally meeting Shannon's. "Are you reopening my case?" Her voice wavered ever so slightly. Hopeful.

"No. Especially since you seem content to stonewall me." Shannon stepped away from the mesh and turned down the aisle.

"Wait."

Here we go. Shannon turned back slowly. "Who?"

"I'm sure there was... I mean, not someone I was with, but someone Derek was with when I was gone. His mom was always fighting with him, maybe that call...maybe it was her at the apartment. Maybe they had an argument."

Whoever had been there had left well before the cops showed up, but his mom? *Right.* "Derek's mother didn't kill him, Ms. Johnson."

"No, but she might have fought with him. She'd been trying to get custody of Diamond, and I think she might have called CPS on us. She had another social worker on us and everything. My friend Angela—the one who watches Diamond—said she saw the other worker at the house earlier that day. A guy."

There was nothing about another social worker

anywhere in the files. Shannon stepped back to the mesh window. "You knew this person was at the house, and you kept it to yourself?"

Johnson shrugged. "Derek's mom was trying to take my baby even though I was doing everything right. And Diamond had already been in foster care once. I didn't want to lose her again."

If Derek and his mother had been trying to get Diamond taken away from Johnson, that was motive enough for murder. But if there had been another worker at the house the day of the killing, the fact that this other worker hadn't come forward was very suspicious. Had they seen something or someone that afternoon that they shouldn't have? Maybe Petrosky knew who the other social worker was. Shit, maybe he'd even told Johnson not to say anything if he thought it made her look worse. *Why am I even here?*

Shannon stepped back from the mesh but paused at a sudden thought about Johnson's visitors. "Your normal caseworker is Frieda Burke, yes?"

Slow nod.

"Did she come to visit you yesterday?"

"Yeah."

"Did she know who this other social worker was?"

"I didn't mention the other worker at all. She just wanted to know how I was holding up, gave me an update on the baby, let me know that Derek's mom was planning to go forward with adoption after they terminate my parental rights next year. Lucinda got exactly what she wanted."

Got what she wanted, my ass. "She lost her son, Ms. Johnson. Because of you."

"It wasn't because of me!" But her eyes radiated uncertainty. "And she *did* want Diamond. She always did." Johnson sniffed. "Ms. Burke said she went over there to check on the baby, make sure she was safe. She said Diamond's trying to walk now. And I'm gonna miss it." Tears welled in her eyes. "I'm gonna miss everything."

9

SHANNON LEFT the detention center as tense as she'd been when she entered. More questions, no answers, and Ashley Johnson was definitely withholding information about what she did after Petrosky left her. So if Johnson wasn't guilty...

She shook her head. No. This was all bullshit. Sometimes the right answer is the simplest one, and no matter how good Johnson was at playing innocent, no one else would have killed Derek over hurting his child. Who else could possibly have benefitted from his death?

Shannon peered into the parking lot, shielding her eyes from the white-hot sun that filtered through the clouds and cast the shadows of still-barren trees on the ground. What had her rental car looked like? Blue? She wiped dew from her forehead.

"Taylor!" Petrosky hustled up behind her, red-faced, smoke wafting from his nose.

If I had a nickel for every time he chased me across this lot... She whirled on him. "Why were you at my brother's house?"

"I was concerned."

"About what?"

Petrosky tossed his cigarette to the pavement and ground it out with his heel. "How's Ashley?"

"Oh, she's hanging in there, *Eddie*." Her fist clenched around her briefcase. "Why were you outside the detention center? You're not tired of stalking my family yet?"

"I saw you leave the office. I had an appointment across the street."

"With McCallum?"

"Yep."

"Good, I'm sure you need it. You better get out of here, you smell like booze."

His eyes narrowed. "No I don't. You just think that. You think a lot of shit that isn't true."

"Fuck you, Petrosky." Every single time.

Petrosky pulled his lips into an almost passable smile, pulled his cigarette pack from his breast pocket, and tapped a fresh one into his hand. "So, what's the deal with Ashley? You got anything new?"

"Nope."

"Come on, Taylor. You're a terrible liar when you're angry. And I'm exhausted from staying up all night outside your brother's house and then trying to finish up other cases today."

Shannon crossed her arms, her briefcase swinging against her abdomen. Back and forth, back and forth. "So, are you finally going to tell me what you were doing there last night?"

"Making sure."

"Making sure of what?"

"That they were safe."

Right. "I'm surprised you'd care what happens to Alex after last night."

Petrosky flinched. "We're all just trying to do our jobs, Taylor."

"Staking out the homes of civilians?"

"We look out for our own." He met her eyes, defiant but somehow kind, and Shannon's fists loosened. "Come on, Taylor. Tell me about Ashley. We're on the same side here."

She dropped her arms, and her case banged against her

hip. "Fine, but I don't think it means much. Johnson thinks Lewis's mother wanted custody of her kid. Says a neighbor saw another social worker going into their apartment earlier that day. A man."

Petrosky's mouth tensed as he lit another cigarette, tainting her air with nicotine.

"Did you know about that, Petrosky? I swear if I find one more thing you kept from me—"

He blew smoke through his nostrils and shook his head. "I didn't know about the other social worker. And if this guy didn't come forward, didn't file any paperwork..." He puffed again and grimaced at the glowing ash. "Probably someone posing as a social worker. What else?"

Shannon pulled her keys from her briefcase and unlocked the doors on the rental car with a beep. "Not now, Petrosky."

"Did you talk to Roger about reopening Johnson?"

She started toward the car. "Yep. He doesn't want—Hey!"

Petrosky's fingers sank through her sleeve into the flesh of her upper arm.

"What the hell, Pet—"

"Wait, Taylor, just wait." He dropped her arm and took off for her car, closing the gap in four frantic steps, his hand jerking to his gun. Shannon ran after him, watching the lot, but saw no one. He stooped and peered at her hood. No...not the hood. At a letter-sized manila envelope on the windshield, oily pockets of moisture seeping through the mustard-colored paper.

"What the—"

"Stay there, Taylor."

"Like hell."

Cigarette in his teeth, he grabbed a corner of the envelope from under the wiper and hefted the bulky package over the hood, pulling a Swiss Army knife from his back pocket.

"What are you doing?"

He ignored her, sliced the top of the envelope, and peered inside. His face went still. Frozen. Like her lungs.

She forced a breath, watching Petrosky's haunted gaze

and the tremble in his hand that might have been alcohol withdrawal but probably wasn't. "Petrosky, what is it?"

Petrosky pinched the envelope between two fingers and lowered it to his side. "I wouldn't look in there, Taylor."

She reached for the package. Petrosky stepped back, trying to keep it from her.

Oh no you don't. Shannon pivoted and snatched at a corner. The envelope fell to the pavement in slow motion, straight down, hitting way too hard with a sickening thunk. The paper tore along oily lines. And she knew. She knew before it rolled from the lip of the envelope where the seam had given way, a mass of fur and blood, a circle of white bone peeking from the severed neck. And those eyes, dead and milky and bulging, tiny teeth unable to hold back the tongue, which protruded like an emerging slug, purple and rotten and horrid.

Bile rose into Shannon's esophagus.

Petrosky stooped and picked up Lucky's head with a piece of torn envelope, covering the dead eyes, the fat tongue, every lifeless piece. And suddenly it was Derry, going into the ground, never again whole, never again smiling or laughing or playing cards into the wee hours of the morning.

The air had thinned, all the oxygen sucked from the universe like her brother's soul was about to be, and Shannon put her hand on the hood and choked back a noise that sounded oddly like a sob. The noise itself angered her. *Those bastards. Those—*

"You gonna let me keep it this time, Taylor?" Petrosky cradled the envelope in one gnarled paw.

She inhaled through her nose, fighting nausea. *Keep it together, Shannon.* Freaking out wouldn't help her—or her family. "So this is...what? A warning? A threat?"

Petrosky nodded, eyes on the envelope, perhaps hoping it stayed together until he could get it inside.

"You knew it—that this was about me. Us. That's why you were at my brother's."

Petrosky took a drag from his cigarette and watched the

smoke curl into a cloud above his head. "I had a hunch." He turned the envelope and held it out to her. Shannon recoiled, but he held it steady until she looked at the pen scratch on the bottom: *It was me*. Block letters in what looked like a child's handwriting, but had probably been written in the non-dominant hand to avoid identification. Because there was no way it was a child who did this. It was not a child who'd murdered Lucky and left him bloody and dismembered. Not a child who had followed her and put a severed head on her car. *It was me*. Johnson might have killed Lewis in a moment of passionate fury, but this was premeditated.

"It was me, huh?" Petrosky's voice was so low she could barely hear him.

Shannon shook her head, but her jaw clenched. "Johnson had something to do with this, Petrosky. I'm not altogether wrong."

"You *are* wrong unless you think Johnson somehow snuck out of jail and tore your niece's pet limb from limb."

"Maybe Johnson knows whoever did this," she stammered. "Wants to punish me for putting her away. She still could have killed Derek Lewis." But the accusation didn't feel right, not anymore.

Petrosky didn't seem to be in the mood for speculating. "It's risky to drop a severed head on a car in broad daylight. Killers like this enjoy the thrill, the rush." He tapped the envelope, and Shannon imagined Lucky's eyeball wobbling in its socket. She inhaled through her nose to avoid vomiting.

"All of this is the work of someone else, Taylor. Not Ashley Johnson. And she doesn't know who the killer is or she'd have told us to save her own ass."

So someone was still out there. Someone dangerous. Her shoulders slumped. "I can't do this."

He eyed her but said nothing.

"My brother is...he's dying, Petrosky. Abby and Alex can't take any more right now. I just... Let me know how it all works out, okay? You can go harass Roger about it if you want. I just can't."

Petrosky sucked hard on his cigarette, the glowing ash nearly touching his fingertips. "That's why they're doing this to you."

"What?"

"No one killed my cat, Taylor."

"You don't have a—"

"No one took Morrison's dog, and he loves that thing like his own flesh and blood. Whoever did this knows you're vulnerable and knows enough about you to figure out exactly where to hit you, so you'll give him what he wants."

"He knows where to hit me, so...what? What does he want?"

"Credit."

Petrosky was an idiot. Credit for killing some low-level drug dealer? She'd be more likely to believe that Reverend Wilson was a kitten-killing psycho than that some random person had murdered Derek Lewis and framed Ashley Johnson and only later decided to get all pissy about it. "I can't do this," she repeated, her abdominal muscles twitching.

Petrosky crushed the cigarette with his heel. "Take care of yourself, Taylor." He turned his back to her and started across the lot, Shannon's throat growing tighter with each step he took.

"Thank you," she called to his back.

He stopped and looked over his shoulder.

"Alex said you were there until he went to bed this morning."

"I just showed up to take the report and hung out for a few hours." Their eyes met. "Morrison stayed the rest of the night, watched the house incognito from up the road. He's on his third cup of coffee already, and you know how California feels about excessive stimulants. You should thank him, too."

She watched Petrosky stride across the lot toward the precinct, the envelope with Lucky's head still clutched precariously in one hand. When he disappeared into the precinct, she finally unclenched her fists, extracting her fingernails from her palms. The bleeding crescents resembled cat scratches.

10

SHANNON SAW Lucky's tongue twice on the way to the hospital: once in the rearview and once peeking through the leather buckle on her briefcase, the image so vivid that she almost swerved into a truck and went to meet Lucky in the afterlife. The windshield had been scrubbed clean at a gas station, yet every time she glanced at it, there seemed to be a blemish there, some invisible filth that made her anxious to get her own car back. Her car. The one everyone expected her to be driving. Her chest tightened.

Someone had been watching her. Stalking her. There was no other way for Lucky's killer to know she'd driven a different car to the office today.

Shannon parked in the hospital garage, every muscle singing with tension as she exited the car and peered around the dimly-lit lot. Though there was no fetid, sulfuric odor to indicate the presence of a murderous beast, the shadows from every corner felt as if they were reaching toward her like creatures from another world, set to tear her asunder and leave her leaking gore onto the concrete.

She hustled into the hospital, ignoring the cold, the smells, the orderlies, the ladies at the reception desk, the buzz of the elevator. It was as if a fog had descended on the hospital, thickening the air around her until she couldn't breathe, let alone use her sanity checklist to tick off all the mundane things around her. None of it mattered. Nothing mattered. They were all dead, sooner or later, every one of them. *Derry. Lucky. Derry. Lucky.*

Derry was leaning back against a pile of pillows, a clear plastic cannula snaking up his nose, blankets drooping around his frail shoulders. Classical music played from an iPhone dock on the end table, piano and cello—or maybe violin. Slow and haunting and melancholic. And he smelled —a ripe, rank, acidic stench. Maybe it had always been there. But today it wrapped around her head and seeped into her brain, forcing her to recognize what that smell actually was.

Disease. Dying. Decay.

Derry opened his eyes as she entered. "Shanny?" His voice had a harshness to it, a whispery quality that did not belong to the vibrant Derry who used to tease her for wearing pigtails. It was the voice of an old man, the raspy whisper of a stooped geriatric talking to ducks at a park. But Derry would never see old age. He wouldn't even see his next birthday.

She sat on the bed before he could register how much her legs were shaking. "How are you feeling? You sound tired."

Derry pulled the cannula from his nose and pushed a button near his hand. The bed hummed him up to a sitting position. "It's all the extra oxygen. Dries out your sinuses." But the bags under his eyes were more pronounced than they'd been yesterday; he hadn't stayed up all night because the oxygen was drying him out.

"Shanny, are you okay?"

Tell him you're fine. But he'd know she was lying, and she couldn't do that, not this close to the end, not when she needed him to know the truth. Or maybe she just needed him to forgive her. Truth and forgiveness. Throughout their dysfunctional childhoods, those elements had rarely come from anywhere but one another. And once he was gone...

She took a deep breath, air wheezing through her nostrils. "Lucky... It was... He died because of me. Because of a case I'm working on."

He gaped at her.

Say something, Derry. She put her hand over his. "It's my fault. I'm so sorry."

His face softened from surprise to concern. He flipped his hand over and squeezed hers, but softer than she wanted him too. Halfhearted? Or was he just that weak?

"It wasn't because of you. People are crazy."

"Yeah, they are. But I just… I can't…*fuck.*" Her chest was heavy, thick; her lungs smashed inside her rib cage. "Derry, I'm so sorry." She wept, wanting to be strong for him but failing with every choked gasp of air. Salt ran into her mouth and covered her shirt as her shoulders convulsed. Derry squeezed her hand again, but it was feeble, Jesus, *he* was feeble, and it made her feel a thousand times worse. She sucked in a breath through her nose and willed her chest to settle.

"Tell me what happened, Shanny."

"The Johnson case, I think. There were some things I didn't know. She might not have done it, or maybe she did it with someone else, I'm not sure. Maybe it's from another case entirely. But someone wants recognition. Someone wants me to… I don't know. Maybe they just want the fame. I don't understand what's happening." She sat and wiped a hand across her face. "But I can't get involved. I can't put you and Abby in danger, have these crazies running around by your house looking for god-knows-what to threaten me with. I just feel so—"

Derry dropped her hand and put his palms on either side of his skeleton—no, his legs. "You need to be involved in this case."

"What?" There was no way. She had no idea how long it would take to catch Lucky's killer and in the meantime…she couldn't risk something else happening to Derry. To Alex. To Abby.

"You need to figure out who did this. And you're going to."

"Derry, this isn't about us. Abby could get hurt. And I

don't even know for sure Johnson is innocent. It might just be someone else who wants to get famous, some crackpot who—"

"You're rationalizing." He smiled feebly.

"I'm not rationalizing!"

"You know she's innocent, don't you?" He coughed, wet and heavy.

"I don't know anything." *Except that Johnson's lying.* And that there was someone else out there, hurting people. Hurting her family. Hurting Abby. Her nerves jittered with electricity, the urge to run, the need to stay, the overwhelming desire to punch something.

"Come off it." Derry hacked again, and the tray table rattled like the fluid in his chest. "You wouldn't be digging around at all if you didn't think there was a chance she was innocent. You're trying to find a reason not to get involved here so that your poor, dead-in-a-month brother doesn't have to put up with people coming to his house and killing his pets. We promised Abby a dog, by the way. If we get one big enough, there's no way someone can hack it up."

"Derry, you can't be serious."

"You expect me to be afraid for what little remains of my life? To have you let this asshole go free? You want to let me die knowing that that the person who murdered Abby's kitten is still out there?"

"Derry, just listen to yourself! I'm not just going to—"

"You are. Because it's the right thing to do. I'm not afraid to die, Shannon, but I am afraid to leave my daughter here with some maniac running around targeting us every time your office doesn't do what the fuck he wants! I don't want to die knowing that this asshole can go rip up my daughter at any time."

"But—"

"Goddamn you, Shanny. You know better. Now get the hell out of here until you're ready to make a dying man's wish come true." His voice was stronger now, louder, as if he were using all his energy to make sure she got his point.

"Derry, you're such an—"

"An adorable, brilliant, dead man, I know. Now go find this asshole, or I will kick your ass." He grabbed the cannula and stuck it back under his nose.

"You're not kicking anyone's ass."

"Ghosts are crafty, Shanny. Do not test me."

Shannon trudged back to the office, her stomach twisted in knots, her neck aching with unspent energy. She needed to fix this, but it wasn't like she had some awesome lead here. She had nothing. And Petrosky was handling it—he was just as motivated to figure out what was going on as she was.

Yet Derry's words kept zinging through her brain as she slogged through her case files, reading and rereading the same paragraphs over and over but absorbing none of the words. The briefs might as well have been written in Greek. She didn't hear the doorknob turning, but when she saw the door move out of the corner of her eye, she jumped up from her chair and leapt to the side of the desk, pen fisted in her hand, ready to stab the ballpoint tip into someone's throat.

"Shannon?"

Sweat trickled between her shoulder blades, down her spine, and into the waistband of her suit pants. She straightened and sat back down behind the desk, feigning calm and probably failing. "What do you want, Roger?"

"Progress on the Lambert case?"

"Arraignment in the morning."

"Expected plea?"

"Not sure yet. He's wavering."

"Drop it to felony murder."

Not now, Roger, goddammit. She fit her fingernails into the still-healing crescents in her palms and squeezed. "That asshole beat a little girl to death while her mother was at work. We can get second degree easy, especially with his priors. History of DUIs, the last time with an unregistered forty-five in the backseat, and three prior assault charges. Almost killed a guy in a Walmart on Black Friday."

His face remained bland, bored, as he gazed out the window behind her. "Doesn't matter. We'd spend twice as much time in court, and we don't have the time or the resources. See if he'll plead no contest. If he will, drop it down."

"I had a case last month, almost the same deal. Why didn't we drop that one?"

Roger didn't appear to have heard her. He just stared over her head out the window. "He'll end up put away where he can't hurt anyone else. Isn't that the ultimate goal from your point of view? Protecting the innocent?" He finally met her eyes and shrugged. "No reason to risk some jury actually letting him walk because they think it was an accident—discipline gone wrong."

Shannon balled her fist, then released it. "Okay."

"Excellent." Roger sat in the chair across from her and smirked.

What's he so smug about now?

"I saw the chief this morning after you left." Roger's eyes twinkled. "Did you know Petrosky and Morrison aren't supposed to be anywhere near the Johnson case or Lewis's murder?"

She stared at him. "So you...what? Walked over there and told on them like a third grader?"

Roger's smile faltered. "They were forbidden from looking at it well before I got there. Seems Petrosky made a big stink with Kimball and the chief, got thrown out of her office. And last night, someone over at the hospital actually filed a report against Petrosky for harassing doctors about test results. Different case, but it didn't help their cause."

Alex. She sighed. "Listen, you should know that I'm involved, whether I want to be or not. Someone broke into my car."

"You told me. And that doesn't mean—"

"Someone killed Abby's kitten."

The arrogance in Roger's eyes petered out a little, but he only shrugged. "Sorry about the cat, but—"

"They left his head on my windshield. With a note that said 'It was me.'"

Roger sat, jaw working. Then: "It was me? Who... What was them?"

"I assume it was in reference to the murder of Derek Lewis." She didn't know that, not for certain, but she was glad she'd said it. The stunned look on Roger's face was priceless. "Someone wants us to know that he isn't pleased that someone else is taking credit for his handiwork."

Roger didn't seem to buy it as his shock morphed into aggravation. He rolled his eyes. "You have dozens of cases simmering right now, and none of them involve kind, calm individuals."

"Yeah, but this is the only one where someone else got credit."

"*If* someone else got credit. Two days ago, you were convinced that Johnson did it."

And maybe I was wrong. "It isn't a coincidence that my car got trashed the night after the trial. It isn't a coincidence that I found a severed head on my windshield the day after that." That rang true. None of this made any logical sense, but it wasn't coincidence—she was certain of that.

Roger's smug annoyance finally mellowed into something that almost resembled sympathy. "How's Abby taking everything?"

"She's upset."

"Did she see it? The cat?"

"No, she didn't."

"Well, thank goodness for that." Roger watched her, his face frozen like an ice sculpture, but his eyes were suspiciously disappointed like he'd hoped to hear that Abby had found the cat herself. Shannon thought about the way his face had twisted when she'd shown him her stretch marks, how he'd hated the idea of children as a general rule, hated that someone had once lived in her body. As if it were an intrusion.

She leaned toward him. "You can't leave the Johnson case unopened. If we don't investigate, whoever killed Lucky is still out there. And I'm in danger. So is Abby. So are Derry and Alex."

His face did not change. Roger didn't give a shit about Derry or any of them. The only person Roger cared about was Roger.

"And," she added, "if they happen to think I like you, you might be in danger as well."

Now the wrinkles around his mouth deepened until he almost looked his age. He pulled his lips into a half smile, half grimace. "Guess it's a good thing you don't like me, huh, Shannon?"

"Guess so." She stared daggers at him, wishing they could actually cut. "All we really need to do is open the animal abuse case, prosecute for malicious animal cruelty. Anything found in the course of the investigation on Lucky will be useful in the Johnson case too." *Assuming they're related.*

Roger tapped his fingers on the arm of the chair, his shoulders slumped ever so slightly. Shannon couldn't remember why she had ever found him attractive.

"I'm sure the chief is looking at it now, Roger, approving investigation into *something*. Might as well look like a visionary and call her first, let her know the prosecutor's office won't take the harassment of one of its esteemed attorneys lying down. Let them know that we are reexamining evidence before they send someone else over here to do it for us."

Roger scowled. He pushed himself to standing, his face drawn, and let himself out without another word.

Shannon unwound her fist and stared at the pen in her hand. Sticky. Sweaty. She cracked it in half and threw it at the far wall, watching the blue ink spatter across the beige contractor's paint in a stain that looked like bulging, dead veins.

11

THE DETENTION CENTER across the road was disturbingly still as if no one living resided within its walls. Not vacant. Not empty. Just lifeless. Even the cars in the precinct lot looked forgotten, like they belonged in some apocalyptic movie where everyone had been wiped out by brain-eating zombies. At the moment, it would not have surprised Shannon to find her own brain missing.

She wrapped her coat tightly around her as she raced from the precinct to her car, the only sounds were her heels on the pavement, her own haggard breath, and the continuous thoughts that buzzed through her head like insects. Did Johnson know who had killed Derek? Did she do it herself? Everything that had happened today had only deepened the mystery, only made her more confused, and the damn parking lot wasn't helping matters. With every step, she felt an imaginary stalker's breath on the back of her neck.

Shannon slammed the car door, flipped on the headlights, and shoved the car into drive, rubber squealing. Had Derry been there to hear her thoughts, he would have told her to buck the hell up before someone slapped her. Probably him. Or Jesus. Derry had always insisted that Jesus was surely a slappy fellow. "He'd throw a chair at your ass, Shanny. I saw it in a painting. Probably whip your behind, too." Thoughts of Derry almost made her smile, though any grin would have been tinged with raw and utterly incurable heartbreak.

She eased her foot off the gas and drew her eyes to the rearview, blinded for a moment by the brights from the car behind her. *Asshole.* She peered into the side-view mirror as the brights dimmed to normal, but Shannon remained unsettled. The leathery chemical smell in her car suddenly felt like it was strangling her. The headlights were probably nothing to worry about; just some idiot driving too close. *Hopefully.* Once she hit the freeway, they'd drop from her tail, and she'd scoff at her own paranoia.

She watched the sign for the freeway creep from the post-twilight haze toward her. One mile. The twin beams cut through the blackness behind her, eerily blue instead of the typical muted yellow, like some formidable blue-eyed wolf tracking her through a herd of yellow-eyed deer. She gunned the engine. The car behind her followed suit, accelerating until she was sure he'd clip the bumper if she tapped the brakes.

Her hands tightened on the wheel. *No way. You can't intimidate me, you sorry shithead.*

She cut onto the freeway, shot down the on-ramp, and flew around a green truck that honked angrily in response. *And fuck you too.* Behind her, the blue lights wove around the truck and accelerated toward her side door, trying to come up level. To shoot her? Run her off the road and then dismember her like he'd done to Lucky? Her palms wet the steering wheel as she slammed her foot to the floorboard, cutting over rows of cars, the angry blare of horns almost drowned out by the thunderous beating of her heart.

The car was definitely tailing her. Not overtly, but diligently, letting her put distance between them, then cutting around other vehicles and gaining on her until she had a break in traffic and could shoot ahead again. She groped for her briefcase, trying to get at her phone, but she was going too fast. Gravel and broken asphalt spun beneath the tires. Her heart slammed into her rib cage. She dropped the bag onto the floor of the passenger seat and maneuvered the car back into the lane.

Her exit approached, the green of the sign a beacon of safety, or maybe it was just yelling at her to slam on the gas. She bit her lip, cut into the second lane over, and waited for the car to switch behind her. Half a mile. The blue-eyed wolf gained ground. Quarter mile.

Shannon put on her left blinker. The car behind her closed in. One hundred feet. Then she jerked the wheel to the right and bulleted up the off-ramp, tires screeching all around her.

Her heart throbbed in her ears. She pulled into the left exit lane, stopped at the light at the end of the ramp, and stared into her rearview. Nothing. The light stayed red. Then—

It was there, flying up the ramp behind her. *Fuck you, dickhead.* She gripped the wheel and scanned the street in front of her. Too many cars. She'd cause a wreck if she blew through the light. The red circle glared down at her from above.

The moment it turned green, she squealed into the intersection. The car behind her honked, but she ignored it. One mile up. Two. Eyes on the rearview. No blue headlights. She pried her hands from the steering wheel, shaking one hand then the other, replacing them more loosely, trying to force herself to relax. She looked in the rearview again. Still no headlights from the offending car. Her neck ached from playing lookie-loo.

As she neared her street, she took a final glance in the rearview but saw nothing suspicious. Her eyes were strained, irritated from the constant scanning, but she was almost there. Almost home.

She was stepping from the car with her briefcase on her shoulder when the lights returned, streaming up the road, blinding her. Her throat went dry. She ran for the house.

The car honked. Why would he be calling attention to himself if he had unlawful intentions? She leapt up the porch steps, and the honk came again, two short bursts. A car door slammed. Shannon turned back to the street, blinking hard, every muscle taut and ready to pounce, her keys positioned between her fingers like a weapon. She made a pitiful Freddie Kreuger, but it'd hurt if she drove her fist into someone's face.

Her eyes focused. She lowered her hands. "Morrison?" Her back went limp with relief.

He met her on the lawn, stainless steel coffee mug in his fist. "Pretty tricky moves, Shannon, I'll give you that."

"I thought you were... I didn't know it was you."

"Yeah, I figured after that off-ramp maneuver." He rubbed the back of his neck, a move Roger used to pull when he was lying to her. But maybe Morrison was just nervous? Or maybe *she* was just nervous and seeing shit that wasn't there like Roger had always tried to convince her she was guilty of. Maybe she was crazy.

"Why didn't you just call?" Shannon asked, hating that it sounded plaintive.

"I did. You didn't answer. And I can't very well watch for jerks who might be following you unless I follow you too."

Her red brick colonial loomed, empty and quiet and lonely. The white shutters on the upper windows were like eyelashes that she almost expected to blink. Behind Morrison, the street slithered away from them, hushed save for the occasional cricket, empty save for the occasional car in the road. The other houses already glowed from within. Probably lights from dining rooms where residents were eating dessert and doing homework, blissfully unaware of all the dirty bullshit going on out here.

"I'm going to sit outside your place tonight. Petrosky has your brother's."

"You don't need to protect me, Morrison." But her limbs suddenly felt weak and unwieldy. She needed to rest. And the fact that there was police presence at Derry's place...she might actually sleep tonight. "But I'm glad you're here."

The porch light haloed Morrison's hair and glistened

against his forehead. Somewhere a night bird called, long and lonely.

Exhaustion settled onto her shoulders and neck like a boulder. "I just want to go to bed. I had an incredibly shitty day."

"Yeah, I know." He blew into the hole in his coffee mug and sipped. Calm. Undisturbed.

Her muscles were suddenly taut again. "How would you know? Where were you all day, anyway?" *Some friend.* She had expected him to be there. To bring her coffee. To…show up. He had to have known about Lucky. Right?

Morrison lowered the mug, a blue peace sign on the back of the cup garish and out of place. "Didn't Roger tell you?"

"Tell me what?"

"I saw him outside the office on my way in. Brought some tea for you, chamomile. To help you calm down. Roger said you were in court and that you would be indisposed until later in the afternoon."

Goddammit, Roger. Her knuckles ached as she balled her fists. "He lied."

"So he stole your tea, that rat bastard."

"He's an ass," she said, but the twinkle in Morrison's eyes almost made her smile.

"He loves you." It wasn't a question.

Like hell he does. "Roger only loves himself."

If Morrison had any thoughts about her statement, he didn't show it. "I did swing by the courthouse, but I didn't see you."

"Why didn't you come back to the office if you knew I wasn't in court?"

"I was trying to get everything together on a few other cases, so we don't all get fired if Johnson is a no-go."

"You mean, so Petrosky doesn't get fired." The heaviness in her neck spread into her back. Morrison was always looking out for this grown-ass man who could surely take care of his damn self. It was about Petrosky, always about Petrosky. She focused the tension into one clenched fist, wanting to drive it into Petrosky's junk. "If Petrosky gets fired, it's his own damn fault."

"I guess." He shrugged. "Will you be in court all day tomorrow?"

"I've got a case before the judge in the morning. Why?"

"Trying to figure out where I need to be."

"Be wherever the hell you want."

He frowned into his coffee mug, and her shoulders softened.

"Sorry."

"No need to be. I understand." He nodded toward the house. "I'm going to go in and check out the house to make sure. You wait in the car with the doors locked. Anything seems weird, take off. Otherwise, I'll come out to get you in a few. Code still the same?"

"Yeah. You still have your key?"

He held it up and jangled it.

THE QUIET PRESSED in around her as she waited, the throbbing in her head achingly soft compared to the steady hoof beats in her chest. She peered out the windshield at the hood where the envelope had rested. *Poor, poor Lucky.* And poor, poor Abby. How much loss could one little girl be expected to take? The image of the cat's severed neck smeared across her memory, and she looked away from the hood to see Morrison coming down the front steps, broad shoulders square against the porch light, his silhouette domineering but soft—protective.

Shannon grabbed her briefcase and exited the car. She pulled her suit jacket tight against the bitter breeze that had arisen while she was locked in her vehicle, the gusts of chilly air kicking up dirt and the scent of last season's decomposing leaves. Or maybe she just hadn't noticed the wind before because she'd thought she was running from a killer.

Morrison nodded to her. "Everything looks good inside. I'll wait out here, watch the street."

"You're not staying outside, Morrison."

"If someone's after you, they probably aren't going to walk in. They'll watch first."

"You can see the street from the upstairs bedrooms." She gestured to the windows on the top floor.

His gaze swung from the house to the road. "I won't be able to see all the way down the street, but it might be better to do occasional rounds anyway. Make me look like a… houseguest." His voice was quieter than it should have been as they trudged to the front door. Tired? He had to be exhausted after last night.

"You *are* a houseguest. Not like it's the first time." The knob didn't want to turn. The front door felt as if it was made of lead. "Plus, it'll be nice to have someone to talk to when I can't sleep tonight. I think I need to keep my mind off of…everything."

"Distraction I can do." Morrison followed her into the foyer and pulled cards from his pocket, nodding to the dining room table in the next room. "Gin rummy? I'd guess we have about an hour or two before anyone would dare show up. But I can sit at the window if you believe differently."

"No, no. Sit. I appreciate you being here. And rummy's fine." She dropped her briefcase beside the door and sank into the chair across from him. Pajamas would be nice. Bed would be nicer. But her legs were too tired to scale the steps to her bedroom despite her too-active brain.

"I figured you might need a break from poker." His fingers flew as he shuffled and dealt. "Saw Derry earlier. He said you've been sucking at five-card draw all week."

"Sounds like him," she said, but the cards froze against her fingers.

"I already owe him three lunches and twelve packs of bubble gum, so you're in good company."

She lowered her hands. "He never said anything about that."

"Why would he?"

"No, I mean, I guess he wouldn't." Her brother was allowed to have friends, and he and Morrison had hit it off the moment they'd met. So why did Morrison visiting feel so...secretive? Deceptive? She must be tired. Or maybe she was just overly protective of Derry's last months or weeks or days or—

"He probably doesn't want you to know how much practice he's getting. So you don't feel bad about losing...or should I say, letting him win."

Shannon tapped her pinky against the table, watching Morrison's face as he examined his cards, features placid and still, to avoid giving away his hand. She waited for him to ask her about Lucky's head. About the hospital. Did he already know she had been there? That Derry had talked her into getting involved? Or maybe Morrison had convinced Derry to make sure she stayed on the case. But no, Morrison would never do that. *What the hell is wrong with me?*

Morrison picked a card from the pile, discarded another, and looked at her. She exchanged her own cards, her throat hot and tighter than it should have been. They repeated the pattern in silence, one after another, the constant thrum of the crickets outside spiking the shuffling and the thunk of cards on the table until the knot in her throat melted.

Shannon beat Morrison six times in a row, but he grinned every time she laid down her hand and offered to deal the next.

"You suck at this, Morrison."

"It's all in the cards. Can't control them."

"You say that about a lot of stuff."

"That's because it's true about a lot of stuff."

He was so accepting. Relaxed. "You are relentlessly chill."

His eyes dropped to his cards. "I had a mean streak when I was younger. Angry at life."

She had known Morrison'd had a rough time as a kid, but she hadn't realized he'd been aggressive.

"I guess that's why my folks thought it'd be a good idea to put me in karate." He frowned as if disturbed by a memory, but he didn't look up.

So that was where he got all that martial arts stuff he did with Kimball. Shannon pulled a card from the draw pile. Four. She tossed it into the discards.

"I do less martial arts these days and more yoga," Morrison said. He selected a card and laid it on the pile. "You should try it, Shanny. Very relaxing."

"I guess you need all the help you can get dealing with Petrosky."

He finally met her gaze, and there was sadness there, though he seemed to be trying to hide it behind a smile. "You'll learn to love him."

"Love's a strong word, Morrison."

Morrison shrugged and turned back to his hand. "He's human too."

TEN ROUNDS. Shannon had won eight. She might have been annoyingly self-satisfied if she could have managed to lift her lips into a smile.

Their banter, and the card games themselves, had managed to pull her focus from the stress that had been suffocating her all day. But as they climbed the stairs, the twisting in her gut returned. Lucky. Derry. She had to find a killer. But her entire body was too heavy to go chasing after anyone tonight. Exhaustion pulled at Shannon's eyelids.

Morrison gestured to the unicorn poster staring out at them through the open doorway to the spare room. "How often has Abby been here in the last few weeks?"

"Once a week, at least. Whenever Alex has to work the night shift."

"She always brought the cat, right? Any other pattern that

someone watching might have noticed? Was she just here on certain days?"

Shannon shook her head. "Nope. It was usually in the evenings, but no pattern week-to-week unless they happened to know Alex's schedule." *Poor Lucky.* She ignored the tightness in her chest, crossed to the bedroom window and pulled back the curtain. "You can see the backyard from here, and the road behind it." They both looked past the ten-foot concrete wall that separated her patch of green lawn from the office buildings beyond.

"I forgot your yard backs up to an office complex. That's where I'd come from if I was trying to sneak up on the place. But I'll watch the front too."

They headed for Shannon's bedroom, decorated in muted blues and greens with a bright-white comforter on the bed. A massive black dresser stood across from the bed, a remnant from Roger's brief stint at playing house. Some nights, a fantasy of burning the dresser out back was the only thing that helped her sleep.

Morrison's footsteps stopped in the center of the room. "Nice."

Men. She sighed, looked at the dresser again and realized Morrison was not admiring it but rather was staring at the art above the bed: an oil painting of three sunflowers twisting toward an azure sky. "Oh. Thanks." She'd won the picture from Derry last month in a particularly intense poker game. She purposefully hadn't won a game since. Part of her suspected that Derry was trying to give his things away, and she wasn't ready to accept the pieces of him that would be left after he was cold and buried.

Morrison peered through the gauzy curtains. "Leave the door unlocked, and I'll rotate through here. I'll be quiet, so I don't wake you."

The thought of him coming in while she was dead to the world made something jerk around inside her belly. *Seriously, what the hell is wrong with me today?* "You can't stay up all night," she said.

"I'll rest in the spare when I need to."

"You think they'll assign anyone else to the case?"

"Not to do this. They're still farting around with exactly what to open. Oh, and that reminds me: Petrosky filed the report for you on...the envelope. Lucky. You need to come in and sign it tomorrow."

Her stomach lurched. "I will."

"I'm going to go scope out the parking lot at the office back there." Morrison dropped the curtain and turned from the window.

She nodded, struck by the set of his jaw, the shadow of stubble creeping across his chin.

"I'll set the alarm," he said. "Let me know if you need me."

When the door closed behind him, Shannon disrobed and pulled on a flannel nightgown. Soft and cozy. Morrison had seen it before, and she'd felt perfectly fine about it then. But this time...

She looked down at it: frumpy material, old and faded, and the plaid made her look ten pounds heavier. Why did she care?

Her face warmed. Nope. *No way, Shannon.* Roger had been enough man trouble for ten lifetimes. *And I'll screw it up —he's my best friend. I can't lose him right now.* But...it was warmer tonight, definitely getting to be springtime. She didn't want to sweat to death. She pulled the flannel nightgown off and rummaged in her drawer until she found one in silk.

Crickets chirped as she flicked off the light on the night table and slipped under the covers before she could consider her pajama choice further. Outside in the night, a dog barked —someone's not-dead pet. Her skin crawled as she pulled the covers tighter.

Morrison's footsteps sounded from somewhere on the floor below, steady and calm. She listened to him pace the kitchen, the stairs, the spare room. He was on the stairs again when she finally closed her eyes and slept.

12

SHANNON WASN'T ALONE. Still bleary and half-immobile with sleep, her breath caught as she registered the rustling and scuffling of an intruder. Close. So close to her that she could almost feel the heat coming off them in waves, tightening her muscles. Every part of her was ready to bolt as she shot to seated and—

Her shoulders relaxed. Morrison stood at the window in an unwrinkled button-down shirt, coffee cup in hand, his frame silhouetted against the outline of the bleak, gray dawn. But why was he... Oh yeah. *Lucky*. She blinked sleep from her eyes.

"Did I wake you?"

Yes. She stretched her legs. "No."

"Good."

She swung her feet to the floor, the chill of the morning, sending goose bumps shivering up her arms. She pulled the blanket back up around her shoulders. "Anything overnight?"

"No one suspicious," he said, shaking his head. "Though I did find a raccoon eating your trash. I lured it across the road with the hamburger Petrosky left on my passenger seat."

"Sounds like you just invited him to come back the next time he wants a burger."

"Yeah, maybe. I'm not very scary."

She yawned. "True enough."

"I made that special coffee," he said.

"The stuff you keep in your trunk?"

He nodded. "Yup. Won't make you jittery. It's got mushrooms in it, you know, more antioxidants. Supposed to be good for cholesterol."

"Chol—" She cocked her head. "That's what I've been drinking for the last three years?"

He grinned like a schoolboy. "You've always said you liked the taste."

He's got me there. She dropped the blanket and stood, the air kissing her legs and sending a fresh prickle of goose bumps from toes to thighs. She wrapped her arms around her chest. "I've never seen you jittery in my life. And how did I not know this about your coffee?"

"Gotta have a few secrets," he said hurriedly. "Okay, well, there's more downstairs." He lowered his eyes and headed for the door. "I'll let you get ready." It wasn't until the door closed that she remembered she was wearing her silk nightgown. Not that it mattered.

WHEN SHE CAME DOWNSTAIRS ALL SHOWERED and dressed, Morrison was at the kitchen table, shoveling food into his mouth. He swallowed and held up his spoon. "Oatmeal?"

She sat across from him where a place was already set for her and moved the porridge around with her spoon. Red and black peppered the beige mush. "Goji berries and chia seed again?"

"You know it. And hemp."

If only the hemp were enough to get her stoned. She could use a little high right now. Shannon had dressed too quickly to think about anything unpleasant, but now memories of the day before were trickling back into her consciousness. Derry's thin face. Poor little Lucky. The tears on Abby's cheeks as she clung to her father's skeletal frame. *Make a dying man's wish come true, Shanny*. She needed to figure this case out and fast.

Morrison picked up his spoon again. "Your arraignment is at what time?"

"Nine." She spooned a bite to her lips and chewed. Good. Bland but good.

"After that?"

"Just paperwork. Got a few things to file."

"I'll drive us." He put up a hand when he saw her face. "I'm supposed to be watching you."

"Like I need a babysitter."

"Like you wouldn't be hanging out with me anyway." He winked, and she couldn't help smiling back.

"Anyway, I'll drop you at the courthouse. You can get your filing completed, and I'll meet you back there after I visit Ms. Lewis."

Derek's mother. A spoon of mush froze halfway to her lips. "What makes you think you're going over there alone?"

"You don't need to be there, Shannon. If Derek's killing really is related to her—"

"It isn't."

"I kinda thought you wanted out of this."

Of course he thought that—she had been pretty clear on the point with Petrosky. And from the look on his face and the way he was encouraging her to stay home, he obviously hadn't told Derry to convince her otherwise. But...she *had* been convinced. She needed to find this bastard. She needed to see Derry's eyes when she told him, "It's over now, Derry, Abby'll be fine, just worry about getting better." Except...he wasn't ever getting better. She dropped her spoon into the bowl. "I interviewed Lucinda Lewis three times before Johnson's court case began, and I just put away the person she thinks hurt her son. Maybe I can help make things go more smoothly."

Morrison chewed silently and sipped his coffee. "Okay. After court, we'll go to Lewis's. I'll clear it with Petrosky."

"You don't have to clear it with him."

"I know I don't have to, but I'm sure he'd appreciate it. And asking him won't hurt anything. Win-win."

"And if he says no?" She crossed her arms. "What then, smart guy?"

Morrison stood and took one last bite on the way to the sink. "If he says no, we'll do it anyway."

She approached to set her dish beside his, and the scent of his lavender soap and shaving foam overpowered the oats.

Morrison glanced at her bowl, still mostly full. "I thought you liked oatmeal."

She shrugged.

"You'll get used to it. You want to grab some workout clothes? We can hit Kimball's class tonight if we have time." *We.* He took the bowl from her, brushing her fingers, and a jolt of electricity shimmered up her arm and into her chest.

Shannon stared at his fingers. *Nope. Not happening. I am not losing my best friend to some hormonal whim.* She wouldn't make it through Derry's death without his support, and shit had a way of falling apart once you played pants-off dance-off.

"Shanny? Hey, you all right?"

She nodded. *I just need to get out more. Maybe fuck a stranger. Win-win.* "Yep, fine. I'll get my gym bag."

IKE LAMBERT WAS ALREADY SEATED in the defendant's chair when she entered, his brows furrowed, glasses askew. His snub nostrils flared and settled as she sat across the aisle. Beside him, Griffen tapped the desk, adjusting his own glasses and ruffling papers with the twitchy dexterity of a rabbit. No one sat behind Lambert, no friend or family member to offer an affectionate gaze or a pat on the shoulder. *Good.* Lambert was a piece of shit. The pews behind Shannon were empty as well—not even the girl's mother had shown up to watch this bastard enter a plea.

Shannon stood to the rustle of fabric around her and faced the front. The judge had a shock of white hair and cheekbones that looked like they'd cut anyone who touched them. His voice was just as sharp, as were the punishments he doled out. He sat and picked up the gavel.

"Come to order, court is now in session, the Honorable Judge Klein presiding." The gavel sounded, and fabric rustled again as everyone sat.

"Is the prosecution ready to proceed?" he barked.

Shannon stood. "Yes, Your Honor."

"The defense?"

Griffen winced and rolled himself to standing until his shoulders were square. "Yes, Your Honor."

"Ike Lambert, a complaint has been filed against you, case number 43277901A that alleges in count one, the felony homicide of Cindy Waters, age seven, committed on the fourth of March..."

Shannon turned to Lambert as Klein rattled off the list of crimes, the numbers, the dates. Lambert locked eyes with her. Not a twitch of the mouth, not a quiver of the lip. Only his nose betrayed his true emotions, nostrils flaring with anger and malice. No remorse, just like the killer she was still looking for. Lambert was probably proud of murdering another human being. Someone like him would be just as proud of killing a cat. Icicles tore up her back and raced along her arms.

"How does the defense plead?"

Griffen's fingertips danced on the table in front of him. "No contest, Your Honor."

Lambert ran his tongue over his lips. Like a reptile.

Shannon responded to the judge when prompted and spent the rest of the time grinding her teeth together, the sound of them creaking in her ears as Griffen and the judge spoke back and forth, back and forth. Even in profile, Griffen looked tired, blue tinting the skin under his eyes. He hadn't been sleeping. Though the bags might have been guilt—he couldn't be happy about getting a better deal for this murdering asshole. Griffen was too good a guy for that. Which was the problem with defense; even when you won, sometimes you felt like you were failing humanity. It was the reason she'd flipped over to prosecution.

Not that it was all that much better on her side.

Griffen finally nodded at the judge and ran a jerky finger over his watch—the face looked like it was made of wood—and then the band on his wrist—red was for...AIDS awareness, right? Definitely not for justice, that was for damn sure. Lambert smiled, self-assured and heartless. *What a psycho.*

The gavel sounded over her creaking teeth and the whoosh of blood in her ears. She grabbed her briefcase and was turning to stride from the courtroom when Griffen stepped in front of her. "Oh...hey, Griffen."

"Hey." He glanced back over his shoulder at his client, who was being escorted from the room in handcuffs. Lambert was still grinning. Her skin bristled.

"You have a moment?" he asked.

She looked longingly at the door and dragged her eyes back, hoping he'd take the hint. When he just stood there waiting for her answer, she sighed. "Sure. What's up?"

His mouth opened and closed like he was trying to figure out what exactly to say to her. He still hadn't met her gaze. "Well...there's been some talk, Shannon. Are you okay?"

Talk? Probably about Lucky. "Yeah, I'm okay. What exactly did you hear?"

"You know how I feel about Roger." His eyes flicked to her and away again. "How I've always felt about Roger since the day you started dating him."

Shannon said nothing, just waited while Griffen's face reddened.

"He's had a lot to say, as of late. He seems to... It's about you; that you may be...in a precarious situation." He was trying to be judicious, diplomatic. What he meant was that Roger was talking a bunch of shit, trying to play the martyr who wanted to save her from herself. Some things never changed.

"I thought it was ridiculous, of course, but then it came up again, this time from someone out of the chief's office and—"

"You know you can't believe everything Roger says." Or everything out of the chief's office if it came from Kimball, Roger's BFF. But her throat tightened anyway. If Griffen had heard about Lucky, everyone else probably had too.

"But is it true? About the cat?" He finally looked at her, and his face was drawn, his eyes searching. He really was worried.

She sighed and peeked behind them at the pews. Everyone else had gone, but still she lowered her voice just above a whisper. "Listen, between you and me, off the record…"

"Of…course." But his face was pained like it would kill him to keep it to himself. Jesus, he really had changed. Or maybe he was just different to her because she no longer gave him her secrets to keep.

"There've been some…issues," Shannon said. "Someone is none too happy about the fact that Johnson got put away. And now I'm scrambling, trying to make sure I got everything right."

Griffen's mouth dropped open, and he closed it again, but his eyes flicked to the wall, and back to her like someone behind her was telling him it wasn't true. "You believe it now? That she's innocent?"

"I don't know what I believe. But I could use anything you have." She shifted her briefcase to her other hand. Roger was going to be pissed as hell when he discovered she'd thrown doubt on their conviction, and to the defense attorney at that. "Did you know about a second social worker going to Johnson's house the day Lewis was murdered? Seems he was there earlier that afternoon."

"What? No!" His eyes widened. "This could be—perhaps they saw something or someone or maybe—"

"Between you and me, *counsel*, I'm doing what I can. And I'll keep you posted. We'll attack this together, okay?"

"Yes, of course. Here…let me give you my new cell number." His face was bright with excitement, though the corners of his eyes remained tight. "Shannon, this could be amazing. I mean—"

Amazing that she'd convicted an innocent person? She silenced him with a look, happy her ability to do that hadn't changed over the last few years.

"Okay," he said more subdued. "Just let me know what else you find. Petrosky already has copies of all my files." Griffen adjusted his pocket square; the material red and faded. She wondered if it was the one she'd given him half a dozen years ago for Christmas. It wouldn't have surprised her, and the familiarity of him, of them, tugged at her.

"Listen, I told Karen about what happened between us," he said, seemingly reading her mind. "About how our friendship...ended." He winced like it hurt to say, and maybe it did —guilt at walking away? Or maybe he was wincing because Karen had reacted the same as his ex. Her cold eyes at the bar sure hadn't looked very understanding.

"Karen thinks I miss you. And I believe...that she's right. We did make great friends, Shan."

Shannon balked; recovered. "Yeah, we did." She forced a smile, but hearing his nickname for her on his lips felt wrong after so much time had passed. And now her memories of hanging out at the bar with him and working long hours prepping for court together were bittersweet—tinged with the pain he'd caused when he severed their friendship. When he'd proven to her, yet again, that people are not to be trusted, even in a platonic capacity.

"Maybe we can all get together some night," he began slowly. "You and me and Karen and Morrison?"

Her heart slammed against her breastbone, drowning out the background noise of a courtroom door closing somewhere in the hallway. "Morrison and I aren't a couple." Morrison hadn't even glanced at her in that silk. Not that it would have mattered if he had.

He frowned. "Oh. Well, bring whoever you want then. Friend, boyfriend, whatever. Anyone but Valentine. I think he hates me. He always looks at me like he wants to kick my ass."

That was true enough. Life got tricky when one friend was content to beat the snot out of another. Not that Valentine was particularly violent, but he had no time for those who defended criminals and made law enforcement's job harder. If she'd known Valentine back when she was on the defense side, maybe he would have hated her just as much.

13

SHANNON'S back was still tense when she exited the courtroom and headed into the hall. Around her, other attorneys scuttled their clients through the halls like rats in a maze, urgent whispers of what to do—and what not to do—in court echoing off the walls. She kept her eyes downcast, avoiding the clamor. Trying to think. Trying to figure this case out while Derry could still high five her and offer her a medal, or keys to his vast fortune, or whatever thing he'd presume to be funny when she told him he no longer had to worry about cat-killing assholes running around his neighborhood.

Think, Shannon.

Lucinda Lewis wouldn't know much, but it was critical that Shannon go today with an open mind. Last time she'd spoken to Lucinda, both women had been convinced Ashley Johnson was guilty. Maybe Shannon had heard what she wanted to hear. But this time, she wasn't going to make any errors in judgment.

Shannon skirted a man in a pinstriped suit, yanked open the heavy wooden front door, and winced against the damp, biting wind. The parking lot was thick with dreary mist. She stepped over the threshold, eyes on her shoes and the cracked concrete, and plowed directly into someone: Dr. McCallum.

Shannon managed to keep hold of her briefcase, but his fell to the pavement. *Seriously, I'm spending the rest of the day locked up somewhere.* "I'm so sorry, Doctor."

"No worries, Ms. Taylor." McCallum's cheeks were rouged with the effort of walking across the lot, or maybe from embarrassment. The buttons on his jacket strained against a girth larger than Lillian Valentine's baby bump. He bent and grabbed the handle on his case.

"How are you?" she asked. "Haven't seen you around for a few weeks."

"Oh, you know how it is. Clients all day long, don't get out much." McCallum met her eyes, and she flinched under his stare: that I-see-into-your-soul look that all shrinks seemed to have. "How have you been? And Abby?"

"She's…big."

He appraised her as if looking for a chink in her armor. She averted her gaze. Under her shoes, the pock-marked concrete threatened to swallow her heels.

Shannon drew her eyes back to McCallum. "Who are you here on? You testifying?"

"Stanley case." McCallum glanced over her shoulder at the parking lot. Twitchy. Nervous? Or was it just her? "Did a psychological evaluation to determine whether the girl could consent to the relationship and on the implications of the trauma."

"Ah." More information than she needed. Though she'd offered little in response, his eyes were alight as if the conversation was the best thing he had experienced all day. She tried to recall ever seeing McCallum with anyone else—a friend, a colleague at a lunch meeting—but came up empty. Shame for him to be so lonely. He was always so kind to her. Though the fact that he knew her darkest secrets didn't make her feel entirely comfortable with him outside the confines of his office.

She glanced at the lot, looking for Morrison's car. "I'd better run."

McCallum looked into the lot and back at her, raising a brow in question.

"I'm meeting Morrison on a case." Now who was giving away too much information?

McCallum's pudgy face broke into a smile. "Ah, well, tell him I said hello. And send my salutations to his partner as well. I haven't seen them around in weeks either."

Weeks? Hadn't Petrosky told her he'd been with McCallum just the other day?

Alarm must have registered on her face because McCallum patted her arm, kindly, almost fatherly. "Come down and visit sometime. My services are always covered for those on the force. Perk of the job." He stepped toward the door.

"Alas, I'm not on the force."

"Close enough." He grabbed the door handle.

No, she had paid him out of pocket after Abby was born, when the raging postpartum depression had tried to eat her alive. Though, he had come to the hospital to see her after the birth, free of charge. He'd probably just forgotten.

"I'll see you around, Doctor."

"Until we meet again, Ms. Taylor."

Something about the exchange was off; she felt it in her gut, but could not place it. Why had McCallum been so fidgety? That wasn't like him—at least the him she knew from her time as a patient. And what the hell was Petrosky trying to pull?

The lot was silent as a graveyard, not a car on the road, not even a rustle from the single tree that perched precariously at the curb near the precinct. She found Morrison's Fusion behind a truck, Morrison in the driver's seat writing in a notebook propped against the steering wheel. When he saw her, he flipped the book closed and leaned over to push open the passenger door. She tossed her briefcase into the back and climbed in beside him, unease gnawing at her chest.

Morrison raised an eyebrow but turned to the windshield and put the car in drive. She watched the precinct roll by, then the courthouse, then her office, as he pulled onto the main road.

"So...you going to tell me what's wrong?"

She drummed her fingers on the console. "Petrosky lied to me. About going to see McCallum."

He kept his eyes on the road, but not a muscle twitched with surprise. "Huh." He stopped at a light.

"That's it? Just 'huh'?" She wanted him to be just as irritated as she was by Petrosky's behavior. Anger heated her chest. It was bad enough to know that Petrosky was a lush—worse, that she was impotent to do anything about it. If she turned him in, Morrison would never speak to her again. "Petrosky needs to see McCallum. You're enabling him. In the parking lot the other day, he reeked of liquor."

"You can't force these things." The light changed, and Morrison gunned it through the intersection. The softness in his voice was betrayed by the hardness in his jaw. "He's been a little messed up since the Hannah Montgomery case, but he's still doing everything he needs to do at work."

Hannah Montgomery was a girl taken by a serial killer a few years back, after her boyfriend, prominent businessman Dominic Harwick, was brutally murdered along with seven others. They'd never found a body, only her blood on the steering wheel of an empty car three states over, any trace of the killer gone. Petrosky had taken leave, but judging by his boozy breath, not for long enough.

"He always has other people's best interests at heart."

"Not an excuse."

Silence fell over them as buildings rushed by outside the windows—gas stations, fast food, strip malls. But the silence wasn't necessarily uncomfortable, just strange. Different. Like they were slowly becoming something besides what they'd always been. She hoped she wasn't losing her best friend over this case, though if it came down to it, maybe Morrison would choose Petrosky over her anyway. Not that she'd give him an ultimatum like Griffen's ex-girlfriend had done. But eventually, Petrosky might do something worse than simply withholding evidence or telling little white lies, something that she'd not be able to ignore, especially if he kept drinking, and then—

Morrison's voice pulled her out of her head and back into the car. "He takes it all real hard, you know? He doesn't like to see people suffer. It eats at him."

"I'm sure it does. But he's got issues, Morrison. He's okay with harassing doctors and lab techs to get what he wants. And he lied to me about Johnson for no reason I can figure except that it didn't suit his version of the truth. Obstruction isn't nothing. If you really care about him, get him some help."

Morrison didn't respond. She turned away.

And then: "Petrosky's not a dick to everyone." He hooked a left and coasted down a side street where neatly trimmed bushes sat in square rows. "And some people deserve it, like the assholes who do stupid shit but won't ever see the inside of a courtroom. He has a knack for getting jerks to back off even if they haven't officially committed a prosecutable crime."

"What? Who?" Probably the boyfriends of his "girls."

Morrison pulled into a lot and parked near the door. Lucinda Lewis's apartment building was five stories of red brick and stone with a heavy wooden door that looked like it belonged on a storybook mansion—or maybe the courthouse—instead of an apartment building. Somewhere nearby, a dog howled. "I'm just saying, there are people who shouldn't be out there hurting people. Then there's everyone else that we need to protect. Petrosky does what he has to."

Shannon searched his eyes. "That's why you like him, isn't it? It's that whole hero complex. Vigilante justice." Maybe that was why he liked Johnson too: even if she'd been guilty, he might not have thought she'd been wrong either. Just like Valentine. *I wasn't the least bit upset that Johnson took care of*

Derek. That asshole, beating on his kid... She pushed the thought away.

Morrison grabbed the door handle. "I just think Petrosky's a good guy. One of the nicest people I know, actually." He kept the focus off himself, she noticed. No response to her amateur psychological analysis.

"It's sad you don't know nicer people," she said.

"I don't think so."

The door to the building's main entrance creaked open ominously, but the inside looked undisturbed, normal, if not ostentatious—thick red carpets, gilded picture frames, and an entry table holding a potted plant beside a wall of copper-colored mailboxes. And yet, the niggling inside her chest remained, a sensation far too common in the last few days. Worry about Derry? But that ache was more poignant, always present in the pit of her stomach, sometimes stabbing at her heart in quiet moments. No, probably from just talking about Petrosky. *Goddamn that man.*

They ascended the stairs to the third floor and started down the hallway toward Lucinda Lewis's apartment. Paisley wallpaper, in reds and golds, shimmered under the glow of bronze fixtures, and every brass door knocker seemed to watch them, the one on Lewis's door especially—the head of a lion perched to snarl and spring. The harsh report of brass on brass drew a threatening growl from behind a neighboring door. Shannon eyed the door beside Lewis's warily, as if the animal could claw its way through the scarred wood and wrench her head from her body. What was her deal? This was routine stuff. She even knew the lady for god's sake.

The door in front of them opened a crack. "Yes?"

"Ms. Lewis? Police, ma'am."

The heavy-lidded eyeball in the crack shifted to Shannon. "Oh, it's you." The dog next door growled again. Lewis's door shut, and the rattle of the security chain being disengaged clanked from the other side. From next door came muffled human shouts, then something thunked against the door. The dog yelped and fell silent.

Lewis opened the door and stood back so Morrison and Shannon could enter. The overpowering smell of potpourri followed them down the hallway and into the living room, harsh and thick as cigar smoke in the back of Shannon's throat.

"Diamond is asleep. The worker always sees her when she comes, though, so you can ask her if you're worried." Her eyes radiated haughty determination, a warning that she was not one to be trifled with. Ms. Lewis sat in a wingback chair striped in white and black like old prison garb and gestured to the flowered love seat across from her. Morrison and Shannon sat, thighs touching, his deodorant sharp and crisp like menthol. On the wall behind Lewis, a framed image of Jesus holding a lamb looked down on them condescendingly, his grip on the animal appearing less nurturing and more corrupt. Shannon blinked at the picture, and Jesus loosened his grip. Nope, nothing sinister about it. Just her mood.

"Has your CPS caseworker been here to see you lately?" Morrison's phone buzzed in his pocket, and he reached a finger inside to turn it off.

"Ms. Burke? She was here yesterday. Been checking to make sure everything is all right with Diamond. Even set me up with some services to get help with meals and diapers and whatnot." She nodded. "Real nice girl."

"Have you ever had another worker stop by here?"

"Ms. Burke asked me about that too." She folded her hands in her lap and studied them. "Never seen anyone but her. There something I need to know?"

Shannon and Morrison exchanged a look.

"Did Derek ever mention another worker?" Shannon asked.

"He didn't talk to me about that stuff. Thought I was the one who called."

"Weren't you?" Morrison said.

Lewis glowered at Morrison and pursed her lips.

"Ma'am?"

She crossed her arms, defiant. "That baby deserves better.

Every time I stopped by, those two were arguing. Yellin' and carrying on. Any good grandmother woulda done the same." Her lip quivered, grief melting the confidence. "And now... now Diamond's all I have left of him. I did the best I could after Derek's father ran, but the street just...took him from me. All that fear, none of the good. What he saw was his friends dying and the drugs taking the pain away. I kept believing he'd get back one day, but—" Lewis shrugged one fleshy shoulder, and her pressed blouse whispered crisply with starch.

"I'm so sorry for your loss, Ms. Lewis," Morrison said. "I wish there was more I could do."

"Yeah, the social worker said that too." She nodded. "You're good people."

From the next room, a screech split the air, and Shannon jumped.

"That'll be her." Lewis leveled a hard gaze at Shannon. "You find out who hurt my boy."

Unease fluttered in Shannon's chest, just a notch below panic. Find out? She'd just tossed someone in jail. But maybe Ashley Johnson hadn't killed Derek, and Lucinda Lewis knew it. Maybe she'd known it all along. Shannon swallowed hard. "What do you mean, Ms.—"

Lewis stood. "Ashley's fine where she is. Won't get a chance to hurt Diamond with her...lifestyle. But something else is going on, or you wouldn't be here. Besides, Ashley never seemed the type to—" Her eyes glazed, and Shannon heard the words she couldn't say: *To kill my son. To smash my boy's skull in.*

Lewis leaned toward her and aimed a finger at Shannon's chest. "But you mark my words, Ashley knows who killed Derek. She ain't innocent." She straightened up and gestured to the door.

The sickly sweet of Lewis's apartment was still messing with Shannon's sinuses as she and Morrison descended the stairs. Morrison was looking at his phone, which was buzzing again.

"What's up, boss?" His voice echoed in the stairwell.

Boss. Shannon sighed, and Morrison winked at her.

"Yeah, we're leaving now. Said her worker had mentioned another... Oh, good. Okay. We'll meet you there."

Morrison pocketed the phone as they escaped the confines of the stairwell and entered the lobby. "Petrosky's got an appointment with infamous social worker Frieda Burke. He wants us to swing by in thirty minutes. Hopefully, we can get a lead on who else was at the house that day, figure out if there actually was another worker from their office poking around over there like Ashley Johnson seems to think." He opened the door to the outside, and the air, slightly rotten with exhaust from the nearby road, was almost refreshing after the thick perfume inside the building.

"You have time to run over there, or do you need to get back to the office?"

Shannon could feel eyes on her back as she walked away from the building. *It's this place. This situation. This...life.* She had a full day's worth of reports on her desk, but half of them would be pleas. And this case was the only one with the potential to protect the people she loved. Maybe. Not that she was psyched about dealing with Burke—her temples were already throbbing.

She nodded. "I've got time."

14

FRIEDA BURKE MET them under the awning outside the social work building just as the rain began to spit on the overhang. Her curly hair poofed around her head in a Little Orphan Annie way, except it was brown, not red, and fell over tense eyes—eyes that seemed to embed her frustration into her face. Or maybe it was residual jealousy toward Shannon. She wondered if Burke knew about the flowers Griffen had sent, the constant apologies that came for months after Shannon had officially stopped speaking to him. He'd felt guilty about screwing up their friendship. Shannon hoped Burke had felt bad too. She searched Burke's face for the slightest hint of contrition but saw only agitation on her lipless mouth.

Petrosky clumped up behind them, raindrops splattering his jacket, and Shannon coughed at the tobacco-mint thing he had going on. Cigarettes. Booze. And the stereotypical mouthwash cover-up. She wondered if Burke might recognize Petrosky's shenanigans from her work with other alcoholics. Shannon hoped not—she wanted Petrosky to get help, but not at Burke's discretion. And the woman already despised Shannon. Morrison was their only hope of getting the information they needed unless Petrosky bullied it out of her.

Burke buzzed them into the building with her key card

and led them into the lobby, then to an office dominated by a poster of smiley face sketches with "How Do You Feel Today?" emblazoned across the top. Petrosky sat in the only chair in front of Burke's desk. Shannon leaned against the back wall with Morrison and watched Burke, who currently looked like the little cartoon face labeled "Irritable." Just as she had at Ashley Johnson's hearing. Though Shannon knew she hadn't been there to testify. Hadn't needed to go visit Johnson in jail either.

"I saw you at the hearing," Shannon said. "Ashley Johnson's closing arguments."

Burke's eyes flashed alarm and settled, but not before Petrosky shifted in his chair. "I wanted to see Lucinda Lewis under pressure and watch the verdict," she said carefully.

Petrosky leaned toward her. "Do you go to the trials of everyone on your caseload? I imagine that's rather time consuming."

Her mouth tensed. She stared back. "I was called in for questioning before that trial, so I suppose it's only natural that I'd want to see it play out in court." Her tone was dangerous. Defensive. Shannon's shoulders went rigid.

"What about your visit to Johnson this week?" Petrosky said.

"Updating her on her daughter. A closing session essentially. I know it wasn't necessary, but...none of us wants to lose a child. No matter what Ashley did, that's a horrible thing to go through." Color had crept into Burke's cheeks like a bad rouge job. "You think that's wrong too?"

"Just being thorough," Petrosky said. "It seemed odd that someone so busy would take the time to visit. Even more odd that you'd spend an afternoon watching a trial when you could do absolutely nothing except gawk. I don't like odd."

Burke's jaw dropped. She crossed her arms. "It isn't odd. There was no other family available. If Lucinda proved unable to care for Diamond or seemed unstable, I would have needed to change my plans and look at fosters. I try to keep them with family as much as possible, but it doesn't always work that way, for obvious reasons. A clean house and cooked meals are more than enough if you ask half the kids in this godforsaken city." Her eyes narrowed at Shannon, perhaps to avoid Petrosky's glare, or maybe for another reason altogether. Griffen had said that Burke wanted to adopt but had been unsuccessful, that Shannon's easy surrogacy had made Burke uncomfortable, distressed. As if it were up to Shannon to shoulder this woman's burdens.

Shannon purposefully loosened her balled fists, but the rigidity in her chest remained. *This is all wrong.* Burke would have known whether Lucinda Lewis was stable before the trial. And breaking down at a trial would certainly not be cause to remove a grandchild from her care. So what was Burke really doing at the hearing? The nagging itch in Shannon's brain intensified.

"Sounds like you don't like your job much, Ms. Burke," Petrosky said.

"Seeing this...stuff every day—it's sad." But her eyes were hard, not sad, as they flicked around the room and finally landed on Shannon. Shannon held her gaze until Petrosky spoke again.

"Did you know another worker went to visit Derek Lewis?"

"No," Burke said and broke eye contact. Shannon leaned forward, off the wall, as if lying had a scent she could catch.

Morrison straightened beside her and laid a hand on Petrosky's shoulder. "No?" Morrison said to Burke, his voice soft but accusing. "You told Lucinda Lewis that if anyone else showed up, she should call you."

Burke dragged her eyes to Morrison but didn't seem especially intimidated. "Oh, that." She waved her hand dismissively. "I believe I heard something about that from Ashley when I went in to meet with her the one day." It rang false, and Shannon knew why: Ashley Johnson had insisted she'd said nothing of this other worker to Burke. Was Johnson lying? Or was Burke?

Petrosky cleared his throat.

Burke's eyes narrowed. "I was worried it was some weirdo trying to get in on the fame after a murder trial. I told Lucinda to let me know if anyone came posing as a worker."

"You think it's a faker?" Petrosky asked, but Shannon already knew he believed that—he'd said as much the day they'd found Lucky's head.

Morrison stepped back to take his place next to Shannon on the wall.

"I'm not really sure, but it happens. On normal cases, we occasionally get some overlap, an accidental second call put through to the wrong worker, and paperwork gets screwed up. But we almost always catch those double-ups quick and make a note in the chart. Worst case, Lucinda calls me if they show up, and it's just someone with a duplicate file. But if it's someone who shouldn't be there, it's that much more important to find out who it is. I work with other care providers all over the city, and things do occasionally slip through. Communication isn't perfect." She smiled, but it was strained. "Is there anything else I can do for you?" She was being dismissive; she clearly didn't want to help them. Or Ashley Johnson.

"We'd like to talk to your boss," Petrosky said. Shannon's chest loosened a touch. Maybe they'd actually manage to get what they needed from someone else.

"My boss?"

"Where's his office?"

"*Her* office is at the end of the hall. She's usually out on cases, but she got back a little bit ago."

"The boss is out getting her hands dirty, too, huh?"

"The lead social worker is still a social worker, detectives, and a damn good one at that." Her eyes were fiery, a little too upset for the occasion.

Petrosky's index finger twitched against his knee as he stared Burke down.

"She might be able to spare a few minutes, but our time is stretched thin these days," Burke said. "All of us are scrambling to pick up Benjamin's caseload since he left."

She shook her head. "I'll call her first to make sure it's okay."

"Benjamin who? And when did he quit?" Shannon blurted out, and Burke's hand froze over the phone. If it was a month ago, when Derek was killed—

"Just in the last few days. And he had a helluva caseload. Like we all do, I guess."

The last few days. After the trial. Around the time her car got ransacked, and Lucky was crushed underfoot. Not that it necessarily meant anything, but—

"He been here long?" Petrosky asked.

"A year or so."

"Anything weird about him leaving?"

Burke glanced at the ceiling—considering, not guilty. "I don't know. You'll have to ask Amanda."

Shit. Amanda Kimball, Park Kimball's wife. How had she forgotten? Amanda was another friend Roger had stolen in the divorce, but Shannon hadn't been shocked by that—she'd never really trusted Amanda. And now Roger would know within hours that they'd been at the social work office, and Shannon would hear about it this afternoon. A knot between her shoulder blades throbbed.

Petrosky stood. "Thank you, Ms. Burke."

She smiled, but her eyes remained guarded. "If you need anything else, just call." She pulled a card from her desk and handed it over, but the look on her face said that she hoped they would never use it.

Burke led them down the hall and rapped on the door to Amanda Kimball's office. The easy grin Amanda gave Burke faltered when she saw who Burke had brought with her.

"Nice to see you again, Mrs. Kimball," Petrosky said.

"Likewise," she said through clenched teeth.

Was there anyone in the free world who didn't want to kick Petrosky's ass?

Three chairs in Amanda Kimball's office, not just one. *Fancy.* Amanda's keys twinkled from a nail in the wall behind her desk, and Shannon wondered how many times she had to lose her keys in a disordered purse or drawer to make slamming a nail into plaster seem like the only solution to keep track of them.

"Nice computer," Morrison said, gesturing at Amanda's shiny laptop in the corner of the desk. "MacBook?"

Amanda's expression warmed when she looked at Morrison. "Park gave it to me. But you helped him pick it out, didn't you?"

Morrison smiled in response and pulled out his notepad.

"Thanks for seeing us on short notice," Petrosky said. Amanda didn't acknowledge him. Or Shannon. That stung more than she wanted to admit, but she couldn't dwell on it —they didn't have time for personal nonsense. Or maybe they did because the tension wasn't going to subside on its own.

Shannon cleared her throat. "Amanda, I know it's been a while and that things have been...difficult in recent months." *Ever since you and your husband decided you'd rather be buddies with my cheating ex.* "But, we need your help with this."

Amanda sighed, finally meeting Shannon's eyes. "I wanted to call."

Sure you did. Shannon bit her tongue and waited.

"With the hours I work these days, I can barely squeeze in grocery shopping, let alone anything else."

Find common ground; then I can get what I'm after. "Yeah, I know. It's hard for me too. And juggling work and everything else...at least Park can pick up a little of the slack with stuff around the house or running Dana to dance, right?"

Amanda's eyes dropped to the desktop. "Dana doesn't have much going on these days." Brusque. Dismissive? Maybe even angry. Mad at her husband? Or at Shannon? Maybe Roger had given Amanda reason to be pissed—he wasn't above spreading rumors about his exes, she knew that all too well.

Amanda side-eyed Petrosky and leaned back in her chair, her shoulders slumped—defeated. "No matter what's happened outside the office, I have no interest in hindering a police investigation. Just tell me what you need."

No matter what's happened? From the way Amanda continued to avoid Shannon's gaze, Roger must have told some fantastic lies. Shannon's stomach twisted. Maybe he'd tried to make Shannon look crazy—or hateful. It wouldn't have been the first time. Roger had once told Morrison that she had spoken badly of him at home, made jokes at her best friend's expense. Morrison had ignored him, thank god, but...

That jerk. It wasn't enough for Roger to just cut her out of their old friends' lives—he wanted them to hate her.

Petrosky cleared his throat. "Do you have any idea which social worker might have gone to Derek Lewis's house on February fifteenth?"

"The Lewis case again?" Amanda shook her head. "You already did quite a number on Frieda, and all she did was her job."

Petrosky must have harassed the crap out of Burke during the trial, but he didn't look sorry. "We got some new evidence, Mrs. Kimball. A witness who indicates there was someone else at the house the day Derek Lewis was murdered. Someone who identified themselves as Lewis's social worker."

Her eyes widened. "You think someone in this office—"

"We'll need to talk to anyone who had reason to be in the area that day. They might be a witness but not be aware of it." He lowered his voice and leaned toward the desk. "Or maybe whoever it was thought they'd get in trouble for fighting with Lewis just before he mysteriously ended up dead."

The blood drained from Amanda's cheeks. "We have incredible people here. Truly amazing. Half of them would offer you the shirt off their backs. Did you know that Frieda even fosters sometimes when kids have no one to stay with? She fostered Diamond twice: once last year, and again while we vetted Lucinda. She's...incredible."

Back to Burke again. Those two definitely had a close

work relationship. Shannon opened her mouth to ask, but Petrosky did it for her.

"You guys seem pretty chummy."

"Frieda and I have been friends for years."

Amanda had never mentioned her friendship with Burke to Shannon, even six months ago, when they were still friends. Not that this was necessarily an issue, but—

"That aside," Amanda said, "no one who works here would do anything that would hurt these children, and that includes withholding information that could be...questionable." The fire burning in her eyes indicated that she believed that. But that didn't mean she wasn't wrong.

Petrosky rubbed his chin. "I'm not saying that someone in your department committed a crime, Mrs. Kimball, merely that if they happened to be at the scene on the day of the murder, they might have been concerned about the implications of their presence."

Amanda clamped her mouth shut and crossed her arms.

"You have a lot of male social workers?" Petrosky asked.

The only noise for a moment was Morrison's pen scratching on his notepad as Amanda paused.

"I mean...no, we don't have a lot of male workers. Just one. Or we *had* one."

That narrowed it down.

"Benjamin?" Petrosky asked.

She nodded warily. "Benjamin Wheatley."

"Tell me about Benjamin," Petrosky said, probably trying not to sound demanding but failing. He needed to take it down a notch, or he'd lose Amanda's tentative cooperation.

"He been here long?" Petrosky continued.

"Longer than some."

Vaguely confrontational. *Hmm.*

"When was the last time you saw him?"

"Um, Thursday morning? He didn't come back to close his day out online. Didn't even send his resignation. I've called four times but no answer."

He had disappeared two days after the trial. Morrison

shifted in his seat and flipped another page in his notebook. "Does that happen often?" Morrison asked without looking up. "People just taking off like that?"

Amanda looked at him and nodded, her face softening ever so slightly. "We lose social workers all the time. We have one of the highest rates of burnout as a profession—low pay, lots of work, tons of emotional strain. Sometimes they just... ghost." She shrugged. "But the fact that he hasn't stopped by is weird. I still have his last paycheck because we can't release it until he gives back his badge."

"So Mr. Wheatley still has access to the building?"

"He'll lose his privileges on Monday when he's officially fired. Would have done it before, but he's damn good, and we don't have a replacement yet." She shook her head. "Every time someone takes off, I'm surprised. You'd think I'd be used to it by now."

"What about records?"

"Frieda is taking some, and I—"

"Not records for social work cases. Records for his security badge." Petrosky put his hands on his knees. "Can you tell when it was last used? If he's been back here in the past few days since he...ghosted?"

"Yes, we can tell when people use their badges." She lowered her voice as if worried an employee would hear, despite the fact they'd seen no one except Burke. Wouldn't Burke already know about the badges given how close she and Amanda were? Looked like Amanda didn't have a problem hiding things from her best buddy. *Serves Frieda right.*

"But we don't advertise that we track entrances and exits," Amanda said. "It helps us verify whether workers are keeping appointments. If someone says they met with a client and they were logged in as being here, we know something's up."

"Does that happen often?"

"Not here. But there have been cases of overworked individuals just charting the notes without doing the required visits. Sometimes the kids fall through the cracks and end up injured or…worse."

"And no one here knows about this tracking system?"

"No."

Not even your good buddy next door? Maybe the issues here were worse than Amanda was letting on if she was worried about Burke lying to her. And Shannon knew all too well how manipulative Burke could be.

Amanda pulled her laptop in front of her and tapped on the keyboard, squinting at the screen. "Okay, here it is. Benjamin was—" Her eyes widened.

"Mrs. Kimball?"

"He was here at two-fifteen this morning."

Petrosky glanced at Morrison, whose pen was scratching furiously on the notepad. "Mrs. Kimball, are there cameras on the door?"

She shook her head. "Just on the parking lot."

"We'll need access to that."

Amanda turned back to the screen, the clack of her fingers on the keys hard and frantic. "The camera system is all online, videos, reports, everything. They oversee it from the security office upstate, but we only use them for maintenance."

"You're expected to monitor this too?"

"Not unless there's a concern, which has only happened once with someone getting a purse snatched. And then we just called you guys." She hit another key and turned the laptop toward them. A grainy image of the empty parking lot filled the screen.

"One o'clock," she said. She hit a key, and the video fast-forwarded. A bird flitted in and out of frame. A piece of paper appeared and vanished. "Two o'clock."

"Did Benjamin have a car?" Morrison asked.

"Yes, he did. It's one of the requirements for the job because we do house calls."

But the car wasn't on the recording. The lot stayed empty.

"Three o'clock." Amanda hit a key, and the video paused, a sparrow or some other bird in mid-flight over the lot.

"So he walked it," Petrosky muttered. He leaned back in his chair. "I'll need access to his desk, any personal effects as well. And a photo, so I can match him with the person seen entering Lewis's apartment the day he died."

Finally, a lead. They had a direction, a plan...on a case none of them were supposed to be touching. Roger was going to be pissed.

Amanda chewed her lip. "His license is in his personnel file, though his desk looked rather...sparse when I went in earlier to check for charts." Her eyebrows rose, face suddenly hopeful. "Maybe that's what he came back for? The stuff in his office?"

Right, because normal people suddenly feel the need to grab all their stuff at two in the morning.

"Are your workers aware of the cameras?" Petrosky said.

"Like with the cards, we don't advertise that we're watching the lot, but the cameras are pretty obvious out there."

So Benjamin Wheatley probably knew someone would see his car, but didn't know Amanda was monitoring his badge. Which meant he didn't want anyone to see him. They'd check his office, but if Wheatley had been there this morning, he'd surely have taken anything incriminating with him.

"I'll pull his privileges immediately." Amanda turned the computer screen back to herself, shaking her head. "I can't believe this."

Shannon glanced at the wall in the direction of Burke's office. Burke might have misremembered where she'd heard about the other worker at Derek Lewis's house, but she hadn't been secretive in inquiring about it. She hadn't been worried about someone finding out. But Wheatley...

Wheatley definitely had a secret to hide.

15

Shannon was inappropriately jealous of Petrosky and Morrison's freedom when they dropped her at the office and set out to locate Benjamin Wheatley. Her day was a predictable whirlwind of paperwork and Roger dropping in to harass her about her other cases while she tried not to punch him for talking shit to Amanda Kimball. That was all he wanted—a rise. A fight. She wasn't giving it to him. When dusk, at last, crept in, she locked up her office and met Morrison downstairs so he could give her a ride over to Kimball's warehouse.

Her chest tightened as they passed the spot where she'd found her vandalized car. Shards of windshield glass still glittered on the asphalt, some edged with white from the shatterproof coating, making the whole mess resemble broken teeth. Shannon shot Morrison a thank-you glance when he parked at the other end of the lot.

Inside, the warehouse was bright, cool, and already smelled of sweat...and bleach. Kimball waved as they entered. "Stone Cold and Silent. Welcome back." He marched from under the weight machine, nodded to Morrison, and touched Shannon's elbow. She tried not to flinch.

"I'm really sorry about your car. I ordered some extra

floodlights and a set of security cameras for the perimeter. They'll be here next week."

She pulled her arm away. "You didn't have to do that, Kimball."

"I should have from the get-go. I just didn't think..." He looked at the back wall as if expecting someone to sneak in through the door to the alley. Had Kimball talked to his wife? Did Kimball know Amanda had possibly spent the last year in charge of a very crazy person? Maybe not since Shannon hadn't heard a word about it from Roger. And Shannon sure as hell wasn't going to be the one to bring up Wheatley and the fact that she'd spent half the day skipping work and prying into a case her boss had specifically told her to avoid.

Kimball pulled his gaze from the wall. "How's Abby doing?"

Shannon faltered, and the lingering knots in her shoulders tightened like her spine was in a vise. "She's...okay. As well as can be expected, I guess." No wonder he was being weird and awkward. There was no good way to ask about a disemboweled cat.

"They don't think that cat thing was connected to your car break-in, do they?"

Of course they're connected. Someone had threatened her with a decapitated head two days after the trial, right after someone had smashed their way into her car. During that same time frame, Wheatley just happened to be doing weirdo stuff in the same office that dispatched workers to Derek Lewis's house. Now Wheatley was gone. Scared or guilty?

Morrison stiffened beside her.

"The cat...is a hell of a coincidence," Shannon said.

Kimball nodded. "Now, I'm really glad I got those new lights." He scanned the room again, and looked back at Shannon, his eyes too narrowed, mouth too drawn like his words and his thoughts were fighting for control of his face. "Well, go get ready. I've got a doozy of a workout for us tonight, then I've gotta run to get Dana from dance class."

Something about the way he said it struck Shannon as

strange, but she had no time to consider it because Valentine had shown up and was clapping Kimball on the back. "Sure, sure. You know you're teaching that dance class, you fancy ass—"

Shannon left them and headed for the bathroom. As soon as she slipped into her shorts and tank top, she felt like she could breathe for the first time all day. Maybe her bun was just too tight all the time. *I need to try a braid.* But the gnawing in her stomach remained as she gathered her things and shoved them into her bag.

Outside the room, Morrison was leaning against the wall. He swept past her into the restroom in a haze of lavender and a smell distinctly musky, masculine. She stared at the door for a beat after he passed through it, then grabbed her weights from the back, and took her place behind one of the eight crates Kimball had set up. Five were already full.

"Today, we've got dumbbell swings, elevators, Turkish get-ups, then power deck squats with weights, and inchworms to grasshoppers." Kimball's voice rose with each exercise he named, and Shannon's pulse quickened with anticipation, or maybe with defensiveness at the posture Kimball had taken like he'd beat the crap out of anyone who tried to tell him they weren't doing his bullshit workout. Maybe he did know about her visit with Amanda and was pissed that neither she nor Morrison had volunteered the information.

Bring it, Kimball. Shannon shook out her legs and arms as Morrison returned from the bathroom and took his place at the crate next to her. The woman beside Shannon groaned quietly.

"Let's do this." Kimball pressed a button on the stereo behind him, and the room filled with Kid Rock yelling over a deep bass beat that vibrated Shannon's marrow. "Twenty. Make it happen."

Shannon bent her knees and hinged forward at the hips, swinging the weight between her legs and back up over her head as if the act would extinguish the disquiet spreading through her like poison from a needle, from her neck, down into the veins in her chest, then to her stomach. Innocent people locked up. Guilty people going free sooner than they should. On the second set, she pushed the weight faster, harder, and her thoughts solidified. She envisioned punishing people from her caseload—smashing baby-killing Ike Lambert's teeth, crushing the reverend's nose—as she brought the weight down again and again and again. Then she envisioned Wheatley standing over Derek Lewis's body and Ashley Johnson staring at her with red-rimmed eyes: *Why did you do this to me, Shannon?* Shannon punched the weights higher, harder, every muscle screaming, and the image splintered and fell apart like a broken mirror.

"Keep it up!"

She panted, punched, lunged. Sweat stung her eyes, and she blinked to clear it. Her mouth tasted like salt. But so help her, she'd sweat this shit out.

"Elevators!"

"Get-ups!"

"Power decks!"

Roll, squat, leap, sit, roll, squat, leap, sit, and it all became one fluid motion; just breath and an aching cramp in her chest.

"Modified inchworms! I want five mock lunges on each side before inching down to plank."

She stood, gasping at too-thin air, then hinged forward before dropping to plank. *You can't fall, Shanny. Everybody needs you.* And, suddenly, there was Lucky, his sweet, tiny face rubbing against Abby's chin, a motorboat engine rumbling contentment under the kitchen table. A lump swelled in her throat, and she wheezed over it, bringing one leg under her body from a down dog-ish position, then back, then the other leg, pretending she was kneeing the asshole in the balls, the person who had killed Derek Lewis, framed Ashley Johnson. The dickwad who had suddenly decided he wanted some credit and sucked Shannon into this nonsense. The person who had made her niece cry by killing Lucky, who had made Abby's life worse than it already was because

Derry was leaving them, he was going to die, and no one could stop it. She jumped to a squat, stood, and started over, every movement of her leg more violent until she was kicking at the air beneath her. Her heart throbbed, but she wasn't sure it was from the workout. She wanted it to be, wanted it to be from the pushing, from the testing of her endurance and not fear and pain. Her hands slipped on the mat beneath her, and she righted herself and tried again, harder this time, her own labored panting mingling with hard rock and bass for a soundtrack born of human suffering.

"Let it go and stretch it out," Kimball called. She stood, shirt stuck to her skin, tears and sweat covering her face, her legs wet and sticky. Beside her, the woman in blue was spread-eagled on the floor like she was about to make a snow angel. Around them, the panting echoed over Kimball's muscle-stretching music—something classical—and she tried to focus on the stringed instruments. But every muscle felt like it was tightened to the point of splitting, as though one more reach would tear her muscles and cause her to crumple like a marionette whose ropes had been severed.

Morrison touched Shannon's arm. His fingers left searing hot imprints on her skin. "Shannon?"

She jerked her arm from his grasp. People were dispersing, toweling off, collecting their things. She could hear the warehouse door opening, the grinding of metal, the crisp splatter of the rain outside growing louder and louder. Morrison sat on his crate off to the side. Still. Quiet.

"You staying?" Kimball called from his spot near the door. He already had his gym bag slung over his shoulder, so she must have been stretching for at least ten minutes. But time seemed to have stopped. If only it would—she'd have Derry with her forever.

"Gotta get Dana from dance," Kimball said, a trace of impatience in his voice.

She barely heard him. She wanted to punch him. For having a normal life. For not having to think about any of this stupid bullshit. For only having to worry about some stupid dance class when she had to worry about very real monsters killing family pets and diseases that could wipe those closest to her from the face of the fucking earth.

"I want to hit the rings for a few," Morrison said to Kimball. "Go on. I'll clean up."

"Sounds good. I'll lock the door on my way out." Kimball's shoes thwacked over the floors toward the exit. "See ya, Shannon," Kimball called, and she wondered at the use of her name, at the lilt in his voice that you used with little kids. Maybe he thought she was fragile. She'd show him fragile. She'd show everyone.

Everyone's counting on you, Shanny...

There was an agitated squeal, an angry clang of metal on ground from the warehouse door, and then silence, stretching around her until she could almost feel a vindictive puppeteer rising above her, scissors poised to cut. The muscles in her back screamed as she pushed herself to standing.

"Want to talk about it?" Morrison's gaze bored into her side, as palpable as if he were physically touching her. "Shanny—"

She whirled to face him. "What?"

He said nothing, but she could read the question in his gaze.

"Fine! No, I don't want to fucking talk about it! Anytime I talk about it, it's like everything just…falls…apart." She put her hands on her knees, her mouth dry, full of ashes. Ash Park: sucking the life out of everything, slowly, methodically, inevitably. But some of them would die sooner than others. Gone forever, and soon. Too soon.

She was weeping when he pulled her to him, her every muscle heaving with the force of her tears. His arms, slick with sweat, slid over her back, marrying with the dew on her skin. She clutched his shoulders. Her legs threatened to buckle.

"Relax. I've got you."

Relax? She shoved him away. "You can't fix this, Morrison. You can't just make everything better by pretending things will be okay. Forget your Zen bullshit for once. No matter how much you meditate, you can't bring people back from the dead." She was yelling at him, her voice echoing over the equipment with a metallic twang.

"I know how much it hurts to lose someone you love. I know there's no fixing it."

She wiped her nose on her hand. "My brother's dying." There. They were out. The words that she had shoved down, choked back, bitten from her own tongue, now hung in the air, sharp and vicious and utterly devastating.

He met her eyes and nodded. "I know, Shanny. And I love him too. I've only known him three years, but he's a great guy."

"You think everyone's a great guy." A shuddering sob wracked her body as the world spun, and then she was in his arms again, her face pressed into his shirt, her fists clenched. He was always so goddamn calm.

When she was steady, she pulled away. "Were you really going to do rings?"

He shrugged. "I will if you want to. Or we can hit the bags. You looked like you wanted to punch something earlier." The bags behind him swung slightly as if taunting her. "Or, you can hit me."

Her hands remained balled in tight fists. She couldn't seem to release them. "Will you hit me back?"

He glanced at his shoes, and his fingers twitched. "No."

"Then what's the point?"

In response, Morrison walked toward the back of the room and tossed her a pair of gloves from the floor. The first one slid on, but she grappled with the second, its enormous padding thwarting her efforts like a dog trying to put on goddamn pants. She blew damp hair off her forehead, grinding her teeth until her jaw ached.

"Here." Morrison took the glove and held it. She wanted

to shove him away, but instead, she slid her hand into the mitt and let him Velcro it closed. He was watching her.

She ignored him, and the moment he walked behind the punching bag, she attacked it. The bag was Lambert. It was Roger. It was Wheatley. It was some masked intruder killing Lucky. It was cancer. It was all of them.

Morrison wasn't sweating, wasn't straining, was just standing, holding the bag steady. "Arms higher."

She lifted her elbows, attacking the bag with her fists, her knees.

"Careful with your wrists. Sometimes restraint is just as important as accuracy."

Restraint. She had heard Kimball say that too, but she suspected he didn't believe it either, with his widening shoulders, his ever more irritable attitude. *Forget restraint.* She envisioned Lambert's nose beneath her glove, splintering, blood flying. Roger's perfect teeth reduced to a row of shattered piano keys beneath her fist. The cowardly shadow who was making Derry's death into a race to find the person who had gone after Abby's kitten—someone she had to find soon so that Derry could die peacefully knowing his little girl was safe. This killer... he was making it into a game. Toying with her. With her brother.

The fury was building, creeping through her veins like a virus. Cancer had a name but nothing tangible for her to annihilate, but their killer, goddamn him, she'd find him and fuck his shit up. Someone had to pay for the shithole that had become her life.

The leather thunked under the force of her gloves, her face heated, her shirt soaked through with sweat, and through it all Morrison stood still, his face quiet and peaceful and accepting. She hated him for being able to turn his emotions off. For being able to hold it together when her life was falling apart. He wasn't supposed to be okay when she wasn't. He was her best friend, goddamn him. *Break down with me. Let me break.* Her breath echoed in her ears, fast as the throbbing in her hollow chest.

She staggered back, her arms already sore. He stepped from behind the bag, and his face was still calm, serene, a paragon of relaxation when every shred of her control had disintegrated. She raised her quaking arms and shoved him hard with her gloved hands.

He stumbled but didn't fall, and when he locked eyes with her, she shoved him again, hands against his chest. This time he didn't even stagger. Just stood like he was made of granite.

"Hit me back."

He shook his head slowly.

She pushed him again, then again, and he stepped back with his right foot to avoid falling backward.

"Hit me!"

He didn't move. She socked him in the stomach, and he gritted his teeth as air escaped him with an *oomph*. He winced. Finally, a reaction.

"I'll miss him too, Shanny. I know it hurts, but—"

"You don't know *anything*. You always think you do, but you don't know shit. Not about this." She struck out again, but this time he dodged the punch and pivoted around her.

"I lost my mom," he said. "My dad. More close friends than I want to think about. I know, Shannon. I know."

"Do you? Have you ever had to watch it for months and months, knowing it's coming, seeing someone you love suffer? *Smelling* them dying every time you enter the room? Knowing it will be on you to pull things back together when it's impossible because there is no way to fix that kind of broken?" She didn't wait for an answer, just went at him again, socking him in the arm, pivoting and striking at his lower back. He danced around her on tiptoes as she punched again and again, the wet thwack of gloves on skin the only sound over her heavy breathing. Sweat dripped down her back, into her eyes, down her legs. "You don't know, Morrison. It's just not the same for you."

"It isn't."

"You don't love him like I do."

But he did care. Deeply. And his eyes held such sorrow

that she regretted the words the moment they tumbled from her lips. What was she doing? She lowered her arms and put her forehead against his chest, gloved hands slack at her sides. "I'm sorry," she whispered as tears trickled through the sweat on her cheeks.

He wrapped his arms around her and rested his chin on the top of her head. "Me too."

16

THE SILENCE on the ride back to the house was so heavy and thick that Shannon half believed she could take it in her hand and watch it ooze through her fingers. Morrison kept his eyes on the road. She was grateful for that. She didn't want to see the look on his face, didn't want to have to say she was sorry again. She was in too much pain to feel sorry for anyone but herself.

And he knew that. He'd known it in the gym too, known she'd wanted—no, needed—to hit him. Her head was sticky on the seat back as she listened to his steady breath and the whir of tires, wondering if she'd ever be able to see into his head the way he did into hers.

Morrison parked in the driveway and waited by the side of the car until she got out and followed him up the steps. Somewhere a crow cawed, and Shannon jumped, but she saw nothing but the infinite blackness of night. No killer. *I'll find you, motherfucker. For Derry.*

She pointed Morrison to the downstairs bath and dragged her smarting legs upstairs to shower. Her pulse was steady now, and the anger, so furious and blistering an hour before, had drained from her during the car ride. By the time she stepped under the water, she felt as though her insides had been sucked out with a straw.

When the last of the soap had disappeared down the drain, she threw on a T-shirt with a picture of The Doors, the one that always made Morrison grin and say, "I was the brother Jim Morrison never knew he wanted." But this time when Morrison saw her in the shirt, he just nodded, a few droplets of water still clinging to his clean forehead.

"Turmeric milk," he said, offering her a steaming mug. It'll calm you down."

Turmeric? She took the cup, sipped, and grimaced. "Strong."

"That'll be the vodka." He picked up his own cup off the counter. His mouth was drawn, and he was looking at her now with one eyebrow just a little higher than the other as if trying to figure out the right thing to say. Or to do.

She didn't need help. And she sure didn't need his pity. But when she searched his eyes, she saw no pity, only frustration—probably at the case—mingling with the gut-crushing sadness they shared, though he was infinitely better at handling it. She wanted to be him, calm like him, just for a minute. Just for one minute, she wanted that kind of peace.

"Just know I'm here, okay, Shanny?"

She set the mug on the counter and wrapped her arms around his waist. He stilled, inhaled sharply, then he set his cup down and held her. He'd always been there for her. More than anyone else, even during the hellish two years she was married to Roger. Hell, even before she'd gotten married. And then during the divorce. Now she'd been divorced for four months, and through it all, Morrison had been the one she could talk to. Morrison had been the one she and Derry had gone out with on the weekends when her husband refused. And when Derry's illness had begun to overtake him... God, had they really only been friends for three years? It seemed like forever. "You're always here," she said.

"Yep. And I always will be."

"Always is a long time."

"Time we have." There was something in the way he said it that sent tingles of electricity down her back as if the words themselves had climbed from his lips over her head and run down her spine on feathered feet.

Don't do it, Shannon. But she couldn't help it. When she raised her lips to his, her insides melted, every inch of her liquid and hot and waiting to be flooded with him—his touch, his scent, his calm. But he made no move to pull her closer, just stood, arms frozen—rigid. The warmth in her belly cooled to ice. She pulled back and looked at him—his eyes were wide, lips open in shock.

Oh my god. She had been reading him wrong. He felt only friendship, nothing more. Shit, maybe Roger was right. Was he gay? No, but she'd have known that, for sure. Had he ever talked about anyone? Dated anyone? *I can't believe I just did that. I ruined everything. No, no, no.* She dropped her arms. "Morrison, I'm—"

But then his lips were on hers, warm and pliable and so soft compared to the hardness of his chest as he pulled her against him, his arms encircling her waist. When he released her mouth, she sought his lips again, but he raised his face out of her reach and lowered his chin to the top of her head. "I don't want to be a distraction," he muttered into her hair.

She nuzzled her face into the crook of his neck, the soft throb of his heart palpable against her lips. His posture was stiff, too stiff. "You could never be only that."

But she had been only that, hadn't she? Friends. Buddies. And she couldn't lose that. *I can't do this.* But she had no time to think; she barely registered that he had moved until his lips were on hers again, the taste of his mouth sweet on her tongue. Her breasts flattened against his chest as his hardness pressed into her groin, and she opened her mouth wider, the gentle caress of his tongue on hers, sending a rush of heat pulsing through her abdomen.

He pulled back, rolled her T-shirt from the bottom, and up over her head, and then they were tugging, groping, stumbling up the steps toward her bedroom. When she tripped midway up, he rolled her over to face him and ran his hands over the roadmap of post-pregnancy stretch marks on her belly, kissing the skin between her breasts until she moaned and arched toward him.

What am I thinking? He's my best friend. But when he slid her shorts and panties down over her ankles, his fingers leaving a trail of brilliant electricity in their wake, she no longer cared about what she wasn't supposed to do. Everything in her life was about what she was supposed to do; what she was supposed to be. *Everything but this.*

He lowered his mouth to tongue the apex of her thighs, searching her, exploring her as she leaned back against the steps, gripping the railing for support. Every nerve vibrated with his energy. She clawed at his shoulders with her free hand, gnarled her fingers in his hair and pulled, daring him to take her—begging him.

But he just smiled, just fucking *smiled*, and slid a finger inside her, barely out of breath while she fought the aching heat that throbbed painfully between her legs and in every stinging muscle in her thighs. *Oh god. This.* How had they gone for so long without this?

She pulled herself up one stair and then another, and he came after her, followed her with his hands, caressing her, pursuing her. Four more stairs up, and his tongue was in her mouth again, his fingers at her rib cage, on her abdomen. She sought him with her hips. When he moved his hand to her nipple, she hooked her fingers under his waistband, pushed down his shorts and stroked him—he was solid and perfect and ready. He scooted around her and stood, trying to escape up the last stair to the landing. But she rose to her knees and took him in her mouth—salty and sweet—and as he sighed her name, she ignored the ache in her body, ignored everything but pulling him to the brink and letting him go, over and over again, until he was panting above her. He reached for her, and she let him draw her up into his arms.

"Shanny—"

"Don't let me go." She wrapped her legs around his waist, locking herself against his hardness, their bodies wet and slippery and warm. She ground against him as he carried her to the bedroom. He laid her on the comforter, and she tried to pull him to her, but he climbed off the bed, leaving her lonely and aching.

"Morrison," She arched her pelvis toward him, but he shook his head and knelt on the floor at the foot of the bed.

"Close your eyes."

She hesitated at first, then did as he'd asked—letting him take over. She embraced the blackness, succumbed to feeling as he took her foot in his hand and rubbed the arch, massaged her calf, her thigh, following his deft fingers with his lips and tongue from ankle to knee as she sighed the tension from her bones. When he reached the apex of her thighs, he put her knees over his shoulders and put his face to her sex, his breath hot, his tongue meandering over her slowly, deliberately, always just shy of where she needed him.

Then he stopped. He lowered her knees to the bed. The pulsing ache at her center took over, seeking release as he climbed toward her, running his fingers lightly over her belly. She widened her legs, but he lay beside her, not on top of her, not where she needed him.

"Goddammit, Morrison, just... god." She was going to lose her mind.

His mouth was at her ear. "Breathe with me."

She squeezed her eyelids together. Her body throbbed painfully. She felt him moving down the mattress again, lower and lower until he was back on the floor. He picked up her foot from the bed, massaging the pad, rotating her ankle, his breath hot on her shin. She followed each of his exhales, matching his breath to her own. He worked her shin, lips at her knee. Then her thigh. He matched his massage to their breathing, every movement a dance they were doing together, the pressure building inside her as he approached the top of her thigh, and finally, he exhaled softly, sweetly, against her most tender part. He held her hips and inhaled deeply, exhaling as she moaned, almost there, one touch, and she was—

His breath on her sent her spiraling over the edge, and

then he was tonguing her open, kissing her there the way he'd kissed her mouth, stroking her internally with his finger as she bucked her hips against his hand. Pressure and release, it became a cycle, his breath, her breath, his tongue, her moans.

"Curt." She opened her eyes and met his gaze, his eyes glittering, blue and deep, and she was lost there, lost with him. They'd never be the same. She didn't want them to ever be the same. All this time, every platonic outing, every dinner, every heart-to-heart conversation. It could have been this. "Curt, please."

She was still shivering with desire when he rose over her and pressed himself against her opening, softly, then harder, sinking into her to the hilt. He stilled then, their eyes still locked, his gaze calm, but there was an intensity there, a need, something feral. He touched her cheek. She matched his breath again as he began to move, slowly, his rhythm matching the pulse in her abdomen as they ebbed and flowed together like the ocean tide, his eyes the sea, their breath the waves, washing over them slowly, then harder and faster as she quivered in his arms, still lost in his eyes. This was what she'd been missing. This.

He pulled himself from her depths, lifted her to the pillow, and crawled up behind her, laying his lips against the back of her head. Her insides were still quaking as he stroked her hair and moved lower with his hand, kneading each tender knot around her spine. Lower. His fingers trailed over her hip and then between her legs for one fleeting moment as he wrapped his arms around her and pressed his chest against her back, the heat of him stoking the warmth in her belly. Then his hand was on her hip, lifting her thigh ever so slightly as he eased himself inside her again, slowly, agonizingly slowly, every aftershock in her pelvis tightening around him. She watched his hands—*Morrison's hands*—as he touched her nipple and stroked between her legs. The low burn in her belly spread until all of her was aflame. Her breathing quickened. Then—

Electricity slammed through her body, every inch of her pulsing and shuddering. She clawed at his arms, and he held her tighter against him, fingers dancing on her clit until she couldn't breathe, couldn't move, couldn't think.

"Curt," she whispered. No more air. He bit her shoulder, forcefully enough to draw blood, and the tenuous hold she had on reality snapped. She screamed his name as the whole world throbbed and broke apart, and he went over with her, grasping her hips so hard it hurt, growling unintelligible words into her hair.

17

THEY SLEPT CURLED AROUND one another, skin to skin, limbs and arms and hair haphazard like a puzzle she didn't want to solve. Every so often, he would rise from the bed and creep downstairs to check, listen, watch, and then he would climb back in beside her and cling to her as if he were frightened she'd float away if he let go.

Dawn broke dismally gray, but there was a peaceful quiet about it, like the mist that remains after a storm. Shannon watched it, breathing in the haze as if she could keep the morning forever. Once day broke, it was all over, but now—now she relished Morrison's arms around her, his fingertips lightly stroking her back, one of his legs over her hip, keeping her close to him. Connected. She blinked hard, taking a mental picture of the moment, of the sound of his gentle breath, of the way her body felt: exhilarated, alive, and deliciously used.

But. There was always a but. The deliciousness faded as the sun rose higher, and anxiety took its place, a nagging in her belly that grew more insistent with every inhale she took. He hadn't wanted to be a distraction. And he hadn't been—he'd been so much more. He had awakened quiet pieces inside her that had lain dormant, tarnished from disuse, and he'd made them shiny again. For a few blissful moments, she'd been complete.

But in the light of day...she couldn't allow herself to be this vulnerable. She had too much to lose. She had *him* to lose. His friendship. Panic was wrapping itself tighter and tighter around her throat with every beat of her heart, every exhaled whisper of his breath. Partly because she wanted this. Partly because she couldn't have it. Partly because of how much this would hurt him—unless she was thinking too highly of herself, though that might have been rationalization too. Dr. McCallum had taught her all about that word. If only he could have taught her how to avoid screwing up her life.

"About last night," she said into his chest.

He kissed the top of her head and ran a hand over her hip. "It was perfect."

It had been perfect. But a mistake. She wasn't ready. She had Derry to think of and Abby. This case. And she couldn't take any more complications, the potential for hurt, for more pain, when she was already stretched to her limit. Just because he was perfect now didn't mean it would last. A few days? A few months? Roger had seemed perfect too when they'd first started dating. But she and Morrison had been perfect before—they'd had the perfect friendship. Jesus, how badly had she messed things up?

"It was...amazing. You were amazing. But it...it probably shouldn't happen again. I've got a lot going on, and I just... I don't know what to do here."

His hand stilled on her thigh. "You're scared."

She wanted to deny it, but how could she ignore the way her stomach tightened imagining opening herself up to him, actually being with him, loving him with all of her for longer than a night? She let out a breath. *Yes. I'm terrified.* "No, I'm just...confused."

"Okay."

Her stomach clamped down at the whispered hurt in his voice. "We can still be friends."

He ran a finger down her backbone. "Of course, Shannon. We'll always be friends. And I'll always be here for you. I'll always take care of you."

He took care of everyone. "You'll be there because I'm human, right?"

"If you say so."

"Is that a dig at my humanity?"

He let go of her and rolled toward the window, away from her. "It was a dig at your reasoning."

She stared past him out the window, willing the burning in her belly to subside. When it didn't, she slid from the bed and headed for the door, scanning the room for a towel, a robe. Friends wore robes in front of each other, right?

His phone buzzed on the bedside table as she put her hand on the knob. He sat and stared at her, mouth opening once, then closing.

Please don't make this harder, Curt...Morrison. Morrison.

The phone buzzed again, and he picked it up and turned it over. "Petrosky," he said to the screen and put the cell to his ear. "Hey, boss." He raised his gaze to the ceiling—listening, thinking. Or maybe avoiding looking at her.

She stared at his back, at the angry, red fingernail gouges from shoulder blade to hip. She'd already injured him. Shannon averted her eyes, hoping the wounds would heal.

"Be right there." His voice was tight. Morrison swung his feet off the bed and laid the phone on the table, still facing the window.

Shannon stepped toward him, no longer concerned about her nakedness. "What happened?"

He kept his eyes on the window and the morning fog. "They found Wheatley's car."

THROUGH THE WINDSHIELD, the bleary sky loomed ominous and heavy, though the temperature teased them with the promise of spring. The ride was silent, tense, but every muscle in her body was still warm and pliable from last night's gentle caresses. Everything today was a contradiction.

Petrosky was waiting for Morrison and Shannon outside the precinct, a halo of smoke following him as he climbed into the backseat. At least he hadn't changed overnight. Morrison handed him a granola bar from the console, and Petrosky glanced at it for a second, then shoved it into his pocket with a grunt. Morrison closed the console without offering Shannon one. She turned to face the window, the sting of tears hot behind her eyes. *This is why I don't need a relationship—bullshit like this.* She didn't need anyone. She just needed to concentrate on the case.

Ash Park passed by the window in an insectile buzz of tires—here a burned-out building with a graffitied smiley face, there a vacant lot where empty plastic bags skittered with the breeze over chunks of broken asphalt. By the time they reached the city limits, the deep ruts in the road were encouraging Shannon's coffee to make a comeback.

The case. *Think.* They'd found no prints or other identifying forensic evidence on Lucky's body or the envelope, save for soil ground into Lucky's fur, common fertilized dirt that might have been there before he was killed. Someone had been careful. Okay, so...Wheatley's car. Had he abandoned it once he found out that they were looking for him? Petrosky had already said they'd had no luck tracking him down yesterday, but maybe someone had tipped him off. Maybe Wheatley was still in contact with his coworkers at the social work office. Amanda had seemed genuinely worried about Wheatley's late-night entry, and Burke...well, she seemed a little off, but then again, she would; she and Shannon had a history.

Still, try as she might, Shannon could think of no possible reason for Wheatley or anyone in the social work department to hurt Derek Lewis. He was a royal dick who beat women and children, but social workers saw that every day. If they felt compelled to kill people over shitty parenting or domestic violence, there'd be a hell of a lot more bodies.

But one of the social workers *had* been there, according to Johnson's friend Angela Perez, the witness they were still trying to locate. If the tip was legit, it had to have been Wheatley. And Wheatley must have seen something; why else would he avoid coming forward and then suddenly disappear once their killer decided he wanted more attention than he'd gotten? Was Wheatley trying to figure out if what he'd seen was important? Or was someone scaring him into silence? He couldn't be the killer, could he? These clues were not adding up.

She rolled her window down, but the stagnant air of the river did little to quell the angry burbling in her stomach. Morrison's silence wasn't helping, either. He wouldn't even look at her. Fine, she'd stop looking at him too.

Shannon breathed through her mouth as Morrison took a left behind what looked like an abandoned factory, all steel and bars and broken glass. And there was the car—a green import of some kind, the rear wheel wells grown over with rust, a spiderweb crack spanning the front windshield. They pulled up beside it and got out.

The air was heady with the stink of moldering vegetation or brackish water, and maybe dead fish. She could almost taste the decay. Petrosky walked to the side door and peered through the glass into the backseat.

"Who called it in?" Shannon walked around to the other side and looked through the driver's window at a seat littered with fast-food bags and an empty two-liter of Red Pop.

"Uniform," Petrosky said. "Came down here because someone was screaming."

"Screaming?"

"Some schizo." Petrosky frowned at a smudge on the window, though Shannon couldn't figure out why that of all things would bother him.

"Isn't 'schizo' a little politically incorrect?" she said.

Petrosky squinted at the door handles. "Not if it's true. Cop took the guy to the ER. Got him some meds and a bed for the night."

Shannon straightened and looked at him over the top of the car. "But, they didn't pull the car to the impound?"

"I told them not to."

Shannon cocked an eyebrow.

Petrosky walked to the hood and stooped over the headlights. "He said it smelled." He bent to examine the tires, then walked to the back and put his face close to the exhaust pipe. Then up to the trunk. He sniffed, grimaced, and reared back.

He said it smelled. Horror washed through her, and her already agitated stomach flipped. "Is that smell…not from the river?" She chanced a look at the front of the car, where Morrison was examining the grille.

Morrison met her eye and shook his head grimly. *Not the river.* They all stared at the trunk.

Petrosky pulled gloves and a knife from his back pocket, and with latexed fingers, he jimmied the trunk lock open. Shannon held her breath. Petrosky gagged but leaned his head over the open trunk cavity. From the look on his face, whatever was in there, was disgusting. Morrison edged closer to him, leaned over too, and turned away.

Shannon released her breath and took another, the horrid, rotting stink stronger than it had been moments before. She swallowed hard and approached anyway. "Is it Wheatley?"

"You sure you want to see this, Taylor?"

"I've seen enough crime scene photos. I can handle it." But she didn't want to look.

"I wouldn't have involved you to begin with if I didn't think you could handle it. But that doesn't mean you need to see more than necessary." Petrosky pulled his head out of the trunk and started for the river. "Get a breath first," he called over his shoulder.

Shannon turned her head and inhaled sharply but couldn't shake the stench of rotten meat and sulfur. She squared her shoulders and stepped toward the car, arms crossed as if that might protect her from whatever was in there. Or whoever was in there. She peered inside.

Not Wheatley, not even parts of Wheatley, but the sight was almost as grotesque.

At the bottom of the trunk, lay a mass of gnarled towels, black and heavy with what looked like semi-congealed blood and writhing with enough maggots that the entire crumpled bundle was almost a living, breathing organism, the squirming brain of some alien creature. Gravel crunched as Petrosky returned. Shannon stepped away and turned her head from the wet mess to get a breath of air while Petrosky poked at the bloody towels with a stick he must have picked up by the water. Maggots suctioned to the wood. He set the stick aside and reached through the wriggling creatures, smearing dark stains across his gloved knuckles.

Maggots didn't just appear. Blowflies needed to find blood and lay eggs before the maggots could hatch. That meant the car had been abandoned long before they'd visited the social work office, probably just after the trial. Wednesday—maybe as late as Thursday. If the blood in the trunk was someone else's, another victim's, Wheatley might be running; but if it belonged to a new victim, then who? And if it was Wheatley's blood, then someone else—the killer—was tying up loose ends. And she was no closer to finding their murderer.

Shannon stepped farther from the trunk, from the mess, from Petrosky, who was leaning into it, face inches from the wiggling pile. Neither he nor Morrison said a thing, but she knew they could feel it too, the dark omen in the air. A whisper that this was a beginning rather than an ending, that bloody towels would be the least of the horrors they encountered. At the horizon line, the sun sat, pale and white, barely illuminating the fog that rose from the river like disturbed ashes.

18

PETROSKY STAYED to wait for the tow truck and the crime techs. Morrison drove Shannon back to the office, the air thick with things they couldn't say, maybe about the bloody scene they had witnessed that morning, maybe about death, maybe about Derry. Maybe about the two of them. Shannon stared hard out the window.

Morrison parked out front and touched her arm. "You okay?" The first words he had uttered since they left the river.

She nodded. "Yeah, I just… I feel like I'm drowning in death lately." Too much. Too vulnerable. These were feelings she could confess to a friend, but…Morrison wasn't just a friend anymore. She gritted her teeth. They had to go back to being just that—just friends. She'd never survive the next few months without his support.

Morrison averted his eyes. "I know the feeling."

She looked at her hands and back at his profile. His jaw was hard. Angry, maybe. He should be furious with her—she'd just fucked everything up for both of them. But at least they were alive. And she had to make sure they all stayed that way. "Do you think Abby needs someone with her at school?"

"Valentine is already over there."

Valentine. She visualized the tight line of his mouth when

he talked about Derek Lewis, his gentleness with Lillian's belly. Yeah, he'd watch out for Abby. He wouldn't let anyone near her.

They stared up at her office building together, and her eyes dropped to Dr. McCallum's window on the ground floor. Maybe she'd take him up on his therapy offer—again. But watching the curtains in McCallum's office gave her a sinking feeling like her life was going backward. She looked away.

"Can I walk you up?" Morrison said.

"No, I'll be fine."

"I know. Maybe I'll follow you anyway, just to make sure."

They were silent in the hallway, their footsteps covered by the bustle of other lawyers in the offices nearby. Odd—she rarely noticed the sound of printers and agitated attorneys on the phone with their clients, and on Saturday the bustle was usually even more subdued. Perhaps it was her senses that were heightened, as if the bloody rags in Benjamin Wheatley's car had made the rest of the world stand out if only for its normalcy. Or perhaps she'd woken up different, her nerves still on fire from the night before. She wondered if the sensations would dull in a day or two, hiding themselves forevermore in some deep, internal cave. Numb but safe. And without someone there to wake them up again...

Not now, Shannon. Her heart ached as she nodded goodbye to Morrison and escaped into her office. Three new folders had arrived on her desk while she'd been down at the river. Shannon stowed her briefcase next to her chair and opened the top one. Maggie Batsom, age four, beaten within an inch of her life, multiple lacerations and seventeen fractures including neck, arms, legs—some injuries old, some new. Two other children in the house, CPS involved. Stephanie Batsom, the mother, was arrested when she took the girl to the hospital, claiming she'd fallen down the stairs, which didn't explain the fingerprints around Maggie's throat. Mom claimed it was a boyfriend who was out of state at the time of the hospitalization. *Bullshit.*

Shannon flipped through the police report to the photos. A girl with a round baby face lay on a bed, eyes closed, a white bandage seeping blood wrapping her forehead. Every limb was encased in a different plaster cast.

Her stomach turned. *Attempted murder.* She frowned toward Roger's office, made a note on the top page, and slapped the file shut. The next file contained more of the same: neglect, bodily injury, bloody bandages, unconfirmed presence of someone else in the home.

She spent three more hours researching and making phone calls and trying to ignore the heaviness in her belly, the tightness in her chest that might have been fear or, somehow, more horrible, loneliness. Shit was going down, and she'd lost the one person she could have talked to. Maybe she did need more girlfriends. Or maybe she needed to not fuck her friends like a goddamn idiot. Mistakes, everyone made them, but she was most upset that she couldn't decide whether sleeping with Morrison actually *had* been a mistake. And she didn't have time to really consider it—or a head clear enough to do the thinking part justice.

Shannon flipped another folder closed and hauled out the files in her briefcase, reviewing her to-do list and scribbling notes. So many people to talk to and not enough time. One lead seemed promising on Reverend Wilson: according to the detective on the case, Wilson had told another bar patron that he was going to "take care of the girl." Leave it to alcohol to loosen one's tongue. It was always the alcohol or a partner that did you in.

She was making final notes in his file when someone tapped on her open door.

Petrosky. "Still looking for Angela Perez," he said, "the girl who told Johnson about the other social worker. But today wasn't a total waste: blood type in Wheatley's trunk matches Wheatley, though they can't tell definitively if the amount that was there would have been enough to kill him. Probably, though." Petrosky leaned his bulk against the doorframe, Morrison's granola bar in his hand. He tore it open, and a hot pang of jealousy ripped through Shannon's chest, even as she grimaced at the thought of eating while discussing Wheatley's bloody remains.

Oh my god, I can get my own granola. She put her pen aside.

"And Wheatley isn't at home. Not that I expected him to be; he's probably buried in a shallow grave." Petrosky swallowed his food. "I went into his place anyway, poked around a bit."

"Poked around?"

Petrosky grunted and took another bite.

She closed the file and pushed it aside. "You're going to get arrested, Petrosky." Not for this, she knew. He had cause after finding the bloody towels in the car, though she doubted he'd followed protocol even there.

"No one's hauling me in over looking in his closets. Which are full, by the way, undisturbed, and with a complete set of luggage sitting there empty. He didn't leave the social work office high and dry."

"You think he was…taken? Against his will?"

Petrosky shrugged one shoulder. "Just because his card went back to the office doesn't mean he did."

Of course. She'd known it didn't make sense for Wheatley to have gone back, especially not in the middle of the night. Even if he had been planning on running away, he still could've gone in earlier without arousing a bit of suspicion. In for a few, get what he needed, and out again, on the road. How had she missed something so simple? "Okay, so someone used his card to gain access in the middle of the night. What do you think they were looking for?"

"Don't know. Something Wheatley had, or something they thought he had. Maybe notes, like in your car, trying to figure out exactly what he knew. Same reason they hit you." He stepped inside her office, put a hand on her desk. and lowered his voice. "Also found a buddy of Wheatley's.

Theodore Ruskin over in Grosse Pointe. Only caller on Wheatley's cell records outside of business calls. Lonely guy." Petrosky took the last bite of the granola bar, and crumbs fell from the wrapper to her desktop.

She glared at them. "Does Cur—Morrison know you're actually eating that?" She nodded at the empty granola package.

He crumpled the wrapper in his palm and shrugged.

Her heart rate picked up. She avoided Petrosky's eyes and tried to look nonchalant. "Where is Morrison?"

"California's busy running down Wheatley's credit cards, knocking on the doors of offices around the social work building, and interviewing anyone and everyone around Wheatley's place. That's why I'm here to give you this." Petrosky pulled another granola bar out of his pocket and dropped it onto her desk. Cranberry white chocolate.

"He said you liked caramel," Petrosky said. "Yelled at me for eating that one. He'll be even more pissed that I ate the blueberry one too. But no one likes cranberries."

Shannon cocked an eyebrow. "He *yelled* at you?" She'd never once seen Morrison yell. Maybe she didn't know him as well as she'd thought. After all, she'd only just learned that he had a "mean streak."

"He frowned at me. Which is as close to yelling as California gets."

"Maybe he frowned at you because you gave him the busywork. He's a good detective, Petrosky."

"Good detectives do busywork. Hell, almost all of it's busywork, just like this lawyer gig. You oughta know that." Petrosky tossed his wrapper into her trash can. "Plus, California takes better notes than I do—says it helps him get his thoughts together. Man's a born writer. Might as well let him put that fancy English degree to use." He kicked the door closed and sat, leveling his eyes at Shannon. "Got some shit on your husband too."

She grimaced. *Roger is not my husband anymore.* She bit her tongue and waited for him to go on.

"There are four on his caseload now that have had sudden changes in charges or even full drops. And more overlap with cases Wheatley was working on than you'd expect based on random chance."

"You think Wheatley and Roger were—"

"Ike Lambert's case was one of Wheatley's. I met with his ex about an hour ago. Lambert's a bad, bad guy. Druggie. Almost killed another little boy a few years back while under the influence of cocaine. Roger dropped him to a drug charge and misdemeanor assault." His eyes glittered in her overhead lights. He was a hair away from outright smirking. "And Lambert had cash. Ex thought he might have paid for his freedom."

Paid for his freedom? Was Petrosky kidding? "Have you found any evidence that Roger's taking bribes?"

Petrosky's face soured. "Not yet."

"There are tons of reasons to plead down, Petrosky. With Lambert, it made sense. It's a judgment call, really." Though that wasn't entirely true—she'd been pissed as hell over the Lambert case. He'd gotten off too easy.

"That one might have made sense, but some of his charges are being dropped way below what could reasonably have been prosecuted. He's a sneaky bastard; I'll give you that, Taylor. He does a good job making it not look too obvious."

What is he getting at? "But Roger never asked me to reduce charges on Johnson. Not once."

"Of course he didn't. Roger never had a relationship with Johnson. But Derek Lewis used Roger as a defense attorney about ten years back, before he was a prosecutor. Roger got Lewis off clean on a drug charge. Funny that he went full throttle on the murder charge when half the people your office prosecutes end up with reductions."

"Maybe he liked Lewis. Wanted to see his killer put away."

"Or maybe Lewis knew that Roger was getting bribed by defendants to reduce their charges and Roger offed him for it. And he was happy to put Ashley Johnson away instead."

What the fuck? "You can't seriously think Roger played a part in Lewis's death."

"Not necessarily." But the hardness in his eyes said maybe.

"That's insane, Petrosky." Her head spun.

"Is it? We both know he's lowering those charges. I don't know how Lewis would have found out, but I'm working on it. And if Roger was using Wheatley to somehow flush out who might have the resources to pay for their freedom, we've got a link there too."

Petrosky had lost his goddamn mind. "Roger would have just paid people off. He wouldn't kill anyone." She never thought he'd cheat either. But still, murder was extreme. And the fact that Petrosky was pushing something so ridiculous, shutting out dialogue where they might explore other valid options... Was there something he was trying to ignore? Something he wanted to hide?

"Fine, okay? Fine. I don't have a good reason for motive, not yet." Petrosky glowered out the window behind her. "But there's something there."

She shook her head. "You just *want* it to be Roger."

"He's got issues, Taylor. McCallum says he's a narcissist, though I suspect you already know that. But he might actually be a full-on psycho. Neither personality gets emotional for shit unless you piss them off. And they're gifted liars."

You haven't seen McCallum in weeks. Roger wasn't the only liar here. Her teeth hurt, and she loosened her jaw. "Roger's just an asshole. Not a killer." He was reducing charges, but only to up their percentage of convictions without going to court—not for pay. And no one was complaining except her. "I just can't—"

"With all due respect, Shannon, Roger has a history of hiding things. From you especially." He glanced at the door as if expecting Roger to appear. "Did he know where you were going to be, Shannon?"

"What? When?"

"When you were at the gym. When your car got vandalized."

"Petrosky, he could have just looked in my briefcase. Hell, he didn't even have to sneak anything. All he had to do was ask."

"Not if you weren't supposed to be on that case. Or maybe he wanted to throw suspicion elsewhere—no one would believe that the lead prosecutor is out smashing car windows." Petrosky touched his shirt pocket as if to make sure his smokes were still there.

"Whoever left Lucky's head on my car wasn't worried about being found out, Petrosky. They *wanted* us to pay attention. They wanted to scare me."

"And whoever did it, knew just how to get to you. Knew what would bother you. Who your family was." Petrosky met her eyes. "Maybe you should hit the training sessions without the classes for a little while. Be less predictable."

Maybe she should skip the workouts altogether since she just had sex with her gym buddy.

Petrosky's phone buzzed, and he glanced at it, then back at the granola bar on the desk. "If you don't eat that, you'll hurt California's feelings."

"Since when are you worried about anyone's feelings?"

The corner of Petrosky's mouth turned up, but he said nothing.

"I'll save it for later. Thanks for bringing it by, though."

"Least I can do for California's girlfriend." He pulled a cigarette from his pack, stuck it between his teeth, and stepped toward the door.

"I'm not his girlfriend," she called after him.

He turned back to her, his face a mask of incredulity.

Does he...know?

"Come off it, Taylor. You know better, and so do I. He yelled at me over food."

"He frowned." But her abdomen tightened like someone had punched her in the gut.

"Just don't fuck with him. Whatever hippie bullshit California might be into, he's a good man."

"What?"

"I'm not repeating that shit, not to you or anyone else." Petrosky pulled a lighter from his coat. "Ever." He cut his eyes to the hall and back to her, lip curling as if he had smelled something bad. Her neck tensed.

Sure enough, Roger's stupid face appeared in her office, a fake and completely inappropriate smile plastered across his maw. "What's going on in here?"

"Consultation," Petrosky said.

"On what, may I ask?"

Petrosky smiled and lit his cigarette. "Nope, you may not." He turned and pushed past Roger into the hallway.

Roger staggered against the doorframe and scowled at Petrosky's back until the stairwell door slammed. "Not a good idea, Shannon."

She fingered the granola bar on her desk, but all she could see was a bloody mass of towels teeming with bugs. She took a deep breath. "I can be friends with whomever I want."

"Petrosky and Morrison are no one's friends. Unless you're a prostitute."

She squeezed the bar, and the wrapper crinkled as if it were trying to scream. "Kiss my ass, Roger." The phone on her desk rang.

He smiled at her, but it looked like a snarl. "Not if you paid me." Roger turned to leave, hand on the doorknob.

There's the man I walked away from. She opened her mouth to tell him to fuck off, but the phone buzzed again. She ignored Roger instead and pressed the receiver to her ear, knuckles white.

"Sorry to call you at the office, but I've been trying to get ahold of you all morning." Alex's voice shook.

She straightened, the sound of Roger slamming her door almost mute under the pounding in her ears and Alex's heavy breathing. "What's happened?"

"I'm taking him home in an hour," Alex said. "I—" His voice caught, and Shannon's heart seized. "His liver's failing, kidneys too, and his lungs... fuck. They can't tell me exactly how long but...they're done treating any of it or the wound on his leg. Maybe the infection even contributed, but they don't... Shit, I'm a doctor, and I knew it was coming, and I just can't..." There was a sharp intake of breath on the line. "He begged them to let him go home, *begged* them, and it looks like he's going fast. They're discharging him into home hospice care. Nurse once a day, a...priest or some shit. I refused that part." Alex sniffed. "I don't know how to tell Abby."

"I'll be there in twenty minutes." She hung up the phone and yanked her suit jacket from the back of the chair. Then she was in the hall, somehow on the stairs, the hollow echo of her footsteps following her as she ran down, every step clanging like a bell that was ticking off minutes until eternity caught up with her. She was running toward doom. Derry's end. Racing toward the last look, the last hug, the last everything. Twice she paused, hand gripping the railing, her body a magnet, her office the North Pole. If she went back, she wouldn't have to face this. Wouldn't have to watch Derry go home to die. And then it would be almost like he never died at all, and for the rest of her life, she could live in a state of delusional bliss, convinced that he was still alive and well but just...somewhere else. She stepped forward, again and again and again, the dread weighting her feet like concrete boots, every nerve in her body screaming at her to stop. But there was no stopping the inevitable. And the fire behind her eyes, the panic buzzing through her chest, even her heavy feet knew that tragedy was coming whether she stood still or not.

She was in the parking lot before she remembered that she didn't have her car. A cab would take an hour to arrive. She grabbed her cell and scrolled through the contact list, past Morrison's number, flinching when she realized there was no one but him she could call, no one but him she could trust to come running. Her finger hovered over the call button. Petrosky? Maybe Petrosky. He'd still be close by, and probably perfectly willing to take her anywhere she needed to go. But...she didn't just need a ride. Tears stung her eyes.

Her chest hurt. She needed her best friend. She needed Morrison.

He answered on the first ring. "Hey, Shannon." But his voice lacked its usual friendliness; his tone laced with something thick and tired and sad.

She stared at the courthouse, at the single ash tree at the far corner, barren despite the impending spring. She'd screwed up. She'd screwed everything up. *Breathe.* But she couldn't catch her breath any more than she could force the tree into a sudden full bloom. "Sorry to bother you, but…are you around?" She was whispering, wheezing. She laid a hand on her knee.

"Shanny—what's wrong? I'm here at the precinct."

"Can you give me a ride to the hospital?" Her voice wavered, and she fought to control it. The phone was silent in her hand. "Morrison?"

Then the shriek of a squeaky door sounded in the phone and from across the lot, and when she looked up toward the noise, she saw him emerge through the front door of the precinct.

He ran. "Shanny."

Her steps were leaden, her feet numb. When she stumbled, he grabbed her elbow and led her to the passenger seat of his car. "It sucks, Shanny," he whispered. "But you've got this." No bullshit. No banality. "I'm here, okay?"

He knew. He always knew. She watched through the windshield as he raced around the car and jumped in, shoving the keys into the ignition. She forced a cough over the lump in her throat, trying to find her breath. "Thanks, Morrison. I appreciate it." But her voice cracked on the last word.

He leaned over the console and put his arms around her shoulders.

She laid her head against his neck and sobbed.

19

THE LADIES at the desk were morose, or seemed to be, staring at their computers and tapping furiously on their keyboards. Wanting to be somewhere else, like she did, somewhere death didn't hang in the air like a cheap perfume.

Derry's things were already packed in a duffel bag by the door. He sat in a wheelchair parallel to the bed, his sweatshirt hanging off his bony shoulders. The skin on his face sagged in a way that made him look thirty years older. She went to him and squeezed his hand. "Derry."

"It's really not a bad weight loss plan," he said, gesturing feebly to his chest. His voice was raspy and strange and grotesque. "I lost thirty pounds in thirty days!"

She blinked back tears. "Where's Alex?"

"Finishing the last of the paperwork. He's going to take me home, then go get Abby."

Shannon's heart throbbed, viscous and sluggish as if the muscle was swimming in glue. "They give you oxygen to take home?"

Beside her, Derry's chest rose and fell, his breath crinkling like paper. "Alex is getting that too."

"Good." She stared at the back wall, avoiding his face.

Derry coughed. "He here for you?"

Right. Morrison. She turned. He'd been standing in the

corridor, but he approached when he saw her looking. "Yes. I mean, for you too, but he drove me here and—"

Morrison poked his head into the room. "What's up, old man?"

"Ahh, nothing better than old man end-of-life references at vulnerable times."

"You sure as hell weren't vulnerable last week when you took all my money."

Derry grinned, but the corner of his mouth twitched with pain.

Morrison winced and nodded to Shannon.

She patted Derry's hand. "Be right back." They took a few steps away from the room, far enough so Derry couldn't hear them. The hospital swam by around her, busy with the effort of hustling death.

"You can head out if you want," Shannon said, though her chest tightened at the thought of being alone with Derry and Alex. "I'll ride back with them."

"Your brother has a Prius. There's no way they'll get him and the wheelchair and you in that car." Morrison glanced back into the hospital room. "Plus the supplies. I'll wait downstairs in the lot."

He knew what she needed. What Derry needed. And the flush in his cheeks had never been more alive, more vital, than now when everything else felt so...dead. She tried to ignore the image of Derry's chalky pallor that had crept into her brain and stuck like a parasite—sucking the life out of her too.

Her arms tingled with the desire to hug Morrison, to draw from his strength, to brush her lips against his warm neck, but she clenched her fists at her sides. "Thank you."

He nodded and headed down the hallway as Shannon crossed back to Derry's room. Her body felt as though it weighed a thousand pounds, every step an almost Herculean feat.

Derry peered at her through narrowed eyes. "Are you guys...a thing? God, please tell me you're a thing. Right from the beginning, I hoped you'd date him instead of Roger, but..." He coughed wetly and struggled to catch his breath, gasping as he inhaled. "So?"

"He's just helping me out."

Derry studied her face. "Spill it, girlfriend. I saw how you looked at him." His voice was higher, inflated with mock flamboyance, but its unusual hoarseness grated over her eardrums.

Shit, Derry, I can't, I... She sighed. "Okay, fine, we *might* be a thing. A little bit of a thing. I'm not sure." *A little bit of a thing?* Out loud, the words sounded trite, dismissive, and nowhere near reflective of what had transpired between her and Morrison.

Derry wheezed in a breath. "Oh, honey, it's not worth wasting your time on a little thing." He leaned toward her, but he groaned with the effort, wincing in pain, and her stomach twisted at the misery in his eyes. "So, is he good?" He smiled, and for one glorious second, they were almost themselves again, the hospital and death and the hissing oxygen tank fading away.

She wanted to stay like that forever, just talking, teasing each other—not dying. "Yes, he's good." *God yes.*

He nodded at the door and slumped back into the wheelchair. "About damn time. I've always liked him."

"You'd like anyone who wasn't Roger."

"Maybe so. But I loved Curt from that first day you brought him out to dinner with us and Abs." He coughed, swallowed phlegm. "He's got...a kindness about him, you know?"

She nodded. She knew. "But we've been friends for so long, and I don't want to lose that. I..."

He shook his head feebly. "You sound just like Mom."

"I'm not like her at all!"

"You are, Shanny. Angry. Stubborn. Pessimistic about relationships because you can't see the potential unless some narcissistic asshole hammers how great they are into your head." He coughed, wheezing air through his nose. "And seriously? You can't be friends with your lover? What the hell is wrong with you?" He closed his eyes for a moment, pain etched on his face.

Everything was wrong with her. She was being ridiculous. But... "I just don't have time."

"Don't have time?" Derry opened his eyes. "Time for what exactly?"

"For a relationship."

"Make time."

"It isn't that easy."

"Bullshit, Shanny. Time is what you have. I'd love to have more." And they were back in the hospital, circling the drain. Her eyes filled with tears.

"Be happy, Shanny. Be with people who make you happy. That's what Alex does for me. Even with all this,"—he gestured to his ruined body—" he still makes me smile." His mouth tightened, and he hissed a breath through clenched teeth. "I'll leave this world knowing someone loves me and always will."

"Abby loves you too." Shannon put her hand on his shoulder, and the bones were sharp under her palm. "And I love you. Always."

Derry put his hand over hers. "I love you too, Shanny. Now stop messing around and letting your long-ass life pass you by. God knows you wasted enough time on your asshole ex." He squeezed her hand, his knuckles whitening. "And grab the nurse."

THE NEXT FEW hours were a blur. Morrison clutched her hand on the center console but stayed blessedly silent as he drove back to Derry's house. Shannon watched the sky, the vibrant blue finally peeking through the storm clouds, and it seemed too hot, too bright, too...happy. She let the tears fill her eyes and watched the city pass through a watery film, pretending that she was drowning. If she couldn't breathe, she couldn't hurt.

When they got to Derry's, Shannon and Morrison unloaded Alex's car while Alex settled Derry into the office on the first floor where a hospital bed dwarfed Derry's antique desk in the corner. When the car was empty, Shannon sat in a folding chair beside her brother's bed, her head resting on the duvet near Derry's emaciated calf. Alex squeezed her hand, said something about groceries and picking up Abby, and left. Derry snored quietly through it all, presumably because of the drugs the nurse had given him before they left the hospital. Morphine. Ativan. Every four hours, to keep him comfortable.

But not to save him.

A car door clanged outside, and Shannon raised her head to look out the window as Petrosky stepped out of his car in the circular drive. Roger's Mercedes pulled in behind him.

Shit. The folding chair clattered to the floor behind her as she left Derry wheezing softly in the office and walked out onto the crowded front porch. Morrison was already out there, facing Roger. Petrosky stood behind them, leaning against the house.

Roger turned to Shannon as the front door swung shut behind her. "What are these guys doing here? You take off from work, don't tell anyone where you're going—"

"No, Roger, I just didn't tell *you*, which is the reason you're upset."

"This isn't about us, Shannon. I shouldn't have to call back the last known number on your office phone to find out where you went."

Narcissistic. Maybe psychopathic. Anger seared through her, boiling her blood, turning her bones to ash. "You shouldn't be doing that at all."

Roger's face twisted into one of concern, and he stepped toward her and reached out to touch her arm. "I'm sorry about Jerry."

Shannon slapped his hand away, and Morrison stiffened.

The hurt in Roger's eyes hardened into rage. "You need to take some time off." His voice was soft, measured, dangerous. "Before you let your instability get the better of you."

I promised Derry. I'm going to find this fucker. She glowered at Roger. "I don't need time off. I need to figure out what's going on with this case."

"Figuring out this case isn't in the scope of your job. Stick to your job."

"The right thing, that's the scope of my job. Finding the truth, that's my job. Putting the right people away, that's my job." Her voice was rising, higher and louder, and she didn't care. A breeze sweetened with spring and new life whipped her words away, and she could feel the vestiges of winter underneath it—the cold, the death. "Don't you dare try to tell me what I need to do. It's not like you have any frame of right or wrong, anyway. You do whatever it takes to get an easy win."

Roger's eyes flicked to Petrosky, to Morrison, and back to her. "You're wrong on that."

"Am I? What about Sandusky? Easily second-degree murder, but we pleaded down despite no shortage of evidence."

"It was easier to—"

"And Lambert. He should have been put away forever."

"We didn't have enough to guarantee he would." Roger shrugged. "Everything isn't always cut-and-dried."

"Some things are." Morrison's voice was low, almost a whisper.

Roger sneered, his jaw working. "This isn't your business, asshole."

Petrosky pulled a cigarette from his pack. "Derek Lewis dead in a lonely apartment, though, that is our business. Decapitated pets, that's our business. Ditto on a trunk full of bloody towels."

Roger turned on him. "What the fuck are you talking about?"

"Oh, I'm sure you'll hear all about it on Monday, Roger."

Petrosky lit his cigarette. "By the way, how well did you know Benjamin Wheatley?"

"Who?"

Petrosky smiled at him, but it wasn't a friendly grin.

Shannon glanced down the street. "Alex and Abby will be back soon. You need to be gone before they get here."

Roger's mouth tightened. "All of us?"

"Just you."

Roger's nostrils flared. He shook his head. "You always were a fucking whore."

There was a flash of activity, Roger smirking, Petrosky straightening, and then Morrison's arm shot out, his fist connecting with Roger's face.

Roger grunted, hands over his nose, blood spurting through his fingers. "You fucking—" He looked at his hands, bared his teeth, and lunged. Morrison sidestepped him, grabbed his wrist, and flipped him over the porch railing and into the flower bed. Roger groaned but didn't stand. Morrison stood above him, hands twitching and ready at his sides.

Petrosky blew smoke rings toward the roof and peered into the flower bed. "You okay there, Rog? You seem a little unsteady on your feet."

Roger clambered out of the bushes, grasping his nose, and shook a finger at Morrison. "You'll regret that." He pointed at Shannon. "You too."

Morrison didn't move.

Roger stumbled back to his car, and they watched him squeal down the drive and out onto the street.

Petrosky balanced his cigarette between his teeth. "You need to watch yourself around him, Taylor."

"What could he possibly do to me now that he didn't already do in our four years together?"

"I'm just saying; he might have more to lose now. And you're no longer married—he's lost his leverage."

She glanced toward the house, her chest tightening.

Petrosky squinted through the smoke. "You should go

inside, get some rest." He met her eyes once more then strode down the porch steps toward his car.

"I don't need rest," she called after him. But every muscle in her body pulsed with a dull ache as if she'd just run a marathon. Her brain felt like it was encased in sludge.

Morrison kept his eyes on the road until Petrosky was out of sight. Then he reached over and squeezed Shannon's hand, sending currents of warm liquid up her arm. Roger's blood was still streaked across his knuckles like an exclamation point. He'd hit Roger. Maybe risked his career. And he was still here, helping her, supporting her.

She was turning to wrap herself in his arms when Alex's Prius turned into the drive.

"I'll be in the car if you need me, Shanny." Morrison released her and stepped off the porch.

She stared after him, her hand burning.

ABBY WAS in Shannon's arms before Alex got out of the car. Shannon knelt and held Abby's quaking body, her blouse soaking through with tears.

"I didn't get the groceries," Alex said, his voice an octave higher than usual as if he were forcing each word through a lake of unshed tears. "I just… couldn't. We went to the park, the one where I…proposed."

Shannon looked into his bloodshot eyes and kissed Abby's head. "I'll take care of it."

"I want to see Daddy." Abby's voice quavered. She let go of Shannon and took Alex's hand.

"Of course, honey," Alex said. "I'll go with you. He might be sleeping, but we can sit with him and just talk awhile, okay?" He kissed her knuckles, and Abby sniffed.

Keep it together. Don't let everyone down now. She straightened. "Alex, can I take your car?" Her rental was still at her house.

"Yeah, thanks, Shanny." Alex handed her his keys, and she squeezed his arm and stepped off the porch, barely registering Morrison's footsteps as she popped the lock. He was at the door before she got it closed.

"Where are you going?"

"Grocery store." *And no one's going to tell me I can't, not now.*

"You need to—"

So much for fucking support. "What, Morrison? What do I need to do right now?"

"Petrosky can grab some stuff."

"Why? You think Roger's staking out the grocery store, so he can off me? That Wheatley's going to miraculously show up and murder me in the frozen food aisle?" And even if someone did come up behind her and slit her throat, would that be the worst thing that could happen? She shook away the dark thought. *Yes. Yes, it would.* Abby needed her. Alex needed her.

Morrison shook his head almost imperceptibly. "No, I—"

"I don't need a babysitter, Morrison. I'll be fine."

"Shannon—"

"Stop." She buckled her seat belt and shoved the key into the ignition. "It's three blocks from here. Just watch them. I'll be back in a few minutes."

Morrison jumped back as she slammed the car door, the edge of it barely missing his already bloodied hand. Her heart hammered in her temples. She put the car in gear and took off, the houses a blur, every passing car shoving her heart into overdrive, every stop sign shrinking the car until it was as confining as a coffin.

Roger. He was an ass. But he wasn't a killer. Petrosky was an idiot. And Morrison with his stupid granola and his shroom coffee and the way he always looked at her like he could fix everything—

Shannon slammed her palms against the steering wheel and turned onto the main road. Why couldn't Roger be the one with cancer? Or Ike Lambert or Benjamin Wheatley? Anyone but Derry. Not her Derry. Alex's Derry. Abby's Derry. The only thing she could do was make his last days as peaceful and pain-free as possible. And find the asshole who slunk up to his daughter's porch and murdered her cat. *I'm not afraid to die, Shannon, but I am afraid to leave my daughter here with some maniac running around...*

I'll find him, Derry. I will find him for you.

Shannon parked in the back of the lot and yanked the keys from the ignition, frustration bubbling inside her chest and thickening near her throat like molten rock, depriving her lungs of oxygen. She checked the windows and locked the doors, and then she screamed, beating her fists against the steering wheel and kicking at the useless pedals. Her hands ached and throbbed as she punched again and again, every impact a welcome pain that brought her back to herself and away from what was happening tomorrow or the next day or the next. The day very soon when Derry would die. Whether he died peacefully...that was up to her.

When her knuckles were throbbing and cracked open with the weight of injustice, she shook out her fists, exited the car, and went into the store to buy groceries. And bandages.

20

Morrison was asleep on the couch when she crept downstairs the next morning. His chest rose and fell with his breath, a tendril of blond hair stuck to his forehead like he was a little kid. She resisted the urge to brush it away.

"Sleep well?" Petrosky walked in from the dining room, coffee in hand. Shannon jumped and banged her elbow against the wall.

Morrison stirred.

She rubbed her sore arm. "I didn't know you were here."

"I came to relieve California. Much as he'll deny it, he needs sleep like anyone else."

Shannon peered past him into the dining room. "Where is everyone?" The stillness of the house was unnerving like someone had died. But that hadn't happened. Not yet. *Had it?* Her stomach turned.

"Alex went to the twenty-four-hour pharmacy to pick up a prescription. Abby's asleep. California will be up to look after them when I leave."

Leave? Shannon raised an eyebrow.

"I've got an appointment in half an hour with Wheatley's best friend, Theodore Ruskin."

Ruskin. Fine. Good.

"You want in?"

She realized her eyes were still on Morrison. She glanced back at the staircase, then at Petrosky. "Yeah. I'm thinking Alex and Abby could use some time alone."

Petrosky sipped his coffee and glanced at her bandaged knuckles. "Good."

He actually wanted her to come? "You could just go yourself," she said slowly.

"So, I could. But it might be nice to have a witness."

"A witness? For what?"

"The chief likes it when I do. Might as well make her happy." He winked a craggy eye.

The chief. She was ballsy, didn't take shit from anyone, especially Petrosky. If she wanted someone to keep an eye on him, she had a reason. Maybe over the hospital complaint? "Did she threaten to suspend you?" Shannon asked.

"Nope. She threatened to suspend Surfer Boy. Even called me on my cell." The corner of his mouth curved up. "It was very special."

Shannon looked again at Morrison's face: unlined and peaceful. "Because he punched Roger?" she hissed at Petrosky. "I can't believe that asshole."

"I prefer 'douche canoe,' but sure."

"What are you—"

"I got it from a blog. I like it." He downed the rest of his coffee. "Anyway, California has a squeaky-clean record and near-perfect attendance. And he brings coffee and donuts to the staff, does shit to keep morale up. They might riot if she lets him go." He waved to the door. "You need breakfast or…?"

She dragged her eyes from Morrison's snoozing profile. "Let's do it."

THEODORE RUSKIN LIVED in a one-story box of gray brick. A triangle of white siding stretched to the A-line roof over a shuttered front window. Shannon and Petrosky exited the car and stepped across the muddy front lawn to a postage-stamp concrete porch. Petrosky rapped twice.

Ruskin opened the door blinking like a mole who hadn't seen daylight in months. Acne erupted over his pasty, sallow chin. He shoved enormous green-rimmed eighties glasses into place on his nose and looked from Shannon to Petrosky.

"Mr. Ruskin?" Petrosky said.

He nodded, and his glasses slipped down his nose. "Yes?"

Petrosky pulled his badge. "Detective Petrosky with the Ash Park PD. We have a few questions about a friend of yours."

"Friend?" Ruskin's eyes widened.

Petrosky peered past him into the house. "Are you alone, sir?"

Ruskin cocked his head as if no one would ever assume anything else.

"Sir?"

"Yes, I'm alone."

"We're looking for a Benjamin Wheatley." Petrosky replaced his badge. "May we come in?"

Ruskin held the door open and pointed to a room directly to the left of the entry. A high-definition television screen hung from one wall, the cords to a variety of gaming systems snaking from the back of it and down to the consoles on a sofa table below. Individual leather theater seats sat within arm's reach of the controllers. On the far wall, a bookshelf bumped up against a wooden L-shaped desk that ran from the corner by the books to below the front window.

Ruskin looked around the room as if pondering where to sit.

"Interesting setup you have here, Ruskin," Petrosky said as he eased himself into one of the gaming chairs. He gestured to the desk. Ruskin took the desk chair and turned it to face the room while Petrosky swiveled both gamer's chairs to face Ruskin. Shannon sat tentatively in one, tensing her legs to keep the rocker from pitching to the floor.

"Thanks. I think," Ruskin said, the question apparent in his voice.

Petrosky put his hands on his knees, feigning calm. "Tell me about Benjamin Wheatley."

"Ben and I have known each other a long time."

"You see him often?"

"No, he didn't go out too much." Ruskin shifted in his seat. "And my wife didn't really like him. Probably why we didn't talk that much anymore."

I'm obviously not the only one who knows how romance screws up friendships.

Ruskin gestured to the desk where a set of framed pictures grinned back at them. In one photo, Ruskin had his arm around a beautiful Jessica Rabbit redhead in a tight white dress.

"That's your wife, Mr. Ruskin?" Petrosky said, sounding far less surprised than she was.

Ruskin smiled. "I know. I don't know what she sees in me." Shannon appraised his doughy body. Ruskin must be a hell of a smart guy. Maybe he was super funny. She pictured her own wedding photos. Superficial attraction only went so far anyway.

Petrosky pulled his eyes from the pictures. "So, Wheatley. Not real outgoing, but you were friends?"

Ruskin shrugged. "Dunno...I guess. We've known each other since middle school. We both wanted to be writers." He looked at his bookshelf and back at Petrosky. "Plus, we were both kinda geeky." Back at the bookshelf again, the clock, the front window. He was avoiding looking Petrosky in the eye. "You think something happened to him?"

"Why would you think that, Mr. Ruskin?"

Ruskin picked at an invisible spot on his pants.

Shannon sat straighter, her muscles taut.

"Do *you* think something happened to him, Mr. Ruskin?"

"No...I mean, I don't think so."

Petrosky stood suddenly enough that Shannon jumped. He stepped between Ruskin and the window and bent so close his breath fogged Ruskin's glasses. The man's eyes widened.

"You're not telling me the truth, Mr. Ruskin, and I can't say I like it."

"I am! I don't know where he is."

"But you know *something*, don't you?"

Shannon stared at Ruskin, who was chewing the inside of his cheek like it was bubble gum.

"Mr. Ruskin, your friend may be responsible for the murders of two people."

Shannon stared at Petrosky in surprise. Did he really think Wheatley'd killed Lewis? Or…two, so Lewis and Lucky? Unless he was just screwing with Ruskin to get him to spill what he knew.

"Wait, wait! You think that Benjamin—"

Petrosky slammed his fist on the arm of Ruskin's chair, and Ruskin's jaw clamped shut. "What do you know, Mr. Ruskin? Either you tell us now, or we take you in and find out the hard way. And if you pick door number two—"

Shannon stood, and Petrosky backed from Ruskin's desk.

"Okay, all right?" Ruskin raised his hands in surrender. "Okay. I mean, I don't even know if it's anything, you know? It might be nothing."

"We'll decide that, Mr. Ruskin."

"Okay, so the only thing I can think of is this thing he told me about at work—like a bust."

"A bust? He was a social worker, Mr. Ruskin, not a cop."

"I know, I know, that's why it was like…secret. He said he saw some guy over at one of the places he visits, maybe buying dope, and the guy was like…important. But he said he wanted to make sure he was right before he turned him in, so he was going to go over there and find out."

Wheatley had seen someone buying drugs. Someone prominent in the community. Someone with a lot to lose if it came out. But that could be a lot of people, right? She couldn't let Petrosky's wild imagination get into her head and snuff logical thought.

Petrosky paced in front of the window. "Did he? Go over there?"

"I don't know."

"How long ago was that, Mr. Ruskin?"

"Maybe... I dunno, a few months?" He chewed harder on his cheek. Shannon was certain he was drawing blood.

"We're going to need you to be more specific on the time."

"I... Shit. Okay. It was before my last book came out. *The Yeti Returns*—I published February twentieth. So maybe... beginning or middle of January?"

"That's almost four months, Mr. Ruskin. Have you talked to him since?"

"Yeah, a few times. Just a quick lunch here and there to catch up. He didn't mention this again, and I didn't ask about it because I pretty much thought he was full of shit."

Shannon and Petrosky exchanged a look. If Wheatley had waited until February to go have that chat with Lewis, he could have been the one arguing with Lewis the day he died.

"Okay, so Wheatley tells you he's going to see some guy to verify that some other guy is buying drugs from him." Petrosky leaned close to Ruskin again. "What was Wheatley planning to do once he got there? Threaten the guy into telling him what he knew?"

"Well, I'm not really sure. He didn't say. But if I know Benjamin, he just planned on talking."

"Did he ever mention a girl? An Ashley Johnson?"

Ruskin's jaw dropped as the name sank in. "Wait...that girl who killed her boyfriend? This is about that? Holy shit." A drop of sweat from his forehead slid through the grease and down onto the side of his nose. "I don't know anything about that. He just said he was going to talk to a guy to make sure of what he saw before he contacted the police. Maybe he'd even be okay with me telling you that part. He was going to call anyway."

"I don't think you have to worry about what Wheatley thinks is okay at this point, Mr. Ruskin. I'd be more worried about going to jail."

Jail? Ruskin hadn't done anything to warrant an arrest. Shannon cleared her throat, preparing to tell Petrosky to lay off before they were the ones in trouble for badgering this twerky idiot.

"But I told you everything! I don't—"

"Obstructing justice is a very serious offense, Mr. Ruskin." Obstruction. Petrosky would know about that. "You know what else is serious? Accessory to murder. And we found Wheatley's car last night with a ton of bloody towels in the trunk."

"Take it easy, Petrosky…" Shannon began.

Ruskin shot her a pleading look. "Bloody…what? I swear I don't—"

Petrosky leaned closer to Ruskin. "If this was such a secret, Mr. Ruskin, why would Benjamin tell you? Were you going to help him?"

Ruskin reared back, his eyes wide.

Petrosky stayed with him, practically nose to nose. "And by the way, I read your book, the one about the little girls on spring break from middle school, written under a pen name, right? Through some shitty indie press for perverts? *Travis.*"

"What? No, that isn't me! You've got the wrong guy! Listen, I—"

"Why would Wheatley tell you, anyway? Did you have an extra set of towels to help him clean himself off after he killed Derek Lewis? After he used a hammer to blast a man's skull clean out? Level with us, or you're going away right along with him."

What the hell is Petrosky doing? He didn't really think Wheatley was the one who killed Lewis, did he? Wheatley had run the day she'd found Lucky's head—without his clothes. Even if he'd done it, he sure wouldn't draw attention to himself with the note and then panic and disappear.

Ruskin leaned back so far the chair tipped. "No! He just told me because he thought I might like the whole vigilante government worker going after drug lord thing as an idea for another book. Said he knew about someone getting all hopped up who shouldn't have been. That's it."

Enough. Shannon paused halfway to Petrosky, trying to decide the best way to intervene.

"Who?" Petrosky growled.

"I'm not sure; he didn't—"

"Who was it, Ruskin?"

"He didn't tell me any names or anything, oh my god, I swear he didn't, and I don't know who Travis is!" Ruskin was panting, his pock-marked face pink and shiny with sweat and oil.

"I'll be calling you, Ruskin. And I'm going to need you to keep in touch. If Wheatley shows up here, if anyone shows up here asking questions, you need to call me, or I will make sure they throw you in jail with the guys who will settle for flabby computer geek tits since they can't get anything else. You got it?"

Ruskin reeled forward and reached for a drawer in his desk. Petrosky leapt forward, snatched Ruskin's hand, and stepped behind the chair, jerking Ruskin's wrist behind his back.

Ruskin's eyes were wide, his mouth gaping like a fish out of water. "In...haler," he croaked.

"Petrosky!" Shannon grabbed Petrosky's arm, and Ruskin collapsed back into the chair, face red, fleshy lips going purple. She reached into the drawer and yanked out a rescue inhaler. Ruskin uncapped it and puffed hungrily, the whoosh like the sound of the air through Derry's oxygen machine. But this guy would live. Probably.

"They don't like guys like you in prison, Ruskin. You call if you see your buddy." Petrosky tossed his card on the desk and walked out, Shannon at his heels.

As soon as the front door closed behind them, Shannon turned on Petrosky. "What the fuck was that?"

"Interrogation." He stepped off the porch and onto the walk.

She hustled after him. "Threats are not interrogation."

Petrosky shrugged. "Well, now we know he probably didn't do anything except keep a secret for Wheatley. And Ruskin was scared enough that he would have told us if he knew more. He'll definitely call us if Wheatley shows up here." Petrosky stomped off the sidewalk and through the lawn, mud splattering his jeans.

What had Wheatley gotten himself involved in? What had he done? He couldn't be their murderer; their killer was after notoriety. "It was me," the note had said. It was a bid for attention, and not a subtle one—definitely not the words of the type of guy who ran away, who hinted to his friends about knowing things but wouldn't spill his secrets. Who kept confidentiality agreements as part of his job as a social worker, just as she did as a lawyer. Hell, maybe he'd heard a confession during a session that had tipped him off, and he hadn't been able to call the police for help because of confidentiality constraints.

Shannon's heel caught in the mushy grass. She hauled it out, squished to the car, and got in, slamming the door hard enough to jar her shoulder. "All that was bullshit, Petrosky. That stuff you said, implying Wheatley was the murderer."

"I don't know yet, Taylor. Just batting around theories. Could still be Roger. If I were a guy like Roger, maybe I'd do a little smack in a place I knew I wouldn't get caught. And maybe I'd kill both the dealer and any potential tattletales to make sure no one ever found out. Maybe I'd even frame the girlfriend since I'd know what it would take for a jury to convict."

"And then you'd leave a note on my car to alert everyone that the wrong person had been put away? Bullshit."

"I'm still working on that part." Petrosky started the engine.

Shannon leaned back against the headrest. "If Wheatley saw something, someone...why wouldn't he have come forward after Lewis was killed?"

"He could have figured that Johnson really had killed Lewis. Not that far out of line, really, since he'd have been privy to her files and would have known about Lewis's history of domestic violence. But if Wheatley's anything like his chickenshit friend in there, maybe he was scared. Scared of the killer, or scared of the fact that snooping around right before a murder makes him look suspicious as fuck."

Had Wheatley thought Johnson guilty? Or was he just scared like Petrosky was saying? Maybe he'd run to avoid being accused of something, but it was more likely he was afraid for his own life. If the blood in the trunk was any indication, he was probably already dead.

Shannon listened to the rumble of the car engine and Petrosky's labored breathing, obviously still recovering from the tongue lashing he'd given Ruskin. "Is Ruskin really an undercover indie author named Travis?"

"Nope. I made that up, trying to throw him off balance, so he'd let his guard down."

She watched Ruskin's house grow smaller in her sideview mirror then turned to Petrosky with narrowed eyes. "You didn't need a witness. You needed a good cop."

Petrosky tapped the steering wheel. "California couldn't be here, and he's usually the good one."

"I'm telling him you said that."

"Don't even think about it, or I'll tell him you think he's hung like a horse."

Shannon's jaw dropped. "He...he *told* you?"

Petrosky's brows hit his hairline, eyes wide. "Told me what?"

"Fuck you, Petrosky." She turned back to the window. "Seriously, fuck you."

21

THE COURTROOM WAS ALIVE, breathing ghastly, frosty breaths down the back of Shannon's blouse. She wished she were out with Petrosky and Morrison, investigating other individuals on Wheatley's caseload, running credit cards, and searching for who knew what else. Instead, she was stuck here with... them. The pews were full today: middle-aged men, young men, and a dozen or so women, all solemn and watchful. Assessing the room. Assessing...her. The gaze of three dozen sets of eyes bored into her back as she stared at the empty judge's chair. She shook her head. They were probably students from some criminal justice class. There was no reason for her to be so rattled.

Her breath caught when the door banged open, and Roger entered the courtroom, his nose splinted and taped with a white bandage from cheekbone to cheekbone. What the hell was he doing there? Roger winked at one of the young women in the pews in true smarmy player style. The thin, pretty woman smiled at his attention until he rearranged his face into "super dickhead" and approached Shannon up the aisle. The woman's eyes followed with thinly veiled contempt as if Shannon were ruining her chances of landing him. If she only knew.

"Ms. Taylor." Roger sat beside her, and the skin on her

arms squirmed. Shannon followed his gaze to the defendant's chair where Reverend Jack Wilson reclined in the seat, eyes more curious than frightened. Three attorneys in expensive suits flanked him, haughty and smug, Rolexes glinting from their wrists. Maybe Wilson would buy them all jets if they got him off.

She turned to Roger. "What are you doing here?" she whispered.

"You've been out of the office so often lately that I've had no time to advise you on this case."

"There's no need for advice, Roger."

"Ah, but there is. You're going too hard here, and the department is concerned you have some personal vendetta that's marring your judgment."

The department? You mean you? "You're out of your mind."

Roger slapped his briefcase on the desk and withdrew a sheaf of papers. "We're charging him with reckless endangerment."

"Reckless endangerment? Roger, what the hell is—"

"Reverend Wilson is an upstanding member of the community at large and—"

"Mr. Wilson murdered his child," she hissed. "He was overheard telling a friend that night that he would take care of the kid before it ruined his family."

"I hardly think saying you're going to care for a child is evidence of intent to harm," Roger said.

"The injuries—"

"Are consistent with dropping the kid on the floor while they were playing, just as Reverend Wilson said, Ms. Taylor. He now admits he threw her into the air during a game. And he called the police right after it happened."

"Because he wanted to be able to play it off as a mistake."

"Because it was an accident."

"If it was an accident, why is he here at all?" No one with Wilson's resources would take a plea deal unless they really thought they'd be convicted.

"He has made it publicly clear that he wishes to atone for his sins, whether committed with malice or otherwise."

"And…he has a book deal already, doesn't he? About his persecution as a holy man." A misdemeanor charge and a slap on the wrist, and he would gain notoriety as a martyr. Shannon glared at Roger, and he shrugged. She looked into the courtroom behind her, avoiding the eyes that were now less solemn and more interested like they were watching *The Bachelor*. "This isn't right. We should be pushing for his conviction, for the victim's sake, for her mother's sake."

Roger set the papers on the desk and snapped his case closed.

"What'd you tell the victim's mother, Roger, to convince her not to go public fighting the decision to let his ass go? That a jury would find him not guilty? That there was no point in taking it to civil court? What?" He'd manipulated that poor woman. All in the name of less paperwork and easy wins and maybe…

Her eyes flicked once more to the Rolexes.

Roger put the case on the ground and nodded to Wilson, who raised one corner of his chicken-lipped mouth and turned to the bench. "You'd know more if you'd bothered to speak to her after the discovery phase."

Ouch. Shannon's heart rate climbed. But everything she'd needed was in the file. What more could she have gleaned from badgering a grieving mother? Evidently something. Roger's eyes were so cool, so confident, so knowing. Maybe she really was losing her touch. Getting sloppy. Then she registered the familiar twitch of his mouth, the one that always told her he thought he was winning. *Not this time, you manipulative bastard.*

She squared her shoulders as the courtroom shrank around the two of them until it seemed there was no one else in the room. Her leg muscles tingled with a repressed desire to kick him in the junk. "He offered her cash." It wasn't a question. She could feel it in the air, the tainted damp of sweaty money on moldering justice.

"Reverend Wilson has agreed to provide restitution as a part of his sentence, in an amount the family has deemed more than fair."

The woman had lost her child. There was no restitution for that. "Why are you trying to protect him?"

Roger opened his mouth to speak just as the door behind the judge's station opened, and Judge Miller entered, swiping a long black braid over her shoulder. She sat behind the bench and banged the gavel, and the courtroom hushed as everyone found their seats. Roger's leg brushed Shannon's. She scooted away, her chair squealing loud enough that the entirety of the defendant's table looked over, eyebrows raised in question, identical smirks plastered on their faces.

Her chest heated. *Fuck them all.*

Judge Miller pushed her glasses up her straight Grecian nose and studied the paperwork in front of her.

"Case number 3834022Z, Reverend Jack Wilson." Shannon watched her rattle off the numbers, the case specifics, everything for the transcription, nothing that mattered for life or death, nothing that mattered at all. None of this mattered—not her presence, not the courtroom, not the judge, certainly not the lawyers sworn to uphold the laws. This asshole had murdered his own daughter and was going to get away with it. He'd serve a few months, and then he'd be free to kill some other little girl who didn't fit into his life plans.

"Ms. Taylor?" Miller peered over her glasses at Shannon. "Again, I understand there have been some changes to the case. Is the prosecution ready to proceed?"

Shannon put her hands on the desk, preparing to push herself upright, but Roger beat her to it, almost leaping to standing beside her in a whoosh of starch and cologne that might have made her gag had she been less shocked.

"Yes, Your Honor," Roger said.

Shannon froze, staring up at him, and removed her hands from the desk, the dampness from her palms streaking the wood. Her mouth was pasty. She could leave now. She could run out of here, and it wouldn't make any difference. But maybe it would make a point to the judge. She eyed the bench as Miller said: "The charges?"

"Reckless endangerment," Roger said.

Miller's eyes narrowed, and Shannon's heart skipped a beat. The judge didn't seem to like this any more than she did, though that might have been wishful thinking. Maybe the judge would deny the plea.

"Reckless endangerment?" Miller said.

"Yes, Your Honor."

Miller met Shannon's eyes, and Shannon tried to hold back the sick sense of culpability she felt standing on this side of the table with Roger. Her ex was a leech, taking what he wanted while ignoring ethical responsibilities, ignoring anything besides making his own life easier.

Miller's mouth remained grim; the mask judges wore, the one they all had to wear. She turned to Wilson. "How do you wish to plead?"

Wilson licked his lips and glanced at Roger, then back to Miller. "No contest."

Miller's eyebrow cocked, her mouth still tense. The air in the courtroom thinned. Sweat dampened Shannon's underarms, and she tried to recall whether she had put on deodorant that morning. Had she even brought it from her house to Alex's?

"Very well," Miller said, her voice pensive. "Bail is set at five hundred thousand dollars. We'll reconvene for sentencing in two weeks after I review this case in its entirety." The gavel rang through the room, and Roger grabbed his case. Wilson stood, cuffs clanking on his wrists, but not for long, that bastard. He'd have no problem coming up with half a million dollars. He could probably just trade in his watch.

SHANNON KEPT her thoughts about Miller and Roger to herself on the way home. Petrosky was driving, face agitated, already brooding, and getting him all worked up over Roger again wouldn't do anyone any good. She wanted the killer to be Roger too, if only because she wanted it to be simple and easy and almost over. But it didn't feel right. It didn't make sense. Still, she entertained the thoughts; they were preferable to considering that these were probably her last weeks with Derry. When she thought of sitting in the house, holding Derry's hand, watching him creep slowly toward his inevitable demise, her breath quickened, and she feared she might pass out. It wasn't until Petrosky parked in front of Alex's house, and she'd gotten out of the car that she realized they'd ridden the entire way in silence.

Abby tackled Shannon at the front door.

"Holy cow, what's—" Shannon gaped as a massive gray pit bull skidded to a stop on the wood floor behind Abby. "Roxy!" Shannon kicked the door closed and knelt to greet the animal. "What are you doing here, girl?"

"Easy, Rox," Morrison called as he entered from the kitchen. Roxy put her butt on the floor, her tail thumping the wood, and licked Shannon's face.

Abby threw her arms around the dog's neck. "Mr. Morrison brought his dog, and he said that she can stay with us while he's hanging out here." The dog abandoned Shannon and turned her attention to Abby, licking her ears, her hair, her chin. Abby giggled maniacally. "Isn't she great?"

Morrison usually left the dog at Valentine's while he worked. Doggie playdates or some such thing.

Morrison knelt and scratched Roxy's ears, talking like a goofball cartoon character. "And she's so excited about it. Aren't you, girl? Who's excited? Who's an excited girl?"

Roxy licked his face and turned herself in a few excited circles, then made a beeline for Shannon and flopped to the ground on her back.

Abby laughed. "Mr. Morrison taught me karate too."

Shannon cocked an eyebrow at him, and he shrugged. "Martial arts and a dog? You've been busy." She sat on the floor to scratch Roxy's belly. "Alex was okay with this?"

Morrison opened his mouth, but Abby beat him to it. Her

grin was infectious. "Daddy said she was awesome and that he wanted to get one just like her one day."

Morrison's eyes sparkled. "Did he now?"

Abby nodded, her eyes on Roxy. "Can she come play out back again? I'll watch her." Roxy leapt up and pushed her huge head into Abby's palm, begging for love, and Abby kissed her nose.

Happy. Content. But something else in the house pulled at Shannon, tugged at a place behind her stomach until she could no longer ignore the discomfort. *Don't look at the office door. Just let Abby enjoy this.*

"You remember what to say?" Morrison asked.

"Funtime, Roxy!" Abby's face lit up with a grin, and Shannon's heart surged as her niece bounded out of the room, Roxy at her heels.

"Funtime? I'd almost forgotten about that."

Morrison shrugged. "It's a good command to let her know it's time to play and not to work."

"She still works?"

"You know, dog stuff. Sniffing shit. Chasing cats." His voice was light, friendly, but he didn't meet her eyes.

"Some job."

"Someone's got to do it." Then his smile was gone, his eyes on Derry's door. Her chest vibrated with a painful thudding. She was going to end up having a heart attack.

"Alex is with him now," Morrison said. "Been about the same today as yesterday, though he is sleeping more. The painkillers, probably." He finally pulled his gaze from Derry's room to the front door behind Shannon. "Where's Petrosky?"

"Parking." But it had been a while. They both looked at the front door. Petrosky was probably hitting a bottle he had stored under a seat. For his sake, she hoped he was just smoking a cigarette.

Morrison leaned toward her and touched her arm. "How are you, Shanny?"

Her heart raced and slowed, a speedball of emotion. "I'm...dealing. Roger was a real ass today. Switched up another set of charges last minute. Totally took over in court. I wasn't prepared for it."

"He showed up unexpected?" he asked, and he finally met her gaze, concern in his narrowed eyes.

"Yeah. Said he hadn't had time to advise me. Made a deal with the defense on the sly."

"That seems...impulsive." Morrison peered at the ceiling. "Aggressive, even. He ever done that before, in court like that?"

She shook her head.

"He ever show signs of instability before? When you were together?"

"Instability?"

"Or impulsivity. You know what I mean."

She breathed through her nose. Morrison smelled like lemon dishwashing detergent. He still had a cluster of stray bubbles on his sleeve near his elbow. "I guess. He used to buy things we didn't need. He came home with a boat once, without talking to me about it, but it wasn't like we didn't have the money."

"Oh, I remember that." He shook his head. "I can take a look at the case tomorrow. Which one was it?"

"Wilson."

"The reverend?"

"That's the one. Roger got the mother some money."

"Maybe he took a little for himself, too. You know...legal fees." He almost spit the words out; his mouth contorted in what might have been rage. Shannon's eyes widened. Roger didn't need to take cash for offering lighter charges—he had an inheritance from his family that would keep him comfortable even if he never worked again. And yet...

From the backyard, Abby's giggling drifted over them like notes on a piano, and Morrison's face molded itself back into the mask she was used to, calm and peaceful and quiet.

She pulled her eyes from him as the office door clicked. Alex emerged, wiping his cheeks on his sleeve. Alex caught Shannon's eye, and she saw her own grief mirrored there, the agonizing knowledge that time was short, a bomb ticking down to inescapable nothingness.

"He's sleeping," Alex said. "Again." He looked down the hall toward the sound of Abby's happy laughter as if confused by it.

Shannon turned as Morrison stepped past her to peer through the window beside the door. As he slid the curtain aside, a shriek of tires cut the muted din of evening. Petrosky's receding headlights bisected the street like lasers, illuminating a row of garbage cans across the street, and then disappeared around the corner.

Morrison stared after the car, his jaw tight. "Petrosky wouldn't have just left like that unless something was up."

She watched the now silent street. "I know."

Abby giggled again from the backyard, and the sound was so full of joy and hope that Shannon wished they could bottle it and keep it on hand for later this week or next month when they'd really need it. When Abby would need it. She drew her eyes from the office door and to the empty space where their garbage should have been, the missing bags of trash a needle in the back of her brain reminding her that the curb was vacant because Derry couldn't do it. Derry had always done it. She could almost see Derry and herself as children, ten and twelve, dragging bags to the curb while their mother yelled drunken obscenities from the house. Derry would stick out his tongue or pretend to gag on the stench of the kitchen trash, and they'd laugh their way back inside. He'd had the same response the night their father had left them in the driveway and taken off for good. And at Mom's funeral, he'd busied himself sticking his tongue out at her every time those around them had looked away. He was her younger brother, but a much older soul.

Morrison's phone buzzed, and he fished it out of his pocket, every muscle in his face rigid. "Hey." Pause. "Really." Not a question. Shannon watched the street as the back door slammed, and a moment later, Alex appeared through the front window, hauling the can up the drive. He set it at the curb and wiped his eyes again. She swallowed over the lump in her throat.

"Shannon."

It took her a moment to realize Morrison was touching her shoulder. She turned.

"They found Wheatley."

22

ALL NIGHT LONG—AS she added drugs, as she watched her brother die—Shannon forced her brain to the case, hoping that Wheatley's death would lead them to the killer. She couldn't bear the thought that she hadn't set Derry's mind at ease—that she might not before he...went. "I'll get him, Derry," she whispered to the darkened room.

She stroked Derry's hand. Derry snored and wheezed and dreamed feverishly, eyes rolling behind his lids, lower lip quivering every few minutes as if in pain, or maybe he was trying to cry. But each inhale seemed more shallow than the last. She held his hand tighter as if that could keep him anchored to their world.

A jostling woke her, a voice growling in her ear. "Get me some of the good shit." The voice was so hoarse that, for a moment, she wasn't sure if some sinister demon had entered the room to take Derry for good. She jolted upright in the chair, blinking sleep from her eyes.

"Jumpy, aren't you?" Then Derry's raspy laugh.

"No, just...the what?"

"The good shit. Drugs. For someone who's seen their share of junkie clients, you're not too down on the lingo." He was nearly invisible in the dim room, but his breathing was fast, his voice tight. He was hurting.

Had she missed a dose? She looked at the clock. Five after three. No, he wasn't due for ten minutes. She reached for the bottle on the nightstand and dumped a few into his palm.

"One more can't hurt, Shanny."

"It's Oxycodone. I don't—"

"I've been on it too long. The lower dose isn't doing it anymore."

"No wonder you know the junkie lingo," she said, trying to keep her voice light. She dropped another pill into his hand and grabbed the water for him.

"Totally. I'm a regular addict." He swallowed the pills and lay back on the bed with a sigh. "This sucks, Shanny."

Her eyes filled. "I know it does." *And I hate this.* "But I'm glad I can be here with you."

He squeezed her hand. "Yeah. Me too." He closed his eyes. For a while his breathing remained pressured and quick, but it evened as the drugs kicked in. And when he finally slept, she did too.

THE NEXT MORNING, she awoke with an aching neck. Derry was groaning—long and deep—but he slept, and she drew her eyes from her brother to the window. In the dawn light that filtered down through the branches of the oak tree, a lone robin scratched at the first shoots of grass. He was searching for something too.

She looked away, trying to think, trying to solve the case before Derry's time ran out. So Wheatley had information about one of Derek Lewis's buyers, someone he knew wouldn't want to get caught. Wheatley had planned to confront Lewis, so he was probably the person arguing with Derek Lewis the day he died—they'd get confirmation on that from their witness, Angela Perez. After the argument, Derek Lewis must have told the killer about Wheatley's visit, maybe even threatened to expose the killer's drug use, which is why he ended up taking a hammer to his skull.

But if it was all over avoiding reprisal for drugs, why

didn't this person kill Wheatley right away? And why try to take credit for Derek's death so long after the fact, with the envelope on her car? Saying, "Hey, look at me! I did it!" wasn't the mark of someone who would frame an innocent girl to buy their freedom. And she doubted he was just messing with their heads. No, their killer had to be someone so obsessed with himself that he simply couldn't stand the thought of another person taking credit for something he'd done. Someone like...Fine, Roger was a narcissist, self-obsessed, but Petrosky's theory about Roger was just crazy. Illogical. Roger didn't fit. Did he? Goddammit all to hell, Petrosky was getting into her head. She laid her face against Derry's bed and closed her eyes, listening to the life leak out of him one breath at a time.

Petrosky arrived at the house around eight with his his hair spiked up on one side of his head. His waxy pallor of the day before had been replaced with bright spots of pink high on his cheekbones and bags of sleeplessness under his eyes. She didn't even want to consider how her face looked. Shannon met him at the front door in sweatpants; her T-shirt rank from her overnight restlessness and fevered checking of Derry's medications. The fact that her brother was able to sleep should have been a good thing, but she knew it probably wasn't.

"Found Wheatley in an old warehouse near the river," Petrosky began as he stepped over the threshold. "Waiting on the autopsy for specifics, but it looks like he died from blunt force trauma to the head, just like Lewis." He toed the door shut behind him. "They dug a bullet out of his abdomen, probably a torture thing or to incapacitate him, because the ME says he lived for some time afterward. Severely beaten, ligature marks over two broken wrists. Some kind of chalky powder on his shoes. No weapons found as of yet."

Abused. Tortured. So Wheatley did have a secret, and

someone needed to know whom else he'd told. And if Wheatley had been killed to keep something hidden, then anyone Wheatley had talked to was in danger. So…who else was in trouble? Maybe nerdy, asthmatic, book-writing Ruskin—but Morrison said someone was already watching his place intermittently. And Petrosky had freaked him out enough that Ruskin surely would have told them if Wheatley had given up names or any other secret worth killing over. Ruskin had nothing to tell. Hopefully, the killer knew that too.

Petrosky swiped a sleeve across his face. "His hands smelled strange too. Like motor oil but sweeter, though it was hard to differentiate between that and the pile of garbage we found him in."

"Maybe he tried to use some kind of lubricant to get out of the restraints? Could have broken his wrists himself, trying to get them off."

"Maybe, but I doubt it." Petrosky coughed wetly, and they both turned as Morrison emerged from the back hallway amidst frantic yelps and the thunk of a tail hitting the wall.

"Easy, Rox."

The dog sat at Morrison's feet and stared adoringly at him, her tail beating a steady rhythm on the baseboard. Shannon looked behind the pair—no Abby, no Alex. Sleeping, still. Hopefully. Suddenly aware of the chill in the air, Shannon hugged her arms around herself.

"The medical examiner's going to call later on Wheatley," Petrosky said.

Shannon dropped her arms. "Today?"

"Maybe. If I harass him enough."

Shannon shook her head. "Give him time, look at other stuff before someone else calls and complains." As soon as she said it, she wished she could suck the words back into her mouth. Just when Petrosky had finally started looking like he didn't want to slap the shit out of Alex… Plus, they needed to do everything they could to expedite the process. They were running out of time.

Petrosky's face darkened as he glanced at the stairway. "Morrison, you've got what you need to investigate remotely from here?"

Morrison nodded and scratched Roxy behind the ears.

"Good." Petrosky turned to Shannon. "And I found Angela Perez yesterday afternoon, the babysitter who told Ashley Johnson that she saw a social worker going into Derek Lewis's apartment the day he was killed. Told her I was coming by. Might as well verify Wheatley was present at Lewis's house. Maybe Perez will even recognize Roger."

Shannon's face heated. Back to Roger again. "Petrosky, Roger doesn't have a motive. He doesn't need to take cash for pleas. He doesn't have any reason—"

"He has some extravagant spending. Some debt you probably don't know about. And he was there last night. At the river."

Roger had gone out on a police call? She wracked her brain but couldn't think of a single other time he'd done that.

"He's all over this case, probably already claimed it for when it filters over to your offices. And he doesn't have alibis for the nights in question. If we're naming him as a suspect, we'll have to do it sooner rather than later."

Her ex, a suspect. Shannon took a deep breath. "I'll go with you."

"You don't have to, Taylor. Stay here with your brother."

Her brother. All she wanted was five minutes to speak to him, but he might not even wake up while she was gone. And if he did, what would she say to him if he asked about Lucky's killer? "I need to move. I can't just sit here all day and...wait for him to...to..." The fire in her cheeks, in her chest, burned hotter than ever. "Look, I made my brother a promise. I need to keep it."

SHANNON WAS ALREADY EXHAUSTED when she and Petrosky set out for Perez's at nine o'clock, both with mugs of Morrison's coffee.

Petrosky sipped from his mug. "Who'd have thought? Fucking fungus."

Shannon watched the city roll by, the sky far too blue and optimistic, and took another bite of the chia-berry oatmeal Morrison had insisted she take with her. It tasted like sawdust. As they neared the river, traffic thinned, and the air grew damper, dejected almost, with the dusty industrial haze blurring their view of the opposite bank. Shannon wondered whether they were close to the place Wheatley's body had been found, but she didn't ask. She didn't really want to know.

They exited the car behind an apartment building ripe with the rotten stink of an overflowing dumpster. Bags and cardboard and food littered the ground outside the container. *Gross.* But at least there was someone to take it out in the first place.

Perez was already outside smoking near the back door, her curly black hair blowing behind her with every gust of breeze. Curvy. Pretty. Perez crushed the cigarette underfoot as they approached.

"Ms. Perez?" Petrosky said.

She nodded, brown eyes cautious. Shannon waited for him to yank out his badge, but instead, he extended his hand, and Perez shook it.

"Nice to meet you, ma'am."

Perez squinted at Shannon. "You're the one who got Ashley locked up."

Guilt swelled in her chest. *I am.*

"She didn't kill anybody."

"That's part of what we're trying to straighten out, Ms. Perez. Will you help us?" Petrosky's tone was soft and gentle, patient even, the same one he'd used with the nurse at the hospital. It was like he had split personalities: Dick and Not a Dick.

"Yeah, I'll help. I want to do what's right by her, you know? We were always friends."

"I know you were." Petrosky pulled out his cigarettes and

offered her one. She frowned at the one on the ground, looked back up at Petrosky, and took a cigarette from the pack.

He lit her smoke and pocketed the pack and the lighter. "Tell me about who you saw at Ashley's house. The day Lewis died."

"Well, it was earlier in the day, you know, because I had just gotten back from school."

"Where do you go to school?"

Why did that matter? He probably intended to check her class schedule to verify the time.

"Over at the community college. I was going to transfer to Wayne State in the fall with Ashley, but—" She looked down. "I've been doing well, but it's real hard. So many classes and tests, and I don't remember learning half this stuff in high school."

She was offering them irrelevant information they hadn't asked about, like witnesses on the stand trying to pad the lies they were about to tell you. Shannon watched Perez's eyes, her hands, her posture as she hit the cigarette, but nothing else wavered. Only her words seemed suspect.

"Tell me about that day," Petrosky said.

"Ashley dropped Diamond off, so she could go to that interview. We played inside for a bit, then I took Diamond up to the roof, so I could have a cigarette. Needed to keep the smoke away from her, or Ashley would have killed me." Her eyes widened. "No, I mean, not really *killed* me, but she didn't want anyone smoking around her baby." She grimaced at the cigarette, puffed again. "Really wish I could quit."

"What time was that?"

"Maybe seven? Eight?"

Eight. After Derek's argument, but before his death. Perez hadn't seen the person who had fought with Derek. She'd seen the killer.

Petrosky leaned against the wall of the building, feigning mellow nonchalance. But she could tell by the twitch in his lip, the subtle tension in his shoulders, that he'd made the connection too.

"So, you were on the roof when you saw someone approach the building?"

"Not the building. Derek was standing outside near the curb, and then this car pulled up, and the social worker got out and walked right up to him. They looked kinda tense like they didn't like each other, but Derek took him inside. I remember thinking that he didn't seem the type who was usually in with Derek."

"He didn't look like a druggie."

She bit her lip. "Yeah. He was in a suit, I think."

A suit? That didn't sound like Wheatley or any other social worker, certainly not at that hour. Shannon scanned the street. A few cars in various states of disrepair lined the abandoned road. Not another soul was out. It was as though the neighborhood had been deserted in the wake of some terrible tragedy.

"What made you think he was a social worker, Ms. Perez?"

"Derek said he was. I had to go to work, and Ashley still wasn't home, so I…dropped Diamond off." She lowered her eyes. "I didn't think he'd hurt her. I mean…he still used. Ashley denied that, but I could see it on his face, you know? But I…"

"It's not your fault, and we can't do anything about that now, okay?"

Perez's jaw dropped. She averted her eyes.

If only guilt could be assuaged with a few words.

Petrosky pulled a file folder from under his arm but didn't extend it to Perez. "So, you went to drop Diamond off…"

"Yeah, and I asked him who that guy was because I knew Ashley'd want to know."

"And Derek knew who you were talking about? Just volunteered this information?"

"Well, I asked him if he had a social worker up earlier, and he said yeah. Though he might have answered just so I'd drop it and leave."

Shannon watched Perez's face, the way the girl bit her lip. How would Perez have known to ask if the visitor was a worker?

"I'm still not sure why you'd ask if the guy was a social worker," Petrosky said, reading her mind. "It's a pretty good guess out of nowhere."

"Ashley was always worried about it, you know? Said Derek's mom kept calling, that she thought she'd lose Diamond. So I always kept a lookout for stuff like that, even though she was doing all the right things. Especially since Derek *wasn't* doing the right things—still sold drugs, didn't want to get a job."

Petrosky's brows furrowed. "Tell me about the guy you saw. What can you remember about his physical appearance?"

"I mean, I didn't get a great look at him because I was above them, and it was kinda dark. And he had on a hat, so I couldn't see his face or his hair or anything."

A hat with a suit? He'd gone incognito on purpose, but had he planned to kill Derek that night? Or was he just making sure he wouldn't be recognized? *Who the hell is this guy?*

"Any idea how tall?"

Perez examined the sky. Thinking up a lie or just thinking?

"Not sure on height," Perez said. "I only caught them together for a second, and perspective can make everything seem different, you know? Smaller, bigger. Sometimes you don't even see things that are right there."

Ain't that the truth.

"You studying psychology in school, Ms. Perez?"

"Yeah. How did you know?"

Petrosky opened the file folder and handed her the first picture, a shot of Benjamin Wheatley. "Is this the guy you saw that day with Derek?"

She glanced at it. "No. But I've seen him in the building before."

"When?"

"Not sure, I just know he looks familiar. Probably a few weeks before all…this."

According to his files, Wheatley hadn't had any families in Johnson's building for a good two months before the killing. If Wheatley had been there, he'd been watching for someone, like a private eye. Too bad Petrosky hadn't found any photos or other documentation at Wheatley's place. Unauthorized search or no, anything could be useful right about now. Maybe they should go back, crawl through the window, and…Holy shit. She was turning into Petrosky.

Petrosky exchanged Wheatley's picture for a photo of Roger; one Shannon had taken on their honeymoon in France. He was in a rare T-shirt instead of his usual button-down, but the same brilliant smile was aimed right at her. Shannon's heart raced.

"Ms. Perez, look closely." So intense. *Just because you want it to be Roger doesn't mean it is, Petrosky.*

Perez shook her head again. "I couldn't really see his face from four stories up, but…this guy doesn't seem right. I'm not real sure why. Just a gut feeling."

Shannon realized she was holding her breath and released it slowly.

"Anything else you recall about the person in question, Ms. Perez?" Petrosky asked.

Perez shook her head.

Shit. They were so close. They just needed one good lead. One good—

"You said you noticed the car first?"

The car. Why didn't she think of that? Maybe she really did need to take a vacation, though she'd never tell Roger that he was right. Her body suddenly felt heavy as if the iron in her blood had thickened and was slowly pulling her down toward the earth.

"Yeah, I hadn't seen it before." She broke eye contact, and Shannon's hackles rose. *Liar.*

"What did it look like?"

Pause. "Black, I think. Or dark blue."

"What kind of car was it?"

"I'm not... I'm bad at cars, and I wasn't really paying attention." Perez studied the ground. "I don't want any trouble."

Perez knew something, that much was clear. Maybe it was why she had moved—afraid of retribution for knowing more than she was supposed to. She should be scared after what had happened to Wheatley.

"Ms. Perez...Angela. I'm here to help. To find Derek Lewis's killer. To help you if you need helping."

Perez raised her eyes to his, but the suspicion remained.

"Please, Angela. Ashley is your best friend, right? You can save her, and I can help you, but I've got to know what you saw."

Perez leaned back against the wall and looked around the lot, finally swinging her eyes back to Petrosky. "I think it was...well..." She sighed. "A cop car. I remember being surprised that a social worker would drive one, but I figured they do work with the police a lot."

Shannon froze. Police cars were pretty recognizable—not like you could mistake the lights on top.

"You *think* it was a cop car?" Petrosky asked.

"Well, the lights were gone off the top, but it had those big antennae things off the back. And one of those huge spotlights over the side-view mirror."

An unmarked? No social worker drove one of those. Neither did Roger. Petrosky's jaw worked overtime. He looked at Shannon, and her stomach twisted.

Even if Wheatley had been arguing with Derek earlier, his green car could never be mistaken for what Perez saw. Neither could Roger's Mercedes.

The killer was one of them.

Their killer was a cop.

23

Roger's phone slammed into the cradle as Shannon scuttled past his office. He was literally breathing down her neck before she even got her office door unlocked.

"Where have you been, Shannon?"

"Working." *On a case I'm supposed to be ignoring. And you were wrong about there being no connection, Roger.* Her keys shook and scraped against the lock but didn't slide home. *We were both wrong. Maybe about everything.*

"Working on what?"

She steadfastly refused to face him, just focused on the doorknob, and listened to the metal clank of keys against the lock. "I was out doing my job. Like it's any of your concern."

"I just got off the phone with your brother."

The latch popped, and relief flooded through her, but it was short-lived, replaced with anger before she'd even gotten the knob turned. The thud of Roger's shoes on the carpet followed her inside. She walked around to her chair and slammed her briefcase between them on the desk. "Why would you be calling Jerry?"

"I was—"

She put her hand up. "I don't even care why. Don't call my brother, Roger."

"Well, it isn't like he can answer the phone himself, Shannon."

So he was mad she'd blown him off and was trying to upset her. He wanted her to lose her shit, just like he had during their marriage, wanted to push her until she cracked in front of their families, their friends, their colleagues. He had wanted to make her look crazy. But why today? So he could fire her? *No way, Roger.* She would not give him the satisfaction.

Shannon leaned toward him. The bandage on his nose was bright against the bruising under his eyes. She hoped it hurt like hell. "What do you want, Roger?" She kept her voice low and deliberate. *Give me shit, Roger, you'll get it back.*

Roger stared at her, his lip twitching.

"You here to make me sorry like you promised the other night? Threatening your ex-wife is rather unbecoming of a lead prosecutor."

His shoulders relaxed first, then his chest, then his mouth, a choreographed transformation she had seen time and time again at dinner parties when someone said something he didn't like. During their arguments when he was trying to convince her that "No really, you're crazy, I never touched her." Then later at the divorce proceedings. From asshole to martyr in three seconds flat. Good time to pull it out, now that he saw she wasn't going to give him what he wanted. *Manipulative prick.*

He sat in the chair across from her, smug smile intact, hands loose on the armrests like he hadn't a care in the world. "I'm sorry about that, Shannon. I was just angry; you know that. And I've been worried about you."

Bullshit. She sank into the chair with enough force that it shuddered backward on its wheels. She hauled herself up to the desk and glared at him. "Nothing for you to be worried about."

"You have crazy people at your brother's house, Shanny. With your niece. That should concern you."

She opened her briefcase, a barrier between herself and

Roger's fake concern, and took her time pulling out her files. When she moved the case aside, his eyes bored into her skull. *Don't let him see you sweat, Shannon. That's what he wants.* "I told you not to call me that, Roger. And they aren't crazy."

"Are you kidding?" Roger aimed a finger at his nose, and Shannon stifled a smirk. "He's unstable. Both of them are."

"I feel safer when they're around." She folded her hands over the files on the desktop and said nothing else. He'd see her nonresponse as defiant. Maybe she was being defiant—and it was about damn time.

He crossed his arms. "Well, I don't feel better about your safety when they're around. About Abby's safety."

"You don't get to make that call."

"So I don't." He leveled his gaze at her. "But one day you'll see, Shannon."

Again, the threat, and a cliché one at that. "You're not the fucking Godfather, Roger," she said.

A smile touched the corner of his lip. "Even at a time like this, you remember my favorite movie."

The only thing she remembered about that movie was a severed horse's head on someone's pillow. Kinda like… Lucky. She shook it off.

He leaned toward her desk, close enough that she could hear the wet sucking sound of air through his mangled nose. "What are you working on?"

"Bartleby."

"How's it going?"

"Why?"

"I'm the head prosecutor, remember? Just trying to stay abreast of your cases, since you've been out of the office so often lately." His tone was condescending and quiet like she was an idiot. "You sure you don't want to take leave? I'll approve it to start now before Jerry's officially gone."

Gone. He's fucking with me. She cleared her throat, pulled Bartleby's folder from the stack, and flipped it open, hoping Roger couldn't see the way her hands trembled. "Bartleby is being charged with felony child endangerment, and his ex-wife is poised to get full custody of all of their children. You have an issue with that?"

"Hey, I'm all about punishing the guilty. It's our job."

It was her job, but not his. Not anymore. Her anxiety bubbled into a cauldron of fury as she watched him shrug, superior and self-satisfied. "Ike Lambert was guilty. Reverend Wilson was too. But Bartleby's poor, so who cares, right?"

Roger leaned back in the chair and laced his fingers over his knee. "They were charged," he said with the careful patience of one speaking to a tantrumming child.

"Not with what they should have been, and you know it. Even Judge Miller seemed surprised at Wilson's arraignment. You saw how she looked at you."

The arrogant glitter in his eye sharpened. "Enough about me, Shanny. Let's talk about what you've been doing lately. Spending a lot of time with your new boyfriend?"

"He isn't my boyfriend, Roger."

"Not what I heard, Shannon. He's not who you think he is."

"Neither were you."

Fire flashed in Roger's eyes but disappeared into a sneer.

She opened the folder on her desk. "Why exactly are you here, Roger?"

"I'll be prosecuting the Wheatley case once it shows up at this office."

Just like Petrosky had warned. She'd love to think Roger was trying to take charge out of concern for her wellbeing, but she didn't believe that he cared about her or about Abby or Alex or Derry, not for one second. "We'll have to look at Johnson too, and that one's mine," she said. "You know they're related, Roger."

"I talked to the chief. Someone other than your boyfriend has been assigned to both cases, so you don't need to worry about them anymore. You need to focus on your own work, the cases that have been specifically assigned to you. We can't run an office with people prosecuting whoever the hell they want."

And once word got out that Lewis's killer might be a cop, Internal Affairs would step in and she and Morrison and Petrosky would be even more out of the loop than they were now. They'd wait to open that box of bullshit until they had something. Until she knew who she needed to protect her family from.

"I'm focusing on my other cases, Roger. Haven't missed a single court date."

"Doing a lot more interviews by phone, also, I see."

"People come in to sign their statements when necessary."

"Didn't I tell you pleas are less work?" Roger sat straighter, but he kept his ankle crossed over one knee. "Spend more time with your brother, Ms. Taylor. Spend some time with Abby too. She needs you now more than ever." Roger's face was impassive, but Shannon's lungs clamped shut. She hated the way Abby's name rolled off his tongue. As if he cared about Abby. He'd scowled at her stretch marks every time she disrobed and had played with Abby a grand total of three times while they were dating. Probably less than that once they were married. Each time, Abby had cried.

Roger released his hands and stood. "I'll be checking on you tomorrow morning, Ms. Taylor. Make sure you're here before nine."

He didn't care about her workload or her family. He wanted to scare her off, just like whoever had left Lucky's severed head on her windshield. Maybe. Then again, he'd always hated cats. Her chest lightened at the thought of watching Roger led away in handcuffs, smirk permanently erased.

PETROSKY KEPT his eyes on the road on the way to the gym, popping antacid after antacid. He'd convinced Shannon to let him drive her. Again. She'd told him she didn't need a babysitter. He didn't agree, but she was too overwhelmed with life and death and work and men to argue the point. Besides, he was probably already pissed that the chief had pulled him off the Wheatley case after Roger's phone call.

She stared out the side window, clutching the door handle, hoping they wouldn't have to talk about it. She didn't need talk—she needed to punch something. Hopefully, this time, she'd avoid hitting Morrison.

Shannon warmed at the thought of him, at the memory of beating his ass and taking him home to...make up for it. Her stomach sank. Sleeping with him had been a mistake—an incredible, beautiful, amazing mistake, but a mistake nonetheless. And even after all that, he was there for her and she for him. They were friends, best friends. Always? *Always is a long time.* But they could pull it off. It'd just be a little... awkward for a while.

Petrosky pulled up in front of the converted warehouse, and she opened the car door before he'd fully stopped. The woman who passed out last time was there already, working the rings, her blond curls hidden beneath a bandana and a look of such grim determination on her face that she might as well have had "I've got this" tattooed across her forehead. Kimball was helping her, hoisting her up as she gritted her teeth and shook. He nodded, and she dropped. There was no way she'd make it through class if Kimball was giving her a private lesson now.

Shannon changed, then took a few minutes to stretch out her arms and legs, neck muscles singing with tension all the way up and around to her forehead when she tried to rotate her shoulders. She exhaled violently enough that Kimball turned her way as she strode past him to grab a crate. The blonde was setting up her own crate near the middle of the room.

"You all right?" Kimball asked Shannon.

"Long day."

"I hear that." But his face looked more alert than ever, eyes bright, cheeks pink. He left her and made his way around the room, saying hello to people who looked appropriately anxious about the evening's workout. One man—all burl and muscle—grimaced as Kimball mimed an exercise. Another furrowed his brows as Kimball pointed out weights. When he reached the blonde again, he touched her lower back, and she smiled at him in a way that was more than friendly. Kimball gave it right back to her and winked, then nodded to the bars in the back.

Fucking cheater. No wonder he and Roger got along so well.

Shannon carried her crate to the middle of the room and set it up near the one belonging to Kimball's new squeeze, trying not to think about his wife, Amanda. Trying not to watch them flirt, as if that would make it better. The punching bag in the back corner swung back and forth, back and forth. She looked away from that too. The bag felt far too intimate now, but it'd pass—a week or two, and she'd be over there attacking it again without feeling guilty. The rings swung of their own accord as if in a nonexistent breeze, or maybe it was the tumultuous energy in the air around her disrupting their rest.

She looked away and stared straight ahead at the gymnast bars, squinting at the metal glistening in the fluorescents. Toe touches. She'd need a little extra workout tonight. But... something was different. It took her a moment to realize what it was, but finally it clicked that the thick mats beneath the bars had been removed, leaving the concrete bare. Maybe Kimball had screwed his girlfriend at the gym and made a mess. *Gross.* Now she was starting to sound like Derry. But way less hilarious.

Someone touched her shoulder, and she jumped as Morrison nudged his crate into place beside hers. "Whoa, Shanny, you okay?" His brows were furrowed, but his forehead relaxed when she nodded.

"Yeah, just...tired, maybe. Glad you made it. Petrosky said you'd be here, but I wondered when I didn't see you."

"You know he wouldn't have left you here alone."

"I'm not alone."

"You know what I mean. He likes being needed. And if you got hurt, neither of us would forgive ourselves." He leaned close enough that she could feel his breath on her ear, and electricity shimmered from her neck down to her toes. "I walked around the warehouse, just checking it out," he said. "No sign of anything weird, and the new lights really do make a difference in the lot." He straightened and positioned himself in front of his crate, pulling an arm across himself to stretch.

"How's everything at the house?" Shannon bent over to fiddle with her already tied shoe, afraid of what she'd see in Morrison's eyes. She was asking how fast her brother was dying, wasn't she? Then there were Roger's words: *Abby needs you now more than ever.* Guilt writhed in her belly. "And how's Abby?"

"The house is fine, no changes. Derry's just tired. Abby seems okay—Roxy's her new favorite thing."

She stood and forced herself to look at Morrison. "Thanks for bringing her over."

"Alex said they were going to get one. I said they could keep her."

"What? You did?" He'd had that dog for years. She belonged with him. "Why would you do that?"

He was watching the rings, jaw tight. "They need her more than I do. And maybe you'll sleep better, knowing that she's there with them. She wouldn't let anyone hurt your family." Morrison bent at the waist and stretched his hamstrings then fingered his own tied laces. Avoiding her eyes.

He was replacing himself. Making his presence unnecessary. So, he could...leave them. *Leave me.* Shit, what was she thinking? They weren't even together. But her chest felt too small.

"I can't let you do this."

"It's done," he said, head still at his knees.

Roxy had gone everywhere with him: jogging, hiking,

even vacation. That dog was family. Her lip quivered, and the tightness around her ribs intensified so that it felt like someone was trying to snap her in two. Morrison loved Roxy. *But he loves me more.* And she couldn't for the life of her figure out a way to make the pain ease, not for any of them.

Down in front, the blonde walked to the bars with Kimball. Shannon looked at the clock. Two minutes until class. *I need to get it together.* But her eyes stung, and the longer she watched Curt's bent form, the more she felt compelled to wrap her arms around him, and that thought was more terrifying than anything else because she knew she'd never come back from it. After that, she'd be his. Right now, she couldn't even handle being hers.

The blond woman ran her hands over the chalk ball next to the bars and slapped her palms together, making a puff of dust. Shannon watched the particles fall to the concrete floor... The bare concrete floor, lighter than the area around it, but it wasn't from spilled chalk. It wasn't...dusty. The floor was always dusty. She squinted. Bleached?

Kimball's hand lingered on the woman's hip as he half lifted her to the bar. She swung her legs up, touched her toes to the bar, and Kimball smiled at her, though she was clearly preoccupied. What the hell was he doing? Class was already late getting started. Kimball touched the lower bar, frowned at his fingers and touched them to the chalk, probably to avoid staining her fancy workout gear with the oily residue from the stuff they used to clean the equipment.

Her heart raced. The oil. They cleaned the bars with... what? Some industrial cleaner—she'd seen Morrison do it before. And every week they wiped them with...WD-40.

He patted the blonde on the shoulder, glanced at the front door, and made another remark. She laughed again and dropped to the concrete floor. Still smiling at him.

Charismatic. Weren't psychos always charismatic? Or was that just narcissists? Roger had charisma—it was how he'd gotten her to marry him. Shannon watched them walk toward her, or maybe it was toward the dumbbells that

Kimball had been hitting so hard lately. Kimball's obsession with his body surely bordered on narcissism, didn't it? But then, everyone at this gym had a little of that. Was his more severe, more noteworthy? More violent? Narcissists got angry, sometimes inexplicably so, but—maybe that was the type of killer that couldn't handle anyone else taking credit for their crimes.

Kimball looked at the door then walked toward the center of the room, near where Shannon stood. Morrison nodded to him.

Shannon licked her parched lips. Had the mats been gone the last time she was here? She hadn't noticed. She'd been too busy socking Morrison in the gut. "What happened to the mats under the bars, Kimball?" *He'll say he doesn't know. That they were stolen or damaged.*

"Someone spilled something on them." He shrugged. "Good opportunity to get a few new ones anyway. Those ones had too much potential for slippage, so I ordered a few with better traction. Should be here by next week." He winked at her. Flirty? No. *Manipulative.* Like Roger.

She looked back at the bar, picturing Wheatley, hanging from broken wrists, his essence shimmering from a bullet wound in his gut. Gore slithering onto the mats. Her blood ran cold.

Kimball squinted at her, and her heart pounded against her rib cage. "Shannon, you okay?"

She could hear Morrison's sneakered footsteps approaching from the side, but she didn't look at him. She was frozen, rooted to the floor. "I'm just a little... I don't feel well."

Kimball walked over to her and every muscle in her body tensed, preparing to flee. "Take a breather before class, okay? I don't want our star prosecutor suing me because she passed out and hit her head." He patted her on the shoulder, and her skin crawled.

Had Kimball known they were looking at Wheatley? He worked for the chief of police, so he'd have access to the case files. And even if there hadn't been any paperwork mentioning the social worker, Amanda might have mentioned Wheatley in passing to her husband—perhaps a snarky remark from Wheatley had made Kimball suspicious without Amanda even realizing it.

She needed to call Petrosky. He could drive over with Luminol, and they could show that there had been blood under the bars. Then they could arrest Kimball. Then she could go home and wait for Derry to wake up, so she could tell him that everything was going to be okay from now on, that he could rest easy. That he could go, and Abby would be safe.

Kimball tossed her a towel, and she jumped—almost fell.

"Hey, Kimball?" Her voice was shaking, but she didn't even try to control it. "I need to sit for a second, but I don't want to miss tonight's workout. Would you mind if I stayed a little later? Maybe I can do some work after class instead?"

"Man, even sick, you're brutal." He looked at the door then grinned at her, and Shannon's throat clamped shut. "But look, if you aren't feeling well, you need to go home. It's a liability."

"I'm fine. It's just stress, and I didn't eat enough. I'm going to grab a snack and come right back."

Kimball squinted at her, sighed, and glanced at the open warehouse door again. Ready to run? Did he know she'd figured him out?

She finally met Morrison's eyes. His face was impassive, but she could see the subtle twitch of his nostrils. He knew something was very wrong. *Don't ask me what it is, not in front of Kimball.*

"Sounds good. But Shannon, seriously, I don't want you to—" Kimball turned to the warehouse door.

She heard the tires then, shrieking through the warehouse and echoing off the walls. In the lot, someone yelled.

Shannon stared toward the entrance as three officers rushed inside, guns holstered but prominent. She didn't recognize any of them—had to be Internal Affairs. But they shot looks of contrition at Kimball, which meant they knew about him. Petrosky knew. It was over. *We got him, Derry.* Shannon's heart soared.

But why didn't Kimball look more...shocked? She backed away from Kimball as he took another step toward the officers. The sweat on her back froze. They weren't looking at Kimball. They were looking at—

"Detective Curtis Morrison. You need to come with us."

Her jaw dropped. She didn't understand.

One officer strode forward more quickly, shoulders tight, eyes narrowed, watching as if he expected Morrison to make a break for the door. Morrison didn't move, just stood. The others inched closer, their hands on their weapons, waiting for a reason to use them. "Hands behind your head!" one of the inchers called. Morrison didn't move, didn't comply. One officer glanced at Kimball and almost smirked. Shannon hated the guy instantly, but her hatred was tempered with confusion. Did she need to put her hands behind her head? After all, if they were taking Morrison, they'd want her too, right? But no, that didn't make sense: investigating a case you weren't assigned to wasn't a crime. Her head felt like it was stuffed with cotton, fuzzy and dense.

The officer drew his eyes from Kimball back to Morrison's stiff profile and pulled his weapon. "On the ground!"

Morrison put his hands behind his head but did not drop. Then officers seemed to be everywhere, only three, but their energy was fierce, hungry, like a pack of wolves circling them, ready to attack. Morrison dropped to his knees beside her and lay on the floor face down. Her stomach heaved.

She stared at Morrison's back, still not understanding. Did she need to lie down too? Then, through the front door, she saw him: Roger, standing in the lot behind the cars with another officer, peering into the warehouse. *He* had done this. And he'd come to watch the carnage.

Behind her, someone was talking about arrest, and then she was being pulled away to the clinking sound of metal on metal, but the cuffs weren't on her, they were on Morrison.

They were doing it wrong, but no one would care, no one would listen because whatever Roger had convinced them of, he had done a thorough job. He had manipulated them all.

Morrison was still belly-down on the mat, hands cuffed behind him. She met his eyes for an instant—saw fear but not surprise—before she was dragged outside to the parking lot by one of the officers.

"Get the hell off me," she said and twisted from the man's grasp.

He went for her arm again, and she tensed, ready to read him his rights, or maybe to sock him in the jaw, but then Roger's voice sounded from across the lot: "Not her. She's good." The officer put both his hands up, stepped away from Shannon, and headed for the warehouse.

She met Roger in front of the cars. "What the hell is going on, Roger? You know he would have come with you peacefully if you had questions for him."

"I told you he was dangerous, Shannon, but I had no idea how dangerous." He shook his head. "You really know how to pick them."

"I picked you, dumbass."

His smugness tightened into anger. "We have more than questions."

But they didn't have proof. Roger was wrong, just like he was wrong about everything else. But Roger could be incredibly convincing when he wanted to be, and the guys who didn't know Morrison...

Her blood boiled. "You told them he'd resist, didn't you?"

"You never know, Shanny."

She ignored the nickname and his idiotic grin. "It was Kimball"—Roger raised an eyebrow and shook his head—" the mats, underneath the bars, Roger. They're missing. And Wheatley had oil on his hands, just like the stuff they use to clean the equipment."

Roger's jaw dropped, and he looked past her, crooking a finger at an officer stationed by the warehouse door. "Kimball has an alibi," he said without meeting her gaze.

Her heartbeat thundered in her ears. "Maybe someone's covering for him, or…" Maybe Roger was covering for him. No wonder Kimball had been staring at the door all night—he'd known they were coming.

"He was at a fundraising banquet with the chief of police the night we suspect Wheatley was killed. I'll bet he's got alibis for the other days too. The beauty of family." He absentmindedly touched his bare ring finger.

Beauty? *Right*. As if keeping someone's lying ass out of jail was clearly the only reason to have a family. Not that Roger was capable of understanding that.

"Morrison has been at my brother's."

The officer Roger had summoned appeared at his side, and Roger whispered something in his ear. The cop took off across the lot. Shannon watched his retreat until Roger spoke again.

"I called your brother's, Shannon. And you know what Alex told me? That he's been having trouble sleeping and has been taking Ativan. That Jerry, the only one sleeping in the room next to Morrison's spot on the couch, is so full of morphine you could run a truck through there without waking him. That Abby sleeps like the dead. That he occasionally heard the door open and close because Morrison routinely leaves the house to pace around outside."

That's why Roger had called her brother's house this morning while she was talking to Perez. Not to check up on her—to fuck Morrison over. He'd known this whole time. Rage burned Shannon's face and spread through her chest and down into her already clenched fists. Roger had finally gone too far.

Across the lot, Kimball's face turned red then blue then red in the flashing police lights. "Did Kimball know you were investigating Morrison?" But if Roger knew, if they'd called in Internal Affairs, Kimball had to know too.

"So what if he did?" Roger said. "It doesn't matter. Your boyfriend has a very big problem."

"You're wrong, Roger. You'll regret this."

"Now who's making threats, Ms. Taylor?" Roger puffed out his chest and turned to walk away.

Shannon grabbed his arm. "What you're saying…it's impossible. I was with Morrison the night someone trashed my car."

"You have no evidence that your car is related to this case. None."

"We have evidence that Wheatley was investigating something he shouldn't have been."

"Maybe he found some nasty surprises about your boyfriend."

"Roger, listen to me! Someone else was there the day Derek Lewis died. A cop."

"And now we've got a cop in custody. How convenient."

"Morrison doesn't drive an unmarked. It was someone else, someone who had—"

"Morrison could easily get access to an unmarked if he needed one. So could most everyone in the precinct. They have a bunch just sitting in the lot to take out anytime someone has a vehicle in the shop. All you need to do is sign it out. You could probably even forget to put your name down."

"Sign it out? Where?"

"The chief's office, I'm guessing."

The chief's office. Where Kimball worked.

Roger was grinning, and she wanted to smash her fist into his nose. Or maybe his balls. *Just give me a reason, dickhead.*

"And anyway," he sneered, "why wasn't this alleged unmarked brought up at trial?"

"The girl who saw it didn't recognize what she'd seen." She needed to go back to Angela Perez's apartment. They'd already looked for cameras, other witnesses, but—nothing. Maybe she'd go back to Ruskin's too. "We're getting there, Roger, just—"

Roger straightened his tie. "You're welcome to go home,

Ms. Taylor." Arrogant. Incredulous. "If we have any questions for you, we'll call."

Either Roger didn't believe her about the unmarked, or he didn't give a shit. Probably the latter—he wasn't going to let Morrison go without a fight whether he was guilty or not. *Not.* Definitely not. She stood in the middle of the lot, watching Roger walk to his car. If only it were legal to run him over.

Shannon jerked around when movement at the entrance of the warehouse caught her eye. *Morrison.* Two officers held either elbow, one of the cops the dickhead who'd tried to manhandle her earlier. He avoided her glare. Morrison's face was impassive, eyes tense and glassy, as they walked him to the squad car.

An officer, with a solemn mouth and eyes the color of Roxy's fur, approached her. "Do you have things inside?"

"What?"

He nodded gently in Morrison's direction. "He was worried about you, wanted me to give you his keys, but we're impounding his car. Do you have someone you can call?"

"Who was worried?"

"Mor—uh, the suspect."

She met his eyes.

"He's a nice guy. Helped me out once." His shoulders slumped. "Just...where's your stuff? I'll get it for you."

"Next to the bathroom. Black gym bag."

"That it?"

"Yeah."

"Okay."

Shannon turned back to the squad car. The back door was open now, and Morrison's eyes flicked around the lot, his head jerking this way and that. The officer at Morrison's left shoulder tensed and tightened his grip. Then Morrison's eyes found Shannon, and he stood there a moment, alternating blue and red in the lights of the squad cars. She held his gaze until he ducked into the car and disappeared.

When the taillights receded from sight, she walked to the corner of the lot behind the trees and vomited into the brush.

24

Petrosky was out of the car and at her side before she had a chance to approach him. "Where the fuck is he?" His jowly face was hard, shoulders tight with rage.

"Gone. I assume they took him to the precinct."

"What about your fuckweasel of an ex-husband?"

"Gone, Petrosky, they're all gone. Just some crime scene techs—"

"What've they got on him?"

"They..." She had no idea. Roger had twisted it and turned it and avoided telling her jack shit. And she'd fallen for it. But they had *something*, or there was no way they could have arrested him. "I don't know."

Petrosky ran a hand over his flaming cheeks. "Fuck."

"I know." She touched his arm, and his bicep was rigid as stone. He didn't seem to notice her hand, just stared at the lot, at the warehouse.

"There's nothing to do here, Petrosky," she said gently, though all she wanted to do was scream. "And I'm sure the guys at the door have specific instructions not to let you through."

"Like hell they—"

"You can't help Morrison if you're in jail too. And you sure as hell can't help me. Or Abby."

Petrosky glanced back at the car, and she followed his gaze. Abby's nose was smashed against the back window, her eyes wide and shining under Kimball's brand-new floodlights. Roxy was licking the window beside her head. "You brought Abby?"

"I brought everyone"—*except Derry*— "because we have a murderer running around who seems to have it in for you, and no one's looking out for your family anymore because they're too busy fucking with the wrong guy. And since I can't be in two places at once..." He turned to her. "You get sick?"

She looked at her shirt, at the wet stain between her breasts. "A little."

"California says peppermint tea works. You have that at home, or should we stop and get some?"

She gaped at him.

"Let's go."

She followed him to the car on legs that felt like they belonged to somebody else.

In the backseat, Abby threw her arms around Shannon, either oblivious to the smell of puke or blessedly detached. Roxy licked her face over Abby's shoulder. "Aunt Shanny! Are you okay? Eddie said you were at the gym and that you were okay, but I was super scared because we had to go so fast and everything."

Eddie? Shannon squeezed her eyes closed to avoid dog saliva in the eyeball and hugged Abby to her, careful her niece's face wasn't being smashed into the vomit on her shirt.

"Roxy, chill," Alex said. Roxy stopped slobbering all over the place and lay on the backseat. Shannon peered at Alex from beneath slimy lids. "Thanks."

He reached over the seat and squeezed her shoulder in that familiar way he'd always done when they were kids. *Everything's okay, Shanny. Friends to the end.* She had never been so grateful for his presence as she was now when she otherwise felt so painfully alone.

ALEX AND ABBY and Roxy settled into what used to be Derry and Alex's room but was now only Alex's. Shannon crept upstairs to the spare, leaving Petrosky on the downstairs couch. Sweat and salt plastered her clothes to her back despite the cool night, and she could still taste the putrid remnants of vomit on her tongue even after she'd brushed her teeth.

And then there was her brain. Images of Morrison's eyes seared through her consciousness every time she let her guard down. His look as they pushed him into the police car —helpless, hopeless. Afraid. Then the eyes belonged to Roger, smiling at her on their honeymoon, deadly angry when she disagreed with him—or full of grim satisfaction like in the parking lot of the CrossFit gym. Then Kimball's eyes, crinkling at the corners as he tried to convince her that he was going to get his daughter, but really he was creeping down to the riverbank with Wheatley's body, his wife yelling "Our daughter doesn't do much dance anymore! My husband just likes to fuck other women!" Then Morrison was there again, eyes calm and blue as ever as he slapped Kimball a high five over Wheatley's corpse. When Morrison began dismembering Wheatley and tossing his body parts into the trunk of a car like enormous bloody branches, she jerked to sitting, soaked in sweat.

Giving up on rest, she left the bed and slunk downstairs past where Petrosky was snoring lightly on the couch and let herself into the office. The heavy wheeze of Derry's breathing croaked through air that reeked of piss and decay. The drainage bag attached to the side of the bed was too dark to be healthy urine, obvious even by the muted light filtering in from outside. She sat in the chair beside the bed and leaned her face against the comforter near his hip, grateful it was dark enough that the yellow of his skin at least could be written off as shadow.

"I don't know what to do, Derry," she whispered.

He didn't stir. He hadn't stirred all day. Had they already spoken their last words? Was it possible that things could go just that quick? If she'd missed her chance... She slipped her hand into his, and it was like touching chicken wrapped in deli paper from the fridge: dry and cold and lifeless.

She'd thought she'd gotten it all figured out. But she hadn't. Now...was she wrong now? About everything? About Morrison? She had definitely been wrong about Roger. But Derry hadn't been wrong—and he had always loved Morrison. That thought lit the tiniest spark of hope in her chest, though any flames were stifled by grief.

She squeezed Derry's hand, gingerly. "You knew from the beginning, Derry. You knew Roger was an asshole. You begged me not to marry him. And he might be even worse than you thought." Her brother didn't respond, but his presence bade her to keep going, to keep talking, as if his shallow breath might suddenly whisper the answer she needed. "Or maybe it's Kimball... I think he lied about taking his daughter to dance, but I just... I don't know. I feel like I don't know anything anymore."

Even about Curt...Morrison. Maybe he was just like Roger, manipulative and conniving, sweet until he got what he wanted, concealing the dark parts of himself until it was too late. But she couldn't put that into words, not even here with Derry. She didn't want to be mistaken about Morrison. Tears slid over her cheeks and onto the bed. "I need your help, Derry. I'm failing."

Derry's breath gurgled through the room, but he did not respond. Not that she expected him to. When had she lost hope? She watched her thumb stroking his fingers, but she couldn't feel him, only the cold. "I'll find this guy, Derry. If they're wrong"— *of course they're wrong—*" I'll find him. Abby will be okay."

Shannon gritted her teeth, buried her face in the bed, and shuddered as the tears came, first a slow trickle then a gushing wound that wet the sheets. Derry's icy hand tethered her to the room, like the fist of a zombie clutching at the heroine's ankle in an old movie she and Roger had once seen. Maybe Roger had always been that zombie. Maybe she had always been the girl handcuffed to the earth by some jerk. She had chosen to marry someone who was very likely a psychopath. She'd put an innocent girl in prison. She pictured Morrison's stoic face in her mind. Maybe this time was no different.

It would not be the first time she had been grievously wrong.

25

MORRISON STRETCHED his arms above his head in warrior pose though he felt less like a warrior and more like a battered piece of meat. His head throbbed with memories of the drug, whispers in the back of his mind telling him to give in, to let go, to forget for just a little while.

He deserved to be here. Maybe he had always deserved it. It was cathartic in a way, an external manifestation of the prison he'd already created for himself. He was, and always would be, a slave, no matter how long he was clean. Now, trapped behind bars of steel, he felt no less a prisoner than when he was roaming free.

Sweat beaded on his forehead as he brought his elbow to the inside of his knee, still deep in a lunge, hands in prayer pose but acknowledging that this was as close as he ever got to praying. Narcotics Anonymous would have frowned on that, but it was no matter. He hadn't been to a meeting in years.

His breath filled the room, and he focused on it, willed himself to sink into it, stay with it, but the chill in the air brought him back to the jail cell again and again. It was a cold that had nothing to do with temperature—it was the panicked realization that he would soon succumb.

He could feel the drug's presence as surely if he were

cloaked in a robe of needles, the prickling of promise at once terrifying and euphoric. One stick and you could soar, above the world, beyond your pain, free of everything. But he knew he'd have to crash back to earth, and then the pain would follow. And this roller coaster, of desire and disgust, pleasure and pain...it wouldn't stop until he was dead.

Was Petrosky clean? Did it matter? Morrison had long pretended it was so, for in Petrosky's sobriety he saw his own, a bit of success held up like a mirror of triumph. But it was a fragile balance—mirrors could crack and falter, shatter into thousands of pieces that sliced at your skin until you were left bleeding hope onto the bedroom floor. Stress always made sober living harder, and lately, it had been a struggle. Now, here, there was no triumph, only vaguely shrouded opportunity to use, potential dealers whispering to him from every corner of steel and stone. And once he was arraigned, he'd be locked up with them.

In jail, there was nothing but the drugs, the cackling of sweet relief. He knew the others in their cells had access. He knew they had needles. He knew heroin was but a rightly placed question away, a look, a nudge in the lunch hall. He could smell it on their sallow skin, see it in their dull, bloodshot eyes, the lids at half-mast—the lonely euphoria of a simple need met. But it was a need met now and only now, because for those men, now was all that existed. Tomorrow would be but a half-intoxicated nightmare. Tomorrow would be a race to resupply before plunging into hell.

And yet, still, he loved it.

Even after years of sobriety, he could not deny the adoration that coexisted with loathing like interwoven threads of lace—though maybe that was how love always was. But not his love for *her*. They'd met three years ago, blistered autumn leaves from the tree next to the courthouse swirling at their feet. Shannon's presence had been a rope, tethering him, sustaining him. Watching her sleep in his arms had been the most blissful thing he'd done in years. She was becoming his drug. Not that she'd love him back if she knew. She couldn't love him, she'd made that plain, though he couldn't let go of this hope that she would come around. But even if she did, how long would she stay? She didn't know what he was—and if he had any say in the matter, she'd never find out.

No one knew everything. Not even Petrosky, and his respect seemed precarious at best. Even on the days Morrison was most certain of their bond, he feared it would soon fray and tear under the weight of the unforgivable things he had done. He wished he didn't have to bear his secrets alone, but what other choice did he have? No one in their right mind would be that understanding, that tolerant.

He could almost smell the blood on his hands, taste it in his mouth. He could still see the body when he closed his eyes, broken and blue, the tops of his shoes speckled with gore.

He deserved to be here in this cell, caged and alone.

He'd committed atrocities no man should get away with. And he still couldn't remember why.

26

THE NAUSEA from the night before made a comeback before she opened her eyes. She leapt from Derry's bedside and raced into the hall bathroom. Bile, thick and yellow, splattered into the toilet, but she could not purge the vile bullshit that was sloshing around in her brain.

Had she been wrong about Ashley Johnson? Probably. But did that mean Kimball was a killer? And what about Morrison? Her doubts about Morrison twisted her insides until she could barely breathe.

He was stoic to be sure. Calm in situations where any other man would lose his shit. She had never seen him cry, never seen him worry, not really. Was that the Zen thing, or did he just not feel anything at all? Emotionless. *Like a psychopath.* She rinsed her mouth and left the bathroom.

The commotion had apparently roused Petrosky, who stood peering at the street, his fingers drumming on the window. *Tap-tap-tap. Tap-tap-tap.* "Got ballistics back on the bullet from Wheatley's belly," he said to the curtain.

"And?"

"Gun was Kimball's." He turned from the window. "Bought it at a police auction four years ago."

She hadn't been wrong. The fist that held her stomach loosened its grip. "So they're arresting him?"

"Nope. He kept it in his glovebox, reported it missing last month, admits he had the car doors unlocked at the gym. With the break-in on your car, Kimball's not looking suspicious to Internal Affairs, and he's definitely not looking suspicious to Roger."

Not suspicious to the rest of the police force, but the look in Petrosky's eyes told her that he thought Kimball looked suspicious as hell. It didn't take a genius or even a detective to know that there was something very, very wrong with Wheatley being shot with a bullet from Kimball's gun, even if Kimball had a solid alibi.

"I think he lied about having to take his daughter to dance," Shannon said.

"I'll look into it." Petrosky frowned at her tank top, the same one she'd been wearing at the gym yesterday, still crusted with dried vomit. He averted his eyes. "You need to eat. Low blood sugar will make you nauseous."

She squinted at him. "Oh...thanks."

Petrosky jerked his chin to the office door. "How is he?"

He. Her brother. Her almost dead brother.

"Not great."

"I had a friend die like that." His mouth was impassive, but his eyes shone dark and deep as he finally looked at her. "We were best buds in the academy. Never smoked a day in his life, yet there it was, lung cancer at thirty. His wife didn't take it well, killed herself the next year, left two little kids to fend for themselves."

Hell of a sad story, but why was he telling her this? Surely Petrosky didn't think Alex would kill himself.

If Petrosky noticed the quiver in her hands, he didn't show it. "It hurts, Shannon. It hurts like a bitch, but it can't own you unless you let it. And you won't let it. No matter how shitty it is, you won't give up."

"That's a little melodramatic." But his words rang through to her very core, hot and sharp as a spear.

"You've thought it, though. We all do, if only for a heartbeat. How the hell am I going to get through this? How am I going to do it without him? But we do." He stepped toward her until she could smell the tobacco stench that clung to his clothes. "We find what we need. And until we get Morrison back out here, you tell *me* what you need." He squeezed her arm, dropped his eyes. "I'm going to walk the perimeter before everyone else gets up. You better get ready for work, Taylor, or we'll be late." He released her and headed for the back hallway, shoulders sagging, leaving her staring after him.

EVERY MUSCLE in Shannon's body felt like rubber as she struggled through her case files, making stacks of things to file, people to call, dates to set. *Derry's sleeping. Just do your job.* The beige walls of her office glared at her, pale and sickly, but still a healthier tone than her brother's skin. The blue stain from her cracked pen looked like a bruise.

Her knuckles were white around her new pen when the knocking started, timid rapping, then harder, swelling to an aggravated pounding: one, two, three, four distinct hits. Shannon knew that knock. She frowned at the door, pulled a sheet from the stack, and wrote a note at the top. Roger had gotten the wrong person thrown in jail last night. He could fucking wait.

He knocked again, four hard raps, but not unreasonably hard, and she could almost see his face melting from anger to faux indifference on the other side.

She laid her latest batch of legal research aside with a sigh and unlocked the door. If she hadn't needed to know what was going on with Morrison's case, she would have let him wait forever.

Roger leaned against the doorframe as if content to stay all day and harass the shit out of her. The purple bruising under his eyes was fading to a sickly yellow-green. Like alien flesh. Inhuman.

"What do you want?"

"Just to talk." His jaw tightened. Bad news?

Bad news for Roger would mean... Her heart leapt. Had they questioned and released Morrison already? No, she'd have heard from Petrosky if that were the case. And Roger wouldn't be here to tell her she had been right—he'd have let her suffer.

Roger pushed past her and sat, folding his hands over his crossed knee. "You working on Anderson?" His face gave away nothing.

Anderson? He hadn't come to talk about Anderson. Fire worked its way into her face as she walked back to her chair, trying to avoid stomping, or he'd know how much his presence got to her. Her back was rigid in her seat. "The asshole who shot his three-year-old in front of two other kids while cleaning his loaded gun?"

"That's the one. What are you charging with?"

She didn't realize her knee was bouncing until the chair chirped underneath her. She stilled her leg. "Involuntary manslaughter."

"Drop the charges, Shannon."

"Every day innocent kids are killed with firearms, Roger. Eventually we have to start holding adults accountable for—"

"Not today, Shannon. It's a hot-button topic. We'll never get a conviction."

"It doesn't mean we shouldn't try." She leveled her stare at him, hating his calm, still face. Why were they discussing Anderson? Was he purposefully avoiding questions about Morrison? Teasing her? Getting ready to rub her face in some perceived victory? "Confuse, deflect, destroy" was pretty much Roger's motto.

"Maybe you just want to avoid all gun-related issues," she said. "After all, Kimball's gun sure as shit pumped a bullet into someone, and you're not even bothering with that." *Because he's your best friend, Roger? Or is he your partner in crime?*

"Your politics are showing, Shannon. Try looking at things objectively, and we'll all be better off."

"Fine." She slapped the file shut. *Enough with this shit.*

"What about Morrison? Are you dropping the charges on him?"

"I've already talked to the judge. There're more than enough to keep him."

Shannon's jaw dropped. "On what grounds?" Roger was insane. Morrison had no motive for killing anyone—not Derek Lewis, not Benjamin Wheatley. Definitely not Lucky. No judge in their right mind would keep him.

He chuckled. "Well, we both know how chummy Morrison's partner was with that family. Those types of people. Maybe he got involved with Johnson, killed Derek out of spite. Killed Wheatley for finding out." His grin fell, eyes sharpening into daggers. "Morrison's not as good and pure as you think he is, Shannon. He's got a history. Aggression, especially after his mother was killed—ironically, brains bashed in by a boyfriend. Sounds like he's replaying her death to me."

His mom's death. Ten years after his dad was killed in a robbery, Morrison's mother had been murdered by an abusive boyfriend. Morrison had many reasons to be angry, but so did she. So did a lot of people. She shook her head. "He isn't—"

"Then there's his drug history, including heroin, which he admitted to. And that's just what we have so far."

"Half the people in helping professions have histories, Roger. That's why they want to give back." But her stomach rolled. An addict? That's something she definitely should have known. *I had a mean streak as a kid.* Wasn't that what Morrison had said? "You have no evidence. You can't hold him forever."

"Kimball reported the gun missing weeks ago. And those towels in Wheatley's trunk? A couple of the ones hidden near the bottom had a recognizable image on them—some logo that looks like a mushroom. Morrison identified the towels himself. They're from his gym bag."

"Anyone at the gym could have gotten hold of them, Roger. Same with the gun. It's all circumstantial."

"You were right about the bars. We found traces of Wheatley's blood in the grooves around the base. He was definitely killed at the gym. And Kimball has an alibi. Your buddy has the only other key."

"No, Roger. This isn't right." They had to have a spare key. She pictured Amanda Kimball's office, the keys on the hook, in plain view. "Anyone could have—"

"We got other stuff from his place too, Shannon." Roger crossed his fingers over his knee. "His writing is especially interesting."

The air left her like she'd been stabbed in the chest. "Who gave you a warrant so fast?"

"He gave us permission to look. And we found a rather interesting piece in his garage: a hammer tucked away in the bottom of a Rubbermaid bin. A hammer that someone had taken the time to scrub clean. No other tools nearby. Odd, don't you think? Equally odd that we never found the weapon used to bash in Derek Lewis's skull."

Roger sat back and smiled. "We've got forensics working on it now. Looks like there's still a trace of something in the wood on the hammer. Preliminaries say it's blood. My guess is it belongs to Lewis."

Her mouth felt like it was stuffed with cotton. *Roxy.* Wouldn't the dog have lost her shit in the garage, smelling blood every time she walked by the door? But no—she was at Derry's now. Was that the real reason he'd brought her to Derry's?

"Roger." She tried to keep her voice light. Patient. "If he really killed Lewis and Wheatley, why would he give you permission to go through his stuff?"

"Maybe he wanted to get caught." Roger shrugged, and Shannon ground her teeth together.

It was me. They'd thought the killer had been bragging with the letter, but what if he'd wanted someone to stop him?

Roger gripped his knee harder, the tendons in his hand straining. "There's also an entire spiral notebook full of what look like poems. Songs. Drawings. Disturbing shit. We saw enough to think he might be unstable."

No way. *There is no fucking way.* "So, what, did he write a song about killing Derek Lewis?" *The hammer.* Morrison had the hammer. The knife in her chest twisted.

Roger released his knee and examined his fingernails. "Found a few other things too. About lovers."

Lovers. She felt naked. Exposed. What the hell had he written? But so help her, she wanted to read it, wanted to know what went on inside Morrison's head. She watched Roger release his knee, his eyes dead and cold and as angry as she'd ever seen them.

"I knew you were fucking him." He stared at her like he wanted her to justify it. To deny it. Maybe to assure him he was a better screw.

Her face blistered with rage. This part of her wasn't Roger's to pry into, not anymore. He had no right. And she hated the way he was looking at her now, leering like he could see clear through her clothes. Depending on what Morrison had written, maybe he could.

"From a marriage to the head prosecutor to shacking up with a killer cop. Quite the nosedive." Roger smiled.

I'll show you nosedive, motherfucker. Her fists clenched, every muscle in her neck screaming with tension. Petrosky was right: Roger was a lying, cheating, douche canoe. Roger was the one who should be in jail.

"Maybe Morrison will pay you to drop it, Roger," she hissed. "Like all the others."

"What did you just say?" In a heartbeat, all traces of amusement were gone. His eyes were icy; his lips pulled into a sneer. She wanted to punch him in the goddamn mouth.

"You heard me. You're fucking dirty, Roger."

"I haven't done anything wrong, Shannon. You might not like the charges, but we're getting through more cases than ever. The whole department is running more smoothly. The other attorneys are less stressed about their caseloads." He flipped his palms to the sky, a magician's ta-da. "And bad guys are still going away."

"Not for as long as they should."

"That's a matter of opinion. Luckily, yours no longer matters to me." A corner of his mouth turned up in a half smile, half sneer. "I think the stress of your brother's death is starting to get to you. If you want to keep your job..." Roger stood and backed toward the door, and she followed suit, advancing on him around the desk.

"You can't fire me, Roger. It'll never stick."

He pursed his lips and dropped his gaze like he felt sorry for her. "You're not a great judge of character these days, Shanny. Why don't you leave the important decisions to me?"

She slammed the door on him, her body thrumming with repressed rage. If someone had told her four years ago that she'd want to stab Roger in the eye, she'd have laughed in their face. Now, Roger was lucky she didn't have a letter opener in her desk.

She laid her palms against the closed door and willed the coolness of it to pull the hot rage from her body. Sanity was fleeting, fragile. Anyone could be a killer.

Anyone.

27

EVEN THROUGH HER OFFICE WINDOW, the afternoon sun was so bright that it hurt her soul. The sounds of spring made her want to kick something. How dare the birds chirp when her life was falling apart. Petrosky had called to tell her about Morrison's preliminary trial—after the fact. Roger had been right. Morrison was staying in jail—a flight risk due to the nature of the charges—though his new attorney, the illustrious Frank Griffen, had done his damnedest to get him released. It had only been a day, and already the loneliness was eating at her so fiercely that she'd picked the cuticle around her nail down to the meat, bloodying it every time she thought of him. Morrison. Not Curt. Maybe if she kept it friendly, professional even, her heart wouldn't hurt so badly.

It already hurt enough. Derry had barely woken in days. It was as if the moment they'd gotten him, home he'd given up. And with his constant, raspy wheezing... it wouldn't be long. She needed to solve this, today. While she could still tell Derry about it. While she could put his mind at ease before—

She shook her head, trying to clear the bullshit. *The case. Think about the case.*

They had interviewed Kimball and cleared him of wrongdoing, or more specifically, Roger's handpicked detectives had cleared Kimball and turned the information over to

Internal Affairs, who hadn't challenged their conclusions thus far. But...the gun. The gym. His daughter's nonexistent dance classes. The irritability that had only increased in the last month. But Kimball had been with her when her car was trashed, which meant...he must have a partner. Someone she hadn't seen in the gym that night. Valentine's face flashed in her brain, but he wouldn't hurt a fly... Well, unless you hurt a child...like Lewis had. She shook her head again. *Stop, Shannon, regroup.* Kimball and Roger? No one had a concrete motive. Nothing made sense. *Nothing.*

Especially not Morrison standing under the bars, kicking Wheatley, watching him bleed. No way. *No fucking way.* Kimball was the one being sneaky. Kimball was the one lying, the one cheating, the one getting more and more aggressive by the day. Kimball was the one—

The telephone rang, and she stared at it like it was a grotesque, hairy mole. Caller ID was someone in Detroit. *Nope, not now.* She waited until it stopped ringing then took it off the hook. If Alex needed her, he'd call her cell. For now, she needed to get her mind off Derry, off Morrison, and into work mode. Not like she could concentrate on the case right now anyway.

She stretched her arms over her head and rolled her neck. *Anderson.* She'd finish the Anderson case. And that bastard wasn't getting off on this one. One of her law professors used to say that regardless of how it happened, whether a premeditated act or an impulsive act of vengeance, everyone needs a reason to stop, a reason to avoid committing the same crime again. She was going to give every one of these dickheads on her caseload a reason. And then, once her head was clear, she was going to figure out who had killed Wheatley and nail them to the wall. For Derry. For Morrison. For Abby. For all of them.

She researched, scrawled notes, typed reports, and signed forms so viciously that she tore a hole in one of her files. No thinking. No more thinking. She needed to step away from the constant analysis. She could almost feel the answer hiding there like a sliver beneath the surface, the kind that pushed a little deeper every time you tried to scratch it up. Maybe time would allow the sliver to work its way to the surface.

Half an hour later, the Anderson file was ready, and her stomach was grumbling. She shoved her folders into her briefcase and left the office, still trying to get a handle on her whirling thoughts. Maybe lunch would help. But the thought of food made her stomach clench as if her gut would reject anything she tried to swallow. She'd go anyway. She started from the office, glanced back at her briefcase, and returned to take it with her.

Petrosky's car was at the curb outside the office. *Has he been out here all day?* He was supposed to be investigating how to get Morrison out of jail. Petrosky waved her over, and she slid into the passenger seat.

"Why are you here, Petrosky?"

"I was just coming to get you." He put the car in gear, and they drove from the lot. "You could have told me you were leaving."

Like she had to answer to him. She'd spent years answering to Roger. Shit, she still had to answer to Roger at work. Once this case was over, she'd move. Find a new job in a place that wasn't full of old baggage. She shrugged. "I needed some time to think."

"This isn't a game, Shannon."

Shannon tightened her grip on the door handle. "You think I don't know that?" Derry needed her to figure this out. She would figure this out. A sandwich, and then she'd be able to focus. "How's Valentine?"

"Good. Following Abby around like a bloodhound." She wanted to ask about Morrison but couldn't bring her mouth to form the words. Maybe she was letting her emotions get the better of her. She'd definitely said too much to Roger earlier.

Petrosky turned toward the freeway. "Taylor—"

"Listen, I fucked up. I was arguing with Roger this morning, and I might've accused him of taking bribes. I kind of... exploded."

"He'll probably think you're just angry, throwing accusations around," Petrosky said, but his eyes were tight, and spots of pink rouged his cheeks.

"It was pretty specific for throwing things around." She looked out the window at the trees, at the brilliant blue sky. But the sunlight didn't feel warm or happy—it was hot, scorching, menacing.

"Won't matter. If anything, he'll get flustered and fuck himself up. That's what usually happens." He took a deep, phlegmy breath and coughed.

"Find out anything about Kimball's daughter's dance classes?"

"His daughter hasn't taken dance in six months."

I knew it. So, what had Wheatley seen that had given Kimball justification to off him? Was Kimball on drugs? Had to be drugs. Ruskin had said—

"I'll look into it more, Taylor, find out what he's been doing. We need to focus on other things."

Right. There was probably tons to do, especially since Morrison was out of commission. Knowing she'd been right about Kimball, even if it was just about dance class, was reviving her brain. Shannon pushed her hair out of her face. "I'll help. I just need some coffee, and then I can start—"

"You need to go home, Taylor." His tone held no demand, just bone-crushing sadness.

Her chest collapsed against her heart. *Derry.* "That's why you were trying to find me. It wasn't about the case?" She'd been so focused on finding the killer for Derry that she'd forgotten to actually be there for him. And now it was too late.

Petrosky stared out the windshield. Shannon blinked back tears and held onto the door handle, the hardness of it grounding her in the moment. But she couldn't hold onto the door—or Derry—forever.

THERE WAS a new guy in the corner of Derry's office-turned-bedroom, a balding man with a hospital ID badge around his throat like a noose. A nurse? Another doctor? Who the fuck had called him?

He nodded solemnly as she entered. "I'm Raj. A colleague of Alex's." She ignored him and looked at the bed.

Alex sat at Derry's bedside, his eyes glassy. Abby lay next to Derry, her head on his chest, Alex's hand on her back. *Derry*. Her baby brother. Under his yellowed skin, something dull and gray had seeped in, blotting out any remnants of the peach and pink of his youth.

Derry's eyes were half-open, his jaw slack.

"Is he awake?" She touched his head, as bald as he'd been when their parents brought him home from the hospital. She had slapped him that first meeting, though she couldn't remember doing it; she only knew because of the story her mom had told her. But she vaguely remembered that he'd been warm then, and now he was cold, or colder than he should be. She swallowed hard.

Alex wiped his eyes with his palm. "Coma. But he's lost the ability to close his eyes due to the wasting in the muscles." His words were clotted with sorrow. "He's close. I knew it the moment I walked in here. And when Raj stopped by—I could barely talk. And I didn't want to be here alone in case it happened...fast." He glanced at the door. "Is Petrosky here? Raj said your line was busy."

"Outside."

Alex sniffed. "I'm glad you made it."

She nodded and sat beside the bed next to Alex, where someone had added an extra folding chair. A shuffling from the back corner caught her attention, then the bedroom door closed, maybe Raj leaving, but she couldn't take her eyes from Derry's body. *So still.*

Abby's face rested on Derry's chest, rising and falling with each of his shallow, ragged gurgles. Every time his breath caught and stopped for a beat too long, Abby's chin quivered, but she did not cry, just stared out past them all with a blank gaze like she could see straight into the afterlife and was watching for the reaper.

Shannon tried to breathe, but the room was suffocating her, the air like molasses. She was drowning. Tears ran freely down Alex's face, his eyes red and raw and helpless. She wrapped her arms around him and let his tears wet her blouse, much like she'd done with her mother when her father had left.

"The blood's pooling and everything is settling," Alex whispered in her ear. "I see people die every day, but he's... cold, my god, he feels so much colder than they do."

They sat. Listened to Derry's ragged breath. Listened to the silence when his body forgot to breathe. Abby was still and silent on his chest, her eyes closed as if she were asleep, but no one could sleep with that rattle in their ear.

Shannon did not know how much time had passed when Alex disentangled himself from her and laid a finger on Derry's jugular. His eyes filled, but he bent to Derry's ear, whispering words she couldn't discern. Alex's chest heaved. He choked back a sob and kissed Derry's forehead, pressing his lips so hard against her brother's face that Shannon expected the skin to split. It didn't, and Alex sat back, his entire body trembling.

Time. They were out of time. And yet it kept passing, achingly slowly. The jangle of air moving through his lungs became a constant, lingering sound even when his body paused, and the silence stretched before them like a road to nowhere. Outside, the sky slowly darkened to a bloody red, then to black. At some point, before the stars emerged, Abby fell asleep.

And still, he breathed. But less. And less.

What time Alex laid his head on Derry's pillow and fell asleep too, Shannon wasn't quite sure. Nor was she certain when Abby moved from Derry's chest to the pillow beside him. But there they all were as dawn broke and birds chirped and early morning commuters went about their normal, boring lives. A new day and all she wanted to do was reverse the clock.

Shannon's neck ached from resting her head on her chest. She stood and put her lips at Derry's ear, whispering low so that Abby couldn't hear her. "Growing up, you always made me better than I was. I'm so grateful that I got to have you as a brother." Tightness wrapped her throat. "I love you, Derry." She blinked hard, willing herself to keep her shit together, to show Abby strength like the strength Derry had shown throughout their entire childhood. She caught a glimpse of Abby's face in her peripheral vision, eyes closed, mouth open in sleep.

She put her hand on one side of Derry's face, the skin cold and dry and horrible. "I'll take care of them, Derry. I won't fail you." She released him and collapsed back into her chair beside Alex as Abby opened her eyes. Looked at her daddy. Laid her hand on his chest. Frowned.

It took Shannon a moment to realize the rattling had stopped. Alex lifted his head from the pillow and touched Derry's neck again. This time he pulled his hand back quickly and picked up Derry's wrist, searching, searching. Then he set Derry's hand back on the bed, patted it gently, and shook his head. Shannon choked back all the stinging tears she wouldn't—couldn't—let fall. *Be strong. For Derry.*

A single tear escaped Abby's eye. "I'll miss you, Daddy. So, so much," Abby touched Derry's face. "And I love you so much too." She kissed Derry's sunken cheek, crawled off the far side of the bed, and ran around to Alex's lap. Shannon's chest felt like it was going to implode, and she forced a breath to inflate it. They huddled there, Shannon's arms around them both, listening to the silence.

28

DERRY HAD NEVER BEEN a fan of funerals or churches, so they skipped the wake and held a memorial at Alex's house the following Wednesday. They had needed at least that long to complete the cremation and to plan what Derry had always called his going-away party. "You fuckers should party all night just to give yourselves an excuse to skip work," he'd said. But the gathering felt anything but festive. The food looked good, though Shannon tasted none of it. Sushi. Mexican. Take out from all his favorite places. They played the songs he'd chosen. She'd never listen to the Grateful Dead again.

All she could do was yearn for her brother as people she knew and people she didn't trudged through offering condolences and cake and lasagna and cards and empty consolations that he was in a better place—as if that was what she needed to accept. As if Derry would have been happier somewhere without them. As if having had him for a brief time rather than not at all somehow made it all okay that he'd died way too early. As if she should be fucking *thankful*.

She'd always hated that flowery bullshit, and she hated it now more than ever. Pretty words wouldn't give her back her brother, wouldn't allow her to hear his voice again. Wouldn't give Abby back her father. Morrison would have known what to say. He would have known when to shut up and just hold her hand too. But he wasn't there. He was gone. *Gone.*

She should have taken time in the past week to visit Morrison in jail. But she couldn't, couldn't face him, knowing she wasn't doing shit to help him get out. There was nothing she could do—not for anyone. The case didn't make sense; her life didn't make sense. Even her own body had betrayed her by completely forgetting how to sleep—in the mornings, she could barely get out of bed. And after the first three days had gone by in a fog of grief and loss, she'd felt guiltier than ever about her absence, and it was even harder to consider Morrison, wrongfully imprisoned in the detention center.

When she couldn't stand the trite condolences any longer, she hid in the office, sitting on the hospital bed that the medical supply place had yet to pick up, watching through the front window as the visitors came, stayed a socially acceptable amount of time, and left. Watching Valentine, who never moved from his spot at the street except to accompany Lillian to the door when she arrived with a bouquet of flowers.

Shannon left the office to meet her. Lillian smelled like talcum powder already, well ahead of her delivery date. Valentine smelled like his car and fast food and Morrison's special coffee, which made her heart ache that much more. But she couldn't think about it, couldn't really think about anything except the hole that seemed to grow in her chest every time she saw the hollow look in Abby's eyes. Shannon offered hugs, but Abby felt wooden, just like the stiff, brittle arms of everyone else today. Eventually, the stream of visitors slowed to a trickle, and she was grateful for the moments of solitude in between the empty apologies.

Griffen showed up as twilight fell, his beanie cap pulled over his ears, bringing a coffee cake on a plate she recognized from his house. The same dishes after all these years. For some reason, that struck her as horribly sad. She saw him coming and met him on the porch.

"Thanks, Griffen. Did you make that?"

"Alas, I did not. But I shall send along your regards to Karen. When I see her." His eyes were watery, mouth tight. Like he was in pain. And he looked thin.

God, not again. In college, he'd had a girlfriend: Natasha... something. Ugly as sin, and equally irritable. But he was down for a month when she left him, barely slept, barely ate. Shannon had been so pissed at him for letting that girl have such an effect. Come to think of it, Shannon had probably been the only woman he'd ever met who hadn't taken advantage of him somehow. Even Burke had given him most of the bills when they'd moved in together, and she'd surely controlled all their social activities. No wonder he missed Shannon. Everyone needs one trustworthy person—someone steady, someone who will just...be there, without demands or expectations. Morrison was her person, though it turned out she was shitty at reciprocation. Then she pictured Alex's bloodshot eyes as he watched his fiancé leave the house for the last time—on a gurney. Her chest lit on fire. She couldn't breathe.

Think about something else, anything else. She glanced at the flower bed where Roger had landed after Morrison punched him. *Morrison.* Nope, not helping.

"How are things with Karen?" she asked.

Griffen shook his head. "Shan, you were always too worried about other people even when you were the one in need of assistance."

She wrapped her coat tighter around her body. "Look who's talking. You had mono, and you still defended that dude with the bum leg who killed his mother."

He smiled, but it looked forced. "Allegedly."

"Yeah, right." She sighed. "It's not like there's anything anyone can do for me. Might as well hear about you." And she could definitely use some distraction from the hole in her heart. "Come on, Griffen. I know something's wrong."

"Ah. Well, it's no big deal, really. I'm...just considering whether Karen and I are meant to be." Griffen shook his head, opened his mouth, and closed it again.

This is new. Something bad must have happened—she'd never known him to break up with anyone. He was usually the one who got left. But he gave her no time to comment on it.

"Perhaps I don't deserve her anyway. I couldn't even keep an innocent girl out of jail. A really, truly, innocent girl. If I'm honest, it's been eating me up. I barely sleep anymore." And there was the Griffen she knew. He kicked at a smudge of mud on the porch, left behind by some well-wisher. Derry would have hosed it off.

She met Griffen's glassy eyes. "I was the one who put her away. If you're feeling shitty about your role, mine was a thousand times more terrible."

He broke eye contact and stared off into the night behind her, his mouth working again. His nerves must have gotten worse over the last few years. How had she not noticed?

"I'm sorry, Shan, I—"

She waved away his apology. "I didn't take it that way. I'm just saying...we all do our best, right? It's like Professor Moore used to say: the truth prevails eventually. That's why we have appeals."

"And where the accused began their trial, so shall it end righteously if the court is just," he recited, rubbing his temple. "I just hope this one ends well."

"Yeah." Her chest tightened. "Endings are always the hardest." She blinked rapidly but was unable to stop the tears from spilling down her cheeks.

"They certainly are." Griffen wrapped his arms around her. He was shaking. Maybe from the cold, she couldn't quite feel. Every part of her was numb.

"I'm so sorry, Shan. For not being here for you. For... everything."

She said nothing, just leaned into him, and watched the sky blacken to ash.

PETROSKY ARRIVED A LITTLE AFTER NINE, the orange glow from his cigarette preceding him in the driveway. He stumbled off the sidewalk, righted himself, and stared into the flower bed as he finished his smoke. Drunk? Or clumsy? *Who cares?* If Shannon didn't have to look out for Abby and Alex, she'd have been completely wasted hours ago.

He turned when she stepped onto the lawn. "Taylor. How are you?" He smelled intensely minty, the reek of mouthwash over tobacco over who knew what else.

How am I? She ignored the question rather than trying to describe the gaping, pulsing wound in her chest. "Valentine took me to pick up my car up today," she said instead, and her voice was lower than she remembered. "I thought I'd go home tonight."

Petrosky shook his head, and she fought the urge to slap him. *Don't tell me no, you asshole.* But it wasn't him she was mad at. She had failed her brother. Shannon could almost hear Derry's voice whispering from the walls: *Why can't you find who did this?* But Derry was no longer around to care, and it was no longer their case. Petrosky would take care of Morrison. She had to get out—she was just so...tired. Tired of smelling death and coffee cake, tired of seeing that office every time she walked into the house, tired of feeling like she was trapped in her brother's crypt. Tired of being alone while Alex and Abby slept in Alex's room, suffering, but together, sharing the burden of grief so that it was less... stifling.

"I was here to be with Derry, but now, I—"

"Taylor, I know, okay? You want to be alone to heal. But there's someone out there who has it out for you."

"No one's looking for me."

He sighed. "Someone *might* be looking for you, Taylor. You need to be worried about your family."

"I can't just sit here and look at his ashes, Petrosky. Alex and Abby are moving on, grieving, but they're together. And here I am, just...sitting. Waiting for something else to happen. I can't spend the rest of my life sitting. You of all people should understand that." *You're the one who threw yourself into your work instead of grieving for your daughter. You're the one who never let it go, who never healed.* Maybe she'd be like that too, consumed by the dead, glaring at the living because no matter how awesome they were, they'd never be the one person she wanted them to be.

Petrosky tossed his cigarette into the barely-there grass, and she had the irrational urge to leap down and grab it. Derry had loved his lawn, though he'd adored ruining it with bounce houses for Abby's birthday. Wait...hadn't he? Or had his eye twitched ever so slightly every time another kid leapt to the ground and exposed the mud? Was she already forgetting him? How much more would she forget? The thought stabbed hot and sharp into her chest, and she breathed over it until the pain lessened.

Petrosky followed her gaze and bent to retrieve the cigarette butt. "Roger held a press conference today with the chief of police. Made it clear there's still another player after they got a different set of latent prints off one of Wheatley's shoes. Got a dark hair too, again, not Morrison's. Male, but not much else. They're claiming it's from the addict that Morrison was coercing because the hair tested positive for heroin, but it's probably from someone Wheatley saw that day. Young's ruling out people on Wheatley's caseload now."

"What? They can't hold him—"

"Roger also said he's got a statement from someone at the rehab center, corroborating that Morrison has a history of preying on addicts, getting drugs or sex in exchange for not arresting them."

Preying on addicts? Taking drugs? Had she really been that blind? "That's—that's fucking—"

"It's obviously not true, Taylor. It's bullshit lies. And Roger's not releasing his source, though he'll have to tell Internal Affairs if he hasn't already. My guess is someone Morrison put away is screwing with him, and Roger made it nice and easy for them to lie, probably asked leading questions." Petrosky grimaced, nostrils flaring. "Unless Roger's lying altogether, which I wouldn't put past him."

The rehab center. "Griffen's girlfriend works at the rehab center—Karen, remember her? I wonder if she knows who said that...if there is someone."

"I asked Griffen. He said she had no idea."

Of course Petrosky had thought of that. "What about Kimball?"

"They printed him to rule out his marks on the equipment. Wasn't his prints on Wheatley either, and with his alibi, they aren't pushing it. And Roger's got a hard-on for California. He's got the chief breathing down my neck to stay away from it, conflict of interest or some bullshit—they don't even want me to see him."

Roger. He was orchestrating everything, from the evidence, to the arrest, to Morrison's confinement. Cutting Morrison off from the people who were trying to help him.

"The detectives are saying Morrison bought drugs from Derek Lewis, Wheatley found out about it accidentally, and Morrison offed them both, though he had assistance on Wheatley from someone at the rehab center, someone who's now missing. I think they're speculating that Morrison killed his junkie partner too and dumped the body."

Insanity. "What about Lucky? What's their opinion on that?"

Petrosky grunted. "That Morrison's a psycho. Unstable. Wants the fame. Maybe a drug-induced moment of insanity. The usual."

"But Morrison doesn't do drugs, right?" *Anymore.* "Didn't they test him?"

"I'm sure they did. Not that they'd let me see the file. But Roger isn't rubbing it in my face, so it's a fair bet the test was negative."

A fair bet, but not certain.

Petrosky's face was cloaked in the shadow of the awning,

but she could feel the tension. The heaviness of whatever he was holding back.

"What else?" she asked, not sure she wanted to know. But there had to be more, or they'd have let Morrison go once they found someone else's DNA. The night breathed around them, fast and sharp, almost panting with the tense energy of revelation.

"They got the forensics back on the towels in Wheatley's trunk—Morrison's DNA all over them, though that isn't a surprise. But the hammer found in Morrison's garage..." Petrosky averted his eyes and stared into the night. "There was some hair, Taylor. And blood. Stuck in the groove between the handle and the top. DNA matched Derek Lewis."

Her pulse went into overdrive, beating a frantic rhythm in her temples.

"He never should have let them search," Petrosky said.

Because he's guilty? But she knew what he meant: with someone on the force implicated in the crimes, Morrison should have known it'd have been easy for them to plant something at his house, especially now that Roxy wasn't there.

"California's not an idiot—he'd have gotten rid of the hammer and the towels. But it doesn't look good from the outside. Morrison's a loner, quiet unless he's being charming in that goofy beach boy way of his. He doesn't show much emotion. All marks of a psychopath if you spin it right."

A psychopath. She'd sometimes thought Morrison's incessant calm was strange, but in a passing way: a little too relaxed here, oddly unaffected there. After four years with Roger, she was sensitive to people who didn't respond normally—almost too sensitive. But wasn't calm good?

"Plus, he has a little bit of a...history that doesn't bode well for him right now." Petrosky jerked his cigarettes from his pocket, a tremor in his fingers.

A history. Same thing Roger had said. So maybe it wasn't

just schoolyard shenanigans, but still… "What exactly does that mean?" *Besides the drugs*, she wanted to add.

"He did some things that Roger will argue are markings of antisocial personality disorder, psychopathy, you know? Minor legal infringements. Drugs, mostly, when he was a kid. Juvenile detention after beating the shit out of a bully at school."

Drugs. Juvenile detention. Turned born again yogi? Best friends and he'd kept it all from her, hiding his secrets behind his placid facade. Though…he *had* hinted at a past, and she hadn't asked him for details. And she hadn't exactly spilled her elementary school secrets either. *Because they aren't relevant anymore.* The present was what mattered. The future. She could almost feel Morrison's hand stroking her back, but she brushed the thought away before it could take root. "Did he tell you all this?" If he'd told Petrosky and not her, maybe they weren't as close as she'd thought.

Petrosky shook his head. "He's a quiet guy, Taylor. I don't push him. But I always know who I'm working with."

He'd investigated Morrison. "Now you're the one who sounds like a psycho," she said, but his words loosened the knot that had formed in her chest.

"Married to Roger, you can probably pick them out of a lineup."

She clenched her fists. He was right—she had often thought the same—but the words felt different coming out of someone else's mouth.

"Sorry, below the belt."

Her shoulders stayed high and tight, but her balled fists released. "What are you going to do tonight?" The house behind her suddenly loomed like a prison, cold and unforgiving.

"Poke around. Our best bet at getting California out is giving them the person who actually did it. But stick around here, don't let your guard down. And take care of yourself. I know how easy it is to stop giving a shit after something like this."

"I'll be fine, Petrosky. Maybe I'll take a run around the lake, get some of this energy out. No one's coming for me." *No one.* She was...alone.

"I don't know how you can be so sure. Unless you think California's guilty." His voice was low, dangerous, but pained. Challenging her to say she thought Morrison was responsible.

"I don't think Morrison did it. You know that." But did she really believe it? She wasn't sure. He had the hammer, for god's sake. Maybe she was just afraid. Afraid that he was guilty. Afraid that the one person she thought she could rely on had turned out to be worse than the rest. Or was she afraid he was innocent and would come home, ready to...be with her? She really was fucked up if she couldn't decide. Not that it was a good time in her life to be deciding anything, but—

"Good. Then stay here for him, Taylor."

Her heart was beating too fast, her lungs too tight. *I can't stay here. I'll suffocate.*

"I'm going to get him out, but I can't do that if you're running all over the place like—"

You can't make me stay. "Like what?" Shannon's heart was in her throat. "Like some idiot who doesn't know what's good for them? Like your partner's plaything?" Petrosky stared at her, eyes widening with surprise. But she couldn't stop. "I don't need your permission. I'm not a prisoner."

"I was going to say like you don't care someone might be following you," Petrosky said slowly. "And I never wanted to make you feel like a prisoner, Taylor. I just need to know you're safe."

"You don't need to know shit. I'm not your fucking daughter." Her chest was on fire, all her grief channeling into fury.

Petrosky froze, his eyes locked on her face. "So you're not." He lumbered off across the lawn to his car as Shannon stalked into the house and slammed the door behind her.

. . .

Conviction

TEN MINUTES LATER, Shannon emerged wearing one of Derry's old sweat suits and a pair of her own sneakers. Petrosky's car was gone. *Good.* Though her heart was already aching over what she'd said to him. If only she could take it back; she of all people knew what it was like to lose someone —and to want to protect those you had left.

Valentine got out of the car, his gaze swinging from one side of the road to the other. "Taylor? You're not leaving, are you?"

Goddammit, not you too. She bristled. "I can do anything I please, Valentine."

"Hey, I'm not here to manhandle you like Petrosky. I'm just your friend, you know? We've known each other a long time."

Since before she'd had Abby. Since before she'd gotten married. Since before Derry got sick. But they'd never been close. Even when he'd come to see her in the hospital, he'd only stayed long enough to drop off flowers and hold the baby before disappearing. He hadn't known what she needed. No one had; even Derry was too wrapped up in his new daughter to worry about Shannon, and rightly so. But the thick, suffocating aloneness she'd felt then was much like the ache she felt now, even in Valentine's presence.

The space left by Morrison's absence gaped like a black hole in her chest, already hollowed out by Derry's loss. She wanted to scream. To cry. The panic that her best friend might be gone for good thrummed in her veins, far hotter than any worry about what he might expect of her once—*if*— he got out.

Valentine knowing her "a long time" hadn't translated into knowing shit about her. Without Morrison, having company was superficial—pointless. She needed to be alone. She needed to get away. She needed her brother back. Her shoulders sagged.

Valentine put a hand on her arm. "Hey, Taylor, why don't you go inside, eh?"

She pulled her arm away. "Just watch the house. I'll be back."

"Where are you going?"

I don't have to answer to you either. But she didn't feel like arguing, didn't have the energy. "I'm just going to run around the neighborhood. I might circle the lake."

"At least—hey, Taylor, wait!"

She ignored him and took off down the road. Fuck Petrosky. Fuck Valentine too, and his fake concern. And Morrison. And Roger. And cancer. Fuck them all. She could run all night, and she'd be perfectly safe. And if she wasn't—hell, maybe if someone bludgeoned her with a hammer too, she'd finally get a little sleep.

Her feet were a blunt metronome on the sidewalk. Living room lights and the blue glare of televisions glowed behind curtained windows in happy houses where people were alive and intact and unburdened by death. People who had brothers and fathers they probably didn't even appreciate. *Fuck them too.* She ran faster, channeling all her worry, all her rage, all her grief, into her legs.

Her thighs were aching by the time she turned onto the side street that led to the lake. No asphalt here, just dirt and rocks that crunched underfoot as she made her way down to the water where the surface sparkled under the light of a half-moon. To her other side, the houses were more scattered, separated by patches of scrubby woods. She wheezed in the acrid air from someone's wood-burning fireplace and kept going. Her shirt stuck to her back. Her exhales fogged in front of her, and then the glistening houses stopped entirely, and it was just her and the water kissing the shore and the raccoons shuffling through the brush on the other side. The breeze whipped against her back, angry, stinging, then went still.

The rustling grew louder. A stray dog? A coyote?

Shannon was turning to peer into the trees when movement behind her caught her eye. *What the—*

It was too late. The dull thunk of wood on bone rang

through the night. Hot, white pain shot through her leg as she tumbled and went down, and a fist—a knee maybe—smashed into the back of her skull. Stars exploded behind her eyes. Then an arm was around her throat, closing off her airway—

No, fuck, no. She slashed at the arm around her neck with her nails, listening to her assailant's breathing, the sound loud and ragged in her ears. In front of her, the lake was placid and still. Derry would have liked it. Her vision wavered. And there was Abby's face, tear-stained, mouth open in a silent wail.

No. Abby could not lose anyone else, not now.

Shannon heaved herself up on one foot, driving her attacker backward. The grip on her throat lessened, and she sucked in a frenzied breath of something spicy-sweet. Then the fingers on her throat clamped down again, harder, tighter, and her sweaty palms slipped and slid as she tried to tear the gloved fingers from her throat. Black tugged at the corners of her vision. She drove an elbow into her attacker's chest and felt a pop, maybe the snap of a clavicle, and a sharp exhale hit the back of her neck. But no sound from the person behind her, nothing but the water on the shore and the throbbing of her pulse. The pressure on her windpipe remained.

She closed her eyes and heaved backward, toppling herself and her attacker to the dirt. The pressure on her neck disappeared, and she surged to her feet and hurtled backward along the road. Her shin screamed. Her attacker leapt up—short, wearing a ski mask, wrapped in a puffy jacket, or maybe that was bulk. Behind the mask, eyes shone black and beady in the gloom.

Shannon ran forward, intending to drive a shoulder into her attacker's gut, but the asshole stumbled back and fled. She watched them go, gasping air into her burning lungs, coughing blood from a split lip.

Headlights shot around the corner and cut through the night, exposing her and blinding her at the same time. She hurtled toward the woods, scrambling over dead leaves and brush, frantically feeling for trees to hide behind—not that a tree would help much if the car jumped the curb to mow her down. Her heel caught in a rut. She stumbled and hit her knees and tears sprang into her eyes, but she did not stop—Shannon ripped at the underbrush, groping for a branch, anything that she could use as a weapon if they got out of the car.

The car screeched to a halt, its headlights sending a cone of light around her. *Not like this. Not tonight.* She missed Derry, but she was not ready to meet him again just yet. She scrambled for the trees and slung herself behind a fir, grabbing a branch to use like a baseball bat. Her throat felt hot and swollen. Dizziness pulled at her.

"Shannon?" Shoes crunched from the car. *Petrosky. Petrosky?* "Jesus Christ, Taylor."

She dropped the branch and slumped against the tree, the world already hazy and fading around her. The last thing she remembered was Petrosky scooping her into his arms.

29

SHE WAS WALKING with Derry along the shore, hand in hand, watching Abby scamper ahead of them at the edge of the surf. "Wait," Shannon yelled, but Abby was gone, leaping into the ocean, disappearing under the waves. Shannon ran, screaming into the sea, but she could not hear Abby's cries. There was only the steady pulse of the ocean. Then a wave, high and white-crested, swelled in front of her, and Morrison rose above her on a surfboard, his hair flying like King Triton. "Help me!" she yelled to him. He threw his head back and vomited water tinged red with blood.

"Ms. Taylor?" A soft female voice, tense but confident, cut into the remnants of her dreams. Then: "I don't think she can see you now, sir."

"It's important for an investigation." *Petrosky.*

Shannon tried to force her eyes open, but her lids felt as if they were weighted down. "I'm... He's okay."

"You've had quite a scare, Ms. Taylor. You need rest."

I can't let him leave. "I need to talk to him." Her tongue felt twice its normal size, and her voice crackled like the rasp of Derry's final breaths. And it reminded her of the sounds, the whispers in the woods, the crunch of gravel beneath her shoes, the snapping twigs she'd assumed were coyotes. She could practically feel the pressure on her neck. Could almost see those eyes, beady in the dark, and the puffy, thick shoulders. The scent of herbs and sweat still clung to the back of her throat. The gloves, she realized, had been to protect his skin—he had been watching her. Waiting for her to be alone. He'd been ready to kill her.

She coughed, and the pain in her throat caused her to clench her eyelids together more tightly.

"We need some water," Petrosky said.

"On the table, sir." The nurse's voice had lost its edge. Then the sound of plastic on plastic, the wet whoosh of liquid, and the cup was pressed against her lower lip, carrying with it the scent of cigarettes from Petrosky's hand.

She let the liquid rush into her mouth and swallowed. "Thanks." Her eyelids still didn't want to open, but she dragged them into a squint, trying to focus on Petrosky's face as her vision adjusted. The light was blinding. "How long have I been out?"

"Six hours." He grabbed the remote and pushed a button to incline the bed.

Her shoulders tightened. "Oh, shit. Abby. And Alex."

"They're sleeping, and Valentine is still posted outside, watching them. I'll let them know in the morning."

She relaxed against the pillow. The back of her head throbbed. "What happened? I mean…what's wrong with me?"

"To start with, you're crazy." His eyes twinkled then dimmed.

She almost smiled, but everything hurt too much. "Physically, Petrosky. I think we both know I made an error in judgment. Is anything broken?" She tested one leg, then the other. Sore. Bruised, certainly, but she'd know the sharp agony of a fracture.

"No breaks. Blunt force trauma to the head, probably a concussion. Lots of bumps and bruises. Nothing too major."

"They go over everything in my chart with you?"

"Nope. Swiped it from the nurses' station. I also took swabs from under your fingernails. Looks like you got cloth, no skin, so if you scratched anyone, their DNA is still inside their jacket." Petrosky sank into the chair beside the bed. "I never should have left. I'm sorry."

"I told you to."

"No excuse. And Valentine is a fucking pushover."

"And you're a fucking asshole." She sighed. "I'm sorry too."

He squinted at her as if trying to remember what she'd done. Finally, he shrugged. "No worries, Taylor. Let's just find the dickhead who attacked you. Then we can both be pissed at them."

"Deal." She almost smiled then closed her eyes, trying to think. There had to be something. Why hadn't she heard anyone? "No one followed me running, and there was no car…until you. I don't know where they came from."

"There's a back road there, runs behind the lake houses. Anyone who saw you leave, and had a vague idea of where you were headed, could have pulled up there and waited in the woods until you ran by." He drew something out of his coat, a bottle barely bigger than his hand. Jack Daniels.

"They're going to throw you out, Petrosky."

"Can't throw me out. I'm the *law*." He unscrewed the top and put the bottle to his lips.

"How much have you had already?"

"Not enough."

"Morrison's going to kick your ass."

"Ohh, too bad Morrison's not here."

She looked down at her hands, the backs scraped and raw. All her thoughts felt fuzzy around the edges. "I know."

Petrosky rested the bottle in his lap. "What do you remember about the person who attacked you?"

Gloves. And a mask. And they were strong, but it might have just felt that way because they'd gotten her from behind. "They were on the shorter side, shorter than me."

"Could it have been Roger?"

She shook her head, and pain shot from the back of her skull down into her neck. "Roger's not short." Nausea rolled through her abdomen and upset the water sloshing around in her belly.

"You sure, Taylor? I could use something on him. I've been watching his bank accounts, his credit cards, his computers, for evidence of bribes. Nothing. You'd think after your outburst he'd have panicked, done something, but..."

She pushed herself up, straighter on the bed. "How do you know that, about his accounts, and his computers?"

"Morrison set up a tracking device on his computer before he got put away."

What? "That'll never be admissible, Petrosky. Even if you did find solid evidence, he'd get away with all of it. And Roger didn't do this to me."

His eyes darkened. "You didn't get a good look at his face."

Petrosky wanted it to be Roger as much as Roger wanted it to be Morrison. "I would know his hands."

"Maybe not if he never hit you before."

Roger almost had, the week before she left him. And she'd been just as ready to punch him back. "The person who grabbed me was short," she repeated, thinking. "About my height, because their chin was digging into my shoulder."

"Kimball's height?"

She stared at him. "Maybe."

"A few witnesses say Kimball's had a temper on him lately."

She pictured Kimball frothing at the mouth, how angry his eyes had been at the gym. But...it couldn't be him, could it? Internal Affairs would have found something. "If there was a real problem, they'd have suspended him by now."

"Not everyone notices real problems, Taylor. Look at Columbine."

"That's completely different," Shannon said. She pushed hair out of her face and winced as she brushed a tender spot near her temple.

Petrosky raised the bottle again and took a long swallow. "Maybe. Or maybe in both cases, we're talking about psychos. And power." He reached a file folder off the end table and set it on her lap. "Got these too. Interesting, I think."

Pain throbbed through her forehead and splintered down across her cheeks to her ears, but she blinked rapidly to force her eyes to focus on what he'd put in front of her. Papers. Photos. The first picture was of Kimball and his wife, her in a blue dress, Kimball smiling and dapper in a suit.

"Mrs. Amanda Kimball was a product of the system herself. Broken home, tossed from one foster home to another. The Kimballs even tried to adopt a few years back—guess they wanted to add a little boy to their clan. But it never happened, and they never had another one of her own." His voice was lower, gruffer. Maybe drunker. "Know what causes infertility, Taylor? Steroids. And they mess with your brain. Mania, depression, instability, aggression, impulsiveness—all things he's been tagged for in the last few months."

Infertility. The Kimballs had talked about it once at a dinner party. Later, Roger had said it was Amanda, but maybe he'd lied about that too. And Kimball had bulked up so quickly. Were they looking at roid rage?

Petrosky belched and wiped his mouth. "Derek Lewis wasn't known for selling steroids, but who knows? Maybe Kimball went to buy and, due to some overreaction to an argument, Lewis ended up dead. The rest was cover-up, trying to get rid of anyone else who knew anything that could lead back to him."

Was steroid use big enough to risk murdering someone over? It wasn't like Kimball was using cocaine—he probably wouldn't have even gone to jail. Might have lost the gym, but...

The bottle clanked against the arm of the chair as Petrosky shifted in the seat. "Found some interesting financial statements too. Seems Kimball's been hurting since he opened the gym—nearly forty thousand in the hole. Maybe he and Roger had some kind of agreement going on. They both could have been in on that plea deal thing."

This again? She fought a wave of dizziness. "Kimball wouldn't have known anything about the cases, would have had no contact with the families." Roger wouldn't have needed him.

"But his wife knew all about the cases—she would have been perfect to vet who might pay for a reduction in charges."

And Roger wouldn't have had to do anything but change the plea.

"Plus, the social work department works close with the rehab center—if they want Morrison to stay put away"—he took another drink—" they've got people who will say whatever it takes to keep out of jail themselves. Hell, half of them would give a false statement for one clean drug test."

Shannon flipped to the next photo, which showed Frieda Burke in a ball gown laughing at a grinning Kimball. Same tux. Same party. "Where'd you get these, Petrosky?"

"The photographer always takes some candids at the policeman's ball after he does the posed ones. For the website. 'Look at us! Cops are just like you!'" Petrosky's jazz hands were unnerving. He lowered them before she had to say anything.

"Social workers always go to these parties?" Her voice came out a half groan, and she immediately wanted to take the words back. She sounded weak.

"Nope. Not sure why Burke was there."

Pain sliced through her brain. She dropped the photos back into the file, put her hands to her head, and inhaled through her nostrils.

"You okay?" Petrosky leaned toward the bed, hands on his knees.

"I'm okay. A little…nauseous."

"A concussion will do that." Petrosky settled back into the chair and took another slug from the bottle. His eyes looked...worried, sad even, but that might have been a trick of her wavering vision. "Does Morrison know, Taylor?"

"Know what?" She put her hands at her sides, every movement painfully sharp.

"About the baby."

"I..." Dizziness unfocused her eyes. "Whose baby?"

"I didn't think so." He lifted the bottle again.

The room around Shannon pulsed, and nausea pulled at her, harder this time, her stomach slithering around, trying to creep up into her throat. *No. I can't be pregnant.* "I'm gonna be sick."

Petrosky reached from the end table and thrust a plastic kidney under her face. He held her hair as she vomited bile and the water she'd just sipped. When she was done, he handed her a towel and set the kidney back on the table, all nonchalant, like it wasn't full of puke.

"Water?"

"Not now." *The baby.* She stared at him. "I'm pregnant?"

"You didn't know?"

"No!" She watched him squint at her. *Is he fucking with me?* "How did you—"

"Read your chart, remember?" He raised the bottle again. "And listened in on the residents discussing your condition during shift change."

She put a hand on her stomach. *A baby.* A baby? What had she done? She wasn't ready for this, was she? "Is it...okay?"

"Yep. But it's real early. Probably wouldn't have shown on a home test for a couple weeks." Petrosky collapsed back into the chair. "Morrison's a good man, Taylor. You should tell him. He's not even pissed that you haven't been over there, just keeps asking if you're okay."

"I just found out, Petrosky. Give me a minute to process before we discuss who I need to tell." And it wasn't true anyway. Couldn't be. Could it? She tried to recall her last period, the date that she and Morrison had... Shit. And he was in jail, accused of murder. She thought he was innocent, but that was no guarantee—Roger had held himself in check too, calm for years before the bullshit started. She couldn't risk being wrong again. She'd do this baby thing herself if she decided to do it at all.

"I don't need a good man."

"Enough with the feminist bullshit."

"Excuse me?"

Petrosky waved a hand in the air like he was waving away a bad smell. "I know, I know, you don't need him. He doesn't need you either. But you want each other. Not all of us tell our friends that we want them around. Morrison? Hell, he told me years ago he was going to marry you."

"Sounds like he only confides in you." *Instead of me.* The thought made her already sensitive stomach burble, but she couldn't tell if it was from the pain of hearing Morrison's secrets from someone else or the...*pregnancy*.

"You know he doesn't just say it out like that. He said you were his kind of awesome. Which seems like Surfer Boy speak for, 'I want to fuck her,' except that California has never said anything like that about anyone."

"Or maybe you're reading too much into it."

Petrosky appraised the bottle, picked at the label with a fingernail. "He doesn't trust that relationship shit, much, Taylor. Doesn't get involved easy." He met her gaze, eyes clear and focused and earnest. "But he'd marry you in a second."

Bile rose in her throat again, and she swallowed it back. "I'm never getting remarried," she spat. And if it turned out that Morrison really had... She couldn't finish the thought. Her limbs felt like they were sinking into the bed. "So, you've been to see him?"

Petrosky scowled at the wall like he wanted to shove his fist through it. "Once. Cook said I was on a list—he had to escort me back, and Morrison and I didn't really get to chat. Cook said Roger cited some Supreme Court bullshit about restricting non-family visitors for drug users, but I assume he mostly told them I'd be a troublemaker if they let us alone." The alcohol had thickened Petrosky's voice. "I don't necessarily disagree."

"Am I on the list?"

"Don't know. Probably. Roger's convinced that we're covering for Morrison. That Morrison's been buying drugs from Lewis for a long time. Roger'll probably be over at the detention center himself tomorrow, trying to convince Ashley Johnson to testify that it's true in exchange for her freedom. As it is, he probably won't be able to hold her much longer."

Ashley Johnson was going to go free. The weight on Shannon's chest grew heavier. She'd put Johnson in jail for a crime that she hadn't committed, and if Johnson was innocent, someone else was guilty. And Morrison was a druggie. Maybe he did do it. Maybe he'd been so high he didn't even remember doing it. Maybe this baby was doomed to be a totally emotionless psychotic freak too. But...no. Jesus, what was she thinking?

"I was going to write a strongly-worded letter to the warden, but now I think I'll just throw eggs at Roger's house. Maybe a Molotov cocktail." Petrosky pulled at the bottle. "I fucked up, Taylor. I'm sorry. I shouldn't have left." His words were definitely slurred.

"Lie down and rest, Petrosky. We've got a big day tomorrow."

He leaned back in the chair and stuck the half-empty bottle under his shirt. "I was afraid you'd say that."

30

They let her out the next morning, shaky and disoriented, but with a furious fire in her belly that wouldn't relent. Someone had tried to kill her. Someone had fucked with the wrong girl.

Petrosky appeared unfazed by his night in the rigid hospital chair or by the now empty bottle of whiskey hidden in the hospital trash. He dropped her at her house—her own house—and waited in the kitchen while she showered and dressed, eating leftover cookies from the wake. She tried to choke down a bite of chocolate chunk, but it stuck in her throat. What she wanted was chia-berry oatmeal.

Petrosky brushed crumbs from his shirt. "Morrison leave any of that mushroom coffee over here?"

"I don't think so." She could almost taste the coffee, almost smell it, almost smell…him. And it wasn't enough.

Petrosky was watching her like he knew exactly what she was thinking. "How you feeling, Taylor?"

"Tired. Weak." She shook her head to clear her thoughts and winced at the pain radiating from the back of her head down into her neck. *I need to go see Morrison.* "I thought… Can you drive me to the detention center? I should go, you know? Talk to Morrison."

Petrosky glanced at her stomach.

"Not about that. About the case." But guilt tingled in the back of her brain. *You can't tell him, Shannon. Not until you decide what you want to do about it. About...her. Or him.* "Maybe I'll visit Ashley Johnson, too. See if Roger got to her yet."

"California's had a lot of time to think. Maybe he came up with something." Petrosky wiped chocolate from his lips with the back of his hand. "I'll drive you to the detention center and wait outside."

Shannon grabbed her jacket. "You don't need to go with me."

"I know. But need is a funny thing, Taylor." He opened her front door, and chill air stung her face. "Lots of shit you don't need to do," he said to the driveway. "But you do it anyway."

AT THE DETENTION CENTER, Cook gave her a sideways look but admitted her into the holding area and stepped back to the entrance with a whispered, "Sorry, Shannon." She ignored him and headed for the stalls, for the mesh, for her best friend.

She gasped when she saw Morrison. He looked ten pounds lighter, shrunken as if the cell walls had sucked the meat from his bones. Stubble crawled along his jawline, ragged and angry.

"Hey," he said. The word hung in the air between them, burgeoning with the possibility of things that needed to be said but couldn't be, not right then. Or maybe ever. If he was guilty, if she decided to get rid of the baby... She cleared her throat. "We need to get you out of here."

"Give it time. They'll figure it out." His eyes were bloodshot, but his shoulders stayed square.

She gripped the ledge so hard her fingers ached. "Roger doesn't want to figure it out. He wants to lock you up forever."

"I'd imagine so." The corner of his mouth turned up, and her heart quickened. *Not normal.* Not a normal response at all and his eyes weren't as downcast as she'd thought they would be. He looked almost... *What the fuck?* Did he want to be here? Did he really not care? But he did, she knew he cared. Just as she knew she wanted to curl up in his arms and shut out the world. The worst week of her life and she had needed him to be there. Wanted him to hold her and tell her things were going to be okay—even if they weren't.

"I'm sorry about Derry," he said. "I hate that I wasn't there, Shanny."

"Me too." Heartache blistered her insides. *The case; focus on the case.* "Morrison, someone at the rehab center is telling Roger that you...coerced them into doing things they didn't want to do."

They stared at one another through the mesh, his breathing harsh but even, hers shallow so she didn't puke again.

"I've never taken advantage of anyone. I've put a lot of people away, though, so..." He shrugged. Same thing Petrosky had said, almost as if Petrosky had coached him. One addict enabling another? And if that were true, what did that make her? After all, she was in love with a druggie. Maybe a psycho.

But she was in love, and when he met her eyes, she didn't doubt her feelings. She needed help. A therapist. She put a hand on her stomach. Love wasn't enough to justify rash, life-altering decisions. She had a month to make up her mind, maybe two, but she couldn't wait that long to decide—the thought of dragging everything out made the throbbing in her head begin anew.

Talk, Shannon, say something. "Had any epiphanies while you've been in here?" Her voice was strained, and she cleared her throat instead of dwelling on why that was.

"More just...wonderings. Wonderings that I can't do anything about." He leaned toward the mesh. "Months before Lewis's death, Wheatley was doing Google searches on drugs, on charges for drug crimes, probably trying to ascertain how bad things would be for the person he saw at Lewis's apartment. Eventually, Wheatley must have talked to Lewis about what he'd seen, maybe even warned him against dealing. But our killer saw Wheatley leaving, or else Lewis mentioned Wheatley to the killer. Then panic, and goodbye, Derek."

Other than the Google searches, it was nothing she didn't already know. But there was still something that didn't make sense about any of these alternative killer scenarios. How had she not seen it before? Maybe she hadn't wanted to. "But Johnson didn't just wander in, say, 'Oh look, he's dead,' and go attempt suicide in the bathtub. Framing someone like that requires premeditation."

"I don't think the killer intended to frame her. I think he planned to kill her too. She might even have been the target."

"You think Ashley and not Derek was the… That doesn't make sense, Morrison."

"Just hear me out, okay?" His voice was strained, pressured, any hint of his earlier smile extinguished. "If Lewis was the target, the killer was probably someone who'd been to the house before—someone Ashley knew. She'd have been able to pick him out. Maybe the killer snuck up and stuck her in the neck, then carried her to the bathroom, not to frame her, but to kill her to make sure any traces of himself were gone. Then, later on, he realized the scene looked like Ashley could have done it and called it in from the pay phone, thinking she'd be dead by the time anyone got there."

The coffee Shannon had forced down in the car, bubbled up in her esophagus. It was a stretch and a big one at that. "Why not just wait? If he wanted her to die, why risk calling and saving her life?"

"Maybe he was worried about the baby."

The baby. Her heart shuddered, and she inhaled sharply through her nose, then forced out the air along with any lingering thoughts about her situation. "Morrison, this guy murders two people in cold blood and has a soft spot for their child?"

Morrison scratched at his stubble. "So let's pretend Ashley Johnson was the target. That Lewis and Wheatley died because they saw someone with *her*. What if that someone was Kimball?"

They had just cleared Kimball...again. Shannon shook her head. "I don't follow."

"I mean...you know he's a little flirty. But I think he had other women on the side."

Wow, Morrison's a regular rocket scientist. She couldn't decide why she was so angry at him, but she could feel the rage sizzling in her belly, mingling with the coffee, trying to escape.

"Specifically, I think Kimball had Ashley Johnson on the side."

The rage mellowed to agitated curiosity. He knew better. Unless he was trying to throw her off on purpose. Or... maybe, he was right. But he sure as hell needed more than just a gut feeling. "Kimball wasn't screwing Johnson in the apartment she shared with her boyfriend, Morrison. Derek Lewis hardly ever left the house because of his business, and when he did, he had friends in the apartment complex who would surely have noticed a guy like Kimball sauntering in there to keep Ashley company. We'd have more bodies if he was covering that up."

In another row, someone coughed, maybe Cook, and she jerked toward the sound and back to the mesh. Morrison looked like he wanted to say more.

"Time's up," Cook called through the room, but he sounded apologetic.

Morrison's gaze locked with hers, and the corner of his eye twitched. There was more, another secret he wasn't telling her. "Morrison?"

He peered past her and into the hall behind her.

"Morrison, what?"

He leaned so close his face almost touched the mesh.

"There were some strange cash withdrawals," he whispered, and his scent was unfamiliar, no coffee, no oats, no lavender, just the harsh tang of mint and laundry soap. "From Kimball's bank accounts. Stopped the week Johnson went away."

That's it? She shook her head. "Those withdrawals could have been for anything. There's no way to trace that, Morrison."

"There is. Because when Ashley Johnson had funds, she called Petrosky. He didn't connect it, but I recalled a few of the dates on the month prior. Dates we picked her up and dropped her at the bank. Or days she asked to stay at Petrosky's house, saying she was scared. Maybe she was just scared Lewis would find the money and take it."

But the cash flow wasn't a definite connection, and it certainly wouldn't pass the standard of reasonable doubt. Plus, it was all inadmissible. There was no way he'd gotten a warrant to look at Kimball's stuff, which meant... "You hacked into Kimball's accounts, didn't you?" Shannon watched as he nodded, almost imperceptibly. Hacking into the bank's server was illegal. *And impressively tricky.* But still illegal. "Petrosky doesn't know this yet?" He'd probably jump right on board with this crazy theory.

Morrison shook his head. "I got put away before I could tell him. And I didn't really connect it in my head until this morning, sitting here alone."

Alone. Her gut clenched.

"And I know Kimball wasn't giving Johnson money for drugs. It was hundreds of dollars at a time, always the same amount, like a payoff. Not even close to a junkie's pattern."

He'd know about a junkie's pattern, right? She pushed the thought aside. If Kimball was paying Johnson for something, and that was a big if, Derek and Wheatley could have found out. Then Kimball would have had motive to kill both of them. But still not the opportunity if he was at the policeman's ball. Not that he couldn't have snuck out for half an hour, especially if someone else—their mystery heroin-addict-hair-donor—was watching Wheatley for him.

"Kimball's a cheat," Morrison said. "But he's charismatic. I think Johnson fell for him. I think Diamond's his."

She sucked in a breath, and the dry air burned the inside of her nose. That would explain the call to the precinct to make sure the baby was taken care of. "But even a narcissistic asshole like Kimball is too smart to leave a note on my car." Though he'd certainly have been able to—he worked right there at the precinct so no one would think it strange for him to be in the lot with an envelope. "Even if you're right, he could have made Wheatley look like an accident, let Johnson rot. Why on earth would he have thrown doubt that we had the right person by leaving that envelope?" It was illogical. Morrison was losing his shit.

Morrison slapped his hands onto either side of his head, peering through the mesh, his eyes darting around like a caged animal. "I just can't think. I can't get my head around all this. I..."

Shannon's stomach turned, watching his face contort as if, inside him, something was coming unhinged.

THE FIRST SET of bulletproof doors buzzed closed behind her, and with everything silenced, the world felt stiff and unwieldy, the pressure of the mere air humming in her ears as loudly as if someone were screaming.

If Morrison was right...could Kimball really be Diamond's father? And who else knew about it that might need protection? Perez had moved out of the building—so maybe she'd been frightened of Kimball too. But no...she'd met them in broad daylight in front of her building. And Perez would have mentioned a secret like the paternity of Ashley's baby. She wanted to get Ashley out of jail. No, any bribes from Kimball, any information about Diamond's father, Johnson had kept to herself.

The door in front of her opened. She walked into the next

chamber and waited. *Whoosh.* She was trapped between the walls of bulletproof glass, trapped inside her head. And no matter how insane Morrison's ideas were, he had been right about Ashley Johnson from the beginning. She owed it to him to look. And she owed it to herself—if there was any truth to this theory, she could get Morrison out of there. And home. With her.

At the front desk, Shannon headed to the bulletproof window, where Cook was already seated. He shrugged at her. "Sorry, Taylor."

"No worries." She lowered her voice. "Can I see the list of people who have been in to see Ashley Johnson since her arrest?"

"Aw, hell, Taylor, you know I'm not supposed to give you that."

"What? Why? I've taken those before."

"I wasn't even supposed to let you back, but I figured it couldn't hurt. But this isn't your case, and from what I understand, Internal Affairs wants all you guys separated while they investigate."

All of them separated? "Who told you that?"

"Roger."

"Fuck Roger."

His caterpillar brows lifted into his thinning hairline.

Shannon leaned toward the window. "You think Morrison's a murderer, Cook?"

His face fell. He shook his head.

"Help me out. I won't say a word. Maybe you can just happen to leave it on the desk for a minute." Like they were in some cheesy murder mystery.

"You know, I am due for a bathroom break," he said slowly and disappeared into a back room. Shannon paced and stared out the front window into the gray drizzle, half expecting Petrosky to be standing outside smoking a soggy cigarette. She was a little disappointed that he wasn't, but she had little time to ponder that; a door closed, Cook's footsteps receded, and she stepped to the window and peered down at the piece of paper left on the desk.

The visitor list for Ashley Johnson was short. Her. Petrosky. Burke.

And Park Kimball.

She waited, pacing, until Cook returned. "I need to see one more person," she said.

Cook nodded. "I thought you might."

31

ASHLEY JOHNSON HAD STARED. She'd cried. She'd avoided the questions about Kimball. But in the end, Shannon had blown up and told Ashley they were going public with Kimball's bank records and that the money Kimball had given her would be seized. That had done it.

Kimball and Johnson had met innocuously enough, at a bar. One broken condom later, and they both had a secret to keep. Kimball had offered Johnson an allowance, four hundred, paid every other week, but told her it would end if she opened her mouth about Diamond. The night Derek died, Johnson met Kimball at a hotel to pick up the money. The pocketful of cash was one reason she'd snuck past Derek that night, hoping he'd stay asleep until the morning when she could get to the bank before he discovered her secret.

Shannon didn't tell Ashley that Kimball had more to lose. She didn't mention that child support was a legal obligation once paternity was verified. She left the detention center, head pounding, and ran for Petrosky's car.

It wasn't Kimball who had attacked her last night: Petrosky had already verified his alibi, and he was too strong for her to fight off anyway. But someone had attacked her. Someone who might be concerned about their progress on the case. Someone who would have wanted to punish Ashley Johnson.

Amanda Kimball smiled at Shannon—self-assured, almost haughty—a far cry from the awkward guilt of the other day. But the look she gave Petrosky was the same as before. He could have been an insect she wanted to smash under her heel. "Back again?" she asked, eyes on her computer screen.

Shannon peered at Amanda's throat, but little was visible behind the collar of her sweater. Had she worn her hair down the last time they'd seen her? Or ever? Maybe she was hiding a bruise from Shannon's elbow beneath her waves.

"Just following up on a few things about your former employee," Petrosky said.

Amanda raised an eyebrow. "Mm-hmm. I actually thought you guys had been removed from that case." Half smile. Definitely haughty. *Smug bitch.*

Petrosky didn't appear to have heard her. "We're looking into the Johnson case too."

Amanda chewed the inside of her cheek, probably torn between telling them to leave and the desire to find out what they knew. Surely her husband had told her that Shannon and Petrosky had been booted off Johnson as well.

Amanda sighed. "What can I do for you?"

Never underestimate curiosity. Unless she was trying to figure out whether to leave the country.

"Mrs. Kimball, I'm having a little trouble remembering… can you tell us again where you were on the evening of February fifteenth?"

Amanda cocked her head. "I'm sorry?"

"We're just trying to figure out if any workers in the area might have seen something that would help us. I gotta admit, this case is a doozy." He ran a hand over his forehead, and Shannon squinted at him. "Makes me feel like a real idiot," he said and cut his eyes at Shannon until she turned away.

The hard lines around Amanda's mouth softened. Less anxious now. "Sounds like you're reaching, but I'm not sure I can help. You already have my statement about that day."

"Maybe you can tell me again. Who from your office was scheduled to be in the area around Derek Lewis's apartment that evening?"

Amanda paused, her shoulders tense again, and she pulled her keyboard closer to her and resumed tapping. "We've been over this. I visited a family on Vista Marie about four. Frieda was three streets up, with a family on Dover at five-thirty, but she would have been there at least an hour or so. And Wheatley was scheduled to see someone up the road on Henrietta at three-thirty, but I don't have anything for him after that." She pushed the keyboard aside. "That all?"

Petrosky splayed his fingers on the desk. "And where did you go after your appointment?"

Her expression hardened. "Not sure what you're getting at with that question. I'd feel better if I talked to my husband about this."

"Why, does he know where you were the night Derek Lewis gasped his final breath?"

Amanda's jaw dropped.

"Does he know where you were last night? Funny, he has an alibi with the department, but no one seems to know where you were."

"What's this all—"

"It's a little warm in here, isn't it?" Petrosky nodded to Amanda's arms, thoroughly encased in navy cotton. "Can you roll up your sleeves, Mrs. Kimball?"

The hard line of her mouth whitened as she pressed her lips together. She crossed her arms. "Please leave."

Petrosky touched Amanda's elbow, and she glowered at him but didn't move. "Where were you last night, Mrs. Kimball?"

"At home. Not that it's any of your business."

"Anyone else there?"

"No, just me." She jerked her arm away.

Petrosky's eyes darted around the room. "Where's your coat, Ms. Kimball?" *The coat.* If they could match the fibers from under Shannon's nails—

Amanda reached for her phone, touching buttons rapid-fire.

Petrosky smiled. "You calling your husband? Make sure you ask him what he was really doing on the nights he was supposedly picking up your daughter from her nonexistent ballet practices. Maybe getting into drugs? Or maybe he was busy screwing someone else? Before he got her tossed in jail, maybe he was hanging out with his baby's mother and their year-old daughter?"

Amanda's fingers froze over the buttons.

"You can't possibly tell me you didn't know." Petrosky leaned his bulldog face over the desk. "You never wondered where all that money was going?"

Amanda dropped the phone and shot to her feet, her hands planted on the desk as if she needed the furniture to bear the weight of her rage. Her lips pulled into a snarl like a rabid dog. But Shannon was not looking at the curl of her lip—her eyes were trained on the gap in Amanda's sweater, now hanging slightly open. No bruise on her neck. Nothing on her upper chest. Even if Shannon hadn't broken Amanda's clavicle, there would be a mark.

"Get out," Amanda hissed.

"Touchy, touchy." Petrosky backed toward the door. "We'll be back, Mrs. Kimball."

Petrosky slammed Amanda's office door behind them, the sound reverberating through the hallway like growling thunder. In the back of Shannon's brain, something snapped, the sound of the rolling hall morphing into the pop she had felt under her elbow, and suddenly she could smell the lake air and the spicy stink of the person who had their fingers around her throat. Shannon's head throbbed dully. *I have to get out of here.* She didn't realize Petrosky's hand was on her elbow until his fingers tightened.

"Wait," he said.

The door to Frieda Burke's office opened, and Burke hurried into the hall, turning toward Amanda's office. She stopped short when she saw them. Shannon's heart thundered in her ears like the slamming door had moments before.

"She came running fast, didn't she?" Petrosky muttered. He advanced on Burke, and she backed toward her office, snagging her heel on the carpet. He caught her by the arm of her turtleneck sweater before she could fall.

"Everything okay, Ms. Burke?"

She righted herself and leaned against the doorframe. "I heard the door. I thought maybe Amanda had an unruly client." Burke scanned the hallway, avoiding Petrosky's icy glare. Avoiding Shannon too. "I was just…surprised because I didn't know she had anyone coming in."

"You always keep tabs on her?" Petrosky asked.

"I… Not really. I don't know."

Petrosky cocked his head at her, his eyes roving over her sleeved arms. "What happened to your wrist?"

Burke shrugged. "Nothing."

"Looked like it hurt to touch. You winced pretty good there," he said wryly.

She shook her head. "No, just surprised. You grabbed me hard."

Burke was small. Thin. What did her clavicle look like? Adrenaline thrummed through Shannon's bloodstream. She trained her eyes on Burke, who was still frozen against the doorframe and staring at Petrosky with unconcealed hatred. Petrosky gave it back. Burke had been involved, in some capacity, with every person who had been murdered. She was Lewis and Johnson's caseworker. Wheatley's coworker. And Lucky…well, she had a history of hating Shannon, and she'd been living with Griffen after Abby's birth. Burke would have known where to hit to scare Shannon. But why?

Petrosky stared at Burke as she pushed past them, curls bobbing in time with her steps as she approached Amanda's door. Shannon stared after her, trying to ignore the rage blistering her abdomen. *Something isn't right.* Whoever was after Shannon had hurt Lucky. Whoever had hurt Lucky—*It was me*—had hurt others. Lewis. Wheatley. She could hate Burke all she wanted, but the woman wasn't a killer. Burke had no motive.

But Park and Amanda Kimball, they had motive for killing Ashley Johnson and Derek Lewis too, if they thought he knew about Diamond's paternity. Ditto on Benjamin Wheatley. And Lucky's murder, Shannon's attack, everything had to be connected. It wasn't coincidental—couldn't be.

"Feisty, isn't she?" Petrosky said as they walked down the hall and out the front doors to the parking lot. "Wonder what's under her sweater."

Outside, the air was muddy with tension and an impending storm. Shannon followed Petrosky to the car, massaging her aching neck. "If anyone but you had said that, Petrosky, I would have thought it was a come on."

He didn't smile. Derry would have smiled. She suddenly missed her brother so terribly it felt like the world was collapsing around her. She could almost hear his voice in the deep gray sky above, but there was no hint of her brother's warmth, only streaks of a deeper black, a storm ready to unleash hell on earth. Someone needed to pay. For killing Derek Lewis. For murdering Lucky. For the fact that Derry had died without knowing his daughter was safe. For everything.

But...there was more, she knew it. There was something she was missing. Something she'd been told.

"Mrs. Kimball seemed a little shocked to hear about her husband's love child, didn't she?" Petrosky said, too quietly, like he was trying to avoid waking a child in the backseat.

Amanda had seemed surprised. Shocked, even. Either she really hadn't known her husband was cheating or she was a damn good liar. "I'm not buying Amanda Kimball as a killer. She had no marks on her, and I hit my attacker pretty hard... or I thought I did."

"We still have our mystery person. With the prints and the hair. Maybe they hired out."

She rubbed her still smarting head, thoughts solidifying at the pressure on her temples. "Wait." She put a hand on Petrosky's arm. "Burke lied to me. To us."

Petrosky raised an eyebrow, but he stopped. "About what?"

"The first time I spoke to Ashley Johnson after the trial, she told me she didn't say anything to Burke about the other social worker being there. But Lucinda Lewis said that Burke knew about it, mentioned it. And last time we met with Burke, she herself admitted to knowing another worker had been there." At the time, it hadn't seemed like much, a misunderstanding. But now...it might be something.

Petrosky pulled a cigarette from his pack, looked at Shannon's still-flat belly, and replaced it in his pocket.

"How'd she know, Petrosky? How'd she know about the other worker? It wasn't in the file, or I would have known. The police didn't know. Even Griffen, Johnson's own defense attorney, didn't know another social worker had been to Lewis's apartment that day."

"Good enough for me." Petrosky cut his eyes at the building behind them and turned toward the car. "Can I drop you at home?"

Her head throbbed, and every step she took felt like slogging through quicksand. But nothing waited for her at home except utter silence and her dead brother's picture on the mantel, reminding her that things had once been happy. "I'm coming with you." *For Derry.* For Morrison. She put a hand on her stomach. *For all of us.*

"Suit yourself."

A whoosh of dank spring air still laced with the chill of winter kicked up around Shannon's feet, and she shivered involuntarily. "Where are we going?"

"We'll check out Burke's place." He unlocked the car and climbed inside as Shannon scrambled into the passenger seat. "We'll get Roxy too. In case."

In case Burke's a fucking psycho? Shannon squinted out the windshield. Could Burke have been as jealous of Ashley Johnson as she had been of Shannon, everyone having babies when she couldn't? That would mean Wheatley and Lewis were just collateral damage, which made no sense. Shannon turned to Petrosky, examined the set of his jaw, the twitch in his temple that screamed determination—or wrath.

"We getting a warrant?" she asked. They didn't have enough for a warrant. And they couldn't just go through her stuff. Above, the clouds loomed lower, and the air thickened with soggy humidity.

"I don't need it to be admissible." Petrosky started the car and pulled out of the lot. "I just need to know."

SHANNON LEANED her head against the seat back and watched the sky through the car windshield. The headache she'd been fighting all morning clawed at her brain. *If the rain starts before we get inside, we're screwed—she'll know we were there. We shouldn't be doing this at all.* "Are you sure this is a good idea?"

Petrosky's fingers beat a frantic rhythm against the console. "I never said it was a good idea. But we need more than what we've got right now." He popped his neck and turned into a neighborhood near the gym full of cookie-cutter houses and the occasional tire swing.

She gestured behind her, where Roxy was panting out the back window. "I'm still not sold on bringing her."

"Roxy's a good girl, aren't you Roxy?" *Tick tick tick*, fingers on leather. From the backseat, Roxy yipped.

Shannon raised an eyebrow, and a sharp pain shot into her forehead. "Good girl, my ass. You know she used to be a police dog. You want her to search." *Tick tick tick.* "But you know we need a warrant, and if she ruins something—"

"She won't ruin anything. We need to see if there's anything worthwhile to find first. If we need to, we'll figure out probable cause after." *Tick tick tick tick.*

"Not the way it's supposed to work, Petrosky."

"Sue me, Taylor."

Eventually, someone will. She straightened and put her hand over his vibrating fingers to still the racket before her head exploded. "What's up with you, Petrosky?"

Roxy put her bull head over the console and licked Shannon's arm.

Petrosky shrugged and put his hand back on the steering wheel, muscles still taut with nervous energy. If Petrosky was this jittery, he had a reason to be. And it wasn't about the search—he did stuff like this all the time. Did he know something she didn't? Her hand tensed over Roxy's head, and the dog's ears pricked forward. They were there.

Burke's house was a red brick colonial, complete with picket fence and hyacinths in the garden just barely shooting green sprouts through the dirt, electric in the gloom. Two, maybe three blocks from the gym. Walking distance. Petrosky parked four houses up.

Shannon hesitated with her hand on the door handle. She wanted to tell Petrosky yet again that they needed to get out of there, that they should get a warrant, that getting arrested themselves wouldn't help Morrison. But doing things the right way hadn't helped them at all so far. They were dealing with someone who had framed the man she…loved. *Loved.* She cleared her throat. "You really think Burke's involved?"

"She knows all the victims. And she's got quite a vendetta against people who hurt kids. Spends her life trying to make things better, right? It's gotta be frustrating."

True. Burke had also— "And you know what? She fostered Diamond too. Maybe she has a vested interest in punishing anyone who injured that little girl—Derek for hitting her; Ashley for not protecting her." Shannon relaxed her grip on the door, but the rigidity in her arm remained. "But why would Wheatley have been scoping the place out for months before Derek's murder? It can't just be unconnected." Unless…Burke was one of Derek's customers. Beat Wheatley to make sure he hadn't told anyone. And Burke could easily have taken Amanda Kimball's gym keys, though there was no way in hell Burke dragged Wheatley into the warehouse by herself.

"We'll find out more soon enough." He held up two silver keys and a gold one, all dangling from a keychain that read "Hug a Social Worker."

"Where did you—"

"I took them out of her pocket when she rammed into me."

"You mean when you grabbed her."

"Whatever." He shrugged. "Now come on, Taylor, I need a smoke." He popped open the car door and nodded to Roxy, who leapt from the backseat and onto the sidewalk.

Since when doesn't he smoke in his car? No wonder he'd been jittery on the way over.

"You coming, Taylor?" he said, smoke already thick around his face. "You can always stay here, claim innocence, if you don't want to get your hands dirty."

Fuck that. She followed him around the car as he started up the walk, scanning the neighborhood and flicking the ash from his cigarette on the muddy spring lawns as they passed. But there was not a soul to interrupt the subtle melody of still-bare branches rustling in the breeze. Any other time, the rustling might have been calming, mere white noise, but today, the hushed rippling sounded crass, almost dangerous, the whisper of a nightmare you couldn't shake. Roxy turned her face to the sky as if she too could feel the unsettled hum of the very air they breathed.

They turned up Burke's driveway and headed through the gate and around to the back. The back door opened into a blue and yellow kitchen straight out of a fifties home decor magazine. They'd barely stepped inside when Petrosky patted the dog on the head. Roxy's nostrils quivered.

"Seek, Roxy," Petrosky said.

Roxy took off, her nose at the cupboards, along the baseboards, poking into the next room. Petrosky opened the kitchen drawers, peered inside, and closed them again.

"What are you looking for?"

"Anything unusual. Maybe a bloody glove. It didn't help convict OJ, but..." He left the kitchen and strode into a cozy living room with traditional furniture—heavy wood. The air was thick with the smell of cinnamon, just like at the office. Shannon's stomach roiled. Spicy. Sweet. Potpourri? Was that what she'd smelled on her attacker?

Petrosky peered at the fireplace mantel. "Lots of pictures of her and Amanda."

On the mantel? That was prime real estate, not the place you'd expect to see a shrine to someone's coworker.

Shannon joined him at the photos. In the first one, Amanda and Burke were holding hands on a beach...or rather, Burke was holding onto Amanda's wrist, eyes on her friend, while Amanda smiled into the camera clutching some fruity drink. On either side of the vacation picture were more photos: Amanda and Burke at a fundraiser, Amanda with a child Shannon didn't recognize. In some of them, Amanda's face was turned away from the lens. Had she known those photos were being snapped?

"Wonder if we have a single white female situation. An obsession with Amanda and Burke's screwing Kimball on the side? We already know he's a cad who will put his dick in anything that moves."

"A...cad?"

"Trying to watch my mouth."

Shannon narrowed her eyes at him, then turned her attention back to the mantel. "Burke does seem awfully protective of Amanda. Maybe she found out that Kimball was Diamond's father and decided to get rid of the evidence before Amanda found out. Took out Lewis and tried to take out Johnson. Then Wheatley for knowing about it." Shannon shook her head. "But Burke couldn't hurt the baby, so she made that midnight call to the station to make sure someone took care of Diamond." Shannon peered at another photo on a nearby built-in bookcase: Amanda and Burke at some marathon, numbers pinned to their shirts, faces pink and shiny with a post-race glow.

Again, Burke ignored the camera in favor of looking at Amanda.

Petrosky snorted from the desk and held up a torn photo of Burke sitting on a boulder. At some point, there had been someone else in the picture, but now all that was left of them was half a severed arm, two orange bracelets on their wrist. Burke held the bracelet-clad hand with her own. "Looks like trouble in paradise."

Disquiet settled in Shannon's bones. "That's—I think that's Griffen's hand. The bands. On his wrist."

Petrosky cocked an eyebrow. But the torn picture wasn't really that unexpected—Griffen and Burke had gone through a dramatic breakup. Although...why would anyone keep half a photo? Why not just throw the whole thing away?

They combed through Burke's bedroom and the spare and found nothing unusual. Shannon headed to the bathroom to peek through the medicine cabinet—a few pain relievers, Q-tips, cotton balls, makeup. Normal. *What did I expect, a severed limb?* Shannon was rummaging through a cabinet drawer when Petrosky called her from the office, and she went to meet him.

"These pictures of Griffen too?" He turned a computer monitor her way and scrolled. "Can't see his face."

A dozen shots of Griffen and Karen: Karen on her own, here standing in a garden, there walking into an aluminum-sided colonial. Griffen coming out of his office, getting into his car, going to the grocery. Facing away from the camera in every picture. Burke couldn't very well snap them with Griffen or Karen looking at her—it was clear the couple didn't know the photos were being taken. "Yeah, that's Griffen. I recognize his hat. And Karen."

"Creepy."

"Yeah."

"Where's Griffen live, Taylor?"

"Used to have a place a few blocks up. Close to work so he could ride his bike. I think he lived here with Burke for a little while, but I'm not really sure when he moved out."

Roxy's howl split the silence and pain splintered the back of Shannon's skull. Petrosky was through the living room and gone before she could swallow back the grossness creeping up her throat. She followed his staccato footsteps into a small but tidy mudroom, where Roxy sat rigid in front of a door, barking—thin and high and acute.

Petrosky yanked the knob. Just outside the door, a chest freezer hummed like the monotonous drone of sitting monks. But like the twittering leaves, there was nothing calming or meditative about it—Shannon's brain buzzed with pain and the harsh sound of Roxy's toenails scraping the concrete as the dog skidded to a halt and sat, nose against the mat by the door that led to the outside.

Petrosky patted Roxy on the head. "Good girl, Roxy. Off." He peered at the mat. Shannon approached, stepping lightly to avoid jarring her already throbbing skull. Goddamn concussion. Unless that was the...baby. But no, it was too early for symptoms. She pushed her thoughts aside and squinted at the dark stains littering the mat. Looked like dirt. Or...

Petrosky put his thumb next to a tiny brown drip smeared into the grime.

"Blood?"

"Maybe." He snapped on a pair of latex gloves and pulled a vial from his jacket.

Shannon stepped back and hit her elbow on the wall as Roxy whined. Petrosky scraped some of the stain into the tube with an enclosed plastic scraper and dropped it into his coat pocket. Then he walked to the window, squinted at the pane, and hoisted the window open. The shrill screech of an alarm split the air.

"Petrosky, what the—"

"I was out walking the dog, Shannon. And Roxy just couldn't wait to get in here, with this window being open and all..."

"You're going to get arrested." The alarm. *Shit.* She pressed her fingers to her temple.

"Nah. Might not be admissible, might get sued, but…" He headed for the front door. "I'll finish up here and make some calls to find your buddy Griffen and his new girlfriend. Make sure they're okay. You go back to the car and wait for Valentine. You're pale as hell."

Shannon wanted to fight him on it, to stay there to see what happened. God knows she would have, but the dizziness rolling over her soured her stomach and pulled the room out of focus. "I'll wait across the street. Tell him to hurry."

VALENTINE DROVE Shannon home while Petrosky headed back to the station. Her head was pounding so violently that she had a hard time responding to Valentine's questions, and eventually, he gave up, leaving her to her pain and her thoughts. *Illegal search and seizure.* Petrosky was an idiot. Nothing they'd found would be admissible. Though maybe he was looking for something bigger—probably figured he'd get a confession. For Morrison's sake, she hoped he was right.

The nausea had crept up and stuck. She had thrown up twice on her way across the road, and again as Valentine pulled up. Her head throbbed more forcibly every time she retched. But even now, with her stomach empty and Valentine silent beside her, Shannon's brain ran wild. So many questions, so few answers. Revelations struggling toward realization but collapsing, frustratingly flat, before coming to fruition. Every pulse of pain from the lump on her head brought a new, disturbing idea. Yet each grisly scenario was preferable to the thought that Morrison was a murderer.

Shannon could see Burke going after Lewis and Johnson for hurting Diamond. She could see her going after them for Amanda's sake, too, regardless of whether Amanda had known about the affair before. Either way, Wheatley had been in the wrong place at the wrong time. And either way, whoever was after Shannon knew where to hit her to make it hurt—and they had.

But not everything fit. The note on her car was a broken spoke, jamming the cogwheel of every theory she produced. *It was me.* Would Burke have wanted to get caught, or wanted the credit? She didn't strike Shannon that way. Burke was insecure, needy even, if her response to Shannon's friendship with Griffen was any indication. Obsessive. But if Burke was that unhinged, why hadn't she attacked Karen? Brutal enough to kill to hide a secret for her best friend, or to protect a child, but she didn't go after the girlfriend of the dude she's obsessed with? And if Burke was obsessed with Amanda, she'd have gone after Kimball, right? It didn't add up. Then there was the car. As a social worker, Burke would have had no access to the police car Perez had seen outside Lewis's apartment—nor would Perez have mistaken Burke for the man she'd seen. Maybe Burke had a new boyfriend who'd helped her move Wheatley's body. That would explain their hair donor, and also why Burke might have left Karen alone. But there was no evidence of a boyfriend at Burke's house. So who had helped her, and why?

Valentine parked in her driveway, cut the engine, and took an enormous bite of the donut he held in wax paper. Morrison would have frowned and offered her a parfait or a granola bar or some coffee. *Mushroom coffee.* The thought made her heart hurt. As she approached the house, the rustling tree branches sighed a mournful ballad of grief and loss and sorrow. Somewhere above, a bird screamed. It sounded like the animal was crying.

She paced the silent hallways of her house, trying not to collapse. Everything felt empty. Cold. Lonely. As hollow as her chest. She tried to find solace in her office, but Derry's photo smiled at her, and she didn't deserve that grin—she hadn't been able to figure this case out, the one thing Derry had asked her for. And Morrison was still locked up, taken from her because she couldn't prove he was innocent. Karma for falsely imprisoning Ashley Johnson, maybe. Or for not being able to…save her brother.

The grief crashed over her like a ton of stone. They were closing in on their killer. Derry would have been so proud. But Derry wasn't here to tell. Even Alex and Abby were gone, off to his mother's in Georgia.

She was alone. Utterly alone.

She headed for the bedroom, but the bed loomed silent and huge, and she could almost smell Morrison's skin—lavender and musk and salt. *Almost.* She grabbed one of Derry's T-shirts she had brought from Alex's house and slipped into it on her way across the hall to Abby's room. The unicorn poster on the wall stared down at her, its horn more deadly than mythical. She lay down on the bed and buried her face in the comforter, curled up among Abby's pillows, and slept. She dreamed of a smiling Frieda Burke, half of someone else's arm wrapped around her body, sitting on a rock that looked suspiciously like Lucky's severed head.

32

PETROSKY WAS SITTING at Shannon's dining table when she awoke an hour and a half later. She raised an eyebrow but found she didn't give a shit that he'd walked in and made himself at home. He passed her a cup of coffee. She sipped it, willing the pain in her head to subside. At least the nausea had passed.

"You get ahold of Griffen?" she asked.

He watched her with that bitchy-but-concerned look on his face. "Not yet. He's not at the office. No answer at home either."

Dammit. Couldn't just one thing go smoothly? And where was he? She felt like she was on the verge of understanding, but there was some bit of information a touch beyond her reach. Maybe it was just leftovers from her dreams. Or from her life. "You try his cell?"

"I was looking Karen's up when the chief told me to go home before Detective Young—the dickwad who's supposed to be handling the Wheatley case—beat my ass. I figured I might as well listen, stay on her good side."

"You care about being on the chief's good side?"

"I do if it makes it easier to get Surfer Boy out."

"Yeah, right." She stared at the coffee cup, wishing it was Morrison's stainless steel mug.

"Shannon?" His voice was soft, concerned.

She swallowed hard. There was a twinge in her stomach, and it wasn't the baby or the caffeine or the concussion. It was deeper, murkier, some abstract thing hiding in her gut waiting to burst free.

"You okay?"

"Yeah, I just... I feel like we should know the answers here."

"You and me both." Petrosky pulled out his cell. "I guess I can shoot Griffen an email so he'll get it whenever he shows up at work...or home." He grimaced. "I hate email, but we don't have much choice since he got rid of his cell. Said he was simplifying his life or some shit. But now, with those pictures at Burke's...maybe she was harassing him."

"No." She rubbed her temples and put the coffee down. "He just gave me his number the other day. Hang on." She rummaged in her briefcase on the countertop. "When did Griffen get rid of his cell, anyway?" Maybe the number she had was no good. After all, a lot had changed in the last couple weeks; when he'd given it to her, she still had a brother.

Petrosky's cough stopped her throat from clamping shut. "Hasn't been long. I met with him the day we found...the envelope, the day you talked to Johnson, to see if he knew anything about the social worker she mentioned. I asked if I could call him to follow-up, and he told me to use the office line because he'd canceled his cell."

"Weird." Shannon pulled out a Post-It and reached for her cell phone. *Wait*...Griffen had seemed shocked when Shannon mentioned the social worker to him in court, but if Petrosky had told him about Wheatley earlier...A female voice answered on the second ring.

"Hey...oh, uh, Karen?"

"Yes. Who is this?" Polite, friendly, nothing more, not the least bit concerned. Burke's polar opposite.

Shannon relaxed just a touch, though Petrosky's eyebrows hit his hairline. "Hey, it's Shannon."

"Oh, hey! Frank said you might be calling me because he canceled his phone. Men, right?" She had a laugh like the peal of a bell.

Did men do shit like that? Roger would never have given someone her number if he'd lost his phone—but then again, Roger was a lying, cheating bastard. Just like Kimball. And... well, if Karen suspected Burke was still into Griffen, *she* might have told him to cancel his phone. Knowing him, he'd have done it. "Right. Men," Shannon said slowly. "So, is he there?"

"Oh, sorry, I'm not with him. I'm out running errands while he picks up a *friend* from the precinct." Her voice was suddenly tight.

Shannon's heart rate climbed. "Is he picking up Frieda Burke?" Why would he be picking her up? She didn't think Griffen was still involved with Burke...and if he was, he wouldn't have told Karen, would he? There had to be more, a connection she wasn't seeing.

"Yes—how did you...how did you know?"

And finally, like pieces snapping together, everything fell into place. Griffen in his knit cap, the one he always wore. Perez saying, "He had on a hat so I couldn't see his face or his hair or anything." Not a disguise, just him. His worry about Johnson, his insistence on her innocence. His sleeplessness over her being put away. Even the note: *It was me.* It hadn't been someone trying to steal the glory—Lucky had been about guilt, a dramatic cry for help, a plea to be discovered. A cry to *her*, the person who'd stuck it out with him through college and their early working days. But...why hurt Lucky? She couldn't quite see it, and yet—

Her heartbeat was thumping in her ears, in her head, but she could barely feel it. He'd seemed so thin lately. Sickly. In pain, probably more than usual, twitchy with it, even. Maybe Griffen's addiction had started honestly, something stronger for his headaches, and then...he'd needed more. He'd found Derek. Maybe Derek Lewis had told Griffen someone was over there asking questions, but not who. The moment

Petrosky had asked Griffen about a social worker at the apartment—the only male social worker in Ash Park—he'd signed Wheatley's death certificate.

No. There was no way. Griffen was passive, quiet. He couldn't even break up with a woman. Shannon's disbelief must have shown on her face because Petrosky stood abruptly, the chair scraping across the floor behind him as he came around the kitchen table to the opposite side of the counter.

Karen was still waiting for a response. *Frieda Burke...* Shannon knew he was picking her up, but not why, at least not enough to explain to Karen. Were Burke and Griffen in this together? Maybe Burke was manipulating him. *No way.* Burke could convince Griffen to drop his friends, but to murder someone? She hadn't even been able to get him to leave Karen. "Lucky guess," Shannon croaked.

Karen paused, sniffed. "You know, between you and me, she doesn't really seem stable. Sad, really, calling him all the time." She lowered her voice. "I hope Frank can talk her into getting some help."

Griffen. It couldn't be, just couldn't. The idea that Griffen was a killer—it meant Griffen had tried to kill *her*. Her friend had tried to murder her in cold blood. And he could try to murder his girlfriend just as easily if he thought she suspected something. Which Karen might after this phone call.

"Karen, he isn't bringing her back there, is he?" She tried to keep her voice even, but the words came out rushed.

"He said he was just going to drive her home..." She trailed off, each word more tense than the last. "What's wrong? You sound weird."

"Karen, listen." Shannon grabbed the countertop as the room spun. "Tell me where you are, and I can send someone to you."

"I don't understand. What's—"

"I'll explain later. Trust me here, okay?"

"Okay, okay. Where am I supposed to go?"

"Just tell me where you are. I'll send Officer Valentine to get you."

"I'm near the precinct. Should I—"

"Yes. Go inside and tell them who you are and that you're waiting for Officer Valentine. I'll be there soon."

"Shannon..." Her voice was higher, tighter. Afraid. "Should I be worried?"

This poor woman. She at least deserved the truth. "Yes. You should be worried."

Shannon shoved the phone into her pocket, Petrosky's eyes boring a hole in her head. "It's Griffen."

33

"THAT PASTY FUCK?" Petrosky jerked out his phone and stalked to the other side of the room with it plastered to his ear, barking something about searching for a car. *Griffen.* Could it really be Griffen? Across the room, Petrosky clenched the phone so hard his knuckles were white.

Maybe she should have known. Would have known if she'd rekindled their friendship after he broke up with Burke, but she had been far too upset and far too afraid that he'd hurt her again. Though at the time, she'd only been concerned about her feelings—not that he wanted to put her in a pine box.

Petrosky yanked the phone from his ear, tapped the screen again, and put it back to his face. "Guess who picked up an unmarked police car at the auction last year?" he snapped over his shoulder.

Of course. Of course Griffen had an old police car. And unless she'd watched him get in, she'd never have noticed it in the lot, not amidst the sea of other cop cars.

"Yeah, need to talk to Detective Young..." Petrosky barked into the phone. "I don't give a fuck what he's doing—" Every word vibrated in Shannon's temples until it felt like her head might explode. She was right; she had to be right this time. But if she wasn't, oh god, if she was wrong again—

They're all counting on you, Shanny. Don't screw it up.

Petrosky's voice rose with each word. "When? How long? Fuck." He shoved his phone into his pocket. "Griffen already picked Burke up—half an hour ago."

"Petrosky—"

"Stay here." He started for the door.

"Fuck you."

"Shannon—"

"Fuck you, Petrosky. Goddammit."

He held the door for her. "No wonder California likes you."

EVERY MUSCLE in Shannon's body was wound like a spring as they drove through town toward Burke's house, though her head throbbed less thanks to the stash of ibuprofen Petrosky kept in his glovebox. She had pretended not to notice the airplane bottles of Jack Daniels, nearly all of them empty.

There was no car in Burke's driveway, unmarked or otherwise. Shannon squinted at the dark windows. "You think they came here? Maybe he took her to his place."

Petrosky stepped onto the front porch and peered through the window beside the door. The air around them hummed with energy. Birds chirped, telling them to turn around. Tree branches clacked together, angry. A van full of yelling children passed, a soccer ball sticker affixed to its rear bumper. Petrosky tried the doorknob. It turned.

Is she here? "Did you leave it open earlier?" Shannon asked.

He shook his head. "Young showed up quick, said we'd bring her in for questioning, and closed the place up again. Didn't even take samples of his own."

If the door was open…someone had been here.

"Come on, Taylor, and stay low."

The moment the door closed behind them, taking with it the rushing cars and the twitter of birds, Shannon's heart went into overdrive. Something was very wrong inside this house. She could feel it in her bones, not so much a presence, but a lack of essence. No noise. No life. The house didn't just feel empty—it felt abandoned.

Like a tomb.

Burke's boots sat in the entry hallway, still-wet mud dribbling onto the linoleum. Had Griffen just dropped her off? Or maybe they'd swung by here to grab a bag so they could run off together.

Petrosky obviously didn't think so—he'd pulled out his gun. They crept down the hall to an alcove. "Stay here, back against the wall, Taylor," he whispered, and she did as he asked. "Now call her," he said.

"Ms. Burke?" Shannon's voice trembled through the house. Petrosky set his sights on the kitchen doorway. Not a sound. Not a swish of a door, a creak of a floorboard, or a whisper of breath from any direction. Shannon jumped when Petrosky threw himself through the kitchen doorway, gun in front of him. He skidded to a halt before she got there too and tried to push her back but wasn't fast enough.

Burke lay on the floor, knees bent as if she'd been standing, and just keeled over backward. But she hadn't fainted. She wasn't sleeping. Her chest was covered with ugly, weeping holes that had only recently stopped bleeding, the blood soaking her shirt and pooling around her head—gelatinous and shiny. Her dead eyes stared at the wall, and her head lolled awkwardly, nearly sawed clean off so that her spine was visible through her neck, all of it gaping like a ghoulish smile.

Shannon's heart was in her throat. She felt suddenly alone and exposed—deserted in the doorway, waiting to be slashed apart by a predator. By Griffen. By her...friend. Where was Petrosky? Why wasn't he at the body?

She dragged her eyes from Burke's mangled corpse, her breath coming erratically, too fast, too hard. Petrosky was bent over something on the counter—a notebook?—peeling back one page after another with his pocket knife. Shannon couldn't remember him taking it out, and his weapon suddenly seemed more violent and sinister than it should have. She wanted to flee, screaming, into the street.

Petrosky was speaking, but Shannon couldn't hear him. Her mind was deathly silent. The birds had quieted, frightened and hiding. Even the tree branches outside had ceased to move. Then he was next to her, his arm on her elbow.

"Taylor? Did you hear me?"

She shook her head.

"Read it. Last entry. You know him better than I do."

Shannon tiptoed around the body to meet Petrosky at the counter, trying not to smell the death that lingered in the air, but she couldn't help it; the tang of metal, a musk that might have been urine, and the smooth, hot cinnamon underneath it all from a candle still burning on the kitchen counter.

The journal page was speckled with blood, but the words on the page Petrosky had chosen were readable:

I am possessed by a demon. Not a demon in the traditional sense of the word, the kind who rises from hell and has fingers long as knitting needles and teeth like knives. It is inside me, as if my brain hates me, like it's turned dark and alien, and I have become a mere host for its lunacy.

Shannon breathed through her mouth, trying to avoid the stench. Her friend. Once, her best friend. He was as foreign to himself as he was to her.

Rage eats at me night and day, piercing the center of my forehead like a steel rivet and sending sparks of incoherent fury through my mind. I no longer try to calm myself, for the harder I struggle against the thoughts, the more insistent they become. And when they scream at me to act, particularly her voice, I do not feel entirely in possession of myself. I know this explanation is irrational, but I cannot explain it any other way.

Her voice? Hallucinations? She tried to picture Griffen in court, the way he'd look off into space. She'd always thought he'd been thinking. Had he been listening to more than just his own internal ramblings?

> *I tried to tell her to let me turn myself in and be done with it. But she will not allow it. Her voice attacks me at all hours, insisting I do more. It is a thorn in the core of my being, a barb scraping and tearing and gouging until there is nothing left but a gaping hole. I have this idea that I can fill the empty hole with blood, and that my pain will stop. It is a strange dichotomy, the way the vision of this battlefield horrifies and pleases me at the same time. It strikes me as a valid sentiment even as I register its illogical nature. These fascinations are a thing of repugnant beauty, oxymoronic only in the nature of how I feel about them: confused, disgusted, exhilarated.*
>
> *Today will end in bloody warfare. Destruction. Ruin. Misery. I am not brave. I am only sorry.*
>
> *Back where it begins, where it ends, where all hope dies, so shall they. So shall she.*
>
> *And so shall I.*
>
> *I am so sorry, Shannon.*

Griffen. But not the Griffen she'd once called a friend. Sanity was fragile…fleeting…and apparently, he thought she should have known. Maybe she should have. *Back where it begins, where it ends, where all hope dies, so shall they. And so shall I.*

She turned to Petrosky. *Where all hope dies.* She could almost smell the weed that had clung to them freshman year, could almost hear Griffen talking as they explored the darkened courthouse in the dead of night. And because of the faulty wiring around the back window, they'd always had a way in. Now Griffen could still get in through that same window—then he'd find a place to sit and wait until morning when he could inflict the most damage.

She ran from the house without a word, Petrosky at her heels.

34

Petrosky waited until they were in the courthouse parking lot before he called for backup, something about other officers distracting him or not letting him do his job. Not that it would take long for them to arrive—cops in the precinct would be over in minutes from the building next door, and officers patrolling the area would race in here moments later, sirens blaring. Petrosky just wanted a head start. And he'd get it.

But Shannon had stopped caring about his reasons. Griffen had tried to kill her. He'd threatened her and her family, murdered Lucky and taken the one thing that had given Abby joy. They'd been friends once—until Burke. And now there was no more sweetened regret when she considered him, only fury. She wanted him alone for just three minutes.

A courtroom. He'd be in a courtroom. *Where it all started.*

Johnson's case? Was that the beginning of the end for him? "Room seven," Shannon said as they opened the car doors.

"Wait. Floorboard."

She leaned down and felt around beneath the seat. "A vest?"

"Either put it on or stay here. But it won't help you if he

shoots you in the head, so stay low, or California will have my ass."

She slid it on and stepped out of the car. Petrosky nodded and pulled a gun from his ankle holster and handed it to her, its cold weight at once disconcerting and exhilarating. She wasn't a marksman, or so Morrison had told her the one time they'd gone to the range—she'd need to be close. She clicked the safety into place and shoved the weapon into her waistband.

Sweat popped out on her forehead as she and Petrosky tore along the side of the building to the back. Their footsteps were hollow, the breeze electric, the world muted with dusk as if the skyline had been drawn with charcoal. She blinked salt from her eyes and squinted at the back facade. Then she saw it—the third window in was open, the thin, severed wire hanging from the corner like a tiny forgotten noose, as it always had been, invisible unless you were looking. Ten years, and it was still there.

Petrosky pulled himself through first and reached to haul her in after him. Their footsteps against the marble floors resounded into the still air, hitting her eardrum like firecrackers, and she switched to running on her toes. But there was no way to escape the sound echoing on the empty walls that had once held a promise of justice and now seemed more like a prison.

They stopped at the door with a brass *#7* bolted to the right of the doorframe, Shannon on one side and Petrosky on the other. Yellow light glowed from the base of the jamb.

Petrosky bent to his knees and put his ear against the bottom of the door, probably trying to avoid getting his head blown off. No sound from inside. The door was oak—thick, heavy, substantial. Like it was conspiring to hide Griffen from them.

Petrosky put up his hand. One finger. *Two*. On three, Petrosky shoved the door open, and they went in low, ducking behind the first row of pews like Shannon had seen in movies but had never actually done. She peeked around the side, her heart hammering in her ears as her eyes adjusted to the light.

Griffen stood at the podium, unmoving, as if addressing a nonexistent jury. An assault rifle hung against his back. Shannon straightened.

Petrosky tried to pull her back down, but she shook him off and trained her weapon on the back of Griffen's head.

"Goddammit, Taylor," Petrosky hissed.

Shannon ignored him. "Griffen?"

He turned, and she saw a second assault rifle swinging at his belly. Petrosky leapt to standing beside her. Griffen made no move to raise either weapon. He smiled, though his eyes remained dull. "You came."

She tensed, training her weapon on his face. Petrosky left her side and slid around the pew to the left aisle. Griffen didn't acknowledge him, just kept his gaze focused on Shannon, so intently she felt like he was using his eyes to peel off her skin.

"Wouldn't miss it," she said, her voice far more steady and sure than she felt.

His hands stayed at his side as she approached, but his eye twitched as Petrosky sidled closer. Then his wrist shifted, just barely, but enough that Shannon tightened her grip on the trigger. Griffen looked at the wall, one eyebrow raised as if he was listening to a voice no one else could hear.

"They think... I mean, I think you'll lose this one. I don't want this, but—"

"You're wrong."

"She promised you'd lose."

She. Frieda Burke? Had she really been fucking with him because he'd left her? Manipulating him, knowing he was sick?

"She told me it would all be okay," he said.

I'm sure she did. She probably told you it was also fine if you guys killed me and tossed me in the lake. "She's a cunt." The thought of Burke's body no longer turned her stomach. She was glad Griffen had killed Burke first.

He stepped from the podium into the aisle, and Petrosky shuttled down the pew toward him. Griffen's eyes did not leave hers.

"I didn't want to do it. She *made* me." His speech was pressured and seemed to consume the air around them. "I had hoped you'd find me sooner. I wanted you to. I thought maybe you could feel the...wrongness in me. But I suppose that was my imagination." He swallowed hard. "I wanted to stop."

He was so sick. Could she have helped him if she'd found out earlier? If she had noticed the strangeness when they were together? But she *had*. She'd seen the eccentricities, the oddities—him staring into space, his constantly moving mouth, and she'd thought it was just...him. He'd always been a little twitchy. But this...*this* was not the man she'd known.

Her gun hand wavered, and he snapped his eyes to the gun, then back up to her. Their eyes met. His gaze was unfocused, maybe confused, but there was no doubting the fury that burned beyond his irises; he was like a rabid animal, unknown to her, but who'd not hesitate to bite. The friend she'd once loved had been snuffed out. All that remained was this wild-eyed lunatic who had tried to murder her like he'd murdered Derek Lewis, Frieda Burke, Benjamin Wheatley. He'd tried to ruin Morrison, tried to take his life as surely as if he'd slit his throat. And Abby...my god—

Her hands no longer shook. *Say you tried to kill me, asshole. That you killed Lucky. That you're a murderer.* She wanted to hear him say it, say he loved the thrill of it. Then she could release her grief and her guilt and embrace the fury that was threatening to explode from her chest.

Petrosky crept down the pew in front of her, headed right for Griffen, but Griffen still didn't look at him. He seemed to see only her.

"Kimball's gun was a nice touch," she said, her voice rising along with her blood pressure.

Griffen's face darkened. "I see now that using Kimball's gun was too vague to link back to me. I should have left another note, perhaps done something more...flagrant. But I didn't really know... I mean...I'm not a criminal."

You are a goddamn criminal. And instead of turning himself in, he'd chosen Morrison as a scapegoat. "And Morrison? He was always nice to you."

"*She* hated him. And you deserved better." Griffen's mouth was moving like a fish gasping its final breath on shore. His nostrils flared, and his eyes darted to the far corners of the room as if an assailant was hiding beyond the drywall.

Nice didn't matter. Not when you had completely lost your mind. But still...not a confession. And the more he watched the room behind her, the more he responded to things that weren't here with them, the more her resolve crumbled. And she needed to do this. She needed to focus and take him down so Petrosky could lock him up for good.

Say it, goddammit. Say you're a killer. "What kind of an asshole murders a kitten?"

He dragged his eyes from the back wall and looked down at his shoes—clean white sneakers. He'd probably stashed his bloody kicks in a closet somewhere after killing Burke. "She *made* me. And it was...regrettable. But I did it quickly. He didn't feel much; I can promise you that."

Close enough. Her blood boiled, thudded in her temples. "'Regrettable?' Seems like an understatement, Griffen." Her voice sounded foreign to her, too soft, too calm, at odds with the storm raging inside her.

"They were all regrettable, but I was blinded by rage. I couldn't even remember picking up the hammer, but then... there it was. There he was." His voice was soft, almost wistful.

She shook her head but kept her eyes fixed on him, on his hands. On the weapons. "Wheatley wasn't an impulsive act of violence. You tortured him."

He looked to the corner again and back to her. "I wish I had never found out who Lewis meant when he asked if I had sent 'that guy' there." Griffen turned his head toward

Petrosky so quickly she almost jumped for cover behind a pew, but Griffen's hands did not shift to the weapons. "Even then, I had no desire to harm Wheatley, but I was convinced his death was necessary. She told me…" He lowered his eyes, and when he spoke again, it was a whisper. "She told me I had to. She's stronger than I am. And she's the only one who understands."

"Who, Griffen? Burke? Is that why you killed her?"

Griffen cocked his head, his eyes narrowed. "What?" But he gave her no time to respond. He jerked his head to the back corner of the room. "No. No!" He wasn't talking to them—to her. He was talking to someone she couldn't see. Fighting. Maybe fighting on her behalf. And the aggression, the hatred, singed into her belly, mingling with the heavy grief of their lost friendship. He'd been normal once. Happy. She raked her eyes over his stubbly jaw—his mouth still moving, his lips almost forming words. She'd spent this entire time trying to work logically on the case. But there was no logic here. Only madness.

"I can't make the voices stop. They are horrible, senseless. And more persistent even than our strictest law school instructor." His face softened suddenly, almost nostalgic, and he took a step toward her, then another, ten feet and closing. Petrosky was a dozen feet from Griffen's right side. "Back in those days, I was free. I yearn for that again, the peace of it." His eyes filled. "Every night, I pray that I will go to sleep and never awaken."

He was close enough that she could smell his stink, the dank, ripe scent of perspiration. He'd killed Lucky, made Abby cry during the worst month of her life. Maybe the stress had killed Derry faster too. And all the while, he'd smiled to her face, asked her how she was, watched her in court, brought her a goddamn coffee cake, and held her in his arms without the slightest bit of remorse. Now…what, crocodile tears? He wasn't sorry. He was just sad it was over. Fire blazed through Shannon's arms and down to her fists. Her muscles tensed.

Griffen bared his teeth, though his eyes remained glassy. "Shan—" He lunged toward her.

Shannon didn't hear the first shot or the second, just a wild ringing in her ears and the stench of gunpowder in her nose as Petrosky took him down. Griffen slammed into the endcap of the pew, writhing and spitting, blood seeping from his thigh and more from his knee. He collapsed into the seat. She stepped toward him and rounded the pew so she could see his face.

Petrosky was yelling, a low growly rumble, but Shannon ignored him—couldn't hear him anyway over the buzzing in her head.

Griffen smiled at her, peaceful. "I'm glad you're here." She intuited the words from the movements of his mouth rather than hearing them, so focused on his lips that she almost didn't see him shift in the seat. But she did. He raised the assault rifle.

Shannon pushed her gun into his eye, pulled the trigger, and watched the back of his head explode against the pew behind him.

Petrosky grabbed her arm, and she looked at him, watching his mouth form unintelligible words. The ringing in her ears intensified.

She looked back to the podium, where Petrosky was pointing at the metal bullets littering the floor.

Bullets. Scattered like they'd been ejected from a gun. She looked back at Griffen's gun, her ears still ringing but not as bad as before.

Petrosky squeezed her arm. "You made the right call," he said, his voice tinny and strained.

She stepped back, with her hand protectively against her belly and watched Griffen's brain matter drip onto the floor.

35

Shannon raised her palm like a visor against the midmorning sun and tried to see the courthouse through the glare. The world felt too bright, too brittle. As it was, she could barely make out Petrosky's bulk a few steps up as he paced back and forth and smoked his seventeenth cigarette of the day. She almost wanted one too. Or a drink. Something to take the edge off, though hearing that Judge Miller had rejected Reverend Wilson's no contest plea helped a little. Knowing Roger was under the microscope helped a little more. Though there was no evidence of wrongdoing so far, it would be a wake-up call; Roger wouldn't be dumb enough to break the law again—if he ever had.

But all was not well. Her hands were clean now, but she could still feel Griffen's blood speckled across her skin like burning oil. Every day, she tried to forget. Forget that he'd raised an empty gun. Forget that she'd shot him, that she'd helped a man who'd once been her best friend commit suicide. The anger at Griffen had persisted, hot and achy in the middle of the night, but...maybe that was grief. It was hard to tell one emotion from another anymore.

Karen had frozen when they'd told her about her boyfriend's murderous rampage. Her shock had made Shannon feel a little better about not seeing Griffen's insanity before, though Karen's tears had turned her stomach. Even if Griffen had been criminally insane, Karen had lost someone she cared about that day. And Shannon didn't wish that ache on anyone.

Though they were still wrapping things up, it appeared that Griffen had acted alone. Except for a note at Derek Lewis's house informing Ashley Johnson of parenting class times—probably from an earlier home visit—no trace evidence of Burke's presence was found at any of the crime scenes. The single drop of blood on Burke's welcome mat belonged to Derek Lewis, but it was smashed into the mat along with fertilized earth consistent with the soil in front of the house. And since Karen admitted that Griffen had gone to Burke's home in the days after the Lewis murder, it was likely that Griffen had just tracked in a speck of dried blood on his shoes.

And it made sense that Griffen had visited Burke—Burke and Griffen had remained in contact, and the journal entries indicated that Lewis had told Griffen someone had come to the house asking about him, but not who it was. Maybe Griffen had decided to pick Burke's brain under the guise of helping his newest client. Burke had probably asked around a little just to help him out. Her conversation with Lucinda Lewis didn't necessarily show that she knew there had been another social worker out there—Shannon had just assumed as much because of what Angela Perez had seen. And Burke, though jealous and more than a little stalker-y, didn't seem capable of murdering anyone or cleaning up crime scenes, even for Griffen's sake. The illustrious Dr. McCallum concurred based on the psychological screenings Burke had completed prior to becoming a foster mom.

Even Griffen's references to "her voice" could be explained without Burke's involvement: hallucinations due to opiate withdrawal. Griffen had filled no fewer than three dozen painkiller prescriptions from various doctors in the last six months—it seemed that once the doctors had stopped prescribing, he had moved on to heroin. Enter Derek Lewis.

And it turned out Griffen had another reason to hear things: the pathologist had found a tumor the size of a dime near his amygdala, amidst central brain tissue. A tumor in that location could easily trigger hallucinations, rage, and impulsivity, the doctor said. Griffen had tried to stop—he just couldn't. Shannon tried not to think about that either, how quickly your mind could snap and take all of you with it.

Petrosky rejoined her on the sidewalk in front of the courthouse, and together they watched women and men milling around, some in suits, some in baseball caps with ponytails pulled through the backs. Shannon could feel their eyes on her, and it made her skin crawl. But that might have been the stains that she couldn't wash away, at least not yet. Maybe one day she'd feel clean again.

"How's Ashley Johnson?" she asked Petrosky as they started toward the street and the detention center. Morrison would be getting out soon, and the thought made her insides flutter with anxiety, or maybe excitement. Or maybe that was the kid making her stomach act up.

"She's hanging in there. I got her an apartment over by Perez. Figured they could start school together in the fall."

"Did you foot the bill for that?" Now that Kimball had been abruptly—but quietly—fired, Ashley Johnson didn't have much outside support.

Petrosky avoided her eyes.

She suppressed a smile. "What about Diamond?"

"A few social work visits and Johnson will be in the clear. Without Lewis around, I doubt she'll have an issue maintaining custody so long as she keeps herself straight. Which she will."

Shannon looked over her shoulder at the courthouse. How could she go back there, practice law in the very room where she'd killed a man? "I still think we should tell them who really killed Griffen."

"He's dead, Taylor. It was my gun, a weapon you should never have touched. If I'd had my way, you wouldn't have been in there at all. Plus, I had residue from the same gun on my hands." They reached the road and Petrosky threw his arm out to stop her as if she was going to walk right into oncoming traffic.

"You had residue on your hands because you shot my gun into the wall." She stared at his hand until he dropped it. "After Griffen was dead."

They crossed the road and into the shadow of the detention center. "Prove it," Petrosky said.

She put her hand on his arm.

He glanced at her fingers as if confused and raised his eyes to the detention center's front entrance. "There's your boy."

She looked up as Morrison walked outside, golden hair glistening in the sun, smile brighter than the hair. His clothes were wrinkled, but they surely felt better than an inmate's jumpsuit. Morrison...or Curt? But no, he'd been Morrison when she'd fallen in love with him. It had happened a long time before she'd been able to admit it.

Petrosky stepped back as Morrison approached. "Good to see you, Surfer Boy. Meet anyone nice in prison?"

Morrison grinned, but it only accentuated the bags under his eyes. "A few guys."

"Made a bunch of friends, eh? Must have stock in Vaseline. Guess that's how they do it in California."

"Yep, that's how we do it," Morrison said, but his eyes were locked on Shannon's. He offered his hand.

She threw her arms around him, and the heat of him melted the rigidity from her back. "I'm so glad you're out."

He said nothing, just held her.

"I missed you," she whispered.

"I missed you too. Hard to be without your friends in jail."

Friends. Were they only that in his mind? She pulled back to look him in the eye, and the warmth in his gaze, the longing she saw mirrored there—it wasn't a glance you'd give a buddy. They were so much more than that, so much...

Morrison released her, and she looked back at Petrosky,

but he was already halfway across the parking lot. "Catch you later, boss!"

Petrosky waved, backhanded, without turning around, and opened his car door.

"So," Shannon said, turning back to Morrison. "What do you want to do?"

He raised one arm and put his nose in his armpit. "Shower."

She smiled. "I'll get you home so you can get cleaned up. You want to grab some food afterward?"

"Only if you're going with me."

She squeezed his hand. "I'll be there." They did have a few things to discuss, not the least of which was why she'd questioned their relationship the morning after they'd slept together. She'd make it up to him—after all, she had helped get him out of jail. There were worse ways to start the reconciliation process.

"We can start with coffee," he said.

"I don't know. Maybe one cup."

He cocked his head. "How about a drink?"

She put her hand on her belly, still taut from the CrossFit workouts, though the button on her pants seemed to press a little harder into her abdomen this morning. Probably her imagination. Though she had heard the second pregnancy always gets bigger faster. "I don't drink."

He nodded in mock chagrin. "One day, maybe."

She smiled again. "Maybe." *Maybe on our kid's first birthday.*

"I'll have to run to the bank first." His gaze traveled across the road to the courthouse. Probably thinking about the day some judge had told him he was going to jail, the day she'd almost lost him.

She wouldn't lose him again. Shannon put her hand on his cheek and drew his mouth to hers, and the guilt that had been eating her insides disappeared in a wave of warmth. She wasn't dirty because of what she'd done. She'd saved the people she loved from ever having to think about the monster who had hurt them. Shannon imagined the cerulean sky was draping them in a protective blanket, the world outside fading into a tranquil haze. Spring, finally in the air, kissed her bare arms.

Their tongues entwined. He slid an arm around her lower back, gentle, so gentle. Tenuous. Maybe he was worried it wouldn't last. Maybe he was as scared as she was.

When their lips parted, they remained nose to nose, wrapped in one another, her hair tickling their cheeks. "I'm so sorry," she whispered. "For not being here. For... I didn't even give us a chance. I won't make that mistake again."

He brushed the hair off her face and tucked it behind her ear. "There's no sorry here, Shanny. You were trying to protect yourself. One day, if I'm very, very lucky, you'll trust me enough to let me help protect you too."

"And exactly what do I need protection from? I just saved your ass, buddy."

He shrugged. "Eh, you know. Killers, though you seem to be doing fine with those pickledicks too."

"Pickle—"

"I learned it on the inside."

She narrowed her eyes.

"Kidding. I heard it from Petrosky."

She had to laugh. "So, you'll protect me from pickledicks."

"That's right. Your ex-husband, too. I've got a mean right hook to help with that." But she could also read what he didn't say. He'd protect her feelings. He'd worry about her. Take care of her. And she'd take care of him right back.

She grabbed him and pulled him to her again, and something hard pressed into her leg from his front pocket. "Hey now, at least wait until we get out of here. Hell, maybe you should just shower at my house." She winked to show she was kidding. Though she wasn't exactly sure she *was* kidding.

"Oh." He reached into his pocket and pulled out a velvet box. "Sorry." He stared at it a moment and shrugged, then went to put it back into his pocket.

She laid her hand over his. "No secrets among friends,

right?" She fiddled with the lid. "Especially ones who saved your—" Her jaw dropped at the diamond and emerald ring inside.

He took it out of the box and held it up to the sunlight. "It was my mother's. I've been carrying it since the day we—" He looked down and stuck the ring back into the box. "I figured I'd just have it, wait for the right time. You never know."

"It looks like an...engagement ring."

"It is."

This was crazy. Too sudden. Had Petrosky brought the ring for him from the house along with his change of clothes? *Shit, he knows about the pregnancy.* She furrowed her brows. "Did Petrosky tell you?"

He squinted at her, earnest confusion in his eyes. "Tell me what?"

"Nothing." She ran her finger over the emeralds. "But you're going to have to slow it down a little bit."

He closed the ring box and put it back in his pocket. "I'll wait. We've got time."

"That we do, Morrison. That we do."

EPILOGUE

THE WAVES BROKE behind Morrison's back as if they were trying to be careful with the earth, the gentle swoosh of salt on sand more a meander than a race. It was the easy pull of love, not the torrid rush of lust. Though the lust was there; it always was. Shannon moved slowly toward him up the aisle, his love, his life, the wind kissing her hair like a thousand breezy fingers. White lace danced around her ankles. Petrosky's arm was linked with hers, protective and fatherly as he marched beside her.

On Morrison's chest, Evelyn nuzzled her perfect face into him, her breath hot and fast and soft against the Hawaiian print shirt that Shannon had said was perfect for the wedding. He would have worn anything she'd wanted. He'd have dressed Evie in anything Shannon wanted too, but Shannon had insisted Evie wear the onesie Morrison had made for her, the one that said: "Will you marry my daddy?"

"I've got you, baby girl, I've got you," he whispered, and Evie settled, this angel, his angel, her trust a balm against all evil, a warm tide cocooning them from all the wrongness in the world.

Morrison smiled down at her, and the love within him multiplied itself ten times over, welling in his chest until he felt he might burst. He looked at Shannon, close now, nearing him. This. Forever and ever. Behind him, the waves sighed their relief.

But then he heard it, that familiar, throaty murmur like a gremlin in the back of his brain trying to convince him that things would never stick. He knew the voice was like the cloud that ensnares the moon, only to release it; it would pass. Behind him, the waves tried to assuage his uneasiness by caressing the shore with salt and sea, but still, the addiction pulled at him, wrapping his mind in gauzy promises. *Come*, it said, *I'll take you back, you'll be happier than you've ever been. Even she can't give you this bliss.* He had almost succumbed when Shannon turned him down the first time. He'd almost run from the fear that she'd never say yes, never want him the way he wanted her. But he had stayed. Waited. And eventually, she had loved him back.

Shannon drew closer. Petrosky's eyes were clear, blue, no hint of irritation or late nights or whiskey in his morning coffee—just him, and Morrison was glad of it. The wind whipped Shannon's hair around her face, and the old needle scars near the crook of Morrison's thigh throbbed once and stilled. Behind him, the waves whispered *no, no, no*, but then Evie gurgled, and the burgeoning panic that had been rising in his throat subsided. Shannon's eyes glistened with love and joy and hope. He'd take this kind of happy. This happy would sustain him.

It won't, the voice whispered and was gone. But it'd be back. The voice always came back, no matter how long Morrison ignored it. It ate at him like a cancer, day after day, a gnawing in his gut that said that life wasn't really getting better, that the ones he loved would eventually leave, that he could never be worthy of such happiness.

That only the drug would do what it promised.

He wanted to believe the drug was a liar, but life was fickle, a twisted roller coaster of pain and loss. Given a long enough period of time, the voice was always proven right.

Nothing lasted forever.

Did you enjoy *Conviction*? Get *Repressed*, the next book in the Ash Park series. When detective Curtis Morrison's wife and daughter vanish, Curtis realizes the kidnapper is tied to his own unsavory, half-forgotten past. Dive into a chilling thriller penned by a "worthy heir to Patricia Cornwell and Tana French" (*New York Times* bestselling author Andra Watkins).

REPRESSED
CHAPTER 1

THE HOUSE WAS HUSHED, steeped in the steely gray of dawn as he made his way to the kitchen and flipped on the lights: the white tile floors, the white cabinets, the light-green soapstone, all of it at once harsh and as vital as the pulse in his veins. Each morning it was that split second of jarring blindness that finally connected him to his body. But that connection wouldn't last. Detective Curtis Morrison was not so much a stranger to his home or to himself—it was his mere existence, the world of men and earth, that seemed utterly foreign.

Around him the noises of morning murmured to him, less sharp than the light, but just as poignant: the click of the heater, the agitated tapping of a backyard woodpecker, the cat's gentle mewl, and, as he moved about his morning routine, the hiss of the coffee pot, rising like an ocean wave and cresting over his eardrum. In these quiet moments, before the present caught up with him, he felt he was on the brink of a precipice, a place where if he concentrated hard enough, he might hear hushed voices from another dimension—from the world where he really, truly belonged.

Telling him how to get home.

From the cabinet, he pulled down Shannon's coffee mug, the one that read "Arguing with a lawyer may prove ineffective," and set it on the counter hard enough that the clatter sent the cat skittering from the room. He stilled, staring at the mug. It was his job to be in control. Thinking like a detective was a skill comprising fire and ice—the passionate pursuit of justice and the cool logic of calculated deliberation, all centered on the *now*. Which was good. The past was hazy at best, and he couldn't bear to consider what it might have been at worst. The ugliness that lurked in his soul was like a malignant blister begging to burst at the first irritation. Common for cops, maybe; guns and violence and blood were a part of the daily routine. Few remained unscathed.

Breathe. Connect. Center.

Morrison padded upstairs to the bedroom where Shannon sat against the upholstered headboard with their daughter, Evie, both wrapped in the blue comforter to ward off the late spring chill. The entire room felt as if it were swaddled—cozy. Shannon said the colors reminded her of the sea. And if the room was the sea, she was a siren, waiting for him as the first rays of sunlight filtered through the curtains and bathed her blond hair in reddish-gold. She raised her hand to block Evie's face from the glare, and he set Shannon's mug on the wooden end table next to her, squinting briefly at his own hands. He knew they were his, yet he'd not have been surprised to learn they'd belonged to someone else all along. Perhaps common for other cops. Perhaps not.

He sat beside Shannon and ran a hand over her thigh, over her leg trapped inside the cotton shell of the comforter.

"What's up, Iron Man?" Shannon's voice was still hoarse with sleep. She put her hand over his fingers, still resting on her shrouded knee. "Ready to go catch some bad guys?"

Nope, not ready. He released her and pulled his guitar onto his knee, relishing the cool of the strings—more familiar than any part of his body. Shannon squeezed his bicep, Evie smiled at him, and suddenly all was right with the world, whether he truly belonged to it or not. They couldn't see the sorrow through his smile, and there was a pleasure in that— not in the hiding, but in the knowledge that they were safe from the pain he carried, the secrets that remained etched on his gut like scars from a jagged blade. Here, with Shannon and Evie, he was just Daddy. Some days he could almost convince himself that he had never been anything else.

While Evie gurgled at him, he strummed and sang: "I loved you from the first, baby, baby girl..." By the time he rode into the second chorus, Evie was squealing with delight, and Shannon was laughing, stroking Evie's head like they were actors in a sappy holiday commercial. But that peaceful tranquility hadn't been easy for her, not lately.

He strummed the final notes of the song and set the guitar beside the bed, then walked downstairs with Shannon to the living room past the white and gray couch Shannon had insisted they buy because it didn't remind them of her ex-husband or of Morrison's bachelor years. He hadn't argued—his pre-detective days were fraught with a wildness he had worried he'd never tame. These days he felt more domestic, but that didn't make him less of a liar.

Or less of an addict.

Shannon touched his shoulder. "You okay?"

"Yeah." He wasn't worried about himself. The bottle of antidepressants on the dresser was some comfort, a safeguard against him coming home to Shannon crying in the kitchen with her hands over her ears, Evie in her crib wailing. "I can't do this," she'd said that night. "I want to drop her at the fire station."

Maybe they should have expected it—she'd had some depression after her surrogacy with her brother's child. Morrison had assumed that episode was related to Shannon going home from the hospital alone while baby Abby went to live with her fathers.

He'd been wrong.

Morrison tried to force the memory from his brain, busying himself by pouring fresh grounds into the coffee maker—one more pot, enough to top Shannon off and keep Petrosky alert and focused for whatever the day had in store.

"You ready to deal with your partner all day long?" Shannon asked from behind him as if reading his mind.

He turned and made a silly face at Evie, and her cherub

cheeks grew wider as she grinned back at him. He tickled her foot and met Shannon's eyes: ice blue and collected...but concerned. About him. "As ready as I'll ever be," he said, forcing a smile.

"Good. You need to get back to work. A month off is long enough."

"Tired of me harassing you, eh?"

"I didn't mean it that way." She shook her head. "Sorry."

"No sorries here, Shanny. Just love." He kissed her cheek. "I'll be back around lunchtime so that I can meet the candidates." He poured the coffee into two stainless-steel mugs and refilled Shannon's when she held her cup out to him, the inscription already marred with a streak of drying coffee.

"Really, I can handle nanny interviews. I've only got two this afternoon." She sipped, then set the cup down when Evie kicked and almost spilled it.

"You didn't let me in on the last ones. You met them at a coffee shop."

"I didn't want you to scare them off."

"I'm not scary!" He stuck his tongue out at Evie to prove his point. Evie tried to kick him too.

She rolled her eyes. "You know what I mean. When it comes to your daughter, you get this 'don't you dare fuck with her' look."

Morrison frowned, but he pulled Shannon close and put his other hand on Evie's back. She was right. He'd have spent all his time cross-examining the potential candidates and scared the good ones off. Interrogating them. Petrosky would have been proud. Shannon would have been pissed.

"I love that you love her, Morrison."

She had never called him "Curt"—he'd been "Morrison" when she'd fallen in love with him. "I love you too, you know," he said.

"I do." She kissed his neck, the highest she could reach. He brushed his lips against her cheek, then over Evie's downy head, inhaling talcum and milk and something sour and ripe that he should maybe take care of before he left. But even if he offered, Shannon would yell at him to get out anyway. And no one in their right mind started the day fighting with a lawyer.

"Go to work," Shannon said. "I've got shit to take care of." She pulled herself from his arms and peeked at Evie's bottom. "Literally. Besides, you know you miss Petrosky. Might as well stop and grab him some donuts. He's going to make you go later anyway."

"Already got him a granola bar."

Shannon smirked. "Oh, he'll love that." She glanced at the clock. "I have to get ready too. Meeting Lillian at the park for an hour early this morning since she's going to meet Isaac for lunch." Isaac Valentine was a good cop and an even better friend with more goofy jokes than Morrison and a brand-new scar on his cheekbone after a run-in with an agitated burglary suspect. Valentine was also married to Shannon's friend Lillian. Even their kids were besties—Valentine was convinced Evie and his son Mason were going to get married one day and officially make them "one big milk chocolate family."

Morrison grabbed the stainless-steel coffee cups off the counter before he could convince himself to call in sick. "Whether he loves the granola or not, Petrosky will eat it. He's probably too swamped at the precinct to get any food at all." He opened the front door, and the still-damp air from last night's storm stuck to his skin.

"Yeah, right. He's probably busy shoving all the paperwork to the side for you." Shannon slapped his ass. "Now stop stalling and get out."

He forced himself not to look back as he headed to his Fusion, struggling with the coffee cups and his keys and the pressure in his chest that was urging him to stay home.

GET *REPRESSED*
on https://meghanoflynn.com

Seven people. A locked storm shelter. Inevitable starvation. What could you do to survive? *A refuge turns into a nightmarish prison in this chilling thriller.*

THE FLOOD
CHAPTER 1

VICTORIA COULD ALMOST SEE IT: the way the cotton pillow would pucker around her fists as she clamped it over his face, how the misshapen lump beneath would wriggle as he tried to force air through the goose feathers, how everything would lapse into silence, nothing to break the stillness but her hushed exhale of relief. On any normal evening, at least. Now, the night breathed wetly, almost as loudly as he did, a thick swooshing against her eardrums. Viscous. Raindrops *plink, plink, plink*-ed against her soaked hair. The shingles caught the skin on the backs of her legs sharply no matter how she tried not to move, like being slowly ground to dust by sandpaper, and water stung in every scrape. Victoria inhaled in the soupy night, stifling her gag reflex when the musky, acidic stench of shit hit her. Her muscles cramped harder. The sound of the rain against the lake of sewage around them was a constant reminder: they were going to die.

Three days they'd been stranded so far, sitting on top of Chad's family home, separated from the nearest dwelling by a mile of farmland and animal pastures. Three days of not eating, of her belly twisting and angry. Three days of filling her hands with rainwater to avoid dying of thirst.

Three days on the roof with the husband she'd been planning to leave.

The forecasters had said it was a long shot, the storm hitting here, and an even longer shot that the enormous storm systems out in the Atlantic would build in strength and aim themselves at their little low-flood-plain section of Louisiana. *That would be ridiculous*, they'd insisted, *unprecedented*. And they'd all been wrong, especially that twit on the news with his gray hair, his eyes an odd purple-blue that didn't exist in nature—"Probably won't be more than a category two, and a little rain the week after," he'd said. Bullshit. And now all the people who'd stayed were fucked. Totally, one hundred percent fucked. *We should have left.* That would have been the rational thing to do, *honey*, the logical thing.

Her heart seized, her stomach cramping too, a burning knot of hunger. Her lungs were far too small. But panicking made you stop thinking clearly—it could only make things worse. She forced air through her mouth as loudly as possible, drowning out the sound of the storm and Chad's equally labored breath. But not his words.

"Are you okay, Vicky?" He said it in a high voice, almost sing-song, the kind of voice he'd use to ask one of his students about a skinned knee.

Victoria wiped her wet hair from her forehead and tried to relax the painful knot in her guts. Raindrops tapped against her flesh, incessant, like a petulant child. The gray of Chad's irises seemed darker than usual in a world haunted by yesterday's storms and pregnant with electricity and anticipation of the second hurricane. She wished they had a radio, a cell phone to check the status of the upcoming storm, but their electronics had been impossible to keep dry. Their phones were sitting on the roof somewhere near the chimney, useless. *Why the fuck did I listen to you?* She turned away from Chad. Couldn't stand to see the guilt in his eyes, like she was supposed to make him feel better.

Chad always felt awful if he gave someone bad advice—he'd once teared up when he realized he'd given a stranger the wrong directions—but he had this way of convincing people not to bitch at him by making them feel guilty or sorry for him. That wasn't going to last. If they stayed on this roof much longer, he was going to get an earful.

In her peripheral vision, off the edge of the roof, the shitty, brackish water rippled like the skin of an enormous serpent, oily scales shivering with the anticipation of finishing them off. Half a block down, the broken post that used to hold their street sign stabbed through the surface of the filth. And to her other side loomed the muscly bulk of the chimney, topped with the grate she'd installed to keep the animals out, now ripped open like snapped metal ribs—some creature had been at it. Maybe whatever had clawed it apart was still there, lurking in the brick tunnel, drowned and bloated, tenderizing in the sea of bacteria.

Her throat closed. She forced it open. Her black leather work boot tap-tap-tapped against the soggy shingles. She tugged on her cut-off shorts, then the hem of her favorite black T-shirt, so dark she couldn't see the film of dirt and wet. The water was still rising, the red of the shingled roof so dark it looked like drying blood, and some of it probably was—Chad had a gash across his shin from a torn aluminum gutter. Behind Chad, the expanse of sky darkened, threatening, and the rush of rain on water seemed suddenly louder; she felt sure he wouldn't be able to hear her unless she yelled. But she said nothing. There was nothing to say.

If only they lived somewhere else, somewhere higher, somewhere the earth wasn't perpetually soggy from April to August, somewhere with some semblance of civilization. All they had in this section of Fossé, Louisiana was the community college, but that was over an hour away by car—and the levees had failed, leaving the paved roads leading to the college impassable by car or truck. The college itself would be underwater too before the week was out, especially if this storm didn't move on, or the second hurricane hit as hard as they'd been saying. And if the next storm hit while the citizens of Fossé were on their roofs... The winds would rip over the flooded streets, tearing shingles and people alike from the tops of their homes, flinging them against the treetops, impaling them on the remains of fences or drowning them in the sewage from overflowing septic tanks. Even if it did pass quickly, the water table was so high that people would be stuck for weeks. No power. No food. No drinkable water once the rain stopped. These might be her last days on this earth, and she and Chad should not be living their final hours together.

They'd been inhabiting their own little worlds for months now, independent planets merely circling the same sun. Even now he was staring out over the water, waiting passively for someone else to come to their rescue, though for once, she had no other ideas herself. They weren't going to swim twenty miles, and the waste products from the farmland—pig and chicken shit—were rife with E. coli and salmonella and other antibiotic-resistant bacteria that would spread through their injuries into their blood before they got to safety. Sepsis. That'd be a fun way to go out. Better than drowning though—she'd done that once, and once was enough.

The rain spit, water on water. The wind howled, an angry beast bellowing from the sky. The expanse of water pulled her gaze, but she refused to look at it, like it was a monster that could only exist if she let herself notice. Victoria shivered.

"Is there more peroxide?" Chad said.

"It's gone."

She sat back on the gritty shingles and turned away from him, squeezing her eyes closed, forcing the sound of the rain and the image of the storm from her mind. But in the blind starbursts of light behind her eyelids, she saw her parents' Chicago apartment and the square of afternoon sunlight that hit the living room floor when the sun snuck between the neighboring buildings. She and her twin brother Phillip used to sit on that little spot whenever they could, which wasn't often—usually the room was occupied, her father out there screaming at her mother, or screaming at Phillip for stealing money, and later for taking their mother's painkillers. Once she'd tried to help and ended up in the emergency room with a broken rib. Phillip had held her hand the whole way there, sung her songs, refused to let go even when the nurses came to ask her questions about her "fall."

Why the fuck am I thinking about this now? But she always

thought about Phillip when she was stressed. He was like...a teddy bear, the memory of his voice somehow comforting. Illogical, sure, but everyone was entitled to one foolish, illogical thing. Better than Chad's foolishness—his was going to get them killed.

She leaned back, resting her head against the sandpapery shingles.

You're going to be okay, Victoria, you know that.

Her brother had said that just before he left Chicago for good. That was why she'd come to Louisiana in the first place, Phillip's last known address—she'd hoped their twin connection would help her do what a PI couldn't. She'd been wrong, yet she'd stayed—too long. Ten years now, fourteen since she'd seen her brother. She did get occasional postcards from him, pictures of historical spots around Louisiana, little notes on the back like "I hope you're doing well. I'm still working on 'well'. See you when I manage to get there." Those cards ripped her wounds open every time, kept her up hearing the words in her brain, his voice whispering to her while she tried to sleep. She could help him. If he'd just fucking *call*.

"Hey!"

Her eyes snapped open. Chad scuttled to his feet, the grating sound ringing through the night as he slid on the gritty roof tiles. The sky was pitch as tar, not even a glimmer of haze on the horizon. Oh god, how long had she been out? Was the next storm here? She'd slept through the last dregs of light leaving the sky. But she didn't feel the harsh gusts of wind, didn't see flying debris, only Chad's silhouette, and she'd not have seen him at all were it not for...

The light.

Far out over the water, a hazy circle swept first one way, then the other, the rippling muck glittering like yellow diamonds in its wake.

Victoria pushed herself to standing, but the roof was slick despite the grit; her foot slid from beneath her and she went down hard on her knees, scrabbling at the tile with her fingernails, cursing under her breath at the wretched shingles.

"Hey!" Chad cried, waving his arms. "Over here!"

The light glided back and forth, back and forth, and only then did she realize the whoosh of rain was muddling the noises around them. She'd become so accustomed to the patter and slap of rain that it had all but vanished from her awareness, but now, looking over the water...the night was *loud*, the wind screaming, the rain hissing into the muck around their little island of house. They'd disappear into the landscape if they couldn't overcome it, and...the water was higher than it had been just hours ago, the ripples licking at the base of the gutters. A few more hours and the nasty water would creep over the shingles, and then—

"Help!" she yelled, still on her hands and knees. The roof and the water went black again as the light swept away off to her left, then to the far side of the boat—the opposite direction. *They can't hear us.* She planted her feet. *Stand up, stand up! Yell louder!* She inhaled once through her nose, put her hands on her thighs, and heaved herself to standing. "We're out here!"

"This way! Hey, help us!"

"Over here!" Her throat ached, her eyes stinging with rain and unshed tears, but the light swept toward them once more. The beam hovered—and stayed. The sound of a motor cut the night.

They were coming to help. Hopefully, they had a place to ride out the storm.

**GET *THE FLOOD*
on https://meghanoflynn.com**

**Love psychological thrillers? Try the Mind Games series!
Start the series with *The Dead Don't Dream*.** *A psychologist*

must decide whether her sleepwalking patient is a victim or a brutal serial killer in this unpredictable psychological thriller.

THE DEAD DON'T DREAM
CHAPTER 1

MOONLIGHT FELL in harsh blades of white against the hardwood floors. It bleached the oak, but it made the filth on his hands appear black, inky and shiny and somehow heavy —tacky against his flesh. It was caked around his wrist, too, pressed into the tiny crevices of his jewelry, smashed into the circular gilded edge, smeared over the leather band. The piece was old as the dirt itself, as reliable as the ground beneath his feet, but it felt... compromised. Soiled.

He stilled, held his breath and strained his ears, but he could not hear the steady *tick, tick, tick* that usually echoed through the room like a second heartbeat—the antique clock from the night table was on the floor. Ticking away for a century, and now it was dead.

Dead. The word ate at the soft spot between his shoulder blades for reasons he could not immediately place. Though he was unable to feel his own heart throbbing in his chest, *he* wasn't dead. He was in his bedroom. A dream—just a dream. But the expanse between the area rug and the floor-to-ceiling window was covered in scattered bits of grass and pebbles. He could smell damp earth, the musk of worms. His feet were bare, cold against the rug. His toes were... wet.

Mud.

He closed his eyes, trying to force his brain to understand, but slivers of memory slipped by without offering explanation. And though he was quite sure that he was alone, he could hear the wet hiss of breath against his ear, less like air and more like the rush of some unidentifiable pent-up emotion. He could still feel the sultry damp of her lips against his earlobe, her teeth like knives, the canines of a hungry animal, tearing his throat as if she intended to sever his windpipe. His wrists hurt as if he'd been tied.

Was it really just a dream? Some of it was. The woman, her long blonde hair, her blade-sharp teeth—those couldn't possibly be real. No injuries marred his neck; no bloody ribbons of skin hung beneath his hairline. Though his wrists were sore, he could not make out any abrasions that might indicate he'd been the victim of some attack. But there were parts that felt more vital—details that stuck out in sharp contrast. He could see the moon in his mind's eye, the outdoor world gray beneath its glare. He could hear the heavy weight of silence broken only by the crackling whisper of skittering leaves. He could feel the rocks, sharp beneath the knees of his sweatpants—he could feel those abrasions even now, the enduring sting from road-rashed skin. And the dirt...

The mud was real. That was definitely real.

He opened his eyes. The dirt... it wasn't only on him, nor was it merely on the floor as if he'd tracked it inside. It was *everywhere*. A swipe of grime marred the window, obscuring the night beyond. The bedspread was crusted in fine streaks of thick black and wider smears of filthy gray.

He touched his face, his fingertips gritty and sticky—mud in his facial hair. The top edge of his cheekbone felt sharper than usual, but the dirt there was dry.

The blood was not. And though the world was a black-and-white movie in the silver gleam of the moon, he knew now that it was blood. He could smell it, woven through with the damp musk of petrichor, the metallic tang of congealing life... or recent death.

Bile rose in his throat. He gagged, his heart thundering to life, pumping furiously as if his body had only now realized that he was being pursued by some predator, his meat snared in a frenzied dance of ichor and panic. Then he was running, wobbling and lopsided, off the rug, over the dirty floor to the marble tile of the bathroom—frigid against his feet. Gooseflesh shivered along his spine. He threw himself onto his injured knees in front of the toilet.

Bile and the bitter remnants of vodka tonic poured over

his tongue and dripped past his lips. But the dirt... oh, the dirt. That was far worse.

This was supposed to be over.

He retched again, again, then slumped back against the wall. He inhaled deeply, trying to steady the frantic throb in his temples, trying to ease the pulse that was turning his vision into a strobe, but he only succeeded in lodging dirt deep in his sinuses. He gagged and snorted, staring in horror at the earth still crusted beneath his fingernails and the slippery weeping chasm along the pad of his thumb. He had tried so hard to stop, but perhaps he'd only been lying to himself. The proof was here, everything he needed to know.

He'd done something terrible.

Again.

**SCAN THE CODE TO GET *THE DEAD DON'T DREAM*
or visit https://meghanoflynn.com**

PRAISE FOR BESTSELLING AUTHOR MEGHAN O'FLYNN

"Creepy and haunting… fully immersive thrillers. The Ash Park series should be everyone's next binge-read."
~*New York Times Bestselling Author Andra Watkins*

"Full of complex, engaging characters and evocative detail, *Wicked Sharp* is a white-knuckle thrill ride. O'Flynn is a master storyteller." ~*Paul Austin Ardoin, USA Today Bestselling Author*

"Nobody writes with such compelling and entrancing prose as O'Flynn. With perfectly executed twists, Born Bad is chilling, twisted, heart-pounding suspense. This is my new favorite thriller series." ~*Bestselling Author Emerald O'Brien*

"Visceral, fearless, and addictive, this series will keep you on the edge of your seat." ~*Bestselling Author Mandi Castle*

"Intense and suspenseful…captured me from the first chapter and held me enthralled until the final page."
~*Susan Sewell, Reader's Favorite*

"Cunning, delightfully disturbing, and addictive, the Ash Park series is an expertly written labyrinth."~*Award-winning Author Beth Teliho*

"Dark, gritty, and raw, O'Flynn's work will take your mind prisoner and keep you awake far into the morning hours." ~*Bestselling Author Kristen Mae*

"From the feverishly surreal to the downright demented, O'Flynn takes you on a twisted journey through the

deepest and darkest corners of the human mind."
~*Bestselling Author Mary Widdicks*

"With unbearable tension and gripping, thought-provoking storytelling, O'Flynn explores fear in all the best—and creepiest—ways. Masterful psychological thrillers replete with staggering, unpredictable twists." ~*Bestselling Author Wendy Heard*

LEARN MORE ON
https://meghanoflynn.com

WANT MORE FROM MEGHAN?
There are many more books to choose from!

Learn more about Meghan's novels on
https://meghanoflynn.com

ABOUT THE AUTHOR

With books deemed "visceral, haunting, and fully immersive" (*New York Times bestseller, Andra Watkins*), Meghan O'Flynn has made her mark on the thriller genre. Meghan is a clinical therapist who draws her character inspiration from her knowledge of the human psyche. She is the bestselling author of gritty crime novels and serial killer thrillers, all of which take readers on the dark, gripping, and unputdownable journey for which Meghan is notorious. Learn more at https://meghanoflynn.com! While you're there, join Meghan's reader group, and get a **FREE SHORT STORY** just for signing up.

Want to connect with Meghan?
https://meghanoflynn.com

www.ingramcontent.com/pod-product-compliance
Lightning Source LLC
LaVergne TN
LVHW040612250326
834688LV00035B/518